Dragonscales Divide
Randi-Anne Dey

Dragonscales Divide

Copyright©2024 Dragonscales Divide by Randi-Anne Dey

©Copyright - All rights reserved. No part of this publication may be reproduced, distributed, or transmitted in any form or by any means, including photocopying, recording, or other electronic or mechanical methods, without the prior written permission of the author, except in the case of brief quotations embodied in critical reviews and certain other non-commercial uses permitted by copyright law. If you see this published on unauthorized sites, Please, contact the author.

This novel is entirely a work of fiction. Unless otherwise indicated, all the names, characters, businesses, places, events, and incidents portrayed in this book ware either the product of the author's imagination or used in a fictitious manner and bear no meaning to where they are placed within the book. Any resemblance to actual persons, living or dead, or actual events is purely coincidental.

Designations used by companies to distinguish their products are often claimed as trademarks. All brand names and product names used in this book and on its cover are trade names, service marks, trademarks and registered trademarks of their respective owners. The publishers and the book are not associated with any product or vendor mentioned in this book. None of the companies referenced within the book have endorsed the book.

This book contains strong language, violence and fade to grey romance. Reader discretion is advised for those with these triggers

LGBTQ Friendly

Published in Canada

Randi-Anne Dey Publishing

ISBN

Hardcover - 978-1-7382843-7-5

Paperback - 978-1-7382843-6-8

eBook - 978-1-7382843-8-2

Spoilers

This book is based in the same world as Madison's Web. While it is separate and can be read as such, some spoilers may occur if you opt to read Madison's after this one. Same can be said for my books The King's Mystic and The Dragon's Mystic as one of the characters crosses over into this world.

To the night-dwellers who refuse to fade, and find strength in the shadows.
To the moon-chasers who run wild, power in their untamed spirit.
And to the fire-breathers who soar above it all with courage in the face of flames.

To everyone that has supported me in this endeavor, from my first book to this one!

Contents

1.	The Attack	1
2.	Realm Shift	5
3.	Compliance	12
4.	The Prophecy	18
5.	The Deal	27
6.	Acceptance	34
7.	The Bond Demands	42
8.	Deceptive Freedom	46
9.	Across Realms	50
10.	Moving Forward	66
11.	Madison Marzire	76
12.	Through the Veil	90
13.	New Inventions	100
14.	Modern Mornings	115
15.	Thrice Loved	124
16.	The Challenge	127
17.	Curiosity Cleansed	138
18.	Mall Crawl	147
19.	Queen Bee	156

20.	Crowned King	175
21.	Red Haze	189
22.	Binding Nine	202
23.	Fangs and Fury	209
24.	Unexpected Delivery	223
25.	Wings of Wrath	226
26.	Ink and Incantations	248
27.	Goddess's Embrace	254
28.	Broken Bond	257
29.	A New Dawn	275
30.	Moonlit Deadlines	284
31.	Realms Align	290
32.	Epilogue	301
33.	People	303
34.	Portraits	307
35.	Contributors	311
36.	Extras	312
	About the Author	313

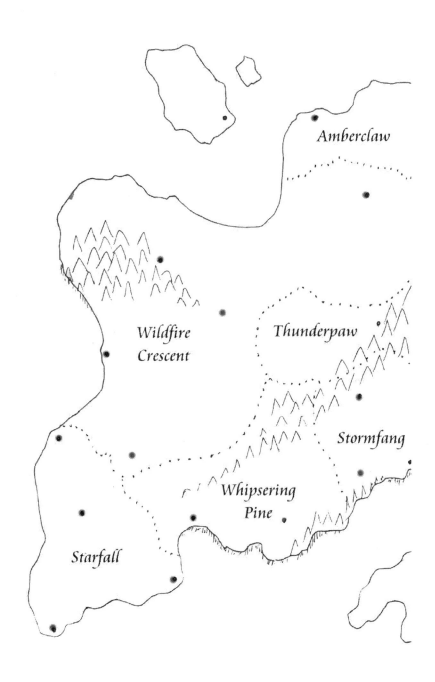

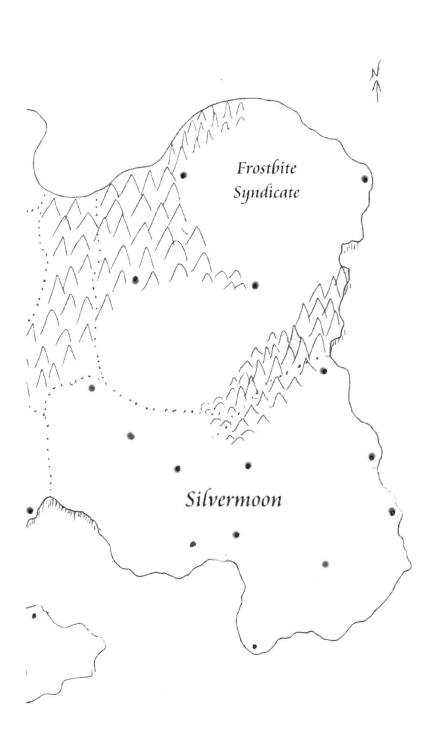

One

The Attack

Darian Ravenwind runs his fingers through his dark brown hair, his broad shoulders slumping at yet another war on his borders, as he sits at his old oak desk, handed down to him by his father. His fingers drum the top of it, staring at the computer screen, lost in thought. Too many battles of late, and he grows weary of them. He lifts his gaze as his Beta Kieran walks in, dressed in jeans and a Henley. His shoulder-length brown hair frames a tan face, rich hazel eyes, and a trimmed beard. Frustration flares within at the fact that he is sending his best friend, a father of three, into yet another battle, knowing that one day, there is a genuine possibility he is not returning, despite being one of the best fighters he has. He gestures to his Beta to sit and sighs heavily.

Kieran studies his friend as he sits down, seeing the weariness written all over him and knowing the fighting is tearing him apart. "Let me guess, Alpha. Another battle on the borders?"

"Yes, down along the southern cliffs. The patrol actually sounded panicked when they contacted me. Said witches are involved just before the link went dead. I did not feel their death, but they are no longer answering."

"Want me to take a look?"

"Not really, but you are the best option. I need to go to the north. Apparently, there is a skirmish there as well."

"Right, so split the pack. Is that a wise idea, Darian?"

"No. I hate it, but it needs to be dealt with. The rogues are getting too brazen, attacking more regularly, and shifters are going missing."

"It's a tough call, Alpha. In a war, there will be losses. It's just a matter of how many."

"I suppose..." Darian frowns. "Take your best team, Kieran. Find out what's happening down there. If they are rogues, just end them. No more prisoners.

They don't talk anyhow, and our cells are near capacity."

"Understood. But what about you? You need men by your side."

"I am taking my Luna and the witch Amara."

Kieran smiles, knowing very well that not much stops the power of that trio. "Right, I do get to pick the best, then."

Darian chuckles. "Well, of the warriors, you do. I will see you later with a report."

Kieran winks and stands up. "Got it, boss. Try to play nice!"

Darian rises, standing the same height as his best friend. "You too."

"Never. Be careful, Darian." Kieran claps his hand on his Alpha's shoulder. He steps out of the pack house, his eyes taking in the winter wonderland that dropped overnight. Snow clings to the branches, dragging the canopy of the forest down, creating a small pocket of peace around them, despite the fights at the border. A smile crosses his lips at the soft crunch beneath his boots. He looks forward to running through it in wolf form. Arriving at the training rings, he watches them fight before calling ten forward, including his daughter Zara. "Alpha received a mind-link from the patrol on the south borders. Something cut it off. We need to find out why. You have ten minutes to inform your mates and family."

He turns to his daughter standing there, looking very much like her mother. Striking blue eyes framed with dark lashes, sparkle in delight. Her tanned skin blends well with her ash blonde hair tied into a tight braid, reaching her waist. He frowns slightly at her yoga pants and a half top, knowing it is her normal fighting attire, but wishes she would cover just a little more. Especially in the cold weather. "Go talk to your mother and put on some decent clothes. It's cold out."

Zara smiles. "Alright, Papa. Thank you for trusting me on this mission."

Kieran sighs and watches his daughter run away, wishing she had a mate, so that he could deny her place on the battlefield. Not that a mate could stop her, either. It is just his wishful dreaming. He pauses on the way to his cottage, seeing his twin boys having a snowball fight with other kids. "Jenson, Jayden. Come here for a second."

The boys race to his side, their ash blond hair damp and stringy, clinging to their scalps with bits of snow. Excitement dances in their hazel eyes as they look up. "What's up Papa?"

"Your sister and I are going to the borders. Watch over your mother while we are gone."

"Got it, Papa. We will stay close to the house."

"Thank you." He ruffles their hair, sending them back to play. He turns and heads to his cottage, unusual for a Beta, as they often live in the pack house with the Alpha, but he prefers it this way, and Darian doesn't mind. Stepping into the kitchen, he sighs at his daughter sitting on the countertop, now dressed in jeans and a sweater, talking with her mother; his wife, his mate, and the love of his life. He flinches at his mate's gaze as she turns it his way, feeling the anger through their bond and mind-link that he is daring to take their daughter on a patrol with him.

'WHAT do you think you are doing, Kieran!?'

'Alpha said the best, and she's one of the best, my love. We can't keep her protected forever. She's earned this right.'

'She's just nineteen! She hasn't even found her mate. You could be robbing her of that chance.'

'Lila, honey, you know I love you, and you know I will do everything in my power to keep Zara safe.'

Lila huffs. *'Fine. You better, or I am taking it out of that hide of yours!'*

Kieran chuckles and draws his wife into his arms. "Deal. I love you Lila. I will see you later this evening."

Lila snuggles into his arms. "I will be waiting. Now go. Before I change my mind and lock our daughter in a cell."

Zara laughs, joining in the family hug. "I will be fine, Mama. I have Papa to take care of me."

"Yes, you do." Kieran offers a hand to his daughter and they head to the gathering.

Once reunited, the group shifts into wolves and races through the woods. A blending of gray, tan, and blond fur, each of them heading to the southern borders. Hours later, they approach carefully and shift back into human form. The warriors look around for the stashes of clothing often hidden throughout the woods, while Zara and Kieran sport the magical necklaces Amara had made for them. Ones that allow them to shift freely with their clothes on. A scattering of bodies, in both wolf and human form, lie in the blood-soaked snow. Some from their pack, others he doesn't recognize.

Kieran directs half of the warriors to find out who is still alive as the remaining five continue forward to where they can hear combat. As Kieran proceeds closer, he hears spell casting and gestures to the others to wait while he stealth's forward, only to find his daughter on his heels. He hisses quietly. "I told you to wait. You disobeyed my orders, Zara!"

"I am not leaving you to fend for yourself. I promised Mama before you arrived."

"Fine, stay close then." He skirts through the trees and around the snow-covered rocks as the sounds of battle grow louder, blending with the crash of the ocean at the bottom of the cliffs. Peeking around a rock, he stares in horror at a gargantuan black dragon dueling with a group of five witches. Dark magic spews from the witches, directed at the dragon, who is fighting back with fire, but bound in place by wisps of dark bindings. Steam rises all around them. "What the hell?" He pushes Zara behind the rocks, only to have the dragon lock its gaze on him, followed by a witch. Kieran mind-links Alpha Darian immediately. *'Alpha, the problem at the border is more than we can handle. Aborting the mission. Black dragon, fighting five dark witches.'*

"Papa?"

Alpha Darian replies immediately. *'Get out of there now!'*

Kieran takes Zara's hand and backs away. Dark magic from the witch surrounds him and binds him. "Run Zara! Run NOW!!"

Zara turns to run, only to have a wispy black snake wrap around her ankle, pulling her off her feet and dragging her into the clearing towards them. She kicks wildly, digging her hands into the rock and snow, struggling to change into her wolf, but finding their magic prohibits it. "Papa!"

Two

Realm Shift

Kieran growls, his hazel eyes shifting to amber as his wolf, Emeric struggles for control. Both fighting against the binding and breaking the magic to the shock of both parties. Kieran rushes forward and grabs his daughter's hands, tightening his grip as he pulls against the magic on her. The witches chant again, sending streams of magic at Zara, with the dragon's magic joining it. Kieran cries out and launches on top of his daughter, wrapping his arms around her to protect her, only to hear silence surround them. Darkness, floating, disembodiment, before crashing onto cobblestone of some kind. He gasps for breath as he rolls off his daughter. "Zare-bear, are you alright?"

"Geez, Papa, you weigh a ton."

He chuckles and draws her into a tight hug. "Your mother never complains."

"Ewww. TMI, Papa!!!" She looks around, spotting a castle looming in the distance, a forest to their backside, and manicured gardens on either side of them. Fresh air, laced with a sweet floral scent wafts over them from the light breeze. "Where are we?"

"I don't know Zare-bear, but I can't feel Alpha Darian."

"Neither can I. It's not good, is it?"

He rises and brushes off his clothing, assisting Zara to her feet as he glances around. "No, it's not."

Zara frowns at the castle. "Who has castles these days?"

"There are a few out there, but they consider them heritage buildings now. Often, the government pays for their upkeep. I don't recall one this size, though."

"Let me check." She pulls out her phone and powers it on, frowning as she spots no cell service. "Damn, no service. We are really in the boonies." Zara lifts her phone and snaps a picture for later, taking a few of the gardens as well, before turning it off and tucking it back into her pocket. "Well Papa, castle? Or the other way?"

"I don't think we are going to get a choice, Zare-bear. Five incoming horses behind us." He backs up, placing Zara behind him as he studies the five approaching. Each one of the riders, striking in their own way; pale skin, dark eyes, and lips tinged redder than they should have, dressed in clothing from an era past. "Vampires?" Kieran hisses softly as his brows furrow. Glancing skyward, he notices an absence of the sun as he turns his attention back to them.

"Vampires? Are we in, like, the Twilight Zone?" Zara steps back to back with her father, knowing the brutality of vampires, and expecting a fight.

"I would like to say no, Zare-bear, but you might be right."

The vampires ride around the pair, circling them slowly, their gazes sharp. One holds his hands up to the others to stop them. "What are you doing back, Zara? You know the boss is unhappy you turned rebel."

Zara shakes her head. "I don't know you or what you are talking about. I am not a rebel."

Kieran takes her hand, holding it tight. "Shhh Zara."

"Of course you are. Serving you on a silver platter will make him happy." He turns to Kieran, watching his hand moving to the girl. "Now, who are you?"

"It doesn't matter."

"It does when you are protecting a rebel." He narrows his eyes, and dismounts, studying the pair closely as he approaches, before sniffing the air in confusion. He locks his gaze on the duo again. "You are not one of us. You smell almost human. Who are you?"

Zara growls under her breath. "Now that's a good question. Clearly not the Zara you are looking for. Just let us go and we will be on our way."

"Not happening. The boss WILL want to meet you."

"Can't say I am entirely interested in meeting the boss."

"Take them." The lead vampire gestures to the others as they dismount and surround the pair.

Kieran strikes the first one. *'Don't shift Zare-bear, keep the wolf hidden.'*

'Got it Papa.'

The leader narrows his eyes at the pair holding their own against his four men. He calls for backup, especially if they are fighting werewolves. A race that is practically extinct, and yet, here is a father-daughter team. They also don't have shields around their thoughts, as everyone else does, which he finds amusing. He steps in to assist as backup arrives. After a loss of some of his men, and taking more time than he expects, they drop the two in question.

"Damn, Nero, they fight like hellcats for humans. Are they from the resistance?"

Nero shakes his head. "No. I don't know where they are from, but the resistance did not enter their thoughts. One Alpha Darian did, who I am guessing is their boss. The others that crossed their minds were a family. I suspect his wife and sons, and that there is his daughter." He looks at his fallen kin, knowing few could take a vampire down the way they did. The fact that they know snapping their necks will kill them is a concern. It is a well kept secret of the realm and yet, these two went right for the kill. Most just assumed that a stake through the heart was enough. Or that pathetic view of garlic would keep them away.

"But she looks just like Zara."

"She does, but it's not her." He moves forward and places a hand on both of their heads, suspecting he will get very little in their unconscious state, but finding some thoughts in their mind. Her in a training ring, surrounded by others, carefree and relaxed. Him with an older version of her in his arms, feeling the love he has for her. "I think they are from another realm. Come, we should get them locked up before they wake. We already lost three men to them."

Nero drapes Zara and Kieran over the horses, while the others carry their dead brethren. Silence fills the air as they make their way to the castle where they part ways, the ones with the dead heading to the back and the others heading to the cells below. He has the captives placed inside and the doors locked, contemplating them for a moment. Twirling the keys around his fingers, he leaves the dungeons and heads into the castle. *'Sebastian, we need to talk'*

'I suspected. I am in the library, Nero.'

Nero winds his way up the stairs, down the hallway lit by torches. Thick woven rugs muffle his steps, not that he is a stomper. He stops at the double doors, knocks lightly, and pushes them open. Smiling, seeing his ruler sitting in a plush blue chair, book in hand and a glass of red wine on the table next to him. The black robes he is wearing only enhance the blue of his eyes, as dark locks fall over his pale face and down past his shoulders.

Sebastian lifts his gaze, the corners of his lips tipping in a wry smile. "Tell me. What did you fight today that cost me three of my men?"

Nero runs a hand through his blond hair. "A pair of werewolves."

The book topples from Sebastian's hands as he rises. "Werewolves? Here?"

"Yes. A father and daughter with a family somewhere. A wife and two boys."

"Where are they now?"

"Downstairs in the cells, unconscious. There is one thing you need to know, Sebastian. The daughter looks exactly like Zara and responds to it as well."

Sebastian frowns. "Are you saying Zara is a werewolf now? That's not possible."

"No, I am saying, if Zara has an identical twin, this girl is it."

"Where did you find them?"

"On the road between the gardens. We were coming out of the woods. No horses, just them. Strange clothes, and a strange accent, but I can't place it. Also, they don't guard their thoughts."

Sebastian bends down and picks up the book, caressing it gently as he ponders the pair downstairs. "Interesting. When they wake up, have them brought here. Use silver chains. It weakens wolves."

"I will return with them shortly. Werewolves heal fast, so they should wake up soon." He bows and strides from the room, closing the door after him.

Sebastian places the book he is reading on the table and lifts his glass of wine. He takes a sip, the liquid bitter to his taste buds, but it is something he enjoys. Moving to the desk, he settles in the seat and pulls a painting out of the right-hand drawer. He looks it over carefully. Zara, his mistress and one that has eluded him for nearly a hundred years. His fingers trace down along the blonde hair, wondering if she is still alive out there. Knowing with her innate stubbornness, she is, and currently plotting his demise. He sighs and tucks the portrait back as he ponders the pair downstairs. Zara's twin. He's certain she didn't have any sisters and even if she did, how could one of them be a werewolf? Zara was human when he turned her and an only child, according to her. She learned to shield her thoughts quickly, but there were times he made it past those defenses and a sister never came into her mind.

Kieran and Zara wake in cells, their wrists burning at the silver chains wrapped around them, matching the chains around their booted ankles. Both knowing their situation is dire as they look at the iron bars penning them in.

Zara pulls at her chains as she looks at her Papa. "How do we get out of here, Papa?"

"Shhh Zara, there are people coming. The less they know of us, the better."

"Got it."

"Good, you are awake. My boss will see you now." Nero gestures at the six vampires behind him to retrieve the prisoners. "This would go easier if you just accept the fact that you are our prisoners. Fight us and we will drag you there anyhow." They open the cell and step in, pulling Zara out first, who fights them to the best of her ability. "I see it's going to be the hard way." He chuckles, not surprised at all, knowing he would too. They drag them through the castle to the library, pausing occasionally to adjust their grip as they slip from their grasp, stopping at the door as Nero knocks.

Not realizing how much time has passed, Sebastian startles slightly at the knock on his door. "Enter." His lips curl in delight at the fight still in the werewolves, each of them taking three of his men to drag them in, despite the silver binding them.

Kieran curses under his breath as they drag him into the room and force him to kneel before the boss, knowing he will do everything in his power to protect his daughter... or kill her if necessary.

Zara stops struggling for a second to stare at the vampire in front of her, fighting with a renewed vigor as she hears Ember yelling in her mind. *'MATE!'*

'NO, Ember. It's NOT!' She pushes her back, refusing to acknowledge her claims.

Sebastian rises to look at them, their thoughts immediately filling his head, meeting Nero's gaze in shock. *'Your right, no shields at all.'*

'No sire, none.'

Sebastian returns his attention to the two brought before him and made to kneel, feeling anger in their gaze as their thoughts and emotions assault him. He looks over each of them quietly, starting with the father. His primary concern is his daughter, and the fear within that this is his fault that he chose her to go on the mission. Knowing his mate was going to be pissed that he didn't keep her safe and that he is willing to kill his daughter to ensure they did not violate her. Sebastian clearly reads the defiance in this werewolf's gaze as he meets his own, understanding immediately how he took down three of his men.

Sebastian turns to the daughter, who avoids his gaze, and moves closer. He lowers himself and places a hand beneath her chin, hearing her hiss at his touch. She is so close to his Zara, but there is a softness in her face that his Zara didn't have, along with unguarded thoughts.

"DON'T touch me!" Zara jerks away from him, feeling a strange warmth at his contact while his scent surrounds her; dark vanilla and amberwood, all with a subtle metallic undertone.

"Then look at me, child."

Zara lifts her gaze, her cobalt blue eyes flashing dangerously as they meet his midnight blue ones. "I am NOT a child!"

"No, but you are his child, yes?"

Kieran immediately mink-links his daughter. *'DO NOT tell him that. He will use it against us!'*

'I don't intend to, Papa.'

Sebastian conceals his surprise, noting the knowing look in Nero's eyes, which suggests that he is already aware of the mind-link. While all vampires within a clan could communicate through a mind-link, only those closest to him could read thoughts. It seemed that wolves possessed a similar ability. "Child?"

"NO, I am not. I am a warrior under his command."

He rises and chuckles. "You know I can smell the lies coming off you. And hear your whispers to each other."

"I don't know what you are talking about."

"Hmmm indeed. Now tell me, this man. What would you give to save his life?" He signals to one of his men, who pulls a sword out and holds it to Kieran's throat.

Zara's body freezes, her hands clenching on her knees as she watches the blade cut through his skin, blood welling beneath it. *'PAPA!'*

'NO Zare-bear. Don't even go there.' Kieran narrows his eyes her way, feeling the sting on his neck. *'I have lived a good life. Fight to get free, every day and get back to your mother and brothers.'* Knowing his daughter well enough to know she will fight to keep him alive because she isn't ready to lose him yet. It tears him up inside. Wanting her to live and be free. Not wanting her to remain a prisoner here with the vampires doing who knows what to her; mentally encouraging her to stand strong and not agree to cater to a vampire, but somewhere, he knows she will. He caught the soft gasp from her as they entered and saw the renewed fighting bordering on desperation. Something is up, and it's tied to the boss, by the way Zara avoids his gaze. His eyes drift to the boss, his pale skin framed by the long black hair. The casual stance he exudes, betrayed only by the piercing blue eyes that study them carefully. He lowers his eyes, his thoughts drifting to his wife and sons. Sadness fills him at the thought that he will not get to see the radiance of her smile again, or feel her lips upon his. To hear his twins laughing

at his wife's cooking and the mess she makes in the kitchen. To hold her tight in her arms as they sleep at night. *Lila, my love. Forgive me. You were right. I should have left Zara with you.*

Zara averts her gaze to the floor, her body slumping in defeat as she struggles with what choice to make. She can feel her wolf Ember fighting with her, telling her the man who is threatening her father is her mate. Spoken as soon as she stepped into the room and her eyes landed on him. A vampire. As a mate. Why the hell would the Goddess even do this to her? She clearly made a mistake. A shifter mate waits for her back in their realm. No! She will never accept a vampire as a mate. They kill people because they are evil, as evidenced by the sword at her father's throat and yet, she couldn't understand why they were still alive. By all rights, they should be dead right now and not talking to this boss. Perhaps it is the weird Twilight Zone they are in. Something to do with the damn dragon and witches. What she needs to do is to escape. To find those witches and get them to send them home because clearly they sent her somewhere abnormal. *'I am not gonna let you die, Papa. Not if I can save you.'*

Sebastian smiles coldly, hearing their thoughts and feeling the struggle in them both; his not wanting the daughter to confess and hers all over the place. He knows he is being cruel because she looks like his Zara, but he can't help it. His eyes drift to the father at her words, his back stiff and proud as he kneels before them. "Child. I need an answer."

Three

Compliance

Zara lifts her gaze in defeat, avoiding her fathers. "Anything. Please. Just don't hurt him."

A growl escapes Kieran as he struggles against his chains and those holding him, despite the blade at his throat. "NO!! Zara, what have you done?"

"Take him back to the cells. His daughter and I are going to have a little chat." The guard withdraws his sword as the five of them drag him away, leaving Nero, Sebastian and Zara in the room.

Zara watches her father leave, a few tears slipping from her eyes as she remains kneeling. She bows her head, not daring to look at the two vampires that remain in the room with her. Pain fills her as her father's voice echoes in the hallway, until there is nothing but silence. She closes her eyes, hoping that she didn't just make the biggest mistake of her life, by having him mad at her and never seeing him again.

Sebastian mind-links Nero as he watches the girl on the floor, feeling the sadness emanating from her at the loss of her father. *'It is refreshing, not having blocks up. So many emotions and it's easy to read.'*

'Indeed, sire, but...'

'But?'

'Are you making her suffer because of her, or because of our Zara?'

'You're right, Nero. I am being needlessly cruel in allowing her to think I am ending her father. But the control in doing that is enticing. She is at war with another entity inside her, telling her we are mates. It is like there are two of them in one body. Just like her father.'

'I heard the father tell her not to shift, to keep the wolf hidden. So it's possible the wolf is one, and she is one. We know so little about werewolves.'

'I think it's time we find out.'

DRAGONSCALES DIVIDE

Nero chuckles. *'And you are just the person to do it. I will research what exactly mate entails for you while you question her. This way, I will be close if you need me. She is just as skilled as her father in fighting and took down one of your men.'*

'Good to know.'

Sebastian watches Nero move to the back of the library before returning full attention to the girl kneeling before him. "You may rise and sit on the couch if that is your desire."

She shakes her head and remains where she is.

"You prefer to be on your knees?"

"I prefer to be with my Papa. If you are to kill him, I want to be with him."

Sebastian smiles. "So you would die for your father, just as he will for you. How valiant. Too bad it's misplaced."

She dares to meet his gaze, fury raging in hers. "It is NOT misplaced. I love my Papa and my family. I know he would die for me as I would for him, but I cannot have him mad at me when he does. He needs to understand. He has a mate to get home to and I... I Don't."

Sebastian rubs the bridge of his nose in contemplation. "And yet, the entity inside you is screaming that you do."

"Ember is wrong. The Goddess is wrong. She would NOT pair me with a blood sucking vamp."

"Ember...So there are two of you in your body. Interesting. We know so little about werewolves. I desire to know more."

A sarcastic edge slips into her voice. "We are not werewolves. We are shifters. There *is a* difference."

"How so?"

"We cannot convert others to be wolves. We are born with it and get our wolf at eighteen. Werewolves bite their targets and convert them against their will... JUST like you."

Sebastian glides gracefully over to the couch and sits, patting the chair next to him. "Come. Sit."

"No."

"Do you want your father tortured before his death? That can be arranged."

Zara pales suddenly, feeling a shake in her hands as she struggles to her feet and stumbles to the couch to sit. "Why? Why are you doing this?"

"Why not? We are evil, are we not? And I need information. You either answer my questions, or he does under duress."

Her shoulders slump as she shifts away from him, putting as much space between them as she can, feeling his scent of dark vanilla and amberwood wrap around her. She places her manacled hands in her lap. "Fine, ask away. Just don't torture him."

"Why are you here?"

"I don't know."

"What do you mean, you don't know?"

Zara shakes her head. "I can't really answer that. Alpha Darian sent us to the southern borders to defend our pack. When we got there, we saw a lot of our warriors defeated. Papa kept me behind him, but I guess they saw me."

"Who saw you?"

"The witches that were fighting the black dragon. I have never seen one up close. I mean, I know there are dragon shifters, but in our world, they remain more hidden than us wolves. Wolves are natural. Dragons are not. Black tendrils bound Papa and dragged me towards them. Papa broke out of the magic that held him and jumped on me. More magic hit us, and we were here."

"Are there a lot of dragons in your lands?"

"I am not sure. I know there is a pack called Frostbite Syndicate. They are mostly dragons, but I don't know how many are part of their pack."

"Interesting. Dragons have been extinct here for centuries. The fact they exist in your world sounds rather fascinating."

"Well. It's not that fascinating. We live in packs, away from the humans, especially the dragons. They shift as we do, hiding in their human form. There are also bear and cat shifters."

"And you all live in harmony?"

"Not all the time. The Lycan King tries to keep control of all the packs under his domain, but I think it's hard. We each have our own territories to defend on his behalf. Our Alpha is in charge of that."

"So you are, in fact, not part of the resistance?"

Her brow furrowed in confusion. "The what?"

"The group of humans and witches opposed to us vampires. My Zara, your doppelgänger so to speak, turned on us and joined them."

Zara looks down at her hands. "That would be why they seemed to know me. Sometimes wolves will turn on their Alpha. They label them as rogues and often kill them on sight."

"Yes, well, had they been paying attention, they should have seen the differences." Sebastian watches her, feeling her thoughts drifting back to the pack, and the battle at his front gates. A slight smile graces his lips, finding himself curious about her. "Tell me more about why you are fighting inside with your wolf about a mate bond."

The color drains from Zara's face as her lips part. "Why? You can't possibly know about that."

"Oh my dear, I know if you speak the truth or not. You do not shield your thoughts, which is a rarity around here, as just about everyone has mastered it. Just as I clearly heard the communication between you and your Papa. It was about as much of a shock as your Ember yelling, mate, the second you saw me."

"No, mind-links are private."

"Not in this realm. Not unless you have the magic to make them so. Now tell me."

Zara chews on her lip nervously, feeling the intensity of his gaze, wanting to run as her eyes slide to the door and freedom.

"You won't make it, but you can certainly try."

Zara scowls at him, frustrated at his ability to read her thoughts. "You can't be my mate. I have a mate back in my realm."

"Yet your heart beats faster when you look at me. When I touched your chin, I could feel your blood warm. I wonder if I should test the theory more." He shifts closer to prove his point.

She shudders and tries to dart from the couch, only to have his hand wrap around her waist and pull her back down.

He breathes against her neck, sniffing her gentle scent of soap, with the subtle underlay of honeysuckle. "You smell delightful, and I can hear your wolf growling contentedly."

Zara closes her eyes, trying to deny the attraction, mentally cursing her wolf at wanting this man. She groans inwardly as she feels his lips kissing along her neck where the mate mark goes, feeling a warmth stirring inside her. Her hands clench in the manacles, trying to push out of his grasp, only to gasp in shock as his lips find hers. Sparks flare through her body, feeling it betray her when she sinks against him. She catches his chuckle as his arms release her. Scrambling back to the other side of the couch, she glares at him. "Never do that again."

"I cannot promise that, my dear, but Nero may return you to your abode downstairs."

Nero rises from behind the desk and moves forward, taking her chains in his hand and leading her back down to the dungeons where her father waits. He unlocks the cell, pushes her in, and locks it behind her, watching the pair a moment, before stepping back and blending into the shadows, feeling Sebastian slide in beside him.

Zara hesitates as she enters, seeing her father's flash of anger at what she has done, before relief floods his face. She looks him over carefully, noticing he is not any more beat up than when they went upstairs. "They didn't torture you?"

Kieran rises and loops his chains over her, hugging her tightly. "Oh, it was torture enough knowing you were upstairs with the vampires."

"I'm sorry, Papa. I couldn't let them kill you."

"Shhh, I know, Zare-bear. I know. Somehow, we will get out of here. Though, to be honest, I don't know how we are going to get back to our realm."

"They have witches. He said so, upstairs. Some sort of resistance, like our rogues."

"You know we can't trust rogues. If they are like ours, then we can't trust theirs either."

"But can we trust the vampires, Papa?"

"No, it's a dilemma." He lifts his hands over her head and steps back, cupping her cheeks and studying her carefully. "Now, tell me what's really going on, Zare-bear."

Zara shakes her head. "I can't, Papa."

"You can and you will. You are not too old to turn over my knee, though it might be a challenge with these chains on."

Zara giggles and leans against her father. A soft sigh escapes her. "Ember says he's my mate."

"And what do you think?"

"She's wrong."

"Zare-bear. Wolves are rarely wrong. They know their bonds."

"I don't want to be bonded to a blood-sucking vampire."

He leads her over to the cot. "To be clear, I am not choosing sides between you and Ember, but after the initial beating, which we started, they have not fed upon or mistreated us. What vampire do you know has the power to resist blood? There were eight in that room with my neck bleeding. Eight, and each held restraint. Perhaps this world is different."

"I doubt it, Papa. They have mistreated us. They shackled us in silver chains." She crawls in against the wall, feeling her father slip in next to her.

"Zare-bear, we are prisoners of war. We do the same."

She mutters under her breath. "I don't want to talk about it, Papa."

"I know. Sleep. I will watch over you."

Sebastian watches the pair with Nero, a pensiveness to his expression, resisting the desire to remove the chains and have them placed in the room upstairs. They are fighters. That much is clear in the way they took down three of his clan. Yet, the father justified they might be different. He is clearly more open to the fact they are not like the vampires of their world. And her laughter at the thought of her father turning her over her knee only soothed the anger that overwhelmed him at the thought of another laying a hand on her. He returns in silence to the library with Nero, picking up the glass of wine and taking a sip. "Nero."

"Yes, sire."

"Did you find anything on mate bonds in that short time?"

"A bit. But not a lot. It says you feel drawn to each other and, when connected, you can feel each other's emotions."

"I can already feel them. She has no shields and it is intoxicating. I struggle because she looks so much like our Zara, but doesn't have the cold, calculated look. This one is soft and open, and when I kissed her, I felt desire. Something I haven't felt in over a hundred years. I wanted to take her back to my room and get to know more about her. I still do. She felt it too. It was all over her aura."

"I know, Sire. I felt it radiating all the way over to my side of the room. There is a lot of confusion in that girl."

"Do you think she's the one?"

"Perhaps. She's definitely life. They both are."

Four

The Prophecy

Sebastian strides over to the wall where an aged scroll hangs, its edges charred and clearly torn in half. The flowing writing upon it has faded with time, becoming barely legible.

When life and death walk as one,
The realms within become undone,
And in the fires of chaos, a new one begun,
Forged....

He touches it gently, caressing the brittle parchment. "It feels different. She feels different. If only we knew the rest of it."

"What are we going to do?"

"Keep them for a week, then we accidentally leave the cage open and let them escape. I want to see what they do. She's looking for witches to send them back, but I don't want her to find them. I want to keep her here."

"Are you going to see her daily?"

"Yes, I believe I will."

"Good, ask her about these. The guards removed them from their pockets when shackling them." He hands over two rectangular objects, one with silver sparkles and the other a forest green. Each having a smooth black face.

"What are they?"

"Not sure, sire. But it is a strange type of magic. When you push the button on the side, they light up and ask for numbers. Then they tell you it's incorrect."

Sebastian places the green one down on his desk and looks over the sparkled one. "This material is very smooth. It is unlike anything I have seen. Tomorrow I will find out more."

"Good plan. Now, I will finish researching mate bonds, sire."

"Thank you."

DRAGONSCALES DIVIDE

The next day, the cell opens and the guards point to her. "She is to come with us."

Zara shakes her head as she remains behind her father. "No."

"We were told to let you know that if you resist, then your father will suffer."

Kieran sighs. "Go Zara. Just be careful."

"I don't want to, Papa."

Kieran turns to her and takes her hands. *'Zare-bear, I know you don't. But for now, we need to get them to trust us and in order to do that, we obey without fighting.'* Kieran turns, catching the chuckle at the door. "What?"

"We can hear your mind-link as if you were talking aloud. No point in even using it."

Kieran growls softly. "You cannot. They are private."

"Indeed, we can. You told her to obey without fighting so that we trust you. Not going to happen. Now, if she comes with us willingly and behaves, the boss will return the gesture in good faith and remove your silver chains for the duration of your stay."

Zara looks down at the shackles on her wrist and steps out from behind her father. "I will be back Papa."

Kieran watches his daughter walk away from him, her back straight and stiff as she approaches the guards. *'Be safe Zare-bear.'*

"That will depend on her behavior. Come." They close and lock the cell after her and lead her back to the library. Guiding her up to the desk where Sebastian sits, they bow and back away, vacating the room and closing the door after them.

Zara scans the library, noticing that only the boss is in here. Brief thoughts flicker through her mind of taking him down before deciding against it. Being the boss means you are in charge and can defeat the challenges before you. It is something she will leave her father to take on.

Sebastian smiles at Zara's thoughts, knowing she came willingly from the mind-links he received from his guards and the conversation she had with her father. Rising from his seat, he gathers the keys resting on the desk and strides toward her, noticing the subtle tension in her body as she averts her gaze. Gently taking her hands, he inserts the key into the shackles and unlocks them, allowing them to fall to the floor at her feet.

With shock, Zara gazes down at her hands and tenderly rubs the silver burns that still mark her wrists. She lifts her gaze to his, her eyes flashing in anger as she raises her hand to strike him. "You lied to me about torturing and killing my Papa!"

Sebastian catches her hand and pulls her close, wrapping his second arm around her waist. "I implied it, yes, but it got me answers and I can STILL have him tortured. As long as you comply, he will remain safe."

Zara struggles against emotions that overwhelm her as his scent wraps around her. She growls at her wolf thrumming inside her. *'Shut up, Ember. He can hear that.'*

'But Zara, open your eyes and look at how handsome he is. I love him already.'

'I DON'T, now STOP!'

Sebastian chuckles and releases her. "You should stop fighting me, Zara. I can make all the difference in how you and your father are treated here."

Zara growls at him, and stumbles back, placing the couch between them. "Not a chance. You are a typical vampire. A bastard."

Sebastian sighs, watching her place distance between them, feeling the race of her heart as she struggles to calm herself. "Don't push me Zara, or you will find out just how much of a bastard I can be. Now sit on that couch. I have more questions."

Zara clutches the edge of the couch and watches him warily.

"SIT Zara. NOW."

Zara begrudgingly jumps over the couch and settles as far away from him as she can.

"Good girl." He moves to the desk and picks up the two objects. "Now, what are these?"

Confusion flickers across her face. "They are phones."

"Phones?"

Zara inspects the room, realizing rather quickly that the lighting is candles or oil lamps. That there is no computer on the desk. She searches around for plugs, recalling she had not seen power poles outside either. Her brow furrows at the fact that this Twilight Zone seemed to have thrust them back in time with no electricity. "Yes. It's like a mind-link but can reach any distance, as long as there is service."

Sebastian looks at the rectangles in his hands. "You're saying these boxes can communicate?"

"Well, not here, I tried. We had no service when I arrived." She rises and approaches cautiously, holding her hand out for the silver one. "I cannot open my Papa's. Only he can." Zara pushes the button on the left, causing the screen to flash and open to a picture of a red dragon with fires surrounding him.

Sebastian's brows furrow. "It did not do that when I tried. It asked for numbers."

"Yes, cause it recognizes my face." She flips through her messages, finding her fathers about making dinner plans one night and hands it over for him to read. "When connected, they also contain a mini library inside it. In our world, you could find anything you wanted in it with Google."

"Google..." Rolling the word off his tongue as he reads through the texts a bit, before handing it back. "Show me."

Zara shakes her head, taking the phone and pointing to the icon. "No service. It won't work. I can show you photos of our world." She opens the albums to the last ones she took of the castle and its gardens.

"Wait, this is here?"

"Yes."

"How is this possible?"

Zara laughs at his frown of confusion and awe. "It's our magic called technology." She flips back to the main screen and opens the camera. She leans in next to him and holds it up, taking a selfie of the two of them. Flipping back to the albums, she goes to that picture and hands the phone over. "See, magic."

Sebastian stares at the mini portrait of them both, stunned that it's done so quickly and with no brush strokes.

"You can zoom in too, by doing this." She places her fingers on the screen and spreads them.

Sebastian zooms in and studies the portrait carefully. "How do I acquire one of these?"

"I don't think you can. I only have 87% left of battery power, then mine is dead. It needs to be plugged in. Even if you had power here, I don't have my cord."

"Do you have other paintings such as this?"

"Photos? Yes."

"May I see them?"

"Sure. Just slide your fingers left or right and it will take you to the next one."

Sebastian moves over to the couch and settles in to skim through photos on her phone. He jumps when a video appears, watching the people moving around a kitchen, laughing and talking. Recognizing her father and her, and suspecting it must be her mother and two identical brothers. A smile graces his lips, seeing the happiness in them all and the close knit family they clearly have. A few pictures later, he looks up at Zara, who remains near the desk. "What is this?"

She moves over and sits next to him, looking at the picture. "It is a car. You drive it places. I guess like a wagon or carriage, if you have those."

Sebastian nods. "Carriage, yes; where are the horses?"

Zara laughs softly. "In barns, we don't need them. Some still ride them, but cars are faster."

Sebastian shifts his gaze over to her, the sound of her laughter warming him inside, wanting to hear more of it. "I want one of these too."

She shakes her head. "You need gas for those, and more technology. I gather you haven't discovered it yet."

"How can you say that?"

She takes the phone and flips through her pictures, finding one of a wall with a plug and blows it up as best as she can. "Here, this box in the wall. They house electricity or power, as people call it. Something that we all rely on in our realm. You don't seem to have any. You have candles to illuminate your room. We have switches that turn on lights." She moves to her video folder and shows him a few more of her lifestyle.

Sebastian grows silent, watching the videos. "Your world has interesting things. It is hard to believe this is real when I have never seen such things and I have lived over five hundred years."

"Five hundred..."

Sebastian offers her a wry smile. "Even your father wouldn't be able to defeat me, but I'd welcome the challenge if he breaks free."

Zara backs away, muttering under her breath. "It's impolite to listen to another's thoughts."

Sebastian rises and moves away from Zara to his desk, where he settles behind it. He dips a quill into an ink jar and writes on parchment. "Zara, it's hard not to miss. You are an open book with your thoughts. Your father is too."

"Still not right." Zara frowns, her eyes moving to the quill, realizing rather suddenly that even pens didn't exist here. "What are you writing?"

"Some thoughts on your world and what I have seen."

"What about me?"

"You are welcome to stay and look around. Perhaps have lunch with me, or you may return to your cell below."

"Lunch?" She hesitates, an edge of accusation creeping into her voice. "As in you feed and I suffer?"

Sebastian carefully places his quill back into the inkwell, fighting the annoyance rising within him at her tone and disrespect. "No, Zara. Unlike what I gather from vampires in your world, we do not feed on those who do not wish to be fed upon. We compensate those who offer generously and allow them to depart freely. Many willingly return to offer again."

Zara hisses softly. "Why would anyone let a vampire feed on them?"

"From what I understand, it's quite euphoric and gold talks."

"So I am not to be lunch then?"

"You are not. Lunch is usually bread, cheese, meat, and whatever else the cook feels like making."

"You have a cook. Why?"

"We *do* eat other foods. Not just blood."

"Will my father get lunch?"

"You both got breakfast and dinner last night, did you not?"

Zara frowns, knowing they did and that it even tasted pretty good. But this was a vampire, and you never trusted a vampire. They are evil incarnate. "Why have you not killed us?"

Sebastian's eyes darken, as he lifts his gaze to stare her down, his fingers drumming the desk in annoyance. "Does your alpha kill all his prisoners?"

Zara shifts nervously under his stare, knowing instinctively that she overstepped and pushed one too many times with him. "No, he doesn't."

"Then why should I?"

'Cause you are a vampire. It's what you do!' Zara's thoughts screamed at him, but she clamps her mouth shut.

Sebastian sighs as he watches her shift beneath his gaze. "I think it's best if you return to your cell with your father. Nero will be here shortly to escort you back. And just to be clear, he's just as old as I am." He returns his attention to the parchment, doing his best to ignore her thoughts, even though he wants to know more.

Zara nods and remains on the couch in silence. Despite being a captive and lying to her about torturing her father, he really hadn't done wrong. Their cell is clean. They receive decent food. She is a bit put out by the chamber pot, but if they have no electricity, it means no running water, or flush toilets. How she longs for a bath to soak in and destress, knowing that is out of the question too. Perhaps even a change of clothes. She picks at the edges of her sweater, stained with dirt and blood, but beggars can't be choosers. They are prisoners of war, so to speak, and she needs to accept that. Her eyes drift to the vampire, clearly focusing on what he is writing, realizing that she doesn't even know his name other than he is the boss. She figures his Beta is Nero, as he feels much like a second in command around here. Nero. Strange name for a vampire, but then, humans often think their names are weird as well.

"Sebastian."

Zara looks up, startled at the break in silence. "Excuse me?"

"That's my name."

Ember hums softly. *'And it fits him perfectly. A regal name for a regal vampire.'*

'Ember, enough!'

'You are no fun Zara. Just think where we would be if you accepted him. I bet he would be most accommodating.'

'Ember, I would rather be in the cell with my Papa.'

'Too bad. I bet he's great in bed.'

'SHUT UP Ember!!' Zara blushes deeply, a growl escaping her as she forces her wolf back into her mind. She glances towards Sebastian, whose focus still seems to be on the parchment, praying he had not heard that exchange. Her body flinches when the door to the library opens.

"Sire, you called?"

"Yes Nero. Zara wishes to return to the cells with her father."

"Understood." He turns his gaze towards the girl on the couch. "This way then."

Zara jumps up and runs to the door, glancing back at Sebastian, who doesn't even lift his gaze, feeling a pang of emptiness inside at his coldness. Following behind Nero, she makes it part way back to the cells before realizing what Nero said. She stops and looks back, her brows furrowing. "Wait...Sire?"

Nero pauses, waiting for her to continue. "Keep walking Zara."

Zara hesitates, her thoughts racing about what she heard. Suddenly, it all made sense. How they all bow and respect him. That they are in a castle, and royals live in castles. Even the Alphas often live in a large mansion style building with other pack members. Not that it matters. He is still a vampire and vampires are evil. A few minutes later, she is back in her cell, where her father and food wait. Nero locks the door after him and fades into the shadows.

Kieran immediately notices her slumped shoulders, her hands twisting the edges of her shirt nervously, and draws his daughter into his arms, free from the chains that bound him. "Zare-bear, are you alright?"

Zara sighs, leaning against her father, feeling tears pricking at her eyes. "Yes Papa, I am fine."

"Do you want to talk about it?"

"Not right now." She shakes her head and pulls away, moving to the cot to curl up, ignoring the lunch that sits there.

Kieran moves over and sits next to her, placing a hand on her shoulder. "We will figure it out, Zare-bear."

Zara nods, tears slipping from her cheeks as she cries softly, slipping into an exhausted sleep.

Kieran waits until he is certain she won't wake up, before turning to the shadows. "I know you are watching. What happened to my daughter?"

Nero steps out of the shadows, a smile playing on his lips that this man is smarter than he appears. "To be honest, I do not know. I expected to return her to this cell after lunch and my boss did not divulge why he called me early. You might suggest she tread carefully, as I could feel the anger in the room, and it wasn't coming from her." With that, he turns and leaves the cells. He returns to the library, knocks lightly and enters. His eyes travel to the desk, seeing it empty, only to find him standing in the corner, staring at the parchment on the wall. "Sire?"

"Nero."

"What happened sire?"

Sebastian glances at his friend. "I don't know. She showed me how those boxes worked, and everything seemed alright. Then when I invited her to lunch, she closed down. I grew frustrated at her mood and figured it would be best to send her back."

"You realize it's been just over twenty-four hours. If vampires are as evil as her thoughts portray in their world, then it will take more time than that to convince her we are not like them. Even with a mate bond tied between you."

"I understand that, but she was full on scrapping with her wolf about it."

"Don't give up, sire. I know you can win her over. Use your charm." Nero winks at him. "We all have it."

Sebastian chuckles. "Indeed. Perhaps tomorrow. Find me clean clothing that will fit her and have it brought to my chamber."

Nero nods. "As you wish, sire."

Kieran watches his daughter remain on the cot for the duration of the day, rising only to pick at her food, and return to the cot. He sighs, and sits next to her, seeing her phone cradled in her hand and realizing he no longer has his. "Zare-bear. It helps to talk to others."

"Why Papa?"

"Well, because people have different views, I suppose."

"No, why did the Goddess pair me with him?" Her fingers trace the image on her phone, staring at the face that called to her and Ember.

"Oh Zare-bear. She has her reasons and we may never know them, but fighting against a mate bond is going to tear you apart. You are better off finding out his name and rejecting him than to go through resisting the bond."

"Sebastian."

Kieran nods, caressing his daughter's back to comfort her, seeing the image of them together on her phone that she is staring at. "Sebastian then. But you need to decide. Especially if we still seek to escape. I cannot have you doubting your decision."

"I won't Papa."

"I know you won't... Now, put your phone away and sleep because if you kill your battery, you cannot use mine. Not that I even have it."

"Sebastian has it. He wanted to see them, but I couldn't open yours."

Kieran chuckles. "You could if you thought about it."

Zara clicks her phone off and rolls over, looking at her father. "I don't know your passcode."

He taps her nose gently. "I think you might."

Zara frowns, growing thoughtful, before looking at him in shock. "You didn't! PAPA! You know better."

"Bah, there is nothing on that phone that I need to be concerned about. If someone wants to see what's on it, they can. And it got you out of your slump."

She giggles and curls up against him. "I am soooo hijacking your phone tomorrow."

Five

The Deal

Kieran kisses her forehead gently. "I am sure you are Zare-bear." He waits until she drifts off to sleep before speaking quietly to the one in the shadows. "You are not Nero, yet I recognize your scent. That means you are Sebastian. What do you want with us?"

Sebastian steps closer, allowing the cloak of shadows to drop. "You know my name, yet I only know yours as Papa."

"Kieran. What brings you down to the cells?"

"Tell me about the vampires of your world."

Kieran rises and looks over at the one standing before him. "You feel the bond with my daughter."

"That is not what I asked."

"No, but it's what you want to know."

"Nero said you were clever. He is not wrong."

Kieran chuckles. "I am a Beta for a reason, as I suspect Nero is yours. Now, what questions do you have about the mate-bond? Then I will trade information about vampires if you tell me your plans for us?"

Sebastian grows silent, listening to the man's thoughts for a moment. His eyes travel to Zara asleep on the cot, her fingers clutching her phone against her. "You have two entities inside you. A wolf and you. It appears your wolf chooses their mate, even if the human side does not."

"Partly correct. Usually the human agrees with the wolf, but not always."

"Then what happens?"

"The human can choose to reject the pairing with a formal declaration, and the partner in question accepts it. Often both suffer intense pain and the wolf withdraws."

"If Zara were to reject me, what of me?"

"To be honest. I don't know. If you were a wolf, you would feel pain as well. Some reject each other and move on, but it is common knowledge that second chance mates are rare, so it's only done in dire circumstances, or idiots."

A wry smile crosses Sebastian's lips. "It seems idiots are universal." His eyes darken as they lock on Kieran. "Is your daughter going to reject me?"

"I cannot say. She is confused. She doesn't understand why the Goddess paired her with you."

Sebastian nods, having felt the confusion within her. "If she accepts me, then what happens?"

"Normally you would mate, mark, and bond with each other. Again, I do not know. It's a complicated situation. I suppose she would stay here, but she is torn. Our family is elsewhere, and it's not like we can just drive to visit each other. So I guess you both have a decision to make. Neither of us can live in the other's realm. When we break free, unless she tells me otherwise, I intend to take her with me and return home... somehow."

"I know. It's in your thoughts."

Kieran nods. "I figured."

Sebastian moves closer to the bars. "This world is not like yours. How would you even know where to go if you got free?"

"We don't, but it's a risk we need to take."

"What if I can offer more?"

"More than my family. I'm afraid there is nothing you can offer to make me give them up."

Sebastian smiles coolly. "Good to know."

Kieran chuckles. "Did I pass the test?"

"In a way. Though you might need to choose. Your daughter or your wife."

"I will never choose. If the Goddess has willed this, then there is a way for both to work out."

"Interesting that you have such faith in this Goddess."

"I have never seen her be wrong."

"So you believe your daughter should be a match for me?"

"Yes, but I cannot begin to understand her reasons for it."

"I might." He unlocks the cage and opens it, gesturing for Kieran to exit.

Kieran glances back at his daughter and steps out, watching as Sebastian locks the door again, wondering if he could take him now and escape.

"I can hear those thoughts and you would not make it far. I am offering an olive branch. Take it." Sebastian turns, watching Kieran bow his head slightly, before turning and leading him back upstairs into the castle. He strides with purpose, knowing Kieran follows by the thoughts surrounding him despite his footsteps being just as quiet as his own. He opens the library door and waits.

Kieran steps in and looks around. "We were here the day you captured us."

"Yes, it is my favorite room in the castle and where I spend most of my free time." He walks over to a parchment hanging on the wall and stops. "I believe this parchment ties your daughter and I together."

Kieran moves to stand beside him and looks at the aging parchment, reading over the words written there.

When life and death walk as one,
The realms within become undone,
And in the fires of chaos, a new one begun,
Forged....

"What does it mean, and where is the rest?"

"Your guess is as good as mine. I have been searching for the missing half for about three hundred years."

"How old are you, exactly?"

"594 years old."

Kieran returns his gaze to the parchment, a smile ghosting his lips. "This is the Goddess's work. It's why you are my daughter's mate. If this is to come true, you need to win her over. Though it doesn't clarify if the new world is good or bad."

"Correct."

"Damn." Kieran runs his hands through his hair. "This is a tough spot to be in."

"Indeed."

"What are you going to do?"

"Try to win your daughter over, for I need to have faith it's for the better. My olive branch is this. I will move you out of the cells and into rooms within this castle if you can convince your daughter not to run or escape for seven days. At the end of those seven days, if I am unsuccessful, then the guards will step aside. The doors will open and none of my clan will stop you. All I ask upon your escape is that do not enter the Dark Woods to the east of here. No one ever returns from them."

Kieran struggles within, and paces around the library, his hands twisting before him, weighing out the pros and cons of the agreement. He knows he can't trust a vampire, and yet, this one seems to be honest enough and is, in actuality, placing the trust in them. It is certainly unexpected from his race. Being free means they can escape easier, but he is offering their freedom after seven days. Choosing this option is better than fighting their way out and ending up dead because it's unlikely they will have a second chance. Overall, Sebastian has treated them well despite being prisoners, though something had made his daughter unhappy.

He turns back to Sebastian, knowing that the same thing angered him according to Nero. He had to wonder if it was on his daughter. She could be stubborn if she set her mind to it, something that she earned directly from her mother. His shoulders slump as he sinks onto the couch, thinking of his mate, missing her desperately and wanting her arms around him. The image of her tearing through the woods, searching frantically for them, especially after the mind-link went dead, weighed heavily on his heart. He can't feel her anymore, but deep inside, he knows she is still alive as his mark still burns with her love. Seven days, and then how long until they can find someone to get them back to their realm? Damn those witches and that dragon. It's like they knew what they were doing. He rises suddenly, spinning to look at the parchment, a frown furrowing his face as he recalls the battle. "Fuck, they planned this."

Sebastian listens to Kieran's thoughts, fully expecting the battle in his mind. He arches a brow at his words. "What do you mean by that?"

"Our pack has been the only one under attack for the past year. Skirmishes, here and there, so to speak. Alpha Darian sent us to the southern borders along with some warriors, where we found our border patrols unconscious or dead. The witches and dragon were fighting each other, but when Zara and I arrived, they both turned on us. Actually, they bound me and started dragging her in. I broke through my bindings and jumped on her to keep her safe, and we both ended up here. They wanted her. I bet the other half of that scroll is in our realm."

"Then you need to take her with you when you leave in seven days. I do not want her harmed." He moves around to face Kieran.

"Spoken like a true mate."

"Do we have a deal then?"

Kieran reaches out to shake his hand. "Deal, but you need to come looking for us if you win her over. If your bond is strong enough, you will feel the minute she leaves this realm and the second you step foot in our realm. Assuming we make it back to ours. Realm hopping is not my expertise."

"Agreed. Somewhere out there will be a witch with that skill and I will find them." Sebastian shakes his hand and moves to his desk. He picks up the phone and hands it back. "Take a painting. Look for the scroll."

Kieran shakes his head. "No, Keep it. Its passcode is 1786. Do not turn it on until you arrive in our realm, then text my daughter. Get her to show you how on her phone and set my phone up."

Sebastian nods. "She showed me some messages and amazing paintings; some of which even move."

Kieran chuckles. "They are called videos. She takes a lot of them on her phone. I will admit she's a bit addicted to it, but there are worse things to be addicted to. She should be the one to take the picture of the scroll, as I know her phone will come home with us."

Sebastian turns the phone over in his hand, before placing it back on the desk. "She is intriguing. It is hard to separate her from our Zara, who is cold and calculated. She is fresh and open, but angry at me all the time." He walks around to sit behind his desk and slumps into the chair. "It felt like I had made steps forward with her when she showed me these... videos on her phone, so I offered her lunch. It was a quick snap back and her thoughts screamed at me with such intensity and hatred that I sent her away. I feel I have been reasonable considering you killed three of my men, but I am finding her difficult."

Kieran sighs. "My daughter is stubborn. That's my fault. Well, actually, no. I am gonna blame my mate on that one cause she's not here to defend herself. What you need to understand is, vampires of our world kill for the delight of it. Ours capture innocents and torture them for days, months even, draining them of their blood. We have found bodies, their skin wrapped around their bones, with hundreds of bites upon them. Others return walking corpses, unaware of their surroundings as the vampires played so many mind games on them, it broke them. They destroy because they can and for the pure pleasure of seeing families decimated. If this was our realm, I would have killed my daughter to save her the torment of what the vampires would do to her, but I knew, even when we fought your men, something was different. They were not seeking the kill the way ours do. You have already proven that in the care of us, but her mind is not accepting it yet. Give her time. Be patient and remember, she is only nineteen. You have centuries of experience on her."

Sebastian taps his fingers on the desk and nods. "Thank you Kieran. If you wish to wake your daughter, I can have you placed in rooms tonight, otherwise, it will be tomorrow morning."

"Morning is fine. It will give me time to talk to her. I should return before she wakes up."

"Nero will take you back."

The door opens and Nero walks in, giving a bow to Sebastian, before turning to Kieran who stands in front of the desk. "This way, please." He leads him back to the cells and opens the door, waiting until he steps in and closes it after him, clicking the lock into place. "I will return in the morning."

"Good night Nero."

"Good night Kieran."

Kieran moves to the cot, shifting his daughter over and crawls in beside her, laying awake for a long time. Drifting in thought about what has happened and where it's going to lead them. He suspects his daughter is going to be stubborn enough to stay in the cell, not wanting to owe a vampire, but somehow he will convince her. It makes no sense why they want her here, but it appears as if both realms may be at stake if half the scroll is here and the other half back home. Something links them together, and he aims to find out what. Clearly, the Goddess planned this when she tied his daughter to the vampire lord with a mate bond, but why?

"King."

Kieran's eyes drift to the darkness, a smile crossing his lips at the fact that Nero still lurks in the shadows. "King it is. What are your thoughts on this, Nero?"

"It is hard to say. My king has remained impassive for as long as I have known him, and yet your daughter ruffles him. It is worrisome the power she has over him, but if they are mates, then he will likewise have the same over her, from what I have read."

"Yes, they are two halves of each other, and if they learn to work together, they will be a force to be reckoned with. It is what mates are. But the question is why. Why now, why them, and how is it tied to that scroll?"

"Something for another day Kieran. Sleep now."

Kieran nods, allowing his thoughts to quiet, and drift off to sleep. He wakes in the morning to his daughter curled up next to him with her arm over his chest.

DRAGONSCALES DIVIDE 33

He brushes her hair aside. "Are you awake Zare-bear?"

"No..." She mumbles and snuggles in closer.

He chuckles. "We should get up. Breakfast is arriving soon and we will be moving."

"Moving?"

"Yes, I made a deal with Sebastian."

Zara snaps awake and bolts away from him as if he has the plague. "WHAT? You made a deal with the enemy?"

Kieran sits up in the bed and feels the anger radiating off her. "Yes. I did."

"HOW could you?"

Kieran's tone sharpens, an edge creeping in. "ENOUGH Zara. We are prisoners. You make deals to better your station whether you want to or not and I have done so."

She sneers quietly, challenging her father. "WHAT deal did you make, Papa?"

"We stay upstairs in the castle, living as a guest and do not seek to escape. We learn and accept their ways. If, after seven days, we do not wish to adapt, we are free to leave, but we need to make an honest effort. If the king decides we are not, we return here for the duration of our lives."

"HOW could you do that, Papa!?"

"It's for the best Zara. You will see it for what it is if you open your eyes."

"I WILL not!"

Kieran draws on his Beta aura, not liking the fact that he needs to use it on his daughter. "You will or I will turn you over my knee. IS that understood?"

Zara kneels and bares her neck. "Yes, Papa."

"Good."

Six

Acceptance

An hour later, the guards escort them into the castle. Nero drops Zara off at the library and takes Kieran to a set of rooms. Inside, the main room boasts two feather beds adorned with brightly colored quilted bedspreads. An ornate chest sits at the foot of each bed. A small dinette sits nestled between a stained glass window and a wooden door. On the opposite side of the room, a plush couch and two chairs face each other near a second door.

Nero gestures toward the doors. "One leads to a balcony. There are guards stationed outside in case you decide to escape from two floors up. The other door leads to the washing chamber. Maids bring fresh water up daily and empty your chamber pot in the evening. Do not harm them, or we will return you downstairs. Sebastian has granted you permission to explore the castle, but be aware that a contingent of four guards will accompany you if you leave this room, including the two at your door. Under no circumstances are you to leave the castle without Sebastian. There are clothes within each of the chests that should fit you and Zara. The maids will wash your current clothing and return them in the morning. Water is being heated and will be here within the hour for a bath. Your daughter will have hers in another room at the same time. You will both join the king for lunch."

Kieran nods and steps into the room. "Understood. Thank you."

Nero returns the nod and closes the door after him, leaving him alone to explore.

Zara steps into the library, her eyes immediately spotting Sebastian sitting behind his desk, quill in hand, his fingers blackened with ink as he focuses on the parchment. She fiddles with her phone, uncertain why she is here and not with her father.

"Sit Zara. I am nearly done."

DRAGONSCALES DIVIDE   35

She bows and moves over to sit on the couch.

After a few minutes, Sebastian looks up at Zara, who fidgets nervously, having heard that her father clearly used some sort of power over her this morning. "Your thoughts are quiet this morning. Zara."

"I suppose."

"Why?"

"Papa told me to behave, so I am."

"And do you always do what your Papa tells you to?"

"No, I..." She scowls at him. "Is that a trick question?"

Sebastian chuckles and rises. "No, pure curiosity. Come, I have a surprise for you." He offers a hand to her, seeing her hesitate before taking it. He leads her out of the library; down another few corridors and up some stairs. He opens the door at the end of the hall and guides her into a plush bedroom.

Zara puts her breaks on as soon as she doesn't see her father, knowing by the scent within that this is his chamber. "I am not sharing a bed with you, *sire*."

"You caught that, did you? I wondered... As for sharing a bed, I am not asking you to. You are sharing a room with your father, but unless you wish to bathe with him, or the maids downstairs, this is the next best thing."

"Excuse me?"

"Zara, you are in three-day-old clothes and I hate to say it, but your scent of honeysuckle is being drowned by the scent of sweat, blood, and dirt."

Zara blushes deeply at Sebastian's kind words of saying she stinks. "How very polite of you, sire."

"Sebastian Zara, just Sebastian. Come." He steps in and leads her to another door. Inside is a large wooden tub with steam rising from it; buckets of water surrounding it. A small table holds a variety of soap. Beige fabric sits folded on a shelf nearby. "The water in the tub is near boiling. Add cold until it's a suitable temperature. There are a couple of outfits on my bed that should fit you. Leave these clothes in here and the maids will collect and clean them when they empty the water." Sebastian turns and heads out of the room.

Zara follows for a few steps. "Wait, you are not staying?"

"Why would I, Zara? But if it is your wish, then I will."

Zara blushes and mumbles something about being a prisoner under her breath.

"Yes Zara, you are a prisoner, but I am not unreasonable. Now, this is your time. Enjoy it. The guards will return you to the library when you are done." He steps out of his bedroom, nodding at the two appearing at his side to guard the door, and heads back to the library.

Zara stands in shock for a moment at the fact she is alone. She runs across the room to open the other door, breathing in the fresh air and stepping out onto the balcony. Peering over the edge, she groans in dismay; both at the fact that it's three floors up and it overlooks a cliff face plunging into the ocean below. Two guards wave at her from nearby on the ground. She frowns deeply and waves back. Stepping inside, her shoulder slump as she heads back to the bathing chamber and strips her clothes. Cooling the water to her desired temperature, she steps in and gasps in delight. Picking out a soap, she scrubs herself from head to toe, enjoying the pure pleasure of being clean; something she took for granted at home.

Half an hour later, she vacates the cool water and dries herself off. Stepping into the bedchamber, she moves to the dresses and looks them over before pulling on the pale blue one. Zara fumbles with the lacings before deciding they are good enough. She spins in a small circle, giggling at the skirts that flow around her, feeling like a lady in one of the fantasy novels she reads. She collects her phone and opens the door, eying the two guards warily. "I am ready to go to the library now."

"As you wish." They step away from the wall, one leading, the other following. A few minutes later, they stop at the library door as she steps in.

Sebastian inhales deeply, the room filling with her familiar scent as desire slams into him, hitting him in the pit of his stomach. He groans inwardly, questioning the wisdom of granting them freedom to roam his castle. Lifting his gaze from the book he's reading, he takes in her appearance as she surveys the room, their gazes locking briefly. Setting the book aside, he rises and approaches her cautiously. "You look beautiful, Zara."

Zara blushes and shifts her stance nervously. "Thank you. I scrubbed myself twice so I hope I smell better."

Sebastian chuckles. "Yes, indeed. Would you care to join me, or would you like to return to the room I placed you in?"

Zara chews on her lower lip as she ponders him for a moment. "What are you reading?"

"It is research about werewolves. I know you call yourself shifters, but we do not have books on shifters."

"Do you have books on vampires?"

"Of course. Would you like one?"

"Yes, please."

"Come." Sebastian moves over to the bookshelves and pulls two out, handing them to Zara.

Zara gasps and staggers at the weight of the books, her gaze snapping up to him as she hugs them against her chest. "Thank you. Where should I sit?"

"Wherever you want, my dear."

Zara nods and settles into a chair across from where he was sitting. She places one book on the table along with her phone and caresses the other. Running her hands slowly over the leather cover and the intricately carved designs before flipping it open, staring in awe at the calligraphy inside. "These are amazing!"

Sebastian settles and pulls his book off the table. "Do you not have books in your world?"

"We do, but they are not the same. They print ours with text and the covers are just cardstock paper."

"Print? Cardstock?"

"Yes. It's like the messages I showed you on my phone. You can get them in all different styles, but books are no longer handwritten anymore. Cardstock is like stiff paper, but they print pretty pictures on the covers."

"I will not say I understand, but perhaps one day I will see your books."

Zara nods, and pulls her legs up into the chair, tucking her skirts around her as she props the book in her lap. A few hours later, she sighs, and places it aside. "Do you have something to drink? Soda would be great, but I bet that's nonexistent too."

"Considering I have never heard of this soda, you are correct." Sebastian lifts his gaze, feeling hesitant to ask after yesterday's mood swing. "Are you hungry? We could get lunch in the dining chamber with your father."

Zara flinches inwardly at the hesitation laced within his voice, knowing she caused it. "I am sorry about yesterday. I will try to keep an open mind."

Sebastian smiles and rises. He takes her hand gently in his, kissing the back of it. "That is all I can ask for. Come, I will take you to the dining room."

Zara closes her eyes at the sparks at his touch, hearing Ember purring loudly at his kiss, giving only a nod as she rises to stand next to him, not entirely trusting her words. She walks beside him as he leads her out of the library and down some stairs, through more hallways and into a grand dining hall. She pauses, her eyes widening at the sight of father already sitting there, casually talking to a few guards lining the walls. "Papa!"

Kieran rises and looks over at his daughter, smiling at her appearance. "Damn! I wish your mother was here to see you dressed in that."

"Papa! I wear dresses!" Her eyes roam over the dark blue tunic reaching nearly past his knees, embroidery on the sleeves and neckline, with tan pants beneath it.

"Really? When was the last time you wore one?"

Zara chews on her lips as she thinks back, unable to recall the last one she did. "I just do."

Sebastian chuckles, as he moves to sit at the table. "To be fair, Kieran, she didn't have a choice. I only placed two dresses out for her. Now, if she had gone through my wardrobe, she would have found tunics and breeches that would be oversized but suitable."

"I never actually thought about it. Next time I will."

"Too late. The chest in your room only contains dresses. You missed out."

Zara pouts, laughter dancing in her eyes. "That's not fair! You didn't tell me the entire room was an option."

"True, I didn't, but I half expected you to search anyway."

She rolls her eyes. "I spent the time soaking because someone said I stunk."

"That's not entirely true. I simply stated your natural scent was being drowned out by others."

Kieran laughs and hugs his daughter. "Oh Zare-bear. You can search our room. Now, I am starving, especially since whatever they are cooking has been wafting this way the past ten minutes, and it smells delicious." He settles at the table with Sebastian, immediately noticing he did not sit at the head of the table as a king normally would. He arches a brow as his daughter moves to sit next to Sebastian, but remains silent on the subject. "What have you been doing for the past few hours, Zare-bear?"

Zara blushes and glances at Sebastian. "Reading in the library."

"About?"

"Vampires. You should see their books, Papa. They are amazing. Each cover is intricately carved leather and inside is all handwritten. Why don't we have books like that?"

"Cost Zare-bear. Our world has simplified everything by the price to make them. Those would be too expensive to make when a computer can make them at a fraction of the cost."

Zara grows pensive. "It's too bad. They really are beautiful."

Lunch arrives, with loaves of freshly baked bread accompanied by churned butter, as well as venison pies. Platters adorned with grapes appear, complemented by pitchers of water, wine, and ale.

Zara remains quiet as she listens to her father and Sebastian talk. Her father explains how the pack hierarchy works and where they themselves fit into the pack, with Sebastian following suit with the vampire clans. She darts occasional glances to Sebastian, his dark eyes softer now that they are not fighting with him. Zara catches him meeting her gaze every so often, causing her to blush and look away.

Lunch passes quickly, and as the platters are being removed, Sebastian rises. He gives a nod to them both. "I will leave you to talk and see you here for dinner."

Zara looks up sharply. "Where are you going?"

Sebastian keeps his face passive as he studies her, feeling the panic and worry inside her. He takes her hand gently in his and lifts it, kissing the back of it. "Where I always am, my dear. The library. It's my favorite place." He turns and strides from the room, feeling Zara's eyes following him. He makes his way back to his corner and settles in his chair. Shortly after, Nero brings in a glass of wine and places it on the table beside him.

"Report."

"Well, you were correct, sire. It was all but a moment before she was on the balcony peering over the edge. Apparently looking rather crestfallen. Her father, on the other hand, opened the doors, but did not step outside. They remained open all morning. According to the guards at his door, he snores quite loudly. I don't believe he slept in the cell downstairs. They had to knock several times to wake him up."

"Yes, her father seems fairly reasonable and I don't sense ill intent from him."

"But you do from Zara?"

"No, she is not as accepting as her father, but as he stated, she is still young."

They both lift their gazes at the knock on the door.

"Enter."

A guard steps in, bowing to Sebastian and Nero. "Sire, they wish to join you in the library for the afternoon."

Sebastian glances at Nero in shock, fully expecting them to explore or return to their room. "Certainly."

Nero chuckles, mind-linking Sebastian as he watches Zara move across the room to the chair in front of him. *'Perhaps she is softening, sire. I will settle in the back corner.'*

'Perhaps.'

Sebastian's eyes follow Zara, smiling as she tucks her legs in again and curls up, pulling the book into her lap. He shifts his gaze to Kieran. "Is there a specific subject you wish to read?"

Kieran shakes his head. "I might just look if I may. I will admit, I am not much of a reader, being that I am often too busy training warriors."

Sebastian smiles wryly. "You understand why I cannot offer you to train with my warriors?"

"One hundred percent. And since you don't have TV, I might as well learn something."

"TV?"

Zara looks up and smiles. "Yes, it's like those moving pictures on my phone, but much bigger."

Sebastian chuckles. "Interesting. Well, there are hundreds of books here. Find one and settle in."

They spend the afternoon in relative silence. Zara and Kieran read while Sebastian and Nero spend about equal time reading and listening to their thoughts as they digest their books. Sebastian answers the occasional question that arises, knowing this world is very much different from the one they came from. As dinner approaches, Sebastian leads them back to the dining chamber, with Nero joining them this time. After dinner, they part ways, with Kieran taking Zara back to their room to explore while Nero and Sebastian head back to the library.

Days pass in much the same fashion, Sebastian showing them the castle, the grounds, reading, and dining with them, all the while carefully courting Zara. He smiles at the fact that her laughter comes more freely and that she banters with him now, hearing the approval in her father's thoughts. On the sixth evening, he shows her the scroll, and she snaps the picture, quickly shutting the phone off because of her battery being dangerously low. The four of them discuss the options and what the scroll may mean. She grows silent as her thoughts whirl in her head. After an hour of being in the library, she rises and gives a bow to

Sebastian. "I am going to wander, then head back to my room to sleep."

"Did you want company?"

She shakes her head. "No, I need to be alone."

"Well, alone is irrelevant. You will have guards following you."

"I know, but they are not you or Nero. They are different. I don't really talk to them."

"True. Enjoy your walk." Sebastian watches her leave the library, listening to the quiet emptiness in the library now that her presence is gone. He rises, giving a nod to Nero. "I am going to sleep. My body is craving it."

"You have not slept since she got here, sire. I am not surprised."

Sebastian chuckles. "Indeed. It is alluring, hearing their thoughts all the time."

"Yes, it is. I will watch over them."

"Thank you." Sebastian heads into his room and pulls his robes off. He slips into the bed and stares at the ceiling, visions of Zara's smile crossing his mind as he drifts into slumber.

Seven

The Bond Demands

In the darkest hour of the night, Zara remains awake and listens to her father's snores. She knows tomorrow they are leaving, feeling pain in her heart at the thought and hearing Ember's whimper. Even if she wants to stay, she needs to go home to find the other half of that scroll. She slips from the bed and pulls a robe on, padding quietly to the door. Opening it, she notices the guards looking at her warily. "I just wish to go to the library." Zara follows them silently, finding herself at the door and stepping inside. Her eyes immediately scan for Sebastian, finding only Nero.

Nero arches a brow, hearing the disappointment in her thoughts. "It's a little late to be visiting the library, lassie."

Zara sighs. "I know. Papa was snoring."

"Is that the only reason you are here?"

"Yes."

"Are you certain?"

Zara rolls her eyes. "Why are you even asking when you already know?"

Nero chuckles. "It tells us whether you speak the truth or lies. Sebastian is sleeping."

"Wait, he's sleeping?"

"Yes, we sleep. Not like you, though. We do not dream, we do not move. We sleep."

"Can I see him?"

"He will not know you are there, lassie."

"I still would like to see him."

Nero studies her for a few minutes before nodding. He rises and leads her out of the library, down several halls and up some stairs. He pushes the door open to his king's chamber, and steps aside, allowing Zara to enter.

Zara moves up silently to the bed, the color draining from her face. "He's not breathing and looks dead."

"We are dead, lassie. We get our life from blood. It gives warmth and color to our bodies."

She caresses his cheek lightly. "Can I stay here with him tonight?"

Nero arches a brow. "You can. But I will be here with you. My duty is to protect my king and in this state, he is vulnerable."

"I won't kill him."

"You are a guest and a prisoner, lassie. I am not taking any chances."

"I understand. I just want to sleep with him."

Nero chuckles. "You may, but he will not hold you, as I suspect you are accustomed to."

"It's alright. Being beside him is enough."

Nero gestures to the bed as he moves over to the stuffed chair and settles in for the remainder of the night.

Zara slips into the bed, adjusting Sebastian's arm so that she can rest her head on his shoulder and curls up against him. She feels the stillness of the room, even knowing that Nero is nearby. Closing her eyes, her thoughts drift to the vampire beside her, knowing it is going to be difficult to leave him in the morning. Wondering when exactly he had won her over. Tears slip down and pool onto his shoulder as she tightens her hold on him, allowing sleep to claim her.

Sebastian wakes in the morning, his eyes snapping open to the warm body beside him. Movement draws his attention to Nero rising from the chair in the corner. *'Nero, what's going on?'*

'The lassie wanted to sleep with you last night. She didn't have malicious thoughts, but I wasn't taking any chances and leaving her alone with you.'

'Why?'

'I do believe she likes you, sire. Now, I will take my leave. I can hear her thoughts waking.'

'Thank you Nero.'

'Anytime sire. Enjoy your morning.' Nero heads out of the room and closes the door after him, giving a nod to the two guards. He heads back to the library to complete the work Sebastian has placed before him.

Sebastian shifts slightly and draws Zara closer, his fingers tracing along her jawline, feeling wonder at this woman who hated him seven days ago and was now bravely crawling into his bed. He smiles when her blue eyes open. "Good morning Zara. What brings you to my bed?"

A blush stains her cheeks as she smiles at him. "Ember and I missed you."

"I saw you for dinner."

"I know, but knowing we are leaving today... I just..."

Sebastian places a finger to her lips. "Shhh, I know, my love. I know."

Zara nods and tightens her hold. "I don't want to go, Sebastian."

"You have to, Zara. You need to find a witch to send you back."

"Make me yours then, before I go."

"Zara, you don't know what you are asking me."

"I do."

Sebastian groans and kisses her gently at first, feeling the instant well of fires within. He breaks the kiss and studies her slightly parted lips, the desire in her eyes. "Are you certain?"

She nods. "One hundred percent."

Sebastian mind-links Nero, knowing damn well her father will come looking for her. *'Nothing is to disturb us till lunch. Take him to the fighting rings if you need to.'*

Nero chuckles. *'I understand, sire. Enjoy.'*

At lunch, Zara follows Sebastian in the dining room, a flush to her cheeks that only deepens under her father's scrutiny. "Papa."

"Zare-bear. Is everything alright?" Kieran notices immediately that she is wearing Sebastian's clothing.

Her fingers twine in the sash at her waist. "Yes Papa."

Kieran's eyes flash as Emeric rises protectively to the surface. "Let's see it, Zare-bear. It better be there."

Zara shifts uncomfortably beneath her father's gaze, her eyes sliding to Sebastian, whose expression remains impassive but his arm tightens around her waist. She moves her fingers up to the collar and pushes it aside, showing him the mating mark. "How did you know Papa?"

"Well, let's see. My daughter was gone before I woke up and Nero took me to the fighting rings to wear off steam."

Sebastian chuckles. "Damn, I guess that was a dead giveaway."

"Indeed, it was. And you, did she return the favor?"

"Are you questioning the king?"

He growls softly. "Yes, but I don't care. It's MY daughter we are talking about."

He slides his collar aside and shows her mark upon him. "We are bound together now."

Kieran smiles. "Perfect. Welcome to the family, Sebastian...?"

"Darkholme."

"Darkholme. Zara Darkholme. It has a nice ring to it, Zare-bear. Well done."

"Thank you, Papa."

The group enjoys their last lunch together as a silent uneasiness fills the air. After lunch, Sebastian kisses Zara softly, whispering in her ear. "Take care, my queen. Stay safe until I can find you."

Zara blinks back tears and nods. "I will Seb." She hugs him tightly before backing away and giving him a bow. "I think I will retire to my room with my father. I believe he wishes to speak with me."

Eight

Deceptive Freedom

Kieran watches the goodbye, knowing the pain his daughter is going through. "Come Zara." He leads her back to their room, where she collects her phone and tucks it into her bodice. An hour later, Kieran and Zara slip from the castle, knowing the guards are suspiciously absent because Sebastian made it happen. Once outside, each of them shifts into wolf form and makes a run for it down the cobblestone road. Not long after, they can hear the horns sounding from the castle at their escape, only to solidify their favor with any of the resistance they might run into. Hooves pound the cobblestone behind them as they give chase. When they breach the walls of the castle grounds, a shadow looms above them, causing Zara to look up and yelp in shock. She veers to the right to avoid it, feeling the claws sink into her hide. *'PAPA, Run!'*

Kieran snarls at the black dragon, lunging at the claws that hold his daughter, only to find one latching onto him as well.

"Enough! Now be good pups and shift back so you can speak." The dragon's voice booms and uses his magic to force them back to human form.

Nero yanks his horse to a stop as the dragon swoops overhead. *'Sire, a black dragon is here, and has the wolves.'*

Sebastian shifts into a raven and flies out the window. He soars through the air to where Nero waits and changes back, standing next to his horse. He walks forward, seeing the dragon with Kieran and Zara in his claws, lifting his eyes upward to the gloating dragon. "What do you want, Dragon?"

"Did you like my gift, King Sebastian?"

"What do you mean, your gift?" Sebastian refuses to look at Zara, feeling her fear and confusion through their bond. Knowing if he does, it will give the dragon an advantage over him.

"The wolf girl. Your mate. I know vampires do not feel emotions like wolves do, but I know of the prophecy. The one that you would bond with. I just needed to find her in order to have power over you. She's it, isn't she? What would you give to stop me from ending her right now?"

Sebastian turns his gaze to Kieran's gasp, his dark eyes warning him to remain silent.

Kieran ignores Sebastian and growls as he fights the claws surrounding him. "No. My daughter has nothing to do with this."

"Be quiet Beta, this doesn't involve you. You weren't even supposed to be here. This involves only the king." The dragon's eyes glint in the light as they narrow on Sebastian. "Do you remember me, sire? I was but a boy when you came into town and killed my father as I hid beneath a wagon."

Sebastian smiles wryly. "You have the wrong vampire. There is no way I killed a dragon."

"My father wasn't a dragon. He was human. I was but a street rat and tried to steal from him. He captured me and took me home to his cottage. He fed me and gave me a bed to sleep in. I ran away, of course, but returned that evening. He welcomed me back with open arms and took care of me for six years as his son. You see, he lost his wife and son to childbirth. You took him from me and now, having given you your mate, I will take her from you. So that you feel the same loss. I have been planning this for a very long time."

"How long exactly?"

"767 years."

"Then you would want my sire, Silas, for I am only 594 years old. He was the one that raided towns and villages. Not me."

Kieran growls and fights against the claws. "You cannot use my daughter as a pawn and kill her because you have a vendetta against the wrong vamp."

The dragon's claw tightens on Kieran. "I told you to be quiet. I can end you just as quickly."

Sebastian draws the dragon's attention back to him. "What do you want?"

"You. On your knees and your kingdom to rule."

"And what will happen to my people?"

"Nothing, if they submit to my rule."

"And if I refuse?"

"Then you lose your mate."

Sebastian's eyes drift to Zara, feeling her pain and love blending along their bond. "By killing her? Seems pointless, don't you think? Yes, I will mourn her death, but I will move on from it and continue to rule as I have been."

The dragon chuckles. "Always the cold, impassive vampire. You are correct, that would be too easy. No, I am sending them back, so that you can live, knowing she will forever be out of your reach. Untouchable. Wondering if she still holds hope for you or if another claims her, all the while not having the answers to those questions. I, of course, can grant you access to her in exchange for your kingdom."

"Then do it. Show me you can back those words up."

The dragon growls, the gem at his neck glowing, the very ground shuddering beneath his feet as a portal opens beside him. He tosses first Kieran through and then Zara, closing it before anyone can react. "Do you feel the pain now, sire?"

Sebastian fights the loss within, and bows to the dragon. "Not at all. In fact, I feel peace, knowing she is no longer in your clutches." Magic flows from the ground, creating a bubble around the dragon standing before him. "Now, as much as I want you out of my territory, I need you contained long enough so that they can return to their pack. After that, you best get out of my territory or you will discover that, in fact, I can kill a dragon. The only reason you are still alive is because you introduced us."

"You tricked me?" The dragon rages against the dome, clawing at the magic that binds him. "Consider her dead now."

"Yes, I did." Sebastian mind-links Nero as they walk back to the castle. *'Now we find a witch with the ability to realm hop. Did you send the notices out?'*

'I did, sire.'

'Good, I want my queen back. The sooner the better.'

Sebastian ignores the roaring of the dragon at his front gates as he strides back to the castle, struggling with the emptiness inside at the loss of Zara. Once inside the castle and out of sight, he leans against the wall and closes his eyes, his body shaking within.

"Sire?"

His pain filled dark eyes open, understanding the question and concern in his voice. "It's harder than I thought it would be, Nero. It is far worse than when our Zara left under the cover of darkness."

"I believe it's tied to the mate bond, sire. You didn't have that with our Zara."

Sebastian nods. "Let's hope your missives find themselves in the hands of a willing witch. I need her back here with me."

"It will take time, but there must be one out there somewhere, sire. I will keep sending weekly missives out until one accepts your offer."

"Thank you Nero, I think I am going to retire to the library."

Nero chuckles. "It's where her scent is the strongest."

"Yes, other than my room, but I don't want to go down that path yet."

"I understand sire. I will have wine brought."

"And perhaps a feeder. I have not eaten all week for fear she would smell the blood upon me."

"I think she accepted you as a vampire, sire. She went to your room and commented that you looked dead. I confirmed you were, and that we used blood to keep us alive. Her thoughts did not rage as they did upon her arrival. In fact, I would say there was a touch of sadness within, so I do not think she would have minded."

"I know. After the second day, it felt like we had an uneasy truce that I wasn't willing to break. Now I know we have a bond, and it won't break if she catches me feeding."

"You will get her back, sire. Even her father feels this. It just might take some time."

"Thank you Nero."

"You're welcome."

Nine

Across Realms

Kieran groans as he hits the ground, feeling a leg and possibly an arm break upon impact, only to have the wind knocked out of him as Zara lands on top of him, adding some ribs to that. He closes his eyes, trying to quell the pain as the mind-links snap into place with his pack and his mate. *'Lila! Gawd! It is so good to feel you again.'*

Lila absently scrolls through the pictures on her phone wishing for many things, that she had taken more pictures of him, that he hadn't gone on that last mission with their daughter and that he was here, right now. Her body was exhausted after the many hours of searching for him, knowing instinctively that he wasn't dead. She would feel it. She startles out her thoughts as the phone drops to the table, certain her mind is playing tricks on her, just as the mate bond clicks back into place. *'Kieran!!! Zara?'*

'Is here... I have missed you so much.'

'I am on my way, Kieran.' She bolts from the house and shifts into a wolf, using her bond to determine where he is.

Kieran mink-links Alpha Darian next. *'Alpha, we need help.'*

Darian rises in shock at the mind-link of his beta after ten days of searching. *'Where are you?'*

'I think south. I hear the ocean. Pretty sure I broke my leg, perhaps an arm and a few ribs. Zara has deep claw wounds from a dragon and I'm not sure about broken bones as she landed on me. Neither of us is moving from the fall we just took.'

'We will be there as soon as we can.' He immediately mind-links Kieran's wife, knowing she would also feel the connection, *'He's back.'* Linking his Gamma and some warriors. *'We need a litter for Kieran, and possibly Zara, though I can carry her. South borders.'*

Lila responds. *'I know. I am heading his way. I can feel his pain through our bond.'*

'I will collect Ashlyn and join you.'

Kieran gathers Zara into his arms, knowing she is in pain, both from the wounds and loss of the mate bond. "Zare-bear, are you alright?"

Zara shakes her head, sobbing, and curls up against her father.

Kieran tightens his hold. "Shhh Zare-bear, we will figure it out."

"I miss him already, Papa. I feel so empty. Is that how you felt with Mama?"

"Yes Zare-bear, but as long as your mark is still there, you need to understand he's with you. Even if it's in another realm."

"I thought I could do it, but I don't think I can."

"You can Zare-bear, you are strong. We will get him back."

Zara nods, crying herself into an uneasy sleep in her father's arms, despite the agony radiating in her body.

Hours later, both Darian and Lila arrive on the southern borders, seeing the pair lying together, dressed in unusual clothing soaked in blood. Kieran's leg lying at a strange angle with one unconscious Zara sprawled over his chest.

Lila shifts out of wolf form and runs forward, dropping to her knees at his side. "Kieran!"

Kieran lifts a hand, groaning in pain, and caresses her cheek lightly. "Lila my love."

A frown mars Darian's features as he does a quick scan, knowing there is nothing he could have fallen from. "Kieran, Ashlyn will heal you, but you need to let Zara go so she can look you over. Where did you fall from?"

"A portal. That bloody dragon threw us through it. I suspect he damn well knew we were well above the landline and hoped that the fall would break us." He releases his hold on Zara.

Darian gently detangles Zara from her father's arms and lies her on the ground, immediately noticing the claw marks on her side, the tears in her clothing, stopping at the mate mark on her neck. He arches a brow, glancing between the pair. "Are you missing someone, Kieran?"

"No. It's just us." Kieran switches to mind-link. *'I will explain later. I don't want my mate knowing Zara is a pawn in a dragon's game just yet.'*

'Understood.' Darian looks over at Ashlyn. "She has deep wounds to heal. While you do that, Lila and I will set Kieran's bones."

"Yes Alpha."

"Lila, hold him down. This is going to hurt."

Lila nods as the pair of them set about resetting the leg and arm as Kieran growls in pain. "I have warriors arriving with a litter. It's the only way we are going to get you back to the pack until Emeric heals you fully."

"Thank you Alpha...Ashlyn." He closes his eyes, feeling Ashlyn's healing magic flow through him and take away some of the pain.

"They will need a few days to rest, Alpha. Both have extensive injuries."

"I will make sure of it." Lila tightens her hand on Kieran's, watching the warriors arriving with litters to carry her mate and daughter home.

Late that evening, Kieran and Zara sleep in their own beds as Lila hovers over them, ensuring they get the rest and care that they need. In the morning Kieran wakes to sun streaming in the window, not realizing how much he missed it in the sunless realm. The color drains from his face, realizing it was something he never thought about when and if Sebastian arrives in this realm. Would it affect him as it did their vampires? Would he need to become a creature of the night? Shit! He hoped it didn't. Zara has already suffered enough in having to leave her mate and knowing she is a pawn in some dragon's vendetta. Damn, he wished it was simple enough to just call him, but had to hope the Goddess knew what she was doing and would have them arrive at night. He pushes himself out of bed, the fresh scent of coffee making his mouth water. Limping down the stairs to the kitchen, he settles into a chair as his wife putters. "Lila, my love."

"Kieran, you are not to be out of bed!"

"Then you shouldn't have made coffee! I have been coffee-less for ten days."

"What do you mean?" She pours a cup and adds his normal teaspoon of sugar.

Kieran chuckles as he wraps his hands around the cup, breathing in deep. "Coffee didn't exist."

She settles into the chair beside him. "Where did you go, Kieran?"

He takes a sip, closing his eyes at the heaven in his cup. "Perhaps we should invite the Alpha so I only need to explain it once. Has Zara woken?"

"No, but I heard her sobbing well into the night, Kieran. What's going on?"

"I will link Darian. He needs to hear this. I need you BOTH to keep an open mind."

"That worries me, Kieran?"

He reaches out to take her hand, squeezing it gently. "Please, just listen. Zara is going to need us more than ever." His eyes glaze over as he reaches out with his mind. *'Alpha Darian. Is it possible for you and Luna Willow to come to the cottage?'*

'Of course. We are already on our way to check on you.'

Kieran chuckles at the knock on the door. "Apparently, my love, they are here."

Lila smiles and runs to the door, bowing to her Alpha and Luna. "He's in the kitchen with his coffee."

They walk into the kitchen and settle in at the table. "Kieran, you're looking better than yesterday. How's Zara?"

"Still sleeping, which is good. She needs it."

"What happened, Kieran? You and Zara both disappeared off the link?"

"More than we expected." He sighs, drinking another mouthful of coffee to settle his nerves. "We went out, as you asked. There was a dragon fighting witches, which you know. We were aborting the mission as planned, but it seems they were after Zara. They bound me with magic and started dragging her towards them. I broke through their shadow wraps and jumped on her to protect her. Immediately after, both their magic struck us and transported us to another realm. We landed near a castle with well-manicured gardens." He looks at his wife. "You would have loved them. Before we could even determine where we were, vampires arrived and quickly surrounded us. Not like ours. These were level-headed and clever. We took down three before they took us down. They tossed us in a cell with silver shackles. I can't tell you how long we were there, but when we woke up, they brought us before their boss. Their King. He threatened my life and Zara caved when they cut my throat."

The three gasp in anger, each looking at Kieran's neck.

He chuckles. "I am fine. I will admit, internally, I was having a panic attack while bleeding in a room full of vamps, but none of them reacted. When have you ever known a vampire to remain calm around fresh blood? The cut was not deep, but it was enough for Zara and she agreed to be questioned. They removed me from the room and kept her. When she returned to the cell, she was angry and despondent at the same time and I knew something more had happened. She admitted when I threatened to turn her over my knee, with chains on I might add, that Ember had claimed the King as her mate."

Darian breaks the silence that ensues. His voice edged. "The mate mark. Was it forced upon her?"

Kieran shakes his head. "No. Both their marks are mutual."

Lila places a hand on her husband. "Are you saying Zara mated a vamp? That she's been crying her eyes out over a bloodsucker?"

Kieran sighs, flipping his hand around to clasp hers. "Yes, but these are different, Lila. The next day, they pulled Zara from the cell again, and she returned within the hour. Apparently, she ruffled the King's feathers, and he sent her away. Nero, the King's Beta, so to speak, and I spoke after the fact. It surprised him that Sebastian had sent her back, expecting it to be after lunch. He warned me to let Zara know not to push boundaries."

"Sebastian? That's our daughter's mate?"

"Yes, Sebastian Darkholme."

Luna Willow lifts her gaze. "Wait, I recognize that name. I recall reading about it in my history class. Sebastian wasn't the name tied to Darkholme though, but it started with an S. I will have to look it up."

"That would probably be his sire, Silas."

"That's right. There was something about the only pure lineage of vampires. The first of the first. But they all disappeared and since then, the vampires have been the crazed ones we see."

Kieran nods. "I am not surprised. These were different. Later that night, Sebastian came down to the cells to watch, and we spoke. He took me upstairs to the library to show me half a prophecy."

Darian glances between Willow and Kieran. "Half?"

"Yes, Alpha, half. I suspect the other half is here, somewhere. Zara took a picture. It spoke of death and life working together. We agreed it is likely tied to them and that the rest needs to be found. As I paced around the library, I realized Zara was the key. They wanted her. That's why all the skirmishes at our borders. The dragon somehow knew Zara was the one."

Darian frowns, not liking the implications. "The borders have been quiet since you left Kieran. Nothing has attacked us."

Kieran turns to his longtime friend. "She won't like it, but she's gonna need guards. She needs to be kept safe. As we escaped the castle, the dragon caught us."

"Wait, escaped?"

"Sorry, I fast forwarded there. Yes, we escaped. Sebastian and I made a deal after agreeing that Zara was likely the life in the prophecy, and that the Goddess knew what she was doing when she paired them. He agreed to move us into the castle, with guards, of course, if I agreed to give him a chance to win her over. After seven days, he would pull his guards so that we could escape and pretend to chase us. He suggested we find their resistance, essentially rogues, who had witches that might be able to realm hop us home. In the end, I was willing, but Zara was a touch stubborn."

Lila laughs softly. "A touch? This is our Zara you are talking about."

Kieran rolls his eyes. "Alright, I had to pull rank and use my aura on her to comply. But over the course of the week, Sebastian proved an excellent host. Other than the four guards, you would never have known we were prisoners of war. Apparently, on the last night while I slept, Zara left to be with Sebastian. He had, in fact, won her over." He chuckles. "Nero even took me to the fighting rings the next morning to blow off steam. They definitely have a different fighting technique, one I plan on teaching here. But I digress. He succeeded, but then a mate bond is hard to deny. After breakfast, he pulled his guards. We shifted and ran, hearing the alarms going off, something that was staged to better our position with the resistance when we found them. We never did, though. That bloody dragon found us first." He grows silent, replaying the attack in his mind. "He specifically asked Sebastian if he liked the gift of his mate. Stating, he would release her if Sebastian forfeited his kingdom. I fought him and he snapped at me, stating I was not even supposed to be there; that I had gotten in the way. So it was Zara they were after."

Darian rises from his chair and paces. "That's not good, Kieran. Had I known, I would not have sent you."

Kieran moves to stand by his friend, clapping a hand on his shoulder. "None of us knew. I could have chosen another warrior and left Zara here, but she earned her right to that fight. This is not your fault, Darian. It's simply circumstance. We need to find the other half of the prophecy before that dragon comes calling for Zara, because I suspect he's pissed that Sebastian tricked him into opening a portal and throwing us through." He glances to the stairs and listens for a moment, ensuring that Zara is still sleeping. "Honestly, I told her he was, but we don't even know if Sebastian is still alive. I need to have faith that if the Goddess willed this, she will protect him. Add that to the fact that he is also over five hundred years old. He might have some skills against a dragon."

"I would like to demand that you move into the pack house, Kieran, but I know that's not happening, so I will have guards placed on your family. Subtly, of course, as I don't want to cause panic just yet. Except for perhaps Zara. You, Lila, one of us. She needs a constant guard. Zach already hangs out with her, but

I will lower his duties so he can be with her twenty four-seven. I don't like the idea that a dragon is going to come looking for her." Darian turns to his mate. "Willow, can you do more research into the Darkholme name and possibly what happened there?"

Willow shifts her chair over to Lila, who looks as if she is about to have a meltdown, and wraps her arm around her. "Of course."

Kieran nods "You're right, we are not moving. People will know something is up, and the pack has been under enough stress with the border fights. Zach would be perfect to guard her. They already are close friends. I am certain Gianna will also be at her side, especially since Zara intends to look for the other half of the scroll. She will browse the internet, but I doubt it's going to be that easy and just show up in a Google search. I suspect she will need to travel to museums, perhaps even the King's archives, and look through the older books and parchments. Sebastian's half appeared quite faded and ancient. The dragon knows it exists. He commented on it. So he's seen it, has it, or knows where it is. Especially since he is over 767 years old and blames Sebastian for killing his father when it was his sire." He pauses, turning to Willow. "Wait, you said pure lineage. Sebastian informed the dragon he did not kill villagers, and that they took care of those they fed from. Silas sounds closer to those that roam here. I wonder if, in fact, they are the same Darkholmes and something tainted the lineage. That's why they disappeared."

Willow ponders it. "It's a possibility. I will see what I can find Kieran, but it might take time."

"Thank you Luna." He lifts his gaze, hearing his daughter moving upstairs, and places a finger to his lips. "Zara is awake. Happier topics now. Keep her focus off being disconnected from her new mate."

Zara stares at the ceiling of her room, her heart breaking at the emptiness within. Hearing the murmur of voices downstairs, she takes a slow breath in and out to stabilize herself, knowing she isn't ready to face them. She wants to say they can't possibly understand, but knows that her mama and papa went through it when they were in Sebastian's realm. How did her papa manage? He seemed so strong there and yet, he must have felt like she was. Her gaze drifts to the window, knowing it was late morning and that she finally actually slept. She recalls the clock flashing two and eventually turned it away, groaning at the light in her room. How did she adapt to the darkness in a week? The utter silence surrounding her compared to the overwhelming drone of noise here. Pushing herself out of bed, she grabs her phone, grateful someone plugged it in and flips it on to his picture. Suddenly wishing she had taken more than the one she did. Tears slip from her eyes as she caresses the screen gently, wondering how he is, hoping the dragon didn't defeat him. Playing with the settings, she sets him to her background and screensaver, intending to print it out later and plaster them on her walls, like her best friend Gianna did with her famous crushes.

Zara pulls her Pjs back and looks at her side, seeing the wounds mostly mended, feeling Ember moping in the back of her mind. Rising, she heads to the bathroom. She stares at her reflection in the mirror, the swollen eyes and dirt stained, tear-streaked cheeks. Grabbing a scrunchie, she ties it around the mess her hair is, knowing it will need buckets of conditioner. Washing her face and feeling her stomach grumble, she heads downstairs. Her eyes open in shock as she steps into the kitchen, seeing the Alpha and Luna there, bowing immediately. "Alpha Darian, Luna Willow."

Darian moves over to her and takes her hands gently in his. "How are you feeling, Zara? You were pretty injured last night."

"I think I am fine. Thank you. May I ask why you are here?"

Darian glances at Kieran. "We just came to check in."

Zara chews on her lips. "You wanted to know what happened to us."

"Well, yes. Neither of you were talking yesterday."

Tears creep from her eyes. "Did Papa tell you I left a mate there?"

Darian draws her into his arms for a hug. "He did Zara, and I saw the mate mark when we found you. We will figure it out. Willow is going to do some research as she recognizes your mate's last name."

"He can't come here. He rules a kingdom there."

"I know. Like I said, we will figure something out. I promise. In the meantime, I want you to accept guards, just in case that dragon comes looking for you."

She nods and rests in his arms. "Thank you Alpha. I just came for some toast, but I think I am going to go back to bed, if that's ok. I didn't sleep and everything was so noisy last night."

"Noisy?" He glances at Kieran.

"Yes, it was so quiet there. Peaceful, no humming... And dark, with no lights at night. All I heard was the waves crashing against the rocks, and Papa's snoring, of course."

Kieran coughs. "Zare-bear, I don't snore!"

Lila and Zara speak at the same time. "Yes, you do."

Darian chuckles. "Alright then, unplug everything, and I will have some blackout curtains sent to you this afternoon. Hopefully, that will help."

"Thank you Alpha." She offers a curtsy and steps away, moving to the counter where she grabs a piece of bread and pops it into the toaster. Opening the fridge, she pours out a glass of juice, waiting on the toast to pop. Once it does, she smears strawberry jam on it. She gives a nod to the others and pads quietly to her room.

Once she has returned upstairs, Darian turns to Kieran. "Quiet?"

Kieran pauses him and steps out of the kitchen, moving to the base of the stairs and hearing her door close upstairs. Once he is certain she's settled, he turns back to Darian with a nod. "Yes, not only were we in a different realm, it was as if we stepped back in time. They had nothing. No running water, no electricity, no cars. They have never even heard of such things. The castle was lit by torches, oil lamps, and candles. Water hauled in by buckets and the chamber pots emptied in the evening. Their books were bound in leather and hand written. Hell, they didn't even know what shifters were. They considered us werewolves. I am surprised they didn't kill us on sight. Also, they can read thoughts and hear our mind-link as if we were talking out loud. The worst part was, they had no coffee, but damn, their beds were soft."

"Shit Kieran. You are lucky to be alive if they thought you were a werewolf."

"I realize that, Darian, hence why these are different. I also think we should neglect to mention Zara mated with a vampire. Ideally, I would like to keep it quiet, but the mate mark is hard to miss and she will still want to train."

"Good plan. A lot will not understand. Perhaps we should tell them she met her mate there and left him behind unwillingly. Keep it at that. Otherwise, we don't volunteer any information about where you were."

Kieran nods. "Yes, saying they captured us and we escaped might draw too many questions such as how she met her mate. Perhaps we don't even tell them about the capture. Not until Sebastian comes for her."

"That might be a better plan. Is he planning on it?"

"Yes, he is going to do everything in his power to get his mate back... She is his queen, after all."

Lila leans on Willow, her voice soft. "We are gonna lose her to him, aren't we?"

Kieran moves to his wife and clasps her hands. "I hope not Lila. There has to be a reason that the Goddess bound them together despite being in different realms.

I have to have faith that it will work out that we won't lose either of them. You will like Sebastian. He is perfect for Zara."

"Do we have an idea when he's coming for her?"

"No, but I know he needs to convince some of their resistance to help him. They are the ones with witches, so it could take time. It would be like us going to the rogues for help. It won't be easy. I will say this, I guarantee, he will do his damndest to make it as fast as possible. I saw the way he looked at her and how he cared for her. Even Nero was worried about the power she seemed to hold over him. I gather he's just as old as Sebastian and has been around for most, if not all, of his life."

Willow squeezes Lila's shoulder. "We will do everything we can to keep her here, and keep them together. I agree with your mate, Lila. There is a reason for this. We just don't have all the pieces of the puzzle yet. Darian and I will cover any expenses Zara needs in order to check out museums and libraries that have old archives. She will not be traveling alone. Someone will go with her."

"Thank you Luna. I really appreciate this."

"Hey, you guys and the kids are family. We grew up together. I know if the positions were reversed, you would help Zach, Ben or Sophie."

Lila nods, her eyes looking up at Kieran. "She's gonna need some support. It was really rough not feeling the link with Kieran and we had time to strengthen it. She hasn't."

Kieran nods. "Sebastian and her bonded yesterday."

"Damn, no wonder she cried all night. I will give her an hour or two and go speak with her."

"If it doesn't work, then I will, because I was there with her."

"Agreed."

Kieran turns to his Alpha. "So it's settled. We refrain from speaking about where we were to the best of our abilities, especially that she's bonded with a vampire, let alone the King. Though I am pretty certain she will tell Gianna because she tells her everything. A guard or two will be with her at all times and several watching the cottage. All the while, we look into the prophecy and the Darkholme's secretly. We also need to keep an eye out for a black dragon; one that somehow knew she was here."

Darian shakes his head, not liking the implications of Kieran's last statement. He runs a hand through his hair. "Kieran. Think about what you just said. The dragon knew Zara was tied to the prophecy, but also that she was a warrior. Hence the fighting at the borders to lure her out. They just bided their time until you took her. That means he's been in the pack and seen her fight."

"Dammit! There are too many that come and go to narrow it down."

"Well, I guess we'll just have to knock them off one at a time. I will talk to Amara and see if she has magic that can determine a dragon in hiding. If not, then we need to look elsewhere."

Willow shakes her head. "I don't think Amara can do it, Dar, but I know one who can. She has fey blood and can see things as they truly are."

Darian and Kieran both turn to look at Willow. "Who?"

"Alpha Madison Martinez, or now Marzire, I believe, of the Wildfire Crescent."

"Shit! I heard the stories about her, Willow. She shut down three packs and the trafficking ring single handedly during the winter festival two months ago. She could extract a high cost to get her to work with us."

"She could, but it never hurts to ask once we narrow the list down."

"I guess we cross that bridge when we get there." Darian turns his attention back to Kieran and Lila. "Consider yourselves on holidays for the week. After that, we will play things by ear. We will figure this out, Kieran. I am not sure how, but we will. Now, Willow and I need to return to the pack house and start things in motion. Take care, my friend."

Kieran hugs his best friend. "Thanks Darian. I really appreciate this."

"You're welcome." He gives a hug to Lila, before taking his wife's hand and heading back to the pack house, lost in his thoughts on everything he just heard.

Zara returns upstairs, knowing her parents and her Alpha meant well, but she just isn't ready to face the world yet, and that includes them. She picks up her phone and scrolls to her father's chat, typing into it, knowing Sebastian won't get the message, but it makes her feel closer to him.

> Sebastian, sorry, this is later than I expected. We made it home.

> The damn dragon tossed us through the portal and we fell. It broke Papa and I landed on him.

> Alpha found us apparently. I think it's the next morning, but I don't know how long I slept for.

> It seems like I didn't sleep at all though.

> I miss you. I want you here...

She flips back to the picture and stares at it a moment, tracing her fingers along it gently and moves to her computer. Booting it up, she plugs her phone in and transfers it over to her desktop. Later, she will send it to the printer, when the house is empty and quiet. Checking her email and Facebook, she sees a lot of messages from her besties, Gianna and Zach, but closes them down, not ready to face them. She rises and crawls back into bed, pulling her teddy close, and cries into it. Gianna and her had always talked about what it would be like to have mates, hoping that they liked each other and that they would be from the same pack so they could move together. Yet, here she was, with a mate; not only from a different pack, but from an entirely different realm. A realm that is away from everything and everyone she loves, yet one she desperately wants to get back to. Hours later, she wakes to a knock on her door and her mama's concerned voice.

"Sweetie, are you up? I brought you some lunch. Toast is not enough to get by on."

Zara rolls over and pulls the blanket up to dry her eyes. "Yes, Mama, I'm awake."

"Can I come in?"

"Of course." Zara watches her mother enter, carrying a tray laden with her favorite foods, making her stomach growl. "You made a meatloaf sandwich? For lunch?"

"Your Papa went to the hives and brought back some honeycomb for you as well."

Zara pushes herself up, knowing they were trying to soothe her, suspecting that, even with muffling her sobs, they would have heard her. "Thanks Mama."

Lila places the tray on the small table in her room and sits on the bed. "I want you to know that your Papa and I are here for you Zara. Even if you want to rant at the unfairness of it all, which we understand completely. We support you."

"I know Mama. It's just too soon."

Lila kisses her forehead. "You know where to find us when you are ready. Now eat your lunch. I will be back in an hour to collect your dishes."

"I can bring them down, Mama."

"Alright sweetie, I will see you downstairs then."

Zara nods, watching her mother leave her room. She glances at the food, not feeling hungry but knowing they went out of their way to cook her favorites. Eating most of the meatloaf sandwich, she switches over to the honeycomb, closing her eyes in delight at the sweet heaven melting in her mouth. Sadness wells within at the thought of all she will miss when she returns with Sebastian, hating that she needs to choose between her family and her mate. Finishing the treat, she curls back up in her bed, and plays with her phone, sending another text to Sebastian before allowing the emotions to draw her away to sleep once more.

I Love you

Lila glances up at the clock, realizing that Zara should have brought her plate down by now. She heads upstairs, knocks quietly. Not getting an answer, she opens the door and peeks in, seeing her daughter curled up on her bed, her phone clutched in her hands, sound asleep. She moves over to the bed, wishing she can help with her daughter's struggles, understanding the loss and fear as she just had ten days of it. She brushes her hair aside. "Oh Zara, I promise we will figure this out." Noticing the half eaten food, she collects the tray and exits the room. After cleaning up, she heads to the living room to find her mate, sprawled on the couch with a book in his hand. Placing a hand on her chest with a gasp. "Who are you and what have you done with my mate?"

Kieran chuckles, placing the book down. "Blame your daughter!"

"How does Zara have anything to do with you reading? I didn't even think you knew what a book was!"

He rises and moves over to his wife, drawing her into his arms. "Well, they wanted her, and so it was her fault we realm hopped. They had no TV there, and they certainly weren't letting me train. Reading was the only entertainment, aside from exploring an amazing castle. I actually enjoyed it, so I figured I'd try here with the books you read."

"Kieran, I don't think..." A flush creeps along her cheeks.

He teases her gently, placing a finger to her lips. "Shhh, it is... most interesting."

Lila avoids his gaze as her blush deepens. "Kieran..."

He tightens his arm around her waist and pulls her closer, kissing her lips gently. "I really don't care that you read that smut, my dear. I just wanted to see what it was like. It does have a certain appeal, though. Enough so that I want to steal you away right now and whisk you up to our room. Especially with how much I missed my wife these past ten days." With that, he lifts her up into his arms and carries her to their bedroom and closes the door behind them.

A week later, Kieran moves up the stairs and pauses at Zara's door, hearing the muffled sobbing on the other side. He knocks gently. "Hey Zare-bear, mind if I come in?" He smiles at the rustling, suspecting she is hiding her diary, something she keeps to herself, even though both he and her mother know she writes in one.

"Of course Papa."

Kieran opens the door and steps into the room, closing it softly behind him. He studies his daughter, sitting in bed, surrounded by blankets, a teddy in her arms and her phone in her lap. He moves over and settles next to her, brushing a few of her wild hairs out of her face. "Zare-bear. You look like hell."

She smiles sadly. "Gee, Thanks Papa... Way to make me feel better. Seriously though, I feel like hell. How did you do it? You didn't even show any signs of missing the bond with Mama."

"Oh, I did Zare-bear, but I knew I needed to be strong for you. I also knew that the mark still called to me, indicating your Mama still searched for me. I know Sebastian is looking for a way to get to you as we speak, just as I know you know."

"How can you be certain?"

"I saw how he looked at you, Zara, even without the mate bond in place."

"Perhaps it was the other Zara. His mistress."

"No, you stop that right now. Do not doubt the mate bond. You will be together again. You need to have faith in that mark, Zara."

"It's really hard Papa."

"I know Zare-bear. But you are strong and can do it. Now, you need to stop writing in your diary and texting him as you know he can't receive them. Hell, his phone's gonna blow up with all the texts you've sent him when he arrives here." He looks around at the pictures of Sebastian plastered over her walls. "Geez, no wonder your Mama had to buy new ink for the printer. Do you think you printed enough?"

She opens her mouth in shock. "How did you know?"

"Cause I know my daughter. It's been a week. Take a shower and get dressed. Eat proper food. You need to stop moping around this room and find the scroll.

What if Sebastian were to walk in that door tomorrow, expecting an answer to your dilemma and you didn't have it? What if he only had twenty-four hours here? Why force a choice between us Zara, when there might not be one in that prophecy? Get out into that sparring ring and get active again. Then we will start searching the web and hit the Alpha's library. Deal?"

Zara stares up at her father, reading the determination in his eyes, knowing he is right. Sebastian would expect her to have information if he made it to this realm, correct that, when he made it. She made a promise, and she needed to keep her end of it. Shifting over, she hugs her father. "Deal."

Kieran envelopes her into a hug, kissing the top of her head. "Right, you really need that shower Zare-bear."

She giggles and pushes him away. "I had one yesterday, Papa!"

"Sure you did." He rises from the bed. "I will see you downstairs in twenty minutes."

She grabs her pillow and throws it at him. "That's not enough time!"

"Twenty-five then." He closes the door after him, listening to her mutterings as she moves about the room, before heading downstairs to find his wife. "She will be down in a half hour."

"What did you say to her?"

"That she stank."

"Kieran!"

"What! It worked, didn't it?"

"You are the worst."

"I know, but you love me."

Thirty minutes later, Zara heads downstairs, dressed in her yoga pants and a half top. Her blond hair is braided into twin braids and tied together at the ends. Seeing both her parents at the kitchen table, she gives them a nod and grabs both a water and a soda out of the fridge.

Kieran arches a brow at the can of pop in her hand. "You are not drinking that!"

"PAPA! I always have a soda before training."

Kieran looks over at his wife for support in this matter. "Did you know about this?"

Lila shrugs her shoulders. "Of course, dear. Who do you think buys her the soda?"

Zara giggles. "Seriously Papa?"

Lila smiles at her daughter's giggle, the first one she has heard in a week. "Kieran, honey. Your daughter is nineteen. If she wants a soda, I am not stopping her. I just buy what's on the list stuck to the fridge."

Kieran scowls at his wife's lack of support in this department, despite the humor dancing in his eyes. "Traitor!" He looks over at his daughter. "In the future, be prepared to see soda scratched off that list, Zare-bear."

Zara moves over and kisses her father's cheek. "I will just rewrite it, or text Mama when she is shopping."

He pulls her into a bear hug. "I will confiscate your phone, then!"

She hugs him back. "Well, I will just steal your new one, cause now I know the password."

"Damn! Never should have told you that."

She laughs, and leans a head on his shoulder a moment, before stepping out of his arms and running from the kitchen. "I will see you in the rings, Papa!"

"Children!"

Lila laughs, nudging her husband. "Hey! Don't blame all your children because you spoiled your daughter."

Kieran chuckles. "Like you didn't spoil Jayden and Jenson."

"Hush!"

He kisses his mate gently, before turning and following his daughter to the training rings.

Ten

Moving Forward

After fighting, Zara hugs her father, feeling her muscles screaming at her from nearly three weeks of not training, suspecting she is going to be soaking in a bath later this evening. She smiles at her bestie, Gianna, waving from the sidelines, knowing there is no way she is getting out of lunch with her. "I will be home later, Papa."

Kieran follows her gaze, smiling as he spots Gianna. "Sounds good Zare-bear. I thought perhaps after dinner, we could ask the Alpha to see his library."

Zara nods. "That sounds great Papa."

Kieran claps her on the shoulder, giving her a bit of a nudge. "It's good to have you out of that room, Zare-bear. Let's see this done so I can see the smile reach your eyes again."

She snaps her gaze back to his. "Thanks Papa. I miss him so much. I never thought I would miss a va…"

Kieran places his finger on her lips. "Shh Zare-bear. Alpha and I have agreed. We think it's best to keep it as your mate and not mention what he is."

Zara grows silent as she ponders it; her eyes scanning the wolves in the fighting rings and those lingering on the borders watching them, suspecting most of them would feel the same as she did when she first encountered Sebastian. Turning her attention to Gianna, who supported her in everything, wondering if she still would. "Can Gia know?"

"Yes, and Zach. Though it's possible Alpha Darian has already told him."

She hugs her father tightly. "I love you Papa. Thank you for being my rock."

Kieran kisses the top of her head. "I love you too, Zare-bear. Now, I see Zach approaching. Go enjoy your afternoon with them."

Zara giggles and runs out of the rings to Gianna. "I need a quick shower. I will meet you at the bistro in fifteen, yes?"

Gianna squeals in delight, taking Zara's hand and squeezing it. "Bout time! Make it a quick fifteen!"

"I will." Zara waves at Zach before racing off to shower.

Fifteen minutes later, she is enjoying a London fog with Gianna and Zach, as they bombard her with questions.

"So Zara, where were you? You didn't answer your phone, or emails, or mind-link. Alpha even said he couldn't access you."

Zara's hands tighten around her cup, not entirely certain what she should say. She takes a sip and closes her eyes, feeling the stress creeping through her, knowing that most would hate vampires as much as she did. "I was in another realm."

"Another realm? What do that mean?"

"It's hard to explain, Gianna. We got hit by magic and transported elsewhere. There was no power, electricity, running water, or even a sun in the sky... SHIT!" She stands suddenly, her London fog spilling over the table as she stares at the sun, her whole body shaking in fear.

Zach jumps up and wraps his arms around her. "What's wrong Zara?"

She sobs against him. "There was no sun... There is a sun here."

"It's gonna be okay." Zach glances at Gianna, who is madly dropping napkins on the liquid, trying to stop the flow of the drink on the table. His father told him she found a vampire mate in the other realm and left him behind. He trusted his Beta Kieran's word and knew damn well if Zara had accepted him, that he differed from the ones they have known from this realm. Realizing that others in the cafe are watching, he leads her out and away from prying ears. "Come. Let's leave the bistro and talk privately."

Gianna collects the two remaining drinks and follows along beside them. "Why does the sun matter, Zara? Please talk to us. You've hidden yourself in your room for a week and now you are in tears over the sun?"

Zach takes her over to the park and sits her on the bench, watching Gianna sit beside her. He kneels before Zara. "Gianna, it's because of who her mate is."

"WHAT!! YOU'RE mated! And you didn't tell me! Bi'otch!!!"

Zara dries her eyes and chuckles. "Sorry, I don't even know if he's *alive*, Gia. I can't feel him at all. I haven't since I got home."

"Shit, Sorry Zara, I didn't mean..."

Zara hugs her bestie and sniffles. "It's alright. I have to believe he survived and is looking for me. It's the only thing keeping me going right now."

"Survived?"

"Yes, a dragon attacked us. He's the one that sent us to the realm and literally tossed us back through a portal. Sebastian provoked him into releasing us."

"Sebastian. Of course, you would find one with an awesome name."

Sadness crosses her eyes as she looks at her friend. "You say that now. How about after I tell you, he's over 500 years old, and the King of the Vampires?"

Gianna jumps up from the bench and spins to gape at Zara. "You mated with a bloody vampire?"

Zach rises and places a hand on Gianna's shoulder. "Just hear her out. Dad says Beta Kieran vouches for him."

Gianna scowls at Zach before staring at Zara, reading the slumped shoulder, the sadness and accusation in her gaze, knowing she wasn't exactly being open with her friend who was clearly in pain. "Fine, I will hear her out."

"Good. This will be a test."

"A test?"

"Well, I want to see how you react before I tell you I am not straight."

"Damn it Zach, we already knew that. I thought it was more juicy than that."

"How the hell did you know that? I haven't told anyone yet?"

Zara laughs, relaxing at their banter. "She's right Zach. We have known it for years."

Gianna pushes his shoulder. "You didn't have to tell us. We can see it. The way your gaze lingers on the men, especially the blondes. Or follow the same backside we watch, except you drool more. How you happily curl up with us and watch chick flicks and have never made a move on either of us. You crushed our egos, Zach!"

"I DO NOT drool more." Zach remarks, teasing them gently. "Your egos? You didn't want me, so you drove me to the other team."

"Next time, I will hand you a napkin for that drool, Zach! Just to prove my point, mister competition for us."

Zara giggles. "That's right. Now, NO stealing my mate when he gets here Zach, cause I know he's just your type, even if he doesn't have blond hair."

Zach moves to sit next to her. "Sooo, do you have a picture?"

"Of course, you would ask first. Yes, I have one picture of him."

Gianna squeals and settles in on the other side. "What the hell Zara? First you keep the fact that you have a mate from me and now that you have a picture. AM

I NOT your bestie anymore? Let's seeeeee him."

"Of course you are still my bestie." Zara pulls her phone out and flips it on, showing them her screen and his face on it next to hers. "That's the only picture I got. I hated him here, but now I regret not getting more. He wanted to know what the phones were and how the mini painting existed, so I snapped a selfie."

Zach growls in approval. "You're right, I would steal him. Do they all look as hot as he does?"

"I suppose. I can't say I paid attention once Ember started fighting with me about him being our mate."

Gianna pauses. "Wait? Hated him?"

"Yes, they were vampires, and we were his prisoners. I did NOT want to be mated to a bloodsucker, but Ember proved difficult. Besides, he forced me to answer his questions with the threat that he was torturing Papa and I couldn't let that happen."

She reaches up to Zara's neck and pushes her shirt aside. "Yet, you let him mark you."

Zara reaches up to caress the mark at her neck, her voice growing soft at the thought of him. "Yes, and I marked him."

"But how? Why?"

"Papa made a deal with him. We would move out of the prison and into the castle, free to roam around; with guards, of course. But we had to make an honest effort for seven days to get to know him. I was so mad at Papa, but I will say the castle's room was much better."

"Castle?"

She flips through to the castle and the gardens. "This is his home."

"HOT damn! It's a real effing castle!"

"Gianna, I did state that he's the King. You caught that right."

"Seriously. I thought you were joking."

"No, he does, in fact, rule the other realm. Though the ones that captured us simply called him the boss to begin with, so we didn't find out till later. After the deal, he moved Papa and I to our own room, on the second floor. Over the next seven days, he courted me and won me over. On the last night, I went to the library to find him but he wasn't there. Nero was, and he took me to Sebastian's room where he was sleeping. Nero allowed me to curl up and sleep with him, but he sat watch the entire night."

"That's creepy Zara, that a man watched you sleep with your mate."

Zara shakes her head. "No, I was still a prisoner of war, despite having some freedoms around the castle. When they sleep, they are helpless. They don't move, shift or wake. They are dead to the world and anyone can kill them. Nero didn't trust me, and that was fair. I fought like a wildcat when they first captured us. Besides, I didn't care. I just cared that I was in Seb's arms. In the morning, when Sebastian woke up, Nero was already gone. That was when we marked each other."

"And?"

"And what? I am not telling you. You will just have to wait till you have a mate." A deepening blush creeps across her cheeks.

"Oh! Zara is blushing Zach! I have never seen her blush like that."

Zach chuckles. "She's right Zara! Details!"

"No." She shakes her head. "Back to my story. The next morning, we had breakfast. Afterwards, knowing we needed to find a way home, he pulled all his guards so we could escape. He had them pretend to chase us, to better our position with the resistance when we found them. But we never made it that far. The damn dragon that sent us to the realm in the first place attacked us."

"Why didn't he come with you?"

Zara rolls her eyes. "Cause he's KING there Gia. Secondly, the dragon wanted us separated. He knew we were mates and so tossed Papa and I through the portal, leaving Sebastian there."

"So, when is he coming to find you?"

"I don't know. He needs to find a realm hopping witch like the dragon. However long that takes."

"So why were you.... Oh shit! We have a sun here and they don't. I get it now." Zara nods.

"Hey, we will figure it out and keep him out of the sun."

"Assuming he arrives during the evening. If he arrives during the day, who knows what might happen to him?"

Gianna hugs her friend tightly. "Then I will pray to the Goddess for rain every day until the day he arrives."

Zach mutters. "Can't you amend that to just the day he arrives? Or perhaps cloudy days?"

Zara smiles, knowing how much her friend hated the rain. "Alright, I will get

Gia to amend her prayers just for you."

"Thank you. So why is the dragon interested in the pair of you?"

Zara flips into the photos of her phone and shows her friends the scroll. "Cause of this. I need to find the other half. Papa and Sebastian both think it's here in our realm somewhere. But we can't tell anyone 'cause we don't know who may or may not work for the dragon. We know at least five witches do 'cause they were pretending to fight the dragon till we got there, and then they turned on us."

"Shit Zara, this is not good."

"No, it's not. That's why I left. Sebastian made me promise I would look for it." She turns to Zach. "So Papa and I wish to start with the pack library and any old books or archives you have. I highly doubt it will be on Google but I am going to try there too. I will probably have to travel to other packs, but I need to find it before Sebastian arrives here."

Zach nods. "I am certain my father will help grant whatever you want. Gianna and I will help you as best as we can."

"Thank you."

A few weeks later, the two girls linger at the fighting rings, watching Zach fight against the others. Zara smiles, catching the wink from Zach as he tackles one warrior, knowing he was in heaven even if no one else had figured it out. They had found nothing in the pack's archives as expected, because that would be far too easy. No, it was elsewhere, and she guessed either in Frostbite Syndicate where the dragons reside or Whispering Pines where the Royals did. She wanted to go straight there, but Alpha Darian had a plan and in that plan, she needed to meet with Alpha D'andre of Silvermoon first. To get him on their side, whatever that meant. Who was she to question her Alpha? But damn, she was feeling impatient and the waiting game was driving her nuts.

"Gamma Luca?"

Gianna turns as she hears her father's name being called, knowing he is out patrolling. A groan escapes her, drawing Zara's attention away from Zach.

"What is it?" Zara's eyes follow Gianna's gaze, landing on the courier driver. Tall, with what one would call black hair, but shown as mahogany beneath the sun. Decently built, even beneath the drab tan uniform he is sporting. She meets his gray eyes momentarily as they lock on hers before drifting to Gianna. "Oh, the one that has a crush on you."

"Yes, I think it matches the crush that Jeremy has on you."

"Ugg, please don't mention his name. Did you want me to get it?"

"No, he won't give it to you. Trust me, I have tried to get others to sign for it. He's unreasonably stubborn and slightly creepy."

Zara laughs, knowing a lot of men flirted with her because Gianna is stunning, with her white blonde hair, flawless complexion and deep green eyes. "It's possible his job would be on the line if he delivers it to the wrong person."

"I suppose."

"How about I be your girlfriend? Come, my darling." Zara takes her hand and leads her over to the courier. She pauses partway, to kiss her cheek and nuzzle her friend's cheek, hearing her giggle and push her away.

"Kitten, you know I don't like that in public. Wait till we are in our room."

Zara grabs her hand and pulls her close, keeping her voice loud enough that the courier can hear. "But darling, you know I love you and I don't care who finds out."

Gianna rolls her eyes and cups Zara's face in her hands. She kisses Zara's lips softly. "Fine, my love. Let me get this package for my father first."

"I will be waiting." Zara takes Gianna's hand and kisses the back of it, lingering there as she offers a small bow to her best friend.

Gianna winks and turns back to the courier, catching the look of curiosity on his face along with the confusion in his gray eyes as he looks between Zara and her. "Hello Colten, my father is busy. I will collect the package."

Colten nods and holds the clipboard out. "Sign here, please." He watches her pen scrawl across the page and accepts it back. Pulling the package from his truck, he hands it to her. "So you and her?"

Gianna looks back at Zara, seeing her wave, and blows a kiss her way. "Yes, we have always been besties, but we just came out a few days ago."

"That's too bad."

"Why would you say that?"

"Just that you are beautiful and so is she. It's sad to see a pair of lovely women such as you, off the market for us men."

Gianna shifts on the balls of her feet, pulling the package close against her chest. "There are plenty of women out there that still prefer a man in their bed."

"I guess." Colten's gaze sweeps around the area, looking at the people wandering around, minding their own business.

"Hey, I am happy, and so is she. Isn't that what counts?"

Colten smiles brightly. "You are right. Have a good day." He gives a last look at the pair and gets back into his van, pulling out of the parking lot and driving off.

Gianna turns and runs back to Zara. "Well, that got awkward."

Zara giggles, slapping her friend's shoulder. "Yes, it did! You bio'tch! You kissed me!"

"Well, I had to make it look real!"

"I want you to know these lips are Sebastian's only."

Gianna giggles. "Until Colten returns and I need them again."

"Never. You are on your own next time. Or use Zach's."

"Use Zach's what?"

They both turn as Zach walks up behind them, fresh from a shower, his hair dripping the remnants of water down his shirt as it clings to his chest. Zara pushes Gianna into Zach's arms. "Gianna here needs a boyfriend for when Colten delivers packages. She kissed me. On the lips even!"

"Damn! I missed that?"

Zara huffs at his comment. "You are no better than her. Shouldn't you still be in the ring?"

Zach chuckles and drapes an arm around her, pulling her in with Gianna. "Awww, Zara. Kiss your girlfriend and make-up. Seriously though, Dad wants to see you. He got through to Alpha D'andre. We leave in an hour."

"What? An hour?"

"Yes, so go pack for ten days away and meet me out front of the pack house. It's you and me this time, babes."

"Thank you, Zach!" Zara rises on her toes to kiss his cheek before racing off to tell her parents and pack a bag.

Gianna looks up at Zach. "Do you think you will find anything?"

"No, but Dad says that's not why we are going there. He says if we win him over, he has the power to put in a good word with Alpha Madison and she's the one we need. She has connections with Frostbite Syndicate and Whispering Pines. Dad also would like her to come to the pack and see if she can find the hidden dragon, so it's a double mission, but Zara doesn't need to know that."

"Got it. I won't tell her. Do you think she's gonna get him back, Zach?"

"Let's hope so. While she smiles and jokes, she still has sadness in her eyes. She's different, Gia, a lot different, and I want the old Zara back. If finding this scroll gets her back to Sebastian and that happiness she's lost, then I want that to happen."

"Yes, me too. Thanks Zach."

Forty minutes later, with a duffle bag bouncing over her shoulder, Zara races back to the pack house. She bows to Alpha Darian, who stands on the porch with his son talking quietly. "Thank you Alpha, for getting me this meeting with Alpha D'andre of Silvermoon. I really appreciate it."

Darian moves down the steps and hugs Zara. "Anything you need, Zara. Remember. Be polite and win Alpha D'andre over. He's your connection and the key to the other packs you want. He's best friends with Alpha Madison, who is the granddaughter of King Caden. Her mate Lucian is from the Frostbite Syndicate and Alpha Pierce's younger brother."

"I understand Alpha. I know I represent you, so I will be on my best behavior."

"That's what I want to hear. Now, Luca will drive you to the airport. It's about a two-hour flight. Alpha D'andre said he would have his Beta Terrance pick you up." He leads her over to the car that pulled around out front and guides her into the back seat as Zach slides into the other side. "Have fun, behave and we will talk when you get back."

Zach smiles at his dad as he buckles himself in. "Thanks Dad."

Zara nods, following suit. "Thanks Alpha."

Zara watches out the window, waving at her family as the car pulls away, before turning to her friend. "Not that I am complaining, Zach, but why are you coming? I thought my Papa was going to help with this."

Zach chuckles and leans back, closing his eyes. "Three reasons. First, to watch over you. Second, to meet Alpha D'andre. Dad wants me to meet the Alphas and get to know them before I take over responsibilities as Alpha. Third, I am still unmated, Zara. He's out there somewhere. This gives me a chance to look."

Zara laughs. "Right, so you are coming to check the men out?"

"Damn right I am and they are all mine cause you have a mate."

"Hmm, I see. That's the real reason Gia's not here with us."

"No competition, babes! I don't stand a chance with her around."

"None of us do Zach."

A week and a half later, Zach and Zara pull up to the pack house empty-handed, having enjoyed their time immensely with Alpha D'andre and Luna Erica, along with their children.

Kieran draws his daughter into his arms, reading the defeat in her gaze. "Hey

Zare-bear. We will find it. You didn't expect it to be there anyhow, right?"

"I know Papa. Still..."

"Did you have fun at least?"

"Yes, Alpha D'andre's family was great. We went to several archives, and they even helped look through the books with us. He's a riot." She glances over at Zach talking with his father and offers a smile. "Thank you Alpha, for allowing me this chance."

"Your welcome Zara. Now, if you did your job right, I should hopefully be in touch with Alpha Madison within the next few weeks, and secure you a trip to Frostbite Syndicate next."

"That sounds great."

Eleven

Madison Marzire

Z ara sits on the patio at the bistro with Gianna, looking out over the small community that surrounds the pack house. It had been three weeks since her return and she still hadn't heard about getting accepted into Frostbite. She was certain things had gone well at Silvermoon; or at least she had thought so, but now, doubts crept in. As the ice clinks together under her straw, she half-listens to Gianna complain about her job. Lifting her gaze, she offers a reassuring smile. "I'm sure you'll figure it out. You always do."

"You're right, I just like to bitch."

Zara shakes her head. "Do the other servers get to hear this side of you?"

"No, only you do 'cause you're my bestie."

"Lucky me..." Zara trails off, seeing a pair of black cars with tinted windows following her father's car into the pack compound. "Who is that?"

Gianna snaps her gaze to the cars and shakes her head. "I have no idea. Didn't your Papa tell you?"

"No, Papa just said he had business outside the pack." Zara watches her father get out and approach Alpha Darian, who appears on the pack house deck at their arrival. She tilts her head, trying to catch their conversation, while her attention remains on the black cars. Five tall, well-built men step out of the second car, while only the driver steps out of the first car. Each dressed in loose fitting black clothes with an air of superiority that radiates around them. Knowing immediately they are shifters and clearly working for someone of power. They fan out and scan the area, as if assessing for danger, causing Zara to look around as well, wondering if they sense something she doesn't.

"Who the hell are they? Shifter gods?"

"Clearly. And if they are, they certainly heard that." Zara chuckles at her friend's comment, seeing all the other she-wolves around them drooling as well.

DRAGONSCALES DIVIDE

She follows their graceful movements as they open the back doors and step back. Gasping at the beautiful woman who slips out of the darkness inside the car and stands next to the man nearby. Another man slides out from the other side and comes to stand beside her, bringing a smile to the lady's lips. "And there is the Goddess that goes with them." The woman has light brown hair, reaching the center of her back, wearing a black silk top, daggered over an aqua skirt. Gold tipped boots match the gold belt at her waist and gold bangles on her wrist. A light cloak hangs off her shoulder, causing a pang in Zara's heart as it draws her thoughts back to Sebastian. Zara lifts her fingers to brush at the tears welling in her eyes just as the woman turns to look their way, the most amazing aqua eyes pinning her in place.

"Damn, she's stunning and pregnant."

"She is." Zara shifts beneath her gaze, watching her attention being drawn back to the older man beside her. Chestnut hair, a touch of gray at the temples, dark brown eyes that wrinkled at the corners as he smiles. Dressed casually in a suit, but clearly sporting the same build as the warriors surrounding them. Perhaps her father, for they clearly loved each other. Her eyes follow them as they approach Alpha Darian, the four men forming a protective box around the pair. Her eyes widen as her Alpha bows to this woman. "Did you see that, Gia?"

"Yah Zara, I did. Who the hell is she? Especially since our Alpha is bowing to her."

"I don't know, but I have suspicions."

"Tell me later. I gotta get to work, and I suspect it's a long story. See ya."

"Sounds good, Gia." Madison watches as they enter the pack house and disappear. She collects her drink and heads home, hiding in her room away from her brothers. Once there, she surfs the web for her daily search of ancient paintings and manuscripts. Finding nothing that matches what she is looking for, she pulls her phone out and sends a few texts to Sebastian.

> I miss you Seb. I love you.

> I hope you are doing fine. How is Nero, I miss him too, even if I found him annoying to start. He's cool.

> I want to come back, I want to be there with you.

A few stray tears slip from her eyes as she closes the chat and pulls out her journal to write her thoughts and feelings down, as well as catching up on her trip with Zach to Silvermoon.

Alpha Darian stands silently with his son Zach on one side of him and Kieran on the other. He smiles and bows to their guest as she approaches, realizing the prestige of having her in his pack. "Alpha Madison Marzire. Welcome to the Stormfang Clan."

"Alpha Darian Ravenwind. Thank you for the invite. This is my Delta, Victor Martinez, and, of course, my four guards."

"Welcome. Please come in. My Luna is busy elsewhere and will join us shortly. I will get you settled before we do business and you meet the pack."

"Thank you."

An hour later, Alpha Darian sits in his office with Alpha Madison, a tray of tea and coffee sitting on the table between them. "I appreciate your help with this, Alpha Madison."

"Just Madison please." She picks up her cup of tea and drops a sugar cube into it, stirring it gently.

"Thank you and no title here as well."

"Fair enough Darian. Now tell me about this scroll and dragon that you are looking for."

"It is actually for my Beta's daughter."

"Yes, D'andre spoke highly of her and your son. But also that they were both quiet about their reasons for the search. Are you going to fill me in? Your queries were rather vague as to why you requested I visit your pack."

"It is not my place to, but I can bring Zara here and you may ask her."

"Do so then."

Alpha Darian nods, his eyes glazing over as he reaches out with his mind-link. *'Zara, please report to my office immediately.'*

'Right away Alpha.' Zara places her journal and pen down. Tucking her phone in her pocket, she races from her bedroom, arriving at the pack house within a few minutes. She takes a moment to straighten her clothes, along with a few deep breaths. Her nerves race inside as the skin prickles on her arms at seeing guards on either side of the office door. Only verifying her thoughts that the woman behind the door is the most feared Alpha of all the packs; The Ruthless Madison Martinez. Hesitantly, she steps between the pair and knocks softly,

hearing Darian's voice telling her to enter. She steps in and bows to both Darian and Madison. "Alpha. Ma'am."

"Please take a seat, Zara. This is Alpha Madison."

"Pleasure to meet you, Alpha Madison. Alpha D'andre spoke highly of you." Zara moves to sit on a nearby chair, not daring to share the couch with her.

Madison smiles, her eyes roaming over the girl, not much younger than herself. Reading the nervousness in her posture, the hands that twitch at her sides and the lack of direct eye contact. "I am sure he did. Now, both your Alpha and D'andre have withheld information as to why I am here. Do you know?"

Zara's eyes dart to her Alpha at the fact he hadn't told her. "Yes, it's because of me."

"And what have you done that has your Alpha requesting my help?"

Zara sighs and pulls her phone out, fiddling with it in her hands. "It's dangerous to know everything."

"Zara, I am certain I can handle it."

Zara catches Darian nodding in approval. "I am in trouble with a dragon because my mate is a vampire that he wants to kill."

Madison arches a brow, her eyes shifting to Darian and reading the truth in them. "A shifter, mated with a vampire? Willingly?"

"Yes. He's different from the ones here. And the dragon wants him dead. Probably me too. He knows this is my pack 'cause he found me here initially so it's possible he's here lurking."

"I have a dragon. Her name is Somoko, and she hasn't sensed another dragon within the area. Are you certain?"

"You have a dragon?"

"Yes, and a wolf named Zuri. I am also fey touched so I can see things as they truly are. Now, please, start at the beginning and tell me what is going on."

Zara turns to her Alpha, suddenly understanding his nuances of befriending Alpha D'andre first. One just didn't approach one as powerful as the woman sitting before her. Not without a cost. She smiles at Madison, hope alighting within that she might actually get Sebastian back and no longer have guards following her every move. "It was about seven weeks ago. Papa and I went to stop a battle at the borders, as per the Alpha's request. When we got there, a black dragon was fighting five witches. Dark magic was everywhere, but when we arrived, they turned on us. Their magic hit us and transported us to another realm. Vampires ruled this realm, and one of them is my mate. During the nine days we were there, he courted me. I didn't like him at first, but Papa made a deal that required me to behave. He really is just like us. Anyhow, he showed me the scroll he showed my Papa when they talked."

Zara turns her phone on, bringing up the picture and handing it over to Madison. "Papa and Sebastian agree it's us and somewhere in this realm is the other half. That's why the Goddess paired us together. I promised him I would search for it when we got back. Sebastian made it look like we escaped so we could find witches to get us home, but the dragon found us first. He's mad at Sebastian. Really, he should be mad at Sebastian's sire, who killed his papa, but he doesn't care. He's blaming Sebastian and wants him dead so that he can rule his lands and his people. Then the dragon opened a portal and threw us through."

Darian speaks softly. "After they disappeared, the battles at our borders stopped. That means the dragon knew who she was, and that she resides in this pack. The only way to know that is to either be here or have seen her. Even then, how did they know she was the one that was the vampire's mate? Unless there is a picture of her somewhere tied to the scroll. What we ask is that you look for our spy, who is likely portraying themselves as a human."

Zara nods. "And to see if you can get me access into the libraries at Frostbite and Whispering Pines. Frostbite 'cause they are dragons and might have something about it and Whispering Pines 'cause that's where the royal archive is. That scroll is old and I need to find the other half to get my mate back."

Madison looks over the picture carefully, daring to ask the question that no one has. "What if it brings darkness and destruction?"

"Then I will go live with Sebastian in his realm. I won't have this land harmed at all."

Madison nods, noting the intricacies in the scroll. The runes scribed over and under the moon. Armies facing each other beneath the wolves and the dragon, with the wolves shrouded in light and the dragon in darkness. She hopes it doesn't mean that wolves and dragons will fight on opposite sides, because Lucian, her mate, is also a dragon. But then, there is only one dragon. A black. Clearly working with dark witches. One that had seen some version of this exact picture. Did he know the rest? Or was he as clueless as them? How do the witches tie into the dragon? She knows her Gran-pappy Caden is going to be less than impressed that another supernatural showdown is happening in his kingdom. She needs light witches. If for nothing else, then to take out the dark witches. "Can I have a copy of this?"

"Of course. I have some printed back in my room or I can send it to you."

Madison hands the phone back and pulls her own out. "Just airdrop it."

Zara nods and sends the picture over.

Madison watches it arrive on her screen and shuts her phone down. "I will have my people search Wildfires' libraries, archives and museums for something like it, as well as talk to the witches that I know. One less place for you to search. I am certain Alpha Pierce will let you into his libraries. Perhaps within the next week. King Caden's will prove to be more challenging. Only the Royals are allowed within, but I will see if I can use my power of persuasion with him."

Zara gasps, her hands tightening on her phone. "Oh no, I don't want you to use magic on the King. You shouldn't get into trouble on my behalf."

Madison laughs and places a hand on Zara's arm. "I won't. It's called batting my lashes and pulling the granddaughter rank."

A slow smile crosses Zara's lips. "Ooh, I get it. The same as the daughter-rank I have with my Papa."

"Yes, that would be the one. I promise I will do my best."

"Thank you Alpha Madison."

Madison nods, then shifts her focus back to Darian. "Would you like me to scan now, or wait until morning? I'd like to walk around a bit, if that's alright. Maybe Zara could give my Delta Victor and I a tour."

Darian nods. "Of course. Once you are done, I will gather the pack. It should take anywhere from thirty minutes to an hour to walk fully around the central pack. Outskirts are much longer, but we can take you on patrols in the morning."

"Understood. Central is fine for now. I will travel in wolf form, if that's acceptable."

"It is."

Madison rises and shakes Darian's hand. "I will see you within the hour then, for the meet and greet." She turns to Zara. "Alright Zara, let's go hunt a dragon. Victor is waiting outside."

"Do you really think he's here?"

"No, he's not. As I stated, Somo sensed no other dragons around here, but there might be a lingering scent."

Zara nods, giving a bow to her Alpha, leading Madison out of the office and to the front doors of the pack house. Standing out front is the older man she saw getting out of the car with her. She smiles shyly at him, catching his warm smile back at both of them.

"So, Maddie. What's going on?"

"Dragon hunting. Vic, this is Zara, Zara, my Delta and father Victor."

"Nice to meet you, sir."

"Likewise, and just Victor. Sir makes me feel older than I am."

Zara giggles. "Yes, Sir...Ah Victor."

Victor turns to Madison. "Dragon hunting. I thought you didn't sense any dragons upon entry."

"I didn't. Zara will explain more while we walk. I am shifting to scent better."

Victor frowns. "Maddie. Not recommended with your pup?"

"He will be fine, Vic. Trust me."

"Madison!"

Madison rolls her eyes at him. "Vic, please. I know my body and I know the pup inside me. I am not ready to put Zuri and Somo on bed rest yet. Give me these three days."

"Don't say I didn't warn you, lass. Clary is gonna be pissed when she finds out."

"I will face Clary."

"Certainly won't be me, lass. I have a witness that will testify that I tried to warn you."

"Indeed, you do." Madison laughs and kisses his cheek lightly. She gives a nod to Zara and shifts into her wolf.

Zara steps back, snapping her mouth shut as her eyes bug out of her head at the size of Madison's wolf and the fact that it is an instant shift, her clothes floating down around her. Taking in the snow white fur with black socks on each of her feet, matching the black ears. "Damn, I want that ability."

Madison's mind touches Zara's while Victor chuckles and picks the clothing up. *It's a Lycan ability.*

Wait, you can mind-link me? How? You are not part of the pack.

Dragon ability. Come, let's go.

Can all dragon's mind-link?

If you are asking about the black, I don't know, but I believe most can. I know my mate's pack members can. Let's tour.

Zara leads Madison and Victor around the compound, the small town and the inner parks, explaining each of the areas to them, as well as filling Victor in on what she told Madison. A few of the pack members stop them, curious about the pair, especially the enormous wolf, larger than even their Alpha. Zara explains she is here at the Alpha's request and that she is giving her a tour of the pack. An hour later, they return to the pack house, where Madison shifts back, and dresses.

"You should get a necklace."

Madison turns. "What do you mean?"

She lifts her hand to the chain at her neck, pulling out the amber stone entwined with a copper wire. "Alpha's witch made them for us. A trial run so we can shift and keep our clothes intact. Kinda like you did, but they stay with us and shift with us when we turn back."

Madison reaches out to the stone and looks it over, giving a nod. "I would like to meet this witch. As for mine, it is a fey ability or my dragon's apparently that instantly removes my clothes. I don't really know. I have always been able to shift that way. But if your witch can make more, my pack would be interested."

"You would have to ask Alpha Darian."

"I will. Now as to what I have found. A dragon has been here, but it's faint, so not for a while. At least a week, probably longer and only in the main area. Right in front of the pack house, the fighting rings and the stores. Not deeper in. This leads me to believe he is an outsider that visits someone on the main drag. Perhaps a shifter that works there. I am still curious to meet your pack and run the outskirts tomorrow, but I will speak with your Alpha now. I will see you when he calls the pack forth."

"Thank you Alpha Madison. I really appreciate all this."

Madison smiles, reading between the lines and feeling the emotions racing around in Zara. She draws her in for a hug, suspecting she probably needs it. "Hey, I know what it's like to live without your mate, to be torn away from him and to be separated by realms. We will get him back for you. I also want to meet this vampire that's won the heart of not only a Beta's daughter, but the Beta himself."

Tears suddenly flood from Zara's eyes. "I really miss him. I can't even feel him anymore."

Madison pats her back gently, understanding the pain. "You are gonna be fine. You will get him back, and this will all seem like a bad dream."

Zara sobs against her, her voice muffled against her chest. "How can you know?"

"Because you are strong and just from talking to you, so is he. I lived without my mate for five years. I know the difficulty of that. Just take it one day at a time. It will happen. A lot of people are helping, and I will say, your Alpha was quite clever, sending you to D'andre first."

Zara smiles and steps back, swiping away her tears while a giggle escapes her. "He said you were best friends and to win you over, we had to win him over. I had to actually behave around him."

Madison laughs. "You didn't because he's a shit disturber himself. His Luna keeps him in check. But you piqued his interest enough that he said I should look into it."

"Thank you."

"You're welcome. Now, I need to talk to your Alpha, and I will see you at the pack meeting."

Zara bows to them both, before turning and running home, hearing the chatter of her parents as she enters the kitchen. She pauses as they both stop and look at her, feeling the questions in their gaze, knowing word will have spread about the large silver wolf touring around the pack center. "It was Alpha Madison. She was looking for the black dragon. He has been here recently. Within the past few weeks, but he is not here now."

Kieran scowls. "I didn't want to hear that Zare-bear. That means he's keeping tabs on you."

"I know, Papa, and I will stay with people unless I am here."

"That's not good enough. You need more people to watch you."

Zara rolls her eyes. "Seriously? Don't I have enough? I see the four guards watching my moves at all times, and Zach is suddenly hanging with Gia and I more. I know you and Alpha Darian did this. He's supposed to be training to be an Alpha. Can't I have some sort of peace at home? Besides, Alpha Madison said she could only scent him near the shops. Not in the back where the cottages are."

"Zara..."

"Papa. I swear. I will be careful. You trained me to fight."

"Not a dragon Zara. We saw what he did to you with his claws."

Zara sighs, her shoulders slumping in defeat. "I know Papa. I'm sorry, I just..."

Kieran draws her into a tight hug. "Zare-bear. It's already bad enough that we might lose you to another realm and Sebastian. We get that. He's your mate. You should choose him, but please grant us some measure of peace to know we are protecting you."

"Are you trying to guilt trip me, Papa?"

"Is it working?"

"Yes."

"Good. Parenting rulebook for the win."

Zara scowls at her father. "I don't think that's in the parenting rulebook."

"Of course it is. It's hidden beneath rule number three."

"And what is rule number three?"

"Do whatever it takes to get your child to agree."

Lila shakes her head. "Don't listen to him, sweetheart. There is no parenting rulebook. He just wishes there was. Though he is correct. We want you safe. Sebastian would want us to keep you safe. Please do not give him a reason to be mad at us when he comes to take you home."

"Alright Mama. You guys can talk to Alpha Darian, and I will keep close to the guards, Zach and Gia. No more running around alone."

"Thank you, sweetie."

"I am gonna go upstairs till the Alpha calls us for the meeting."

"There is a meeting?"

"Yes. Alpha Darian summoned me to a meeting with Alpha Madison. While we were in the office, he said after the tour, he was gonna call the pack forth to meet her and see if the dragon was here, but Alpha Madison didn't find him. Just before I came home, she said she would talk to Alpha Darian about her findings, so he might not call the gathering, but I think he still might."

"Alright."

Zara hugs both her parents and bounds up the stairs to her room, closing the door behind her. She moves to her window and stares out over the pack grounds. A place of safety her entire life, and yet suddenly too dangerous for her to walk alone. Hate races through her at what the dragon has done, playing with people's lives, and yet, a part of her grateful he had. Otherwise, she would never have met Sebastian. She moves over to the computer and wakes it up from sleep mode, flipping through her friends' posts on Facebook absently, while her thoughts focus on another realm. One where her tall, dark-haired, well built, blue-eyed love holds her heart.

An hour later, Alpha Darian calls his pack forward. He stands on the porch with his Luna Willow, Alpha Madison and her Delta Victor. Scanning over the crowd, he reads the confusion on their faces, for he has kept most of them in the dark about where Zara and Kieran had gone. His eyes travel to her family, standing off to the side, seeing one of Madison's guards near her, along with those he appointed. Returning his attention back to his people, he addresses the crowd. "Now, I know you are all wondering what the meaning of this is. I really can't say too much, because the investigation is still ongoing. This here beside me is Alpha Madison and her Delta Victor. You will see four of her guards lingering around the pack. They will be here for three days. During this time, she might have some questions and I ask you to answer as honestly as you can. All I can tell you is that it's connected to the disappearance of Beta Kieran and his daughter Zara."

Zara blushes and looks to the ground, feeling her father's arm wrap around her and pull her close.

Darian's gaze drifts back to Zara. "I have no desire to cause panic, but it appears a black dragon has infiltrated himself into the pack and latched on to Zara, with what we can only assume is ill intent. We need to find him, and Alpha Madison can do that. I know what you are thinking. How can we compete against a dragon shifter? Solo, we can't, but as a pack, we can. If you see anyone unusual lurking around, please inform me immediately." He waits as the pack murmurs in agreement before continuing. "Now Alpha Madison is going to speak." He steps back, giving her the stage.

Madison moves forward, her aqua eyes scanning over all the pack members, seeing them all as they truly are. "I don't really have much to say other than this. Being fey touched, I can see things as they truly are and can feel the lies spoken within words. Your Alpha has asked that you work with me and I hope you do. He will receive my reports and findings." She turns to address Darian quietly. "There is no dragon within the immediate area."

Darian nods and steps up beside her. "Thank you. You may all return to whatever you were doing." He watches them disperse as he leads the visitors back into the pack house to talk.

Zara returns to her house with her parents, heading straight to her room, and spends the night in solitude.

Three days pass, with extra guards on Zara and no dragon in sight. Madison and her team depart with the promise to stay in touch with both Zara and Darian. Zara goes about her daily routine of eating breakfast with her family, then heading to the training rings to keep up her skills. Here she wrestles with the other warriors, reading the questions in their eyes, but grateful they dare not ask. Afterwards, she meets with Gianna and Zach at the local coffee shop for lunch before heading home to scour the internet for any indication that the scroll is out there. Dinner is quiet with her family, with her either returning to her room, or remaining to watch a movie in the living room.

Two weeks later, Zara is once more called to her Alpha's office, finding Madison standing inside. Her eyes stray to the window, having not seen any of her entourage pulling up. "Alphas. How may I help you?"

"Zara, Madison is here to take you and Zach to Frostbite for ten days. Zach is already packing, so you should as well. You leave in an hour."

"Of course Alpha. Thank you Alpha Madison." Zara smiles and runs from the room, not even caring that she has four guards following her. She races upstairs, yelling at her parents. "I am going to Frostbite for a week and a half with Zach." Pulling out her duffle bag, she stuffs her clothes into it as her father steps into the room.

"That's great news, Zare-bear. When do you leave?"

"An hour."

"Good, pack and then come downstairs for a soda with your Mama and I."

"Sounds good Papa. See you in a few minutes."

Forty-five minutes later, Zara races across the compound, her duffle bag hanging on her shoulders, and into the pack house. She smiles as Zach bounds down the stairs. "Hello partner in crime."

"Zara! Looks like we are traveling together again."

She slaps his shoulder. "What did you bribe your father with this time?"

"Wouldn't you like to know?" He leans in and wiggles his eyebrows as he loops an arm through hers. Leading her to the office door, he knocks lightly. "Dad, trouble and I are ready to travel... Greetings Alpha Madison."

Zara giggles. "I am not trouble Alpha, your son is. Hello Alpha Madison."

Darian rolls his eyes. "You are both trouble and together, you are even worse. Feel free to leave them in Frostbite Madison."

Madison laughs. "I can talk to Alpha Pierce. I hear his dungeons are pretty and can have them put there at the end of the week, keeping them there until you want them back."

"That's not fair! I never get into trouble. It's always Zach!"

Darian arches a brow. "And who exactly went missing and took my Beta with her?"

Zara scowls, the laughter in her eyes dampening the effect. "That wasn't my fault!"

"Not what I hear from your Papa."

"Just wait till I get back!"

Darian rises and hugs Zara tightly. "You take care, you hear me? You keep their guards around you at all times."

"I will Alpha."

Releasing her, he faces his son. "You are her personal guard. DO NOT let her out of your sight."

"Got it Dad."

Darian smiles at Madison. "Right then, they belong to you and Alpha Pierce for the next ten days."

Madison laughs. "Only Alpha Pierce. My pup is due sometime this week and my mate would kill me if I had it with his brother. I am simply the transport on this mission."

Zara and Zach glance at each other. "Transport?"

"Yes. Take my hands." She reaches out, taking the hands that are offered and fey steps them to Pierces' castle.

Zara staggers, clutching her stomach as she looks up at Madison. "That's worse than the portal magic."

Madison laughs and pats her on the back. "You get used to it. Now take a few deep breaths and the queasiness will stop. Zach, how are you doing?"

Zach shakes his head, a hand over his mouth. "Fiinnee."

"Great, you are both in perfect shape to meet Alpha Pierce." She gestures to the tall man standing before them, that neither of them noticed.

Pierce chuckles. "First time travelers?"

Madison moves over and hugs her brother-in-law. "My way, yes. Zara has portal hopped twice."

"Interesting." He looks over the pair with their slightly green faces. "Welcome to Frostbite Syndicate. Collect your bags and I will take you to your room to rest. Tomorrow, you can look through the archives. How does that sound?"

"That sounds lovely, Alpha Pierce. Thank you."

Madison smiles at the pair, turning to her brother-in-law. "I leave them in your hands then, Pierce. Have guards around her. A black dragon wishes her dead."

"Understood. No one will get near the pair."

"Thanks. I need to get home in case this pup decides to pop today." She kisses his cheek and fades from the room.

Zara clutches her bag, still unsteady on her feet. "How does she do that with such ease?"

"She's fey. She's used to it. Come, this way." He leads them through the castle to a suite near the center of the castle, suitable for them both. "This is your domain for the week. If you need anything, let the maids or guards know. Dinner is in about an hour, and I hope to see you there."

"Thank you Alpha. We will be."

"Perfect." He closes the door and looks at the guards. "No one except those I approve of are allowed past this door. I don't care who it is. We have a rogue dragon wishing the girl dead."

"Yes Alpha."

Ten days later, Zach and Zara disembark from the plane and collect their luggage. Heading out of the airport, they see Kieran waiting for them. Zara runs over and hugs her father tightly.

"I know Zare-bear. I could read it in your expression." He guides Zara into the car, meeting Zach's gaze and switches to mind-link. *'Alpha Zach. How was your trip?'*

Zach gets into the back with Zara, pulling her into his arms as Kieran gets into the driver's seat. *'No mate for me, but Alpha Peirce was super nice and respectful. He had guards watching over us at all times, even when he was there assisting us. I knew Zara was getting disheartened after about six days of not finding it. I get it. There are so many old books and scrolls and it's hard not to wonder if we missed it. I spoke to Peirce about it privately and we tried to keep things lighthearted, but I don't think it worked. He even had his mate, Violet, bake us cookies. I want the old Zara back, Kieran. This one is not her.'*

'We all do, Zach, trust me. We all see it.' He steers the car out of the parking lot, his eyes on the road, the sun shining in the sky. Flowers bloom along the side of the road as he drives in silence, mulling over their current situations, something he does every time he reads the sadness in his daughter's eyes.

Twelve

Through the Veil

Two weeks later, Zara stares at the ceiling of her room, knowing the morning sun is in the sky, but the blackout curtains are doing their job. Anxiety fills her for unknown reasons. Perhaps because she hasn't found the scroll yet, or that the dragon that hunts her is quietly lurking, waiting for her to be free of the guards that constantly surround her. The only time she is ever alone is here, in her room, a place she is spending more and more time, just to get some peace.

'Em, are you alright?'

'I think so Zara. I just feel something is up but can't place my paw on it'

'Is it bad?'

'I'm sorry Zara, I can't tell.'

'Alright, when you know, let me know.'

'I will.'

Closing her eyes, Zara breathes in and out slowly, doing her best to calm herself, suspecting a few hours in the fighting rings should wear her out. Rising, she readies herself and pads quietly out of the house, knowing everyone else is still asleep because of the silence in the house. She arrives at the empty rings and moves to the punching bags, spending an hour wearing off her frustrations on it as others filter into the training grounds. She spends the rest of the morning wrestling, learning new moves and overall, exhausting herself. After lunch, she wanders with Gianna and Zach, absently listening to their conversation, not even realizing they stopped beside her.

"Zara? Ember? Anyone in there?"

Zara snaps her gaze to them, mumbling quietly. "Sorry, what did you say?"

"We asked if you wanted to head back to the pack house and watch a movie?"

Zara shakes her head. "I don't know if I can sit still that long. For some reason, Ember is antsy, and it's making me nervous."

Gianna steps closer, her eyes scanning the surrounding area. "Do you think it's the dragon?"

"It's possible. I mean, it's been several months. I would have thought the dragon would have made his move by now, but from what I have read, they can be extremely patient."

Zach scowls at the thought. "Do you think he's in town and Ember senses him?"

"If he was, then he was here this morning at dawn. Ember did not have an answer when I asked her why."

"Damn. Perhaps a run instead?"

"Yes, but I can't leave the interior pack grounds. I only get runs when the entire pack goes now."

Zach places a hand on her shoulder. "I'm sorry you have to go through this, Zara."

Zara hugs him. "Thanks Zach. I am glad you and Gia are here."

Gianna jumps in, wrapping her arms around the pair, pulling them to the ground. "Yes! Group hug."

The group laughs and rolls around on the grass, before flopping over and staring at the cloudy sky. A few minutes later, the notification on Zara's phone beeps and she pulls it out, a gasp escaping her lips at her father's name flashing a new message.

Sebastian watches the portal close behind him, before sweeping his gaze around the wooded area they stand in. Glints of the ocean sparkle to the left of him and a soft breeze brings the forest scents to him. He pulls out the small black box and powers it on, punching in 1786. The phone makes strange noises, seeing a multitude of messages popping up on the screen before settling on the last one.

Nero peers over his shoulder. "Is it supposed to do that?"

"I am uncertain." Sebastian types into the phone and pushes the button to send, hearing the soft bleep as it moves up on the screen.

My queen, I have come to take you home.

Zara opens her phone and stares at the text message in shock. "Sebastian!"

Zach and Gianna turn to her. "What about him?"

Zara's fingers fly across the keyboard, her heart swelling inside her at seeing his dark gaze, the smile that barely graces his lips and his touch upon her skin, even if only to hold his hand.

OMG Seb!!!! OMW

Zara rises quickly, stuffing her phone in her pocket. "He's here. I gotta go." She shifts into her wolf and gives Ember full control, racing off before either of them, or her guards, recover from shock.

"ZARA!!! Come back!!" Zach mind-links his father. *'Dad, Zara took off. Sebastian is here.'*

'Shit! Follow her, Zach. And get her guards on her!' Darian shifts his mind-link to his Beta. *'Kieran! Your daughter has taken off. She said Sebastian is here.'*

'Dammit! She can't be alone. The dragon could be waiting for her. I will find her.' Kieran rises and runs for the door, pausing as he spots his wife coming down the stairs. "Zara's mate is here. Best prepare for a guest or two, Lila. I am going after her."

"Kieran, be careful."

"I will."

'Zach, Gianna, and her guards are trying to follow Kieran. I will meet up with you.' Just then, a mind-link comes into Darian from the patrols at the border. *'Alpha, there is a group of six vampires, standing at our borders in weird clothing, staring at a phone. What should we do?'*

'Kieran, the border patrols to the south have found the vamps. We head that way.'

'Darian, do not attack them! Unless they attack first.'

'Vamps usually do.'

'These won't. Trust me, Darian, I was not lying when I said they were different. Especially if my daughter is on her way to them.'

'Got it.' Darian switches his link to his patrols. *'DO NOT attack unless they attack first.'*

'But Alpha, they are vamps...'

'DON'T Attack them, we are on our way.'

Sebastian's brows furrow at the reply on the phone, passing it over to Nero to look at. "What does that mean?"

Nero chuckles, reading the last line. "I believe Seb is you? She calls you Seb? You hate that name. You really do have it bad. As for the rest, I have no clue. Is it wolf talk?"

Sebastian glares at his best friend and snatches the phone back as it shuts off, slipping it into his robes. "I should have left you at the castle."

Nero chuckles. "Yes, you probably should have. I don't believe Mason is gonna run it as tightly as you do, nor keep those witches under control."

"Well, I have to hope he manages it because he is stuck with them for ten days if they are speaking the truth."

"Do you think they are?"

"Yes, I believe they are. But magic is risky in the wrong hands. Still, I needed to take this risk to get my queen back."

"I understand... I hear thoughts nearby."

Sebastian nods. "Yes, wolf patrols. They have already asked what to do about us. I am guessing they are waiting for orders."

"Should we move?"

"No, we wait. I have no desire to fight with this pack if it is Zara's."

Zara can feel the wind blowing through her blond fur, even in the recesses of her mind, having given Ember full control, accepting she can feel the bond stronger because it's tied to the wolf spirit. She can hear the pounding of feet behind her fading as she gains distance on her friends, being faster than they are in wolf form.

'Zara, you can't be alone!'

'Zach, Gia, I will be fine. Sebastian will take care of me. I will see you later.'

'We are backing off now, Zara. My father and yours just passed us.'

'Good, I will see them soon then.' She weaves her way through the undergrowth, clearing logs, her stamina waning after an hour and a half. *'Ember, how much longer?'*

'He is close.'

Twenty minutes later, she spots the wolf patrols, hunkered down behind some ferns, their eyes focused ahead of them, instinctively feeling Sebastian's presence as his scent wafts her way. A low growl escapes her as she jumps clear over the patrol, her feet pivoting to redirect herself to the six standing fifty feet away. Her focus entirely on the tallest one in the middle, her light blue eyes locking onto his midnight blue ones. She bounds towards him, launching into the air, ignoring the four guards who immediately pull their blade to protect their King.

Sebastian places a hand up, stilling the blades as he catches the wolf, not expecting the power behind her as they both tumble to the ground. He chuckles, feeling her wet sloppy kisses up the side of his face, and wraps his arms around her. "Em, I missed you too."

'Alpha!! Ember is attacking the vam... No, wait, she's... What the hell? She's licking him.'

Sebastian sits up and kisses the end of her muzzle. "Ember, my love, it is good to see you too, but may I see Zara? I suspect she's going to need to explain our presence to these wolves watching us. They seem confused."

Ember growls in dismay, nuzzling into his neck, but recedes back and allows Zara forth, who shifts back. She wraps her arms around him and pulls him close, kissing him deeply.

'Ahh... Alpha... Now Zara is kissing him and I mean, kissing him.'

'We are close behind her.' Five minutes later, the pair arrives and shifts back into their human forms, standing with the border patrol, watching Zara and Sebastian, surrounded by five guards.

'Well, they weren't lying. She is kissing a vamp.'

Kieran chuckles. "They are not like the vampires of our realm, Darian. He's her mate. The one that marked her."

'I know you told me she accepted a mate bond with a vampire, but to see it is something else?'

"Yes, it took seven days, but he won her over. Also, there is no point in using our mind-link. They can hear it loud and clear, along with all our thoughts."

'No, they can't. It's not within a vampire's abilities.'

"It is with them, Alpha Darian."

'Can you trust him?'

Sebastian rises, helping Zara to her feet, wrapping an arm protectively over her shoulder. He turns his dark eyes onto the Alpha. "Yes, you can trust me."

Darian coughs, snapping his gaze to Kieran, while the other wolves watch in disbelief as he approaches them just as he would any of the pack members. "Kieran?"

Kieran greets Sebastian with a shake of his hand. "Sebastian! Welcome to our world. Nero, I half expected you to stay behind. Mathew, Anthony, and two I recognize, but don't know."

Sebastian smiles and pulls a hand off Zara, returning the handshake. "Theodore and Julian. They were two of your daughters' guards, just as Nero is mine. We left the others behind to watch over the castle because they have family.

They are not willing to leave in case we didn't make it back. Not that we entirely trusted the witches, but it was a risk I needed to take to find my queen."

Kieran nods. "I understand that. I wouldn't have either if it wasn't forced upon us. Did they give you a timeline?"

"Yes. Ten days before their spell pulls us home."

"Damn, that's not much time then." Kieran catches Zara stiffening in Sebastian's arms, knowing he was losing his daughter in ten days if they didn't figure this out. He turns to his Alpha. "Alpha Darian, this is King Sebastian and his men. I request entrance and acceptance into the pack for them for the next ten days."

Darian observes the interactions between his Beta Kieran, his daughter, and the six vampires, immediately noticing the respect they have for each other. He approaches cautiously, feeling the flood of mind-links from his warriors warning him against it. He turns to Kieran. "I know he said he is trustworthy, but do you trust them within our pack's interior, Kieran?"

Kieran nods. "Yes, they had the chance to kill us and they didn't. Even when we killed three of theirs. They have proven themselves honorable. I explained this to you, Darian."

"I know Kieran, but they are vampires, and I need my own confirmation." He turns to Sebastian. "Do you feed on blood?"

Sebastian smiles coolly. "Yes, we require blood to survive, but we do not feed on the unwilling. We pay well and care for them afterwards."

Darian stiffens at his words, not liking the implication of it. "How so?"

Sebastian chuckles, feeling Zara tense at his words, caressing her cheek lightly to calm her. "When we feed Alpha, it creates a euphoric state that can last anywhere from twenty minutes to an hour. We place them in a room with food and drink, so that no one takes advantage of them as they are incapable of making decisions during this time. In the old days of our world, vampires would feed on the innocent and then take it from them right after, as in bedding them. We do not. Hence protecting and caring for them until their cognitive mind returns. Many come back as we pay well to those that offer to be feeders."

Darian contemplates his words, his eyes drifting to Zara in his arms, seeing her eyes flash in annoyance at his questioning. "Then I will accept you into the pack, but there will be a set of guards monitoring your movements within the pack. Step out of line and I will place you in the cells."

Sebastian chuckles as Zara giggles. "Payback I suppose. I accept those terms."

Darian looks at Sebastian in confusion. "Payback?"

Zara smiles. "Sebastian placed guards on us as we moved about his castle. Papa and I each had four, though I suspect Nero watched us both."

Nero nods. "I did my queen."

"Just Zara, Nero."

"Yes, my queen."

"Uggg, Seb, make him call me Zara!"

Sebastian kisses the top of her head. "I am not making him do anything, my love. It's his sign of respect. I have asked him to call me Sebastian for longer than you have been alive, and he still calls me sire most of the time."

"Fine, but I prefer lassie then, although when you think about it, he's calling me a dog."

"A dog? Are you not a wolf?"

"Bah, wolves and dogs are different Seb and stop teasing me. I will show you who Lassie is when we get home."

Darian chuckles at the banter. "On that note... Lassie, we need to get back to the pack before dark."

"Dark?"

Kieran nods. "Yes, in this realm, it gets dark at night."

"We do too, but not in such a short timeframe. It is seasonal. Light for six months and dark for the remainder. Because of this, we have adapted to seeing as well in the dark as we do in the light."

"Interesting. Our human vision is a touch better than most, but it's our wolves that see in the dark."

"Come, it was a two-hour run. Walking will take longer." The group heads back as the patrols surround them warily, none of them fully trusting the vampires like Kieran and Zara do. Darian makes the occasional glance over to Zara and Sebastian, before drifting his gaze over the others, inspecting the vampires he is leading into his pack. He sighs inwardly at the fact that they stand the same height as them, if not taller, with strikingly handsome looks. All dressing in an old style of clothing that he knows damn well will make the unmated she-wolves swoon. He mind-links Kieran. *'Damn Kieran, I am gonna need extra guards just to keep the unmated she-wolves off them. What do their women look like?'*

Kieran coughs at the mind-link, glancing over at his Alpha as he catches the smirk on Sebastian's lips. *'Darian, they can hear that. You might as well speak out loud. And to be honest, I didn't pay attention, but the few I saw were beautiful.'*

'It's a mind-link. They can't possibly understand this, Kieran.'

"Alpha Darian, I can even hear your thoughts and your concern for your mate. That she loves what you call fantasy movies and that our clothing seems to match that. I assure you, my men will keep their hands and teeth to themselves and not meddle with your she-wolves. I came for Zara and a scroll. I know from hers that she is delighted to see me and worried that she has yet to find the other half of the scroll. She is concerned that I will be disappointed in her for what she perceives as her failure. It is not. I did not expect it to be easy, especially since I have been searching several hundred years for it." He glances down at Zara, feeling her hand tighten on his, reading the mixture of emotions floating through her mind. He kisses her cheek lightly before continuing. "Nero is my best friend and personal guard. I gather what Kieran is to you. A Beta as he calls it. The others are guards with no families who wished to venture into another realm with their king. Each was given a choice, as none of us knew whether it would work or if we would even land in the right realm. It is not something I have ever done, or presumed possible, until Kieran and Zara landed in our realm. I suppose it is feasible that they too could find their mate with a she-wolf, as I have. Should that happen, that discussion is between you and them, because, as I am to understand, you are the ruler of this pack and lay the laws down. I am a visitor and will abide by any you have in place."

Kieran chuckles. "Spoken like a true king there, Sebastian. You and our Lycan King will get along famously."

Sebastian ponders his words as he filters through his thoughts. "He is not here, but you have set up a meeting with him to see the archives with Zara when I arrived."

"Correct. That's the last place she has to look, and she wanted you there for it."

"Do you think it's there?"

"If the dragon does not have it, then it's there. His library boasts the oldest manuscripts, paintings, and books in the realm, so I have hope. The drawback is, the King has only agreed to the two of you, which will make finding it longer. Only those of his lineage have access to it. It was, in fact, his granddaughter, Alpha Madison, that obtained permission for you."

Sebastian turns to Darian, his midnight blue eyes studying him carefully.

"Then my people will be in your hands, Alpha Darian. If you have a need for them, they will obey your commands."

Darian does his best to conceal his shock at the fact that a king was placing his people beneath him. "Thank you. I appreciate it."

Kieran keeps the small talk flowing, understanding completely the nervousness in Darian and the patrols that follow, intending on protecting their Alpha. He asks about the past few months and what Sebastian had to go through to hire the witches, listening as he explains the trials he faced. As well as going over all the libraries and places Zara has traveled to, and that he was more than a little jealous that he hadn't gone with her.

Sebastian arches a brow. "You didn't send her alone. Who is this Zach?"

Zara nudges Sebastian. "My best friend. Him and Gia. Be nice."

Kieran chuckles, catching the concern in Darian's expression at the change in Sebastian's demeanor. "The Alpha's son. To be clear, Sebastian, you are more his type than Zara is."

Zara rolls her eyes. "Papa! He hasn't told people that yet!"

Darian snaps his gaze to Zara. "Told people what?"

"Zare-bear. I am his Beta. I can see it. His father would too if he opened his eyes."

Darian scowls at Kieran. "Can you please explain what you both see in my son?"

Sebastian shifts his gaze to Darian. "It's in your thoughts. You just want confirmation of what you already know."

"Dammit. Why hasn't he told me then?"

"I suspect, having not met him, he worries you might not approve." He turns his gaze to Kieran. "It was the same worry Zara had when I succeeded in courting her. In fact, it's still there, but more so directed at her mama and brothers' approval."

"Does nothing make it past you?"

"Not when you can read thoughts, Alpha Darian."

"Your realm must be fun."

"Actually, most in our realm have mastered the art of blocking their mind from ours. It was rather intriguing to read Kieran's and Zara's so freely."

Zara elbows him in the rib cage. "And I said it's impolite to read another person's thoughts."

Sebastian chuckles, pulling her tight. "Indeed, you did, but I chose not to listen."

Several hours later, they arrive just as the sun is setting. Kieran watches Darian pause, seeing the doubt and uncertainty in his expression. He offers his best friend a smile. "I highly doubt Zara will let Sebastian out of her sight, Alpha, just as I suspect Sebastian's guards are not letting him out of their sight. All of them will stay in the cottage with Lila and I, though I will ask for some cots to be brought around as I do not have enough beds."

Sebastian shakes his head. "We do not need to sleep as you do every night. We can rotate if you have a couple of beds."

"We have a guest room with one bed. We can add a cot to it, or you can sleep on the Hide-a-bed."

"Hide-a-bed?"

"Yes, it's a bed within a couch."

Zara looks up. "That's why I only saw you sleeping one time. You were always in the library."

Sebastian looks down at her, caressing her cheek gently. "Yes. I pushed my sleep for you, which we can do, but my body said I needed it that night." He whispers in her ear, "I will admit, it shocked me to wake up to you curled up in my arms."

Zara blushes and looks away, knowing her father's hearing will have caught that. She mumbles quietly. "Blame Nero. He brought me there."

Nero chuckles. "She is correct, but she came to the library looking for Sebastian."

Kieran sighs. "Zare-bear, He is your mate. It's destined. Speaking of mates, I believe I need to go talk to mine. I didn't exactly tell her how many guests we were getting."

Zara laughs. "Mama's gonna have your hide in the rings tomorrow."

"You might be right about that. Perhaps you should show Sebastian around for fifteen minutes, then bring them home." He races off to the cottage.

Zara watches her father run away before turning to Darian. "Thank you, Alpha, for allowing my mate and his men into the pack. I really appreciate it."

"You're welcome Zara, just keep them in line."

Thirteen

New Inventions

"I will." Zara leads them around, pointing out the pack house, the buildings, the hospital. Smiling as they all stop to gawk at a car pulling up into the parking lot nearby. "That's a car that I showed you, Sebastian. No horses needed."

"Impressive. Can I try it?"

"No, you need a license, but I can take you and Nero for a drive with two guards. Perhaps tomorrow, along with a tour of the pack."

"Very well, tomorrow then." He looks up at the streetlights and the lights in the shop windows. "Your torches and lanterns are so bright."

Zara frowns. "Yes. They are. I will find out where to get more blackout material tomorrow for the spare room."

"Blackout material?"

Zara turns to Sebastian. "Yes, it darkens a room to black. I couldn't sleep when I got home. Everything was so bright and noisy. I missed the quietness of the castle." Her voice drops. "I missed you."

Sebastian pulls her close and kisses her gently. "I missed you too. Every minute of every day. The library was far too quiet without you there."

Zara wraps her arms around him, holding him tight for a minute, enjoying the comfort and bond of having him nearby again. She laughs at Embers humming in her mind. *'Ember!'*

'What, I missed him too, you know.'

'I know, Em, and I know it's why you were withdrawn. Never again. We make it work.'

'Damn right we will!'

Sebastian tightens his hold. "Yes, we make it work."

Zara pushes him away, humor dancing in her eyes. "Hey! No eavesdropping!"

He chuckles. "I can't help it."

She rolls her eyes. "Right. On that note, let's get the group of you home. Papa has had enough time to soothe Mama over." She takes his hand and gently leads him through the cluster of cottages, observing the way they glance over the buildings with curiosity. *'Papa, is it safe?'*

'Yes. Zare-bear. Your Mama and I are in the kitchen with your brothers.'

"I hope you are ready. It's quite different from your realm."

"We are."

Zara opens the door and steps in, seeing them remain outside. She frowns, recalling suddenly that a vampire cannot enter a house uninvited. "Right, sorry, I forgot. You are all welcome to enter."

"Thank you for allowing us entry into your house, Zara."

"I trust you Seb, and I trust your men."

She guides them to the living room and stops, letting them take in all the differences, from the fireplace, with the TV on top of the mantle to the couches and chairs sitting before it. The tall lamps standing in the corner with the small side tables. She gestures for them to move around and explore. "Feel free to sit. I will bring Mama in here to meet you all. Then my brothers, Jayden and Jenson." Zara watches Sebastian move over to the TV, running his fingers over the smooth surface, looking for the button on the side like his phone has. She giggles softly. "I will show you that after Seb. I have one in my room." She peeks her head into the kitchen. "Mama. Sebastian, Nero and their guards are here to meet you."

Lila looks up at Kieran, who nods his head and guides her to the door. "Don't think of them as vampires, my love. Just think of them as supernatural people."

Lila nods nervously and steps out into the living room beside her daughter. Her eyes sweep over the six in her living room. She watches four of them straighten their posture, their gaze bouncing between her and the dark-haired one. The blonde standing beside him smiles and winks at her, relaxing her at his casualness of the whole situation. She turns to the tall, dark and handsome one, a smile tipping at her lips, thinking her daughter would pick him, for he was exactly her type growing up. She walks forward, sizing him up carefully. "So, you are my daughter's mate, Sebastian."

Sebastian takes her hand and kisses the back of it. "Indeed, I am. A pleasure to meet you Zara's Mama and Kieran's mate. He thought of you often while he was in my realm."

"He did?"

"Yes, you were always in his thoughts."

"Ohh." She blushes and looks away at Nero. "And who else is staying in my house?"

"This is Nero, my Beta, so to speak. The four warriors are guards that watched over your family, Mathew, Anthony, Theodore, and Julian. I promise we will be on our best behavior while we are here."

Lila glances back at Zara, seeing her shift nervously in front of the kitchen door, gesturing for her to come up beside her. "Kieran said that you are here for ten days. That you do not have to sleep every night. Should I be concerned that your people are roaming my house while we sleep?"

"MAMA!"

"Enough Zara. I need to hear it from him."

Sebastian chuckles. "Yes, we feed on blood, but we also eat food that you do. No, my people will not feed on you or any of your pack. You have my word on that."

"And you will survive ten days without feeding?"

"Mama, please."

Sebastian takes Zara's hand and pulls her in close. "Your Mama is concerned, my love. It is only natural. I recall the rage you had towards us when you arrived."

Zara mumbles under her breath and shuffles her feet. "That was before I knew you."

He caresses her cheek gently. "And your Mama doesn't know us." He turns back to Lila. "We can survive ten days without feeding. It will not be ideal, but we all came here knowing that would be the case. I trust my men completely. They will touch no one without consent, nor will we use magic, deception, or any other means to trick someone into feeding us. This I swear to you."

Lila smiles. "That's what I wanted to hear. Welcome to the family, Sebastian." She turns to the kitchen. "Kieran, you may bring the boys out."

Kieran leads his two sons out, younger than Zara by five years. He remains behind them, a hand on each of their shoulders. "Jayden, Jenson. This is your sister's mate. Sebastian. Beside him is Nero, his Beta, and watching all of us carefully are his four guards; Mathew, Anthony, Theodore and Julian. They are going to be staying with us for ten days, though your sister and Sebastian will be going on a trip during that time to Whispering Pines."

Sebastian bows to them. "Nice to meet you two. I saw you in a moving painting when your sister was visiting my castle."

"Do you really live in a castle? Zara said you did, but we figured she was just fibbing us."

"Yes, I really live in a castle."

"Is it as big as the pack house?"

"Well, since I only had a glimpse of the pack house, I cannot say, but my castle is three stories high, with many rooms."

"Three stories? That's big."

"Yes, it is, but it houses a lot of my people."

"So does our pack house. I bet you will see it tomorrow."

"I suspect I will. Zara offered me a tour of your pack."

"It will have to be later. She trains every morning. One day, we will be just as strong as her."

"I am certain you will. It takes time and practice."

"Do you practice as well?"

"Yes, but not every day, as I have other duties to attend to."

"What duties?"

"Well, think of me like your Alpha. Does he practice every day?"

"No, he has to run the pack."

"Well, where I come from, I have my pack to run."

"So Zara is going to be your Luna?"

Sebastian glances at Zara, catching her slight nod. "Yes, Zara is going to be my Luna."

The boys turn to look at their father. "Papa! Zara's a Luna! Did you hear that?"

"Yes, I did. Now, I suspect they have suffered enough beneath our interrogation. How about we let them settle in and relax a bit?"

"Can we watch a movie?"

"Sure. You get it set up. Mama will make popcorn."

Zara looks up at Sebastian. "I will take them upstairs and show them the house, Papa."

"Sounds good Zare-bear. You are all welcome to join us."

"Thanks Papa. This way." She leads them upstairs and shows them their room. Stepping inside, she flips the switch to turn the lights on. "This switch turns the lights on. They are all over the house, in each of the rooms. There is no flame, so you don't have to worry about fire. It also turns them off and we turn them off when we leave a room." She moves across the room to the bedside lamps and turns one on. "These also have switches, but they are just more difficult to find. The bed is softer than the cot, but we don't have as many rooms as you do, so we have to bunk you together."

Leaving the room, she crosses the hall and opens the door. "This is our bathing chamber." She steps in, encouraging them all to huddle in the small room. "We have what we call running water. These taps here, if you turn them, produce water." She twists one, then the other, sticking her fingers beneath them. "One is hot, one is cold. It takes a few seconds for the hot to reach here from the tank." Turning the taps off, she moves to the toilet, a soft blush gracing her cheeks. "This is our chamber pot. Beside it is the chamber pot paper, for cleaning afterwards and it can go into the pot. When you are done, you push this lever, and it takes away all the water in the bowl." She shows them how it works, laughing at the gasps of surprise.

Sebastian chuckles. "Now I understand why your thoughts went where they went in our realm. This is incredible."

"It is. I thought you were punishing us with a bucket until I realized you had no power." She turns and pushes the shower curtain aside. "This is our bath or shower. If you want a bath, you put this plug into the hole and turn the taps on. If you want a shower, you pull this lever out." She drops the plug in and turns the water on, watching it fill a bit, before pulling the lever, feeling the spray of water hit her arm. "Showers are fantastic, but close the curtain when you have one, otherwise water will go everywhere. You should make sure you try one before you leave. Now, there is only so much hot water, before the tank reheats. So try not to stay in here too long, or it will get cold on you." Shutting the water off, she points to the cupboard. "Inside there are towels for drying yourself after the shower, bigger than the ones that hang on the rack for drying your hands. Tucked in here are the towels for drying the floor, so we don't step in your puddles." She watches them all nod before exiting the room. Moving down along the doors, she points to them. "This is Mama and Papa's room, and these are my brother's rooms." At the end of the hall, she pushes a door open. "This is our office. As close to a library as we have. Papa is often here, so knock before entering." She reaches out and pulls a book off the shelf, sadness enveloping her at the thought of their books, and hands it to Sebastian. "These are our books. Not as grand as yours, but still readable. We have many, if you desire to read in your spare time."

Sebastian turns the book over, immediately noticing the difference. Lightweight, with uniform, easy-to-read scripture. His fingers run over the well-done painting on the cover, intrigued by the images upon it. "Are there any books you recommend, my queen?"

"Not in here. My favorites are in my room. But I suppose it depends on what you like. I prefer fantasy. Some of these are real-world events, mixed with Mama's smut books and my brother's nerd books." She smiles up at him. "I expect by the end of the week, you and Nero will have read them all, but there are other things to see here and I am going to show you two." Watching Sebastian place the book down, she leads them back down the hall towards her room. "This is my room. Sebastian and Nero will stay here."

Sebastian arches a brow. "Nero?"

"Well yes. I know he won't leave your side and he stayed in the room while I slept with you at the castle. I expect he will do the same here."

Nero laughs. "Oh Lassie! That is priceless. I do believe you might have shocked the King with that statement."

Sebastian mutters quietly under his breath. "I knew I should have left you at home."

"Too late now sire!" He bows to Zara. "I will happily watch over you as you sleep, my queen."

"Nero!"

Zara smiles at his teasing, stepping into her room as the others follow. "But you get the cot when it arrives!"

Sebastian glances back at his guards, giving a shake of his head that they are not to enter. He looks around and immediately notices the printed images of himself all over the wall. His eyes stray to Zara, seeing a blush creeping across her cheeks as she averts her gaze. Returning his attention to the room, he studies it carefully, taking in the lavender and white decor. The bedspread haphazardly pulled up over the bed, with pillows lining the back of it. Sitting in the center is a yellow bear with a sun on its belly. A white night table nestled beside it with a small black box on its surface, matching the white dresser pressed against the wall. Gold jewelry spills out of a decorative container on top of it, surrounded by stacks of books. Beneath the window is a desk, its chair half out with clothing draped over it. Upon it sits a larger black cube, a pad with buttons and a box like the one that played the paintings. An array of clothing spills out of open closet doors, some pooling on the floor, others in a basket nearby.

"I guess I should have cleaned up this morning."

Sebastian draws her into his arms. "No, it is good to see your place. It is truly you, even with my painting all over your walls."

"I wanted you to be the first thing I woke up to in the morning and the last thing I went to sleep to."

"How did you make them?"

"I took them off my phone... Wait, I need yours. It will need to be plugged in."

Sebastian slips his phone out of his pocket and hands it over.

Zara accepts it and moves over to her desk. She pulls her drawer open and rifles through it, pulling out her Papa's cord. She plugs it into her computer, hearing the soft bleep as it charges. "It will take about five hours to charge. Then you can have access to it." She pulls her own out and powers it on. "Remember when I said you had no service? Here we have service." She scrolls to her message, seeing a bunch from Gianna and Zach. She reads through them, ensuring they are decent, before showing them to Sebastian and Nero. "These are from earlier when I took off from my friend Gia. She wanted to know where I was going. Zach has sent a few as well. We can mind-link, but the Alpha can hear them all, so we text to keep things private. Not that we do anything bad, it's just sometimes, we don't want people hearing our thoughts."

Sebastian and Nero both chuckle at her words.

"I know... you both can hear them, but here, it's different. Only the Alpha can, or those we deliberately send our mind-link to, from one person or many. Now I can text her back." She moves over to the group text and responds to them.

> Gia, Zach. Have returned home with my mate. I will introduce you to him tomorrow morning in the training rings.

"Sometimes they answer right away, other times, if they are working, they have to wait to break. It should be quick, though." Zara's phone bleeps within a matter of seconds and she opens the text.

> OMG! That's fantastic Zara. Have fun tonight!!!

> Look forward to it, Zara. Prepare for competition! I might try to steal him away.

Zara blushes and mumbles under her breath. "There you have it. My crazy friends. One encouraging me and one threatening to steal you away from me."

"So all the noises I heard from the box when I pushed the button were messages?"

Zara's blush deepens. "Yes, those were probably me. I texted you a lot. You probably have some that were meant for Papa too, as it was his phone first."

Sebastian grabs her wrist and pulls her in. "And can I read all these texts, as you call them?"

Zara nods. "Yes. They are on your phone, or mine. Yours needs a few hours before it will work again. You can read mine later. I will show you what the computer and phone can do after the movie. That is, if you all want to watch a movie."

Sebastian looks down at Zara, reading her mixed emotions of wanting to be alone with him and being with her family. "We will watch this movie."

"Great." She pulls a blanket off her bed and wraps it over her arm. She sprints down the hall to shut all the lights off, and returns, leading them back downstairs. The scent of popcorn fills the air as they enter the living room. "Did you want something to drink? We don't have wine, but can pick some up for you tomorrow. We have soda, coffee, tea, water, and juice."

"I wish to try both the soda and coffee."

Zara giggles. "Perhaps soda now and coffee in the morning with breakfast. Though I suppose it doesn't matter if it keeps you up all night. Find a place to sit. What do the rest of you want?" Taking their orders, she dashes into the kitchen and grabs a mixture of pops and juices. Carrying them back on a tray, she sets them on the table. "Help yourself." Collecting two Cokes, she passes one to Sebastian and the other to Nero. "There are many flavors, but this one is my favorite. Be careful though, it's very fizzy. Don't drink it too fast to start."

Seeing the couches and chairs full, Zara plants herself on the floor in front of her parents, leaning on their legs, patting the ground beside her.

Nero chuckles as Sebastian sits on the floor next to her, only to settle down on the other side of Zara, whispering in her ear. "Well, my queen, this is the first time I have seen your king sitting on the floor."

"I can hear that, Nero." Sebastian scowls his way as he turns the can over in his hands.

"It's where I usually sit. He better get used to it." Zara giggles as she drapes her blanket over the three of them, snuggling into Sebastian. She smiles, picking up her can, showing him the tab, opening it with a soft hiss and watching as he does the same. She takes a sip and places it on the coffee table, pulling a bowl of popcorn into her lap. "Alright Papa, I think we are all ready now."

Sebastian sips the pop, coughing at the bubbling sensation in his mouth and down his throat.

"Easy there Sebastian. Zara might drink them like they are water, but it's carbonated." Kieran chuckles as he picks up the remotes. He powers the TV on, earning gasps from them and flips to the DVD remote, pressing play. Sound surrounds them, as the screen flashes the opening credits for the movie.

Zara smiles at their gazes, looking around the room. "It's our magic that we call technology. Just watch the show. It's a good one."

Two hours later, the movie ends, earning a round of chatter from the group, wanting to see more, the amazement laced in their voices. A few of them rise to inspect the TV, wanting to know where the magic comes from. Zara remains snuggled in Sebastian's arms. "I suppose you can watch more if you like. But not with the surround sound, because we need to sleep."

"There are more? These are like living books, straight out of the mind, on that magical black box."

Zara points to the bookshelf against the wall. "Yes. That's exactly what they are. Most do come from books. Then movie producers hire actors, film it, digitally edit it, and put it together to make a movie."

Mathew moves over to the cases and pulls a few out, realizing rather suddenly there are descriptions on the back. "It even tells you about them."

"Yes. Some are part of a series, so you will want to watch part one first. Otherwise, it might not make sense. Though I realize that some of the stuff you will see just won't make sense because it's technology based. If you have questions, I can answer them in the morning." Zara shifts over as she feels her parents rising, smiling up at them.

Kieran pats her head softly. "Don't stay up too late, Zare-bear. Your brothers need to get to bed."

The boys groan in dismay. "Aww Papa, do we have to? Can't we stay up and watch another one?"

"No, you have school in the morning. Your sister does not."

"Darn."

Kieran guides them out of the living room and up the stairs with his wife.

Zara reluctantly rises and moves to the desk in the corner. Opening the drawer, she pulls out a pad of paper and a pen, carrying them back to Mathew. "These are our quills. We call them pens." She clicks it open and draws on the pad. "Write your questions here and one of us can answer it in the morning." Moving to the DVD player, she shows Anthony the button to open the drawer and carefully lifts the disc out of the player. "Do not touch this side, fingerprints can cause skips. Place it in its case, and snap it shut. Each disc has its own case because each one tells its own story." She holds her hand out to Mathew, who picks one and hands it over. Zara smiles at the cover and opens it, popping the disc in the player and pushing the tray closed. A soft whirring occurs as it spins up. "This remote, the small one, is for the player. The arrow pointing right is the play button. Point it at the black box and push it down." As Zara does so, the screen flashes up. She taps the remote and pauses it. "Hitting the button with the two vertical lines will pause it, and the arrow will start it again. The button with the square will stop it so that you can get the disc out."

"Why would you pause it?"

"Ba... Chamber pot breaks. Food and drink breaks. Sometimes the phone rings or someone knocks on the door. Not this late, though." She picks up the TV remote and shuts the surround sound off. "Don't worry about this one. It's for the TV. If you tire of watching movies, the TV will shut itself off after five minutes of inactivity. I will show you where to get the food and drinks." She leads them into the kitchen and flips the lights on. Heading to the fridge, she opens it. "The sodas, milk and juice are in here. Water comes from the taps over there or from bottles in the fridge. In this cupboard are the glasses for those that had soda and want water, milk or juice. Chips and cookies are in this pantry. I would stay away from the rest, as it requires cooking and that's a whole other step of training. Too much for tonight." She closes the fridge and moves to the tap. "The one with the blue is cold, and the red is hot."

Sebastian glances at his men. "They will be fine with the drinks and the snacks you have out there."

"Popcorn? It is really the best movie watching snack. We have an air popper for that."

"Yes. It is delightful. I would like to learn how to make it."

"You have corn. It's from heating the kernels suddenly. When we return, we can try it."

Sebastian pauses. "Return?"

Zara nods, looking up at her mate. "Yes, no matter what, I am coming home with you, Sebastian."

A slow smile crosses his lips as he pulls her in suddenly, wrapping his arms tightly around her. "My love, you have no idea what that means to me."

She closes her eyes and leans against him, his scent wrapping around her. "I do. I grew up in this world. It's a lot to take in. All it took was a week in your realm to make me miss it. The peace, the calm, the sounds of the ocean against the rocks. Everything is better there, except for the chamber pots."

Sebastian chuckles. "We can look at adjusting that somehow. Magic has its uses. I believe it's time for you to sleep. We will leave the others to their moving paintings, including Nero."

"I think he should join us."

"He doesn't need to."

"He should, then you have someone to talk to while I sleep."

Sebastian catches his friend's smirk, shaking his head slightly. "Do you not want to be alone with me, my love?"

A blush stains her cheeks. "Not in my parents' house, where the walls are thin. The castle was different."

Sebastian caresses her rosy cheeks. "I think I understand. Nero will join us then."

"Thank you." Zara takes his hand and leads him out of the kitchen, watching as the four guards move to settle in front of the TV again. Grabbing her blanket, she guides Sebastian upstairs, as Nero follows, having heard her quiet request. She steps into her room nervously, a space no one has slept in besides her and her besties. She drops the comforter on the bed and grabs her pajamas. "I will be right back. Make yourself comfortable." She races from the room, breathing a sigh of relief as she steps into the bathroom and closes the door.

Sebastian moves to the bed and sits on it, his thoughts touching Nero's as he picks up the yellow stuffed bear. *'She seems different.'*

'She's not, just uncertain. She wants to be your mate, but this is her parents' house.'

'Kieran supports this. I can read it in his thoughts. His mate is hesitant, but she believes fully in the mate bond.'

'Sire, it's not that. It's sleeping with you. She has only done it once, and not where

her parents could hear. I believe she doesn't trust herself, hence why I am here. And she feels you might get bored watching her sleep.'

He chuckles, hearing the door to the bathing chamber close, placing the teddy back down on her bed. *'I can never get bored watching her.'*

'I understand that, but I don't believe she does. Think about it, you had nine days with her at the castle, seven of which were actual courting. Then three months passed. Now you have ten days here. It's really not a lot of time. You both need to relearn each other. Ideally, not with everyone else around.'

'You speak wisely. Thank you Nero. I suspect I am overthinking it.'

'Sire, she loves you. I see the way she looks at you, the side glances your way, the blushes. They are adorable, by the way. You just need to find your bond again. This place is unusual, with strange objects and things. She seems to understand she needs to teach us how it all works. That side has taken over. It shows she cares about all of us and how we are going to react to a place she grew up. Just as she reacted to ours when she arrived. Give her time. In my estimation, she will relax when she feels we are comfortable here. This world, it's very different. It's like magic surrounds us, but as objects and boxes. Like the box that plays paintings. A box that keeps things cold above ground. The little switches that light candles. Even the box you carried made noises. Ones that send messages to others that even we can't hear.'

'Your right as always, Nero. It is like our ability to mind block is within these boxes.' Sebastian rises and moves to his phone on the desk and picks it up. Punching in the four-digit code, he watches it open to the messages. Reading the last one again, he touches it to bring the keyboard up. Smiling at the soft clicking sounds, he types into it and hits enter.

> What does Omg omw mean?

Her phone bleeps on the desk, and he can see his message pop up momentarily on the screen. Chuckling, he places his phone down and picks up hers. *'I do believe I will have something to read tonight.'*

'On her's?'

'No, on mine. It seems every beep is a message and there were a lot of them when I turned this box on.'

Both turn as Zara enters the room, dressed in soft gray flannel pjs. Little pink bears with a rainbow on their belly printed all over them. Sebastian grins as he places her phone back down. "Are those why your Papa calls you Zare-bear?"

Zara pulls at her shirt hem, a blush crossing her cheeks. "Yes, when I was little, I loved Care Bears. This one's name is Cheery Bear. I know, it's supposed to be a kids' thing, but when my parents get these made for me, it shows they care about me."

Sebastian moves over to her, kissing her cheek softly. "They are adorable, my dear. You will need to bring several pairs home. That being said, with the witches we have hired, it might be possible to visit your parents. Should this work, I intend to keep them in my employ so that you might visit home, no matter the cost. But don't tell them that."

"Really?" Zara blinks back the tears that spring to her eyes.

"My love. I hate that you have to choose between us. I will do everything in my power so that you don't. We just might not visit as often as you like, for I do not know the witches' power and how often they can do this."

She wraps her arms around him tightly. "I love you Sebastian. You are the best."

"I love you, my darling. Now, let's get you to sleep."

Zara nods and moves over to pull the blackout curtains closed. Padding back to her bed, she crawls in and curls up in Sebastian's arms. "Night Nero."

"Good night my queen."

"Right, in the morning, I show him Lassie." She mumbles as Sebastian's scent wraps around her, calling to her in ways no other has. Her breathing stabilizes as she slips off to sleep, happy, content and at peace in loving arms once more.

Sebastian fingers trail over her skin slightly, her thoughts slow to just him, before even they fade. He smiles, looking up at Nero, who sits in the chair beside the desk. *'If you wish to go downstairs, you may. I can call you when she stirs.'*

'Do you want me gone, sire? The little lassie may be unhappy if she finds out and personally, I have seen her temper directed at you. I don't want it directed at me.'

'No, it's always a joy having you here, Nero. I just know your penchant for exploring the unknown, and this place is full of it.'

'Indeed, it is. Tempting as it is, her anger is worse. I will at least wait until they introduce us to the pack formally. I don't need to kill half of them simply because I am a vampire on my own and they feel the need to challenge me. Even on the day we captured them, I thought our men could handle two wolves, stepping in when I realized just how strong she and her father were. There is a whole bloody pack here.'

'True, I can hear the outside thoughts as they spread, each wondering why vampires are in the Beta's place. It seems only a handful were told about us. I have

DRAGONSCALES DIVIDE

to wonder why.'

'It was probably to protect her. They didn't know when or if we were coming for her and telling everyone your mate is a vampire might not go over well in a pack of wolves.'

'That could be the truth of it. Zara knew I would do my best to find her, but neither of us knew whether I would succeed. Tomorrow will be most interesting.'

The pair continue to talk off and on through the night, alternating between reading books that are lying around, and the texts on her phone, bringing both a delight and a sadness to Sebastian. Realizing rather quickly how alone she felt, and just how much she had attached herself to him. He caresses the edge of the phone, understanding her decision to return with him, for he had similar emotions, ones that were completely foreign to him. He glances at all his pictures plastered to the wall, chucking lightly.

Nero looks up from his book. *'What is it, sire?'*

Sebastian gestures to the phone. *'All these messages. How much she missed me, just as I missed her. She had the bonus of having my painting everywhere, whereas I did not.'*

Nero places the book down and rises, moving over to the picture on the wall. He pulls it aside, looking for the hooks to remove it, realizing it is stuck there by clear strips. Running his fingers over them, he gently lifts it off the wall, feeling the stickiness of it. *'Magic hooks. Interesting.'* He studies it carefully, turning to hold it up to compare. *'It is an amazing likeness of you, sire.'*

'Yes, this box, or rather her box, painted it in a few seconds. I will need to get her to show me how that works so that I might have one of her.'

'There is one of her, sire, on her desk.' He moves over and picks up the frame. In it are Zara and another girl, striking in her own way with white blonde hair, very pale skin and green eyes. Both have their arms around a boy half a head taller than them, with auburn hair and the most unusual moss green eyes he had seen in a human; or rather werewolf. He carries the picture back to him. *'My guess with how familiar the three of them are with each other, that this would be Zach and Gia.'*

Sebastian reigns in the protective growl threatening to escape at his queen with her arms around another man. Realizing rather quickly that the picture exudes a strong friendship, with happiness across all three of their expressions. *'Yes, I can see the resemblance to Alpha Darian. Both Zach and Zara have places of power in the pack, being the Alpha and Beta's children. I wonder if this Gia does as well.'*

'I guess we will find out tomorrow. She really is exquisite. I did not realize werewolves were this stunning. Even Kieran's mate is beautiful.'

'Well, I believe that's because they are not werewolves and are shifters. Zara did make a point of telling me there is a difference.'

'True, I recall that discussion.' Nero chuckles, his eyes drifting down to Zara. *'She's definitely a handful.'*

'I suspect it's the way she's been raised. Judging by the thoughts around this place tonight, Kieran's mate rules the castle, so to speak. Even with Alpha Darian, I got the impression that his Luna, as he called her, has the power there. The men might bear the name of Alpha and Beta, but it is the woman that truly holds that title.'

'Do you think you can handle her, sire?' Nero teases him gently.

Sebastian smiles. *'I guess I am going to find out.'*

Fourteen

Modern Mornings

M orning arrives with the blaring of the alarm clock, causing two of the three in the room to jump. Zara's hand reaches out and slams the button down, silencing the noise. She mumbles under her breath and snuggles into the arms that hold her, breathing in the soft scent of amberwood and vanilla.

Sebastian and Nero look at each other, then down to the small box that made an extraordinary amount of noise.

'What do you suppose that is?'

'Perhaps some sort of calling horn?'

'Clearly, it can't be that important. She smacked the box without a second thought. I didn't even sense her waking mind kick in yet.'

'We will have to ask her.' Sebastian reaches over and picks the box up, seeing numbers flashing on the back side of it, with a long cord attached to it. His gaze follows the cord to the wall, recalling the picture of the power box she showed him. *'Interesting. It has numbers on it that flash and glow like fireflies. I wonder why it's facing the wall.'*

'Another thing to ask. I can feel others moving about the house. Should we wake her?'

'No, we let her sleep.'

'Very well sire.'

Nine minutes later, the alarm buzzes again, with Zara's waking mind kicking in and muttering under her breath. She rolls over and slams the clock again, her fingers looking for the switch, only to realize the numbers are facing her. Her brow furrows, feeling an arm tighten around her as recollection settles in whose it is. A blush stains her cheeks as she looks up to Sebastian. She mumbles softly. "Good morning. Sorry, I should have warned you about the alarm."

"Alarm. You mean the blaring noise that broke the peace of the morning?"

"Yes. That about sums it up."

"But you made it stop. Is it not important?"

"It is, but you can hit snooze. Gives you a bit more time to sleep."

"Why not set it to the time you wish to wake up, then?"

Zara chews on her lower lip. "I don't actually know. I have always set it to snooze once."

Sebastian's fingers caress her cheek, gently pulling her lower lip out from her teeth. "No harming those beautiful lips, my dear."

"Ooh!" A deep crimson floods Zara's cheeks, feeling heat flood her core at his touch. She pushes away and rolls out of the bed, placing some space between them. "I should get ready for training." She turns to her dresser, seeing Nero in the chair beside it, amusement dancing in his expression. "G'morning Nero." She opens her drawers, and pulls out her training clothes, racing out of the room before either could say anything.

Nero's shoulders shake with laughter. "Damn sire. I have never seen a woman flee your bed as fast as she did yours."

Sebastian grumbles and rises from the bed. "It's definitely a first."

Nero places the book down and rises from his chair. He clasps Sebastian's shoulder for a moment. "Sire. She loves you and she wants you. That much is apparent. I still believe it has everything to do with her parents being in the house."

"I suppose. Still a blow to the ego."

Nero chuckles. "I think you will survive. Do you think we should wait? Or head downstairs."

"We wait." Sebastian moves to the switch on the wall and flips it, watching the light fill the room. He flips it off and on again several times. "These switches that light the room are most interesting. I wonder if we could figure out a way to have them, rather than having the maids light candles."

"We can always ask how that magic works. She left parchment and a strange quill to write questions with."

Zara breathes a sigh of relief in the bathroom. Moving to the sink, she splashes cold water on her face, trying to quell the heat and desire in her core. She hoped having Nero there would have dampened it, but it had not. Going about her morning routine quickly, she dresses in a pair of black yoga pants and a half top, looking forward to showing Sebastian and Nero her world. She steps out and heads back to her room, hearing their murmur of voices as she pushes the door open and steps inside.

Sebastian's eyes follow her as she moves across the room, desire darkening his gaze at her choice of clothing. "Are you wearing that outside, my dear?"

"Yes, just for training." Zara blushes beneath his gaze and moves to her phone. Clicking it on, she sees the message. "I didn't see you send this. It means, oh my Goddess, on my way. We abbreviate things while messaging. Lol means laugh out loud, though some believe it's lots of love. Rofl is rolling on the floor laughing. Yw is your welcome. Things like that." Her eyes move to the blackout curtains and peeks outside, seeing the sun already rising on the horizon. "We need to check something."

Turning, she grabs Sebastian's hand and pulls him from the room, heading downstairs to the opposite side of the house with Nero following. She stops at the beam filtering in through the window. Taking his hand, she points to the light. "That kills vampires in our realm. I need you to test it with your hands."

Sebastian arches a brow in disbelief. "You want me to test it?"

Nero shakes his head. "NOT happening lassie! I will not allow him to risk his life."

"Neither of you is risking their life. That's why we are here and not immediately outside. Just your fingers. It will burn if it affects you, but you should be able to feel it before it does actual damage."

Nero steps forward. "I will do it then."

Zara steps in his path. "No, NOT your body. You can reach from here; it's a beam through the window."

Nero's eyes shift, seeing the golden orb rising in the sky. "What is it?"

"We call it the sun. Our vampires are creatures of the night. Yesterday, the sun was behind the clouds and didn't seem to affect you, but it was still there. The books I read were unclear whether our vampires can brave the daytime if it's cloudy. It did state that there are three primary effects. First, that the sun doesn't affect you. Second, you will suffer sun sickness and need to feed more often than normal. Third, you burst into flames and die a horrible death. Our vampires only travel at night, so I am inclined to believe they have the fiery death trait, but I wanted to check before taking you outside."

Nero nods, sticking his hand in the beam and waits, staring at the light dancing off his skin. "It's warm."

"Yes, it's warm to us, too. Is it burning, though?"

"No, but it doesn't feel entirely right either."

"Hmmm. I wonder if that is sun sickness. It will require you to feed more often than normal. If that is the case, I will offer myself."

Kieran steps in behind the three of them, having heard the conversation. "I will as well. We cannot have my daughter's mate and his people suffering."

"Papa! You don't need to."

"Your right Zare-bear, I don't, but I want to. Sebastian was more than fair to us when we were in his realm. It's the least I can do."

"Thank you, Papa."

Sebastian and Nero glance at each other, then look at the sun a moment, before turning to the pair standing before them. Sebastian speaks quietly, knowing their initial views on their race and exactly what they are offering. "Thank you. I know what it means for you to offer. If we need it, we will request it. If it is this sun sickness, then we just need to avoid the glowing ball in the sky, yes? Is there a way to do this while outside?"

"Yes. there are. Staying under the cover of trees and in the shade while outside."

"Let's see how it goes and not worry about it. If we are inside buildings, we should be safe. I will try to limit our exposure while outside."

Zara smiles up at the three of them, her gaze drifting to her fathers. "Does Mama need help with breakfast?"

"Probably."

"Right, I will go help before training, especially since I am the reason she's making extra." She passes the four on the couch, chuckling at their expressions at the cartoon dragon on the screen.

"My queen." Anthony picks up the pad of paper and hands it over to her.

She stops as Anthony flags her down, noticing it filled with questions. "Oh boy. I will answer these after breakfast. I promise. Or perhaps Papa can answer them... Papa! Anthony has questions. Sorry, I need to cook your food with Mama."

Anthony frowns and rises. "My queen, you should not be cooking for all of us. I will assist."

Zara chews on her lip, her eyes darting to her Papa, walking back with Sebastian and Nero. "Alright, I will show you how the kitchen works." She leads him into the kitchen, her brothers sitting at the table as her mother places a plate of bacon and eggs before them. "Mama, Anthony has offered to help. What would you like us to do?"

"Zara, sweetie, you should be with your mate."

"Papa is with him. I should help. It's my fault you are cooking for all of us."

Lila moves over and cups Zara's face in her hands. "It's not your fault. Your mate and his people are always welcome. Now, if you really insist on helping, you can start washing dishes. Anthony, I will put you in charge of making toast. Wash your hands there."

"Yes, Ma'am."

When he's done, Lila guides him to the toaster, and places the cutting board in front of him. Picking up the loaf of bread, she pulls two slices out and places them in the toaster. Showing him the lever, she pushes it down. "It will pop when it's done. You will need to spread this on them, and place them butter side together."

Anthony picks up a piece of bread, turning it over. "So evenly sliced. This place is full of magic." He places the bread down and peers into the toaster, feeling the heat rising from it. A minute later, it pops, causing him to jump back in shock.

Zara chuckles, her eyes drifting to the toast. "More magic. Careful, they will be hot." She returns to washing, talking with her mother as she cooks breakfast. "Did you sleep alright Mama?"

"Yes, actually, considering I have a house full of vampires. No offense Anthony. How about you? Your room was quieter than I expected last night."

"None taken Ma'am."

"Mama!" Zara turns her attention to the water as a deep blush crosses her cheeks.

"Just saying. I expected more noise since it was your first night back with your mate."

"We didn't do anything. I slept. He talked with Nero."

"Nero was in the room with you? Why?"

"Cause I asked him to be."

Sebastian steps into the doorway, feeling the embarrassment in his mate. He leans on the wall casually, watching the three of them work. "Mama bear, I will refrain from such activities while we are beneath your roof."

Lila laughs. "Call me Lila, please. You do realize we are wolves and not bears. If she wants to bed her mate, we are not stopping her. It's a natural thing around here, just like nudity is for most of the people that shift out of wolf form. Only a few have necklaces that allow our clothes to remain."

Zara mumbles under her breath. "Mama! I won't do it. It was bad enough facing Papa the next morning, let alone..."

Sebastian moves to Zara, wrapping his arms around her and kissing her cheek. "Whether natural or not, Zara has expressed her desire to abstain while under your roof, and so we shall."

"Well, we will just take everyone out tonight for a few hours to give you some alone time."

Sebastian chuckles. "That could work."

Zara nudges him gently. "You are not to be siding with my Mama on this."

"Why not, my love? We could use a few hours alone. Besides, I can read your thoughts."

"That's right, sweetie. It's been months. I was all over your father when you retur...."

Zara claps a hand over her mother's mouth with a gasp. "TMI!!! Hearing was enough Mama!! I don't need to relive it! And you! You are not to be reading my thoughts!" Slipping out of Sebastian's arms, she races to the dining room where her father is gathering the others for breakfast. "Papa! You need to reign Mama in!" She plops down at the table next to Nero, keeping her gaze actively on the table, a deep blush staining her cheeks. Struggling to force her thoughts anywhere else, knowing the vampires can read them.

"What did she do now, Zare-bear?"

Sebastian follows her out, chuckling at his mate's embarrassment. "She's talking about your bedroom antics when you returned home and giving us a few hours tonight to do the same. Zara, my love, what does TMI mean?"

"Too much information and you just gave the entire room TMI."

Nero chuckles next to Zara. "My Que..."

Zara scowls his way. "Don't you dare read my thoughts too, Nero, or I will drag you into the fighting rings and beat on you!"

Nero places his hands up in surrender. "I would never, my queen."

"Bullshit. You would and you have."

He laughs. "You are correct; I would, I have and I am."

"That's it. You are in the ring with me first."

"I am looking forward to it. I recall your fighting when we first captured you. Then, on your last day, when your father held his own against my best warriors the morning you were, ah, busy with..."

Zara coughs, glaring at him. "NERO!"

Sebastian moves over to sit beside her, pulling her into his arms. "My love. We can work on training you to block your mind, though I will admit it is alluring reading your thoughts."

"So you have said, but it's impolite to read them."

He kisses her forehead. "I love you."

Zara sighs, leaning against him. "I love you too. I am still beating on Nero."

"Fair enough. I shall enjoy watching."

"Better watch it. I might drag you into the ring too if you keep siding with my Mama."

"Duly noted."

"Never a dull moment around here. Now, I will go speak to my wife and bring the food back." Kieran chuckles, heading into the kitchen where his wife is plating all the food. "My love, apparently we are taking everyone out tonight. And where do you think we are going with them?"

"I figured I would talk to Luna Willow and see if the activity room is available. They seem enthralled with the TV. I thought perhaps it would give Zara and Sebastian some bonding time."

He draws his wife in for a hug, kissing her gently. "That sounds like a plan. I am sure Alpha Darian and Luna Willow will agree. Now, what do you want me to carry?"

"The tea and coffee. I got the eggs and bacon. Anthony is covering the toast."

"Got it." He digs through the cupboard, pulling out a tray that he piles coffee cups and glasses on. He carries it back to the dining room, spreading them out before returning for the coffee and tea pots.

"Boys, if you want to carry your plates to the dining room, you may finish your breakfast there." Lila watches Jenson and Jayden collect their plates and run to the dining room. She follows, making two trips, one with a platter of eggs, the other with bacon and sausages. "Help yourselves."

Anthony carries his tray of toast, placing it down before his king. "They have a special box that makes them quickly sire. It is impressive. And they have round things that heat the pots up so that the queen's mother can make the eggs and what they call bacon and sausage. Their pots are so light, unlike ours. I think we need to take some home with us. The cooks will love them."

Zara shakes her head. "Do they cook over fires?"

Anthony nods. "Yes, they do."

"Then those won't work. They are Teflon and will melt in fire. The round disc is special just for them. But we can get some that will."

"Will they be just as light?"

"Almost. Just cast iron instead."

Sebastian chuckles. "This wouldn't have anything to do with the crush you have on the head cook, would it?"

Hints of a blush stain Anthony's cheeks. "I don't know what you are talking about."

"OMG! You guys can blush! What's her name?"

"I believe, my dear Zara, that his name is Kaldor."

Anthony mutters under his breath. "How did you even know? My thoughts are protected."

"They are, but your expressions are not. The way your eyes dart to the kitchens at dinner time. The way they linger on him when he places the food out."

"Damn, do you think he knows?"

"I think he might."

"Do you think I stand a chance?"

"Alas, no. Kaldor fancies himself a ladies' man."

"That's unfortunate."

Zara reaches out and places a hand on Anthony's, causing the soft growl behind her from Sebastian. "Oh, hush Seb. Anthony, you will find the right person for you. It might just take time. Normally, wolf shifters find their mates at eighteen, but I am over nineteen. My friends, Gia and Zach, are the same age as me and have yet to find their mates. Zach even traveled with me to the other packs, searching, while I was scouring libraries. I will admit, I expected mine to be a wolf, and was extremely unhappy Ember picked Sebastian."

"That's an understatement, lassie."

"Be quiet, Nero. You're not helping." Turning back to Anthony. "You will find the right person. I know it."

"Thank you, my queen."

Lila claps her hands. "Right, enough chit-chat. Eat before it gets cold. Boys. finish your breakfast. We need to get you to school. Zara, your training starts in thirty minutes. Let's hustle now."

They eat breakfast together, each enjoying the meal and talking amongst themselves as if they have known each other for years. Kieran and Zara answer all the questions on the pad, doing their best to explain it in terms the vampires would understand. Those that they can't, Kieran marks with a star so Zara can show them on the computer later. At the end of breakfast, Zara collects her and Sebastian's dishes. The others follow suit and bring them to the kitchen. She stacks them on the side and runs fresh soapy water into the sink, testing the temperature. Between her and the others, they wash, dry and put them away quickly. Glancing at the clock, seeing she has five minutes to get to training, she grabs a water bottle and soda out of the fridge. "We gotta go."

"See ya later Mama! Thanks for breakfast." Zara leaves the house with an entourage in tow. She walks swiftly to the training rings, going over the rules and regulations of the fights, what it entails, and who would be there fighting with her. "Papa is the trainer of us all. They pair us up and no matter what you see, do not intervene. Although Seb might want to step in and help Nero when I give him an ass kicking."

Fifteen

Thrice Loved

Sebastian chuckles. "I think not, my dear. I look forward to seeing you fight my beta."

Nero rolls his eyes, humor dancing in them. "I fought her once already and won. I have nothing to prove."

Zara growls softly at him, fighting the laughter in her voice. "You had an unfair advantage. Here it's you and me only. And I won't hold back."

"You aren't going to kill me, are you, lassie?"

Zara's laughter escapes. "Are you concerned?"

"Hell no."

"Good. No deaths allowed. Wolf fighting can get rough. Our wolves heal us fast, so we allow brute force along with claws. That's why you can't step in to save me. I don't need them thinking I can't handle my own battles, not that many can beat me. Zach is one of the few my age that can."

"I look forward to it, lassie."

They arrive at the training ring, seeing a few wolves already there stretching in the rings. Some of them part as Zara leads them to the stands to sit, warily looking at the vampires that casually walk into their midst. Zara places her drinks on the seat next to her mate, realizing that perhaps she should have waited for Alpha Darian to announce them. Sebastian takes her hand and kisses the back of it. "Zara, we will be fine. I can read their thoughts. They are wary but will not attack us. I also hear your Alpha's thoughts, so he is close."

She nods, smiling up at him. "Thank you Seb. Nero, you come with me." She turns towards the entrance, only to hear her friend Gianna's squeal, followed by a second one from Zach. "Mate!"

Zach turns to Gianna. "Wait, which one is yours?"

Gianna points to the group Zara is standing with. "The blonde one."

"Hell no, the blonde one is mine."

"Well, mine's the one standing next to Zara."

"Mines sitting down." Zach grins and grabs her hand, pulling her towards the group. He stops before Zara and Nero. "Zara, my bestie, the one who supports me completely and loves me unconditionally. The one I love dearly. Please introduce us to your friends."

Zara laughs, pushing Zach's shoulder, causing him to stagger a bit. "Right, you just love me cause I have someone you want." She turns, smiling mischievously. "Which one is it, Zach? Nero?" Her eyes lift, seeing Nero's eyes locked on Gianna's and vice versa. "Ooh, No. Nero belongs to Gia!!" She scans the four that sit around Sebastian. "Anthony. Could you please come down here?"

"Yes, my queen."

"Is this the one that has caught your attention, Zach?"

Zach licks his lips, his eyes roaming over the blonde vampire, immediately noticing he stands about an inch taller than him, but otherwise, their builds are the same. His voice shakes gently. "Yes, he's the one."

"I hate to say it, but he's taken."

Anthony shakes his head in denial, panic striking his eyes. "No, my queen."

Sebastian rises and moves to stand beside Zara. "My dear? Are you causing trouble?"

"Never! Isn't it great, though? My two besties have mated with your bestie and your guard."

"It is, but it still needs to be discussed with your Alpha."

"I suppose. I think you will lose a guard, but I will gain a bestie." She turns back to them. "Everyone, this is Sebastian, my mate." Turning to Anthony, she takes his hand and places it in Zach's, catching their sharp intakes of breath at the touch. "Anthony, this is Zach. One of my besties and the Alpha's son. He is next in line to rule this pack when his father steps down. Something for you to consider. Zach, this Anthony. He likes to cook, is a protector of Sebastian and an all around nice guy. He was one of the guards that watched over my Papa when we were in Sebastian's realm." She chuckles as she turns to Nero and Gianna, who are clearly ignoring everything around them. "Nero and Gia! Anyone in there?" She pushes them both, happiness filling her, knowing it is likely Gia will return with her to Sebastian's world. "Gia, this is Nero. Sebastian's Beta and one I am going to beat on in the training rings today, so do not step in. He deserves it! Nero, this is Gia, or Gianna, for those who are not her besties."

Nero bows, taking her hand and kissing the back of it. "Pleasure to meet you, Gianna."

Gianna blushes, averting her eyes to Zara. "You kept this all to yourself last night? Damn, I should have stopped by, but Zach talked me out of it. Said you needed time with your mate! I mean, LOOK at them all! They are all smokin' hot!"

"Gia! Sorry, Nero. Gia's a bit over the top sometimes."

"Damn right I am. I mean, you had six of the hunkiest guys I have ever seen sleeping under your roof, Zara!"

"Well no. They didn't sleep. Anthony, Mathew, Theodore, and Julian watched movies all night in the living room. Nero and Sebastian stayed in my room."

Gianna growls softly. "Wait, you slept with my mate?"

"Yes, I slept. They talked."

"Bi'otch!"

"Right back at you sista."

Gianna laughs and hugs Zara. She turns back to Nero. "So, what did you do that earned you a place in the fighting ring against her?"

Zara scowls at Nero. "Don't you dare tell her!"

Gianna arches her brow. "Ooh, this is good! I wanna know."

Nero chuckles. "I would not dare to discuss what my queen does not want me to, but I will say this. She is upset that I will not refrain from reading her thoughts."

"You read thoughts?" Gianna's gaze snaps to Zara.

"Yes, and he can read yours, Gia, so keep them PG."

"Oh hell no, he can't."

Sixteen

The Challenge

Nero leans in and whispers in Gianna's ear, causing her to stumble back into Zach, a deep blush flooding her cheeks and down her neck. "If you survive Zara, I am beating on you next!"

Zara laughs, her eyes dancing in delight at her friend's discomfort. "I told you. Now, Papa will be here soon and if we are not in the rings, he's gonna have our hides. Come on, Nero, let's see what you got." She leads him to the ring and faces off against him.

Gianna grabs Zach and pulls him away from Anthony. "Right, if you are fighting Nero, I get Zach today."

Zara spars with Nero, testing the range of his abilities, recalling when she was fighting for her life against him. She focuses on him, keeping her mind as blank as she can, knowing he is reading her thoughts on where her next strike is. Once they have warmed up, she smiles. "Are you ready, Nero?"

"Wait, were we not already sparring?"

"That was just a warmup." She leaps on him, catching his shoulder as he attempts to dart away, dragging him to the ground with a thud.

Nero rolls and launches to his feet, realizing she just changed the terms of the fight. "I get it. You were testing me."

"That's right, I wanted to see your movements. I got them now." She rises and prowls around him, watching for the opening. Seeing it, she strikes out with her fist, earning a grunt as she connects with his ribcage.

Nero grabs her arm, twisting it suddenly and flips her over, watching her roll out of his reach before he can land a blow.

She spins low, sweeping her leg out at him, growling in dismay as he jumps over it and lands a strike on her shoulder. "Damn, that was quick."

"I can be quicker, lassie, but then I would have to face Sebastian and I have no desire to do that."

Zara laughs, dancing in, blocking one of his strikes as she slides another in at his arm, feeling him shift at the momentum and elbowing him in the side. "So can I Nero."

Nero growls softly, turning to face off against her again. He circles her warily, keeping the match even between them, with neither of them stepping into the supernatural side of things. He throws a few punches that she expertly blocks. A smile tips the corner of his lips as he notices her attention stray to his left, landing a solid strike on her shoulder.

Zara growls in pain and latches onto his arm. She kicks him in the shins, feeling him jump in shock, then twists, pulling him forward over her extended leg and dropping him onto his back behind her. Her claws and teeth elongate as she swipes at the newcomer, drawing blood as she rakes them over his arm. "Get BACK Jeremy."

Nero groans on the ground, not expecting the force behind it and realizing there was more strength behind that attack than any of her others. Ready to retaliate, he hesitates when he smells blood and hears the anger in her voice. He pushes himself to stand, narrowing his eyes on the one she faces. "Lassie?"

"Stay back Nero. Jeremey here, thought to ambush you with actual claws. That is not in the rules of our sparring."

Jeremy growls. His angry gaze moves from Zara to the man behind her. "He's a vampire. ALL of them must die. You should not be practicing with him."

"He's my friend Jeremy. Back down now."

"No. I am going to finish him. Everyone here is thinking the same thing, just no one is brave enough to act on it."

Zara feels her rage growing at him. "I won't give you another warning, Jeremy."

Jeremy pushes her aside, taking a swipe at Nero, who expertly blocks his attack. "I think you should listen to the lass pup."

Fury takes over as Zara pounces on Jeremy, her claws digging into his shoulders, ripping him away from Nero. She spins him before her, landing two solid punches to the chest, and a roundhouse kick to the head, dropping him into the dirt before her. "Don't bloody well touch him. Stay down Jeremy. You haven't managed to defeat me before. You are not succeeding now."

Jeremy coughs up some dirt and glares at her. "What? Your mate can't defend himself?"

"He's not my mate."

"Don't bullshit me Zara, I know you're mated to a blood sucking vamp. You were supposed to mate with me."

"No, I was not. I know you wanted me to, but I denied you each time. I told you I was waiting for my fated mate."

"How could you do it? How could you choose him over me?"

Zara narrows her eyes. "First, Nero is not my mate. My mate is sitting over there watching me fight his Beta. Second, I didn't just accept him. Sebastian earned his right to call me mate. Now go home Jeremy. You need to cool off."

Jeremy stands, narrowing his eyes on the one in the stands. "Yet, he doesn't fight. He lets you fight with another who has his hands all over you. He's nothing but a coward."

"You don't know anything about him."

"I know enough."

Hearing the conversation in the ring and feeling the rage in his mate, Sebastian rises and moves gracefully towards them. He places a comforting hand against the small of her back as he steps behind her, catching the darkness in Nero's eyes directed at this newcomer. "Zara, my love. What's going on?"

"Jeremy is being an ass. That's what's going on."

Jeremy scoffs at the vampire that approaches, looking him up and down carefully. "How can you even sleep with a man that wears a dress, Zara." Hatred fills his gaze as his jaw tightens. "Sebastian, was it?"

Zara stiffens at his words, her fists clenching at her sides, fighting against the calming aura of her mate. "Would you like to eat dirt again, Jeremy?"

Sebastian caresses her cheek. "Shhh Zara. I got this. Yes, Sebastian Darkholme. You may address me as Sire, or Your Majesty."

"Well, Sebastian Darkholme... Sire." Sarcasm and disgust laced in his words. "It is my right as a shifter to challenge you for your mate. She was mine before you and she will be mine after I kill you."

Zara gasps in shock. "Are you insane? Retract it now!"

Alpha Darian's voice carries over the training grounds. "What the hell is going on here? Kieran?"

Kieran sighs. "We are having some issues with Jeremy not accepting Zara's mate and his guards."

Jeremy turns and bows to Darian. "I have challenged Sebastian Darkholme for rights to Zara. By ancient wolfen laws..."

"I know what the wolfen laws are." Darian snaps, a deep growl emerging, causing everyone in the area to bow to his aura. "Zara is not yours. This is her Goddess given mate you are challenging. Are you certain you wish to do this?"

"Yes Alpha. She should be with a shifter, not a bloody vampire."

Darian turns to Zara, reading the seething rage in her, along with her pale features and a shake in her body. "And Sebastian, do you accept his challenge?"

Zara spins, grabbing his tunic and looking up into his eyes, fear written deep in their depths. "Sebastian. You can deny it. Refuse it. I don..."

"Shhh." Sebastian places a finger on her lips. "Zara, it will be fine. He will not win." Turning back to Darian. "What are the rules?"

Darian's shoulders sink, glancing over to Kieran, who has moved over to calm the guards, each looking as if they are ready to tear Jeremy apart. "There are no rules other than it's a fight to the death or a clear win. This means you can use whatever means necessary to survive, including supernatural abilities."

"Alright then. Challenge accepted."

"Everyone, please vacate the rings, except the two in question."

Tears spring to Zara's eyes. "Please Seb."

"Nero, please take Zara back to stand with her father and the others."

"Understood." Nero grabs Zara's hands. "Come lassie. You mate will be just fine. Have faith in him."

Zara whispers softly. "But Jeremy fights dirty."

Nero chuckles. "Well, whose fault is that? You did faceplant him into it."

"That's not what I meant, Nero."

Nero leans in and whispers back. "Lassie, I know what you meant. I can read your thoughts and Sebastian can read Jeremy's. He won't win. Besides, your Alpha allowed supernatural abilities. I give the fight less than ten seconds before Sebastian drops Jeremey."

"But if he kills him, there will be a war."

Nero draws Zara into a hug. "My queen. Sebastian is King for a reason, and has been for over four hundred years. He thinks before he acts. He knows the consequences of actions. It was his command to let you live, despite killing three of ours. He listened to me when I stated it was fear guiding your attacks. He will read the situation and adjust accordingly. Trust me on this."

"Thank you Nero, I don't want him hurt." Tears creep from her eyes as she leans into his hug.

"He won't be. That pup won't even lay a claw on him."

Seeing Gianna and Zach approaching, Zara leaves Nero's arms and hugs them both as well.

Zach wraps his arms around her and holds her tight. "We always knew Jeremy was crazy, but this takes the cake."

"I don't understand. What can he get out of this? I don't even like him."

Gianna shakes her head, wrapping her arms around them both. "I don't know Zara, but we are here for you. If he takes your mate down, we will challenge him and take you back."

Nero chuckles, earning a look from all three of them. "Come my queen, let's go sit with your father."

She nods, following him to the bleachers where her father waits with the others. She picks up her water bottle and settles in its place, her eyes not leaving her mate, even as she addresses him. "Papa."

Kieran reads the stress in his daughter, doing his best to distract her from strangling her water bottle. "Zare-bear. I saw you were holding your own against Nero. Nicely done."

"Yes. I haven't trounced him yet, but I was getting there."

"Zare-bear... Sebastian will win. He has someone to fight for."

"I hope so. I have never seen him fight, so I don't..."

Nero claps a hand on her shoulder. "He can fight, lassie. He just chooses not to if he can. That's what he has us for."

Zara offers him a half smile, sweeping her gaze over the pack, reading mixed expressions on their faces. Some delight, some concern and some glancing her way, trying to get a read on the situation. She sighs inwardly, turning her attention back to the ring.

Alpha Darian moves into the middle, ensuring that everyone is sitting before he addresses the participants and the pack. He turns to the two in question. "Jeremy Hillock. Sebastian Darkholme. Do you agree to face each other, and only each other, in combat? Understand that no outside sources may step in and assist. Agree to the absence of rules and the allowance of all abilities. That it's a fight to the death or clear surrender."

Sebastian smiles, eyeing up his opponent. "I do."

Jeremy growls. "Yes. I am gonna kill you, vamp. There will be no surrender option for you."

"So be it. Winner receives Zara Lansdowne as their mate." Darian steps out of the ring, signaling to the pair of them. "You may start."

Jeremy shifts around, bouncing on the balls of his feet, studying the vampire who remains motionless before him. A calculated smile crosses his lips, expecting a quick defeat as he withdraws a silver blade from a sheath in his belt. He lunges forward, his hand clenching down on the hilt.

Sebastian readies himself and listens to his thoughts, knowing the blade is there before he pulls it. Seeing the movement give him away, Sebastian uses his right hand to deflect the blade with ease, slamming his left fist into the wrist, causing the blade to drop to the dirt, where he kicks it aside. His claws elongate on his left hand and swiftly rake back across Jeremey's chest, barely skimming him.

Jeremy dances back, looking at the shreds in his clothing. Disgust fills his voice. "You missed vamp. But what can you expect from a man that wears a dress?"

Sebastian arches a brow. "Did I? You might want to check again."

Blood seeps from the wounds inflicted, staining the shirt and dripping into the dirt at his feet. "What the hell?"

Sebastian chuckles. "Immature Pup. You have never faced true vampires before, have you? Our claws strike sharper than a blade and numb the area so you feel no pain. They consider us a dangerous foe and you should have recognized that. I suspect you are in for a shock and it will cost you your life."

"I don't think so," Jeremy growls and shifts to half wolf, launching at him.

Sebastian matches his growl, using his speed and grace to his advantage. He sidesteps, his claws digging into Jeremy's arm as he jerks him closer. Spinning him around before he can react, he clamps his body close, Jeremy's back to his chest, his arm pinning him in place. His other hand twists tightly in Jeremy's hair, as he forces him to bare his neck. Sebastian's teeth lengthen and graze his neck, drawing ever so faint lines of blood from him. "You are defeated. Dead, with your throat ripped out."

Jeremey fights against him, but finds he cannot break the hold Sebastian has on him, resorting to name calling. "Let me go, you blood sucking bastard. Fight me like a real man."

"I did, you lost. Now surrender."

"GO Fuck yourself!"

Sebastian whispers in his ear. "Sleep then." His magic takes effect as Jeremy slumps in his arms. Once Sebastian is certain he's incapacitated, he drops him to the dirt at his feet. "Alpha Darian. I retain my rights on my mate, Zara, daughter to Kieran and Lila Lansdowne. I have successfully defeated Jeremy without death."

Darian nods. "Agreed. Luca, Kieran, take Jeremy to the dungeons. Ten days should be enough to calm his temper." He looks around the pack as his Beta and Gamma carry him away. "Is there anyone else that wishes to challenge Sebastian or his men?" Seeing a shake of heads, he continues. "Good, because all six of them are guests of this pack and are to be treated with respect. They had the chance to kill both Kieran and Zara when they arrived in their realm, and didn't. They housed and cared for them both while they were there. Sebastian had every right to kill Jeremy in the challenge and yet, did not. In these actions, they have proven that they are unlike vampires in our realm. They have honor, and I expect us to match that honor. Is that understood? If it is not, then I am happy to house you downstairs with Jeremy for the next ten days."

Zara rises, but stops when Nero tightens his hand on her shoulder. "Wait my queen. The Alpha and him will speak privately."

Seeing the pack bowing before him, Darian turns to Sebastian. "Right, now please tell me you are NOT stealing my son and my Gamma's daughter."

"I can't tell you that, Alpha. They will need to decide where they end up."

"So it is true. My son and Gianna found mates with two of yours?"

"Yes, Nero, my Beta and Anthony, a guard of mine."

"Dammit, Zach is supposed to rule after me."

"And he will. I will have the witches return Anthony to stay here with Zach, but I suspect Gianna will return with us because Nero will not leave my side. Just as I imagine, Kieran will not leave yours if given the choice."

"Shit, I saw how it affected Lila initially, and Zara when she returned. We need to figure out this prophecy fast so that no one needs to choose, especially as there is a possibility I might lose three more pack members."

"Agreed on all accounts."

Darian shakes his head. "Ten seconds."

"Excuse me?"

"You took less than ten seconds to diffuse him. Impressive."

"You granted permission to use our abilities. Shifters might be fast, but you cannot match our speed if we desire it. Let alone the innate magic we have tied to us."

"How much magic?"

"Enough that there was no chance he was winning."

"That is why you agreed so readily. Vampires of our realm have no magic. Only raw feral strength."

"Yes, Zara is my mate. Even if she wasn't, it is very clear she wants nothing to do with Jeremy. I would have defended her right to be free."

"He's always had his eye on her. She's rejected his advances numerous times. I never thought it would escalate to his challenging her fated mate."

"It wasn't about being her mate, Alpha. It's because I am a vampire."

"Yes. For that I apologize. It's just you are our enemies. Have been for hundreds of years. The pack and its people will not relinquish those beliefs willingly. I should have announced your presence last night, and that's on me. But I wanted you to settle in before Kieran's cottage got swarmed."

"I understand that. Killing him would have only solidified those beliefs about us. Don't get me wrong. We have killed to defend, but only as a necessity. I have no intentions of killing any of your pack. Not only will it harm morale, it will place a distance between me and Zara I do not desire."

Darian offers his hand. "It is good to call you a friend, Sebastian. You truly are a wise king. Take care of her and Gianna."

"I will." He accepts the hand and shakes it.

"Now, we better get up there. I can see your Beta is practically pinning your mate down."

Sebastian's gaze moves to the group, seeing Nero's hand on her shoulder, the tapping of Zara's foot, her hands squeezing the life out of the water bottle in her lap. "Yes, she already wants to beat on him. Perhaps I should step in and save him."

Darian laughs. "If anyone can, it would be her or my son Zach. I hope his mate can fight, because Zach will expect it."

Sebastian chuckles, his eyes straying to Zach and Anthony, quietly lost in their own space talking. "He is one of my guards for a reason."

Darian follows his gaze. "For a guard, he seems a bit distracted."

"He's not."

"How do you know?"

'Nero, Mathew, Theodore and Julian, do not react to what the Alpha is about to do.' Sebastian turns to Darian. "Go ahead, attack me. Do and think your worst. I mind-linked the others. Only he will defend me."

"Are you certain?"

"I am."

Darian grins, turning to pounce on Sebastian, only to be thrown to the ground and sliding a few feet before even connecting.

Anthony stands protectively beside his king, glaring down at him. "I wouldn't suggest it!"

Darian spots his own guards moving in to fight Anthony. "Stand down. It was a test." Turning to Anthony and Sebastian. "What the hell is that? I didn't even get close to you."

Sebastian laughs, reaching a hand down to help Darian up. "A vampire's speed and attention. Thank you Anthony. I am sorry, but Alpha Darian didn't believe you were paying attention. It was simply to prove that I have you as a guard for a reason."

Anthony bows. "You must have told the others to remain where they were."

"I did. You passed, by the way."

"Good to know. May I return to my mate now? He appears to be in shock over there." He scans the pack. "Actually, a lot of them seem to be."

"You may Anthony." He watches his guard casually walk back to Zach. "What happened might also solidify that I am not as unprotected as I seem and that there is more to us than your vampires."

Darian brushes himself off. "Yes, when I said ours had speed, it is nothing like that. He crossed that distance in less than a second."

"Indeed, had you been a genuine threat, they would have split you equally between all five of them at the same time. No longer in the land of the living. It is an ability we rarely use unless we have to, along with our magic. Most creatures we can face with simply the strength of our strikes."

"I would love to duel you, but not today. There are enough tensions in the air already."

"I accept your challenge, Alpha. Name the time and place."

Alpha Darian claps a hand on his shoulder. "Perhaps when you return from Whispering Pines. Alpha Madison is arriving tomorrow to escort you there and introduce you to our royals. Tonight, I hear you have plans with your mate because it seems I am hosting your crew in my games room. Or part of your crew. Gianna might steal her mate away, and I know Zach will."

"Yes, I believe that was Mama-bear's idea."

"Mama-bear?"

Sebastian chuckles "Yes, she is protective like a mama bear and they call her Zare-bear."

Darian laughs at the thought. "That's it. That's her name from this point on."

"I am certain she is going to love that."

"Doesn't matter. Being Alpha has its privileges."

"Indeed, it does."

Zach stares at Anthony, his gaze moving between him and his father. "Anthony. What was that?"

Anthony takes Zach's hand, squeezing it gently. "A test. To see if I was distracted."

"Clearly you were not."

"Oh I was, but I am a king's guard first. Your Alpha started to attack my king."

"But only you reacted?"

"Yes, because my king requested the others not to interfere. It was a test for me."

Zach looks over at his mate once more. "But how fast you moved. Can you all do that?"

"Yes. I should have known it was a test, especially when my king and the others didn't react to the threat, but instinct kicked in first."

"That's impressive. I have never seen such speed, even from Zara, who is one of the fastest wolves in the pack."

"It is one of our gifts."

Zach smiles, desire darkening his eyes as he meets his mate's gaze. "And will I learn more?"

"You will."

Darian and Sebastian arrive at the group just as Kieran and Luca return from locking Jeremy up. "Alpha, We have contained Jeremy. Is everything alright? The pack seems like it's on edge."

Zara pushes Nero off her and launches into Sebastian's arms, holding him tight and burying her face in his chest. "I was so worried."

Sebastian wraps his arms tightly around her, trying to calm the shake in her body. He runs his fingers through her hair, kissing the top of her head softly. "Shhh my queen. There was never a worry. To be honest, I could take half your pack out before they would drop me. Even without my men."

Darian grimaces, catching Kieran's nod of agreement. "I don't want to hear that, Sebastian. Really glad you are an ally and not our enemy."

"Alpha Darian. We are passive, but we will fight if necessary. Nero and I are over five hundred years old. My guards are sitting around four hundred. We have seen a lot and learned many skills in that time, more than a werewolf or shifter will in theirs."

Zach and Gia gasp, each looking at their mates. "Four hundred years..."

Sebastian chuckles. "You have the same expression as Kieran and Zara when they found out my age."

Darian smiles at their shock. "We live longer than the average human, but not even close to your life span. Now, since this morning's training has been interesting, to say the least, you have the rest of the day off. Hell, I think I will give everyone the morning off as I expect some will actually be brave enough to approach you. Zara, what were your plans today?"

Zara turns in Sebastian's arms, not willing to release her hold on him yet. "Alpha. I promised them a ride in a car. I thought perhaps I would take them to the mall, buy them some clothes so they have something else to wear while they are here."

"You will take the van then."

Zach turns to his father. "But dad, that won't fit everyone."

"Sure it will. It seats six plus a driver."

"What about Gia and I?"

Darian grasps his son's shoulder. "What about you? I have paperwork for you to do all day."

Zach groans. "Seriously?"

"You don't want to do paperwork for dear old dad?"

"Are you kidding me? Did you do paperwork when you met Mom?"

"Not a chance. We were all over each other." He teases. "Fine, you may take the Limo because you'll all fit into it, but you are driving."

"Dad! You're the best!" He hugs his father. "Come on, everyone, let's shower and meet back here in thirty minutes."

Seventeen

Curiosity Cleansed

"**G**reat! This should be fun." Zara laughs, dragging the others back to the house. She bounds up the stairs to her room, grabbing a handful of clothing and heading to the bathroom. She pauses at the top of the stairs, seeing Sebastian reaching the top. "Sebastian?"

"I am not leaving you, my love."

"You're going to shower with me?"

"Did you want me to?"

Zara blushes, knowing the house only contained him and his men, but also knowing they too can read thoughts. Her voice is quiet. "It would just be a shower?"

"Yes, we have tonight for everything else."

Her blush deepens, her thoughts drifting back to the castle and his bedroom as she stares at the floor.

Sebastian steps towards her, cupping her face and guiding her gaze back to his. "My queen. You have my heart. I know your desires and sensibilities and I will not overstep them in your parents' house while there are people around. I promise. But I wish to see this shower you have spoken about. Can you tell me a better way to save time?"

Zara lifts her gaze, getting lost in his dark blue eyes, the color of the night sky just after the sun has set and before the stars come out. She mumbles softly, her body filing with heat at the thought of seeing the water run over him. "I am not sure it will save time, but you may join me."

"Thank you."

She leads him to the bathroom and places her clean clothes on the counter, closing and locking the door after them. She drops the bathmat on the floor and moves to the tub, turning the taps and selecting her desired temperature of water.

Pulling the tab out, she jumps back as the water sprays. Smiling, she pulls the curtain closed and turns to Sebastian. Hesitating for a moment, she strips quickly and steps into the shower, feeling the hot water strike her. Within seconds, she feels Sebastian's touch on her backside, turning to face him. Expecting his eyes on her, she follows his gaze to the shower head. Smiling, she shifts over and guides him to stand directly beneath it, laughing at his groan of delight. "Don't get me wrong, Seb. Baths are nice, but showers are pure bliss."

"Why were we not here last night?"

Zara picks up a bar of soap and hands it to him before grabbing her own. "Cause we were watching a movie, then I was sleeping." Watching Sebastian close his eyes and just remain still for a few minutes, her eyes roam over him, resisting the urge to touch him, as she lathers the soap and scrubs herself down.

"I can hear those thoughts, my dear."

Muttering under her breath. "I am sure you can. I can't help it."

Sebastian opens his eyes, a mischievous twinkle dancing in them as he pulls her close, watching the water run over her, creating streams in the soap. "Later, we can have another, yes?"

Zara gasps at his closeness, her desire to touch him growing. "Yes, we can. Assuming my brothers haven't killed the hot water."

He kisses her gently, nibbling her lips and moving along her jaw to her ears. Whispering just loud enough for her to hear it over the drumming water. "Then I look forward to it."

She sways as heat floods her, shivering at his breath upon her ear. "You make it so hard to resist you, Seb."

A smile graces his lips as his hand holds her in place against him. "And you have an amazing strength of will that I admire. More than most I know. Come, we should move or I fear I will break my word to you."

Zara takes in a staggered breath at his closeness, the heat of the shower drawing his scent out and wrapping it around her, suddenly finding she doesn't want to go shopping. She steps back, placing some distance between them. "Agreed." Rinsing off, she vacates the shower, and grabs a towel to dry herself off, leaving Sebastian to enjoy the water, knowing if it was her first time in a shower, she'd stay as long as she could. Dressing quickly, she pulls a brush out and sets to detangling her hair, only to feel Sebastian's hand on hers.

"Allow me?"

"You want to brush my hair?" Her gaze snaps up, before traveling down his body to the towel wrapped around his waist.

"Yes."

"Why?"

"Because it is enjoyable."

"Dress first, then you can. I can't concentrate with you standing there like that."

He chuckles. "So be it." He pulls his clothing on quickly. A few moments later, he quietly reaches for the brush in her hand. His touch is gentle as he lifts a few strands of her hair, carefully running the brush through them, working his way through the tangles.

Zara groans inwardly, closing her eyes as she grips the counter, having never felt such a delight in her life. One that teased all her senses at his fingers grazing her scalp to the soothing calm it created in her. "Damn Seb, you need to be a hairdresser."

"Hairdresser?"

"Right, someone that cuts and colors our hair?"

Sebastian frowns. "Color? I don't understand."

Zara laughs softly, turning around to face him. "You will see it at the mall. Humans wear many colors in their hair. Shifters don't because we lose the color when we shift from wolf back to human. Waste of money but pretty sure we all try at least once; just to see if we will be the one that succeeds."

"Interesting."

"It's hard to explain until you see it."

"There is a lot of magic in your world that is unique. Your way of life differs from ours. Are you certain you wish to return with me?"

Rising to her tiptoes, she kisses his lips gently. "Yes, I am Sebastian. I will miss my family, and some conveniences here, like the computer, phone, TV, but my place is beside you, wherever that is. Now, we need to go."

He draws her into his arms, tightening his hold on her for a few minutes before reluctantly letting her go. "Yes, we should, but first, I have a gift."

"A gift?"

"Yes." He turns her to face the mirror and pulls out the necklace in his pocket. He places it around her neck gently, his fingers tracing lightly over her skin as he clasps it closed.

Zara stares at the necklace, a single heart-shaped ruby with a thin filigree setting. "It's beautiful Seb. Thank you."

"It's bound to my realm." He kisses her shoulders, his eyes locked on hers. "The witches enchanted it to bring the wearer back when they call us home."

She spins in his arms, hugging him tightly. "Thank you Seb. I love it and I love you!"

"I love you too, my queen. Now, we should probably get moving."

Zara nods and collecting her belongings. Unlocking and opening the door, she heads to her room and drops them in a hamper. Grabbing her purse, she rifles through it to make sure she has her keys and money. Moving over to her computer, she unplugs her phone and stuffs it in as well. Picking up Sebastian's, she hands it to him. "Keep that on you in case we get separated."

"We won't"

"We might. There are lots of people at... Wait, are you all going to be okay doing this?"

"Why wouldn't we be?"

"Because of hearing people's thoughts. Likes, a hundred of them, all in the same place."

Sebastian chuckles. "We can block it out, my dear, just as we protect ours from others reading them."

"Will I ever get to hear your thoughts?"

His eyes darken as his expression shifts, giving a shake of his head. "No, not as a shifter."

Zara studies his stoic expression, realizing the humor has drained from him. "There is more going on here regarding my question. You are implying I will hear them eventually were I not a wolf."

"Zara, you are not ready for this discussion and I am not ready to have it with you."

"You mean the one where you turn me into a vampire?"

A pained expression flickers across his features before he conceals it. "Another time perhaps."

"Why not now?"

Sebastian sits on the bed before her. "Zara. You have my heart, and..."

"No, why? You are thinking about it. Yes?"

"Yes, but..."

"But what Sebastian? Don't I get a choice in this?"

He sighs. "Yes, and that is why I hesitate. I will not turn you without your consent. Zara. My queen. I want to. I want nothing more than to spend the rest of eternity with you at my side. But there are other factors involved. Consent means you essentially die and become immortal. It means you will watch everyone you love grow old and die around you. Another thing to consider is we don't know what will happen with Ember. She is another entity within you. If you die, she dies. Yes? And I don't want that. I love her as much as I love you. I have never converted a shifter, and I will not have you lose a part of yourself because of my desires. There is more research that needs to be done before we consider this avenue."

The color drains from her face at the thought of losing Ember, her best friend. Knowing he is right in that the risk is there and she's not taking that chance. *'Ember, do you know?'*

'No Zara, I am as uncertain as he is. He is wise to wait.'

Zara nods, knowing Sebastian can hear their conversation and doesn't need to fill him in. She studies him carefully, reading the caution in his gaze. "You have converted before... The other Zara?"

"Yes, and she ran away from me. I am not ready for that to happen again."

"I will not run from you, Sebastian. You are my fated mate. Mine and Embers. Not the other Zara's." She moves over and sits beside him, wrapping her arms around him. "I couldn't even run from you when I was mad at you for being a vampire."

Sebastian pulls her onto his lap, breathing in her scent, feeling it calm the stress within. "Indeed. You were pretty darn feisty. I didn't think I was ever going to win you over."

"Blame Papa for that one. He placed a beta command on me to behave."

"I know. Nero heard the command and felt the power coming from it."

Zara leans against him, her fingers running lightly over his arms and hands. "Alright, no more talk of converting until we have more info, but you are stuck with me, Seb. I am not running away." She lifts her eyes to his. "Thank you for not killing Jeremy. I mean, I don't like him, but I also didn't want him to die."

Sebastian nods. "That pup has a lot of anger in him, and not just directed at us vampires. At everything. It consumes him and blinds him to what is right in front of him. Like the fact that you are not interested or that I am a formidable threat. Not being able to read the situation will cause deaths of not only himself but possibly others. Something your Alpha needs to know."

Zara closes her eyes, a soft sigh escaping her, as her hands tighten around Sebastian. "I will speak to Alpha Darian about it later."

Caressing her face gently. "As I stated, my queen. I am not killing any of your pack members, no matter how many challenge me. Neither will my men."

"I know Seb. I knew when you didn't kill us back in your realm. You had every right to."

He kisses the top of her head. "I did, but then I wouldn't have the most alluring woman snuggled in my arms right now."

Zara giggles. "Alluring, huh? I think I am more of a handful."

"Well, that too, but right now, you are alluring."

"Thanks Seb... For everything."

"You're welcome, my love."

Ten minutes later, the group of them head out of the house, passing her mom on the way. Zara pauses, her gaze drifting to her mother wagging her pointed finger at Sebastian with an amused expression.

"YOU! I can turn you over my knee just as readily as I turn my daughter over it."

"Mama? What's going on?"

Sebastian chuckles. "Your mother is upset I called her Mama-bear to your Alpha, and he likes it."

"Yes! Cause now it's gonna stick!"

"Is it so bad? You call Zara, Zare-bear."

"That's because she loves Care Bears! There is a difference."

"Would it make you feel better if I called Kieran Papa-bear?"

"Only if you can get Alpha Darian to call him that too."

"Understood. I will work on it."

Lila laughs and turns to her daughter, hugging her. "Your mate is a troublemaker! Have fun at the mall."

"I will Mama. Thank you."

"You be careful." She turns to Sebastian. "And you protect her. She's going without her guards."

"She has my guards, Mama-bear."

"Good. You will be home for dinner, yes?"

"Yes Mama. Do you need anything while we are at the mall?"

"Nope, you just enjoy yourself. You have enough cash?"

"Yes, I have my card and I am sure Zach and Gia will have theirs as well."

"In that case, I changed my mind. I could use a couple of new books. It seems your father has stolen all my favorites."

"MOM! You are not supposed to let Papa read those things!"

Lila turns to scowl at Sebastian. "Talk to your mate. It's HIS fault!"

"Sebastian's? How?"

Sebastian winks at Zara. "It seems Papa-bear decided he likes reading and continued to do so when he returned. I am curious what this word smut is that you think of. Zara mentioned it while we were in the library upstairs."

Both Lila and Zara blush, as their thoughts immediately, unintentionally expand on the term. "It's a need to know basis and you don't need to know."

"Oooh, I understand." Sebastian eyes the blushes, seeing his guards suddenly avert their eyes and pay attention to the siding of the house, or the dirt on the ground. "I think I shall have to read one for myself."

"You know what? I think the others are waiting. Mama, we gotta go. Love you." Zara grabs his hand and drags Sebastian away, trying to focus her mind elsewhere.

'Are you trying to run from the fact that you read about sex, or that both you and Mama-bear just gave me and my guards very clear mental images of what these books entail?'

She can hear Sebastian's thoughts enter her mind, causing her to stumble and come to a full stop, spinning around to look at him, a blush spreading across her cheeks at a swift rate. *'Wait, we can mind-link?'*

'Of course. You can mind-link anyone in my clan. You became their queen as soon as I marked you.'

'HOW did I not know this!?'

'Cause you never asked. Just to be clear, they cannot hear my side, but yours is loud and clear, as are the mind-links that happen within your family and pack members.'

Zara sighs. *'Does it matter? They can already read my thoughts, so can guess what your side is.'*

Sebastian caresses her cheek. *'Indeed, and I love you for it. I wish I could listen to yours all the time, but it is not good for the queen to be such an open book. I will train you when we return to close those thoughts off.'*

'Thank you.'

Switching out of thoughts, he nods. "Now I believe Zach and Gia are waiting. I can hear their impatience at our being late."

"Right! Let's go." She spins and runs to the pack house, knowing they will follow. Zara smiles at the limo, having seen it leave the pack house many times, but never had the opportunity to actually ride it. Bounding over, she hugs Gianna and Zach. "Sorry we are late."

Gianna arches her brow. "Yes, we all know why you were late. On top of that, you are keeping our mates away from us."

Zara laughs. "That is sooo not what happened, but Seb and I did shower together. You should have seen Seb's face."

Sebastian's brows furrow. "My queen? That's... what did you call it this morning, TMI, don't you think?"

"Oh Seb, your men already know cause they can read my thoughts. Pretty sure they are gonna be trying it next and I tell Gia and Zach everything. Besides, it was nice seeing you enjoy the shower."

"It was pretty exquisite."

"Right! And Gia can show Nero and Zach can show Anthony. The others are on their own, though."

"Unless they too find a she-wolf."

"There is that."

Zach chuckles. "Deal, now, let's get going. Apparently, I need to have you all home in time for dinner. It seems my dad has invited you all to eat in the pack house."

Zara squeals. "Yes! Thank you Alpha!" She moves to the door and opens it, gesturing for the others to get in. "Let's go!"

Nero peeks in the car, seeing the leather seats, and steps in, ducking and moving to sit down. Gianna follows and places herself beside him. Sebastian enters third, followed shortly by the three guards. Zara steps in last and closes the door after them, settling herself beside Sebastian.

Zach opens the door to the front seat for Anthony. "You get to ride up front with me." Zach closes the door after him and bounds around to the driver's side. After slipping in, he shuts his door and places the keys in the ignition and starts the limo. Reaching across Anthony, his hands lingering a moment longer than they should, he grabs the strap and pulls it across him. "Buckle up." Snapping it into place, along with his, he reaches out and lowers the window between the front and back. Drawing on a deep, stern voice. "Greetings. I am Zach. I will be your tour guide for the day. This is a Limo, or Limousine. Unlike Zara's bucket of bolts, this is a much smoother ride and seats more passengers than her car. We only use it when we have other alphas to escort into town. There is a full bar in the back with sodas, juice, and water. Dad took the alcohol out." With that, he releases the parking brake and pulls the limo around, heading out of the pack and into human territory.

Zara giggles. "My car is not a bucket of bolts!"

"Your car is too. I swear one of these days, it's just going to fall apart somewhere, and you'll be calling me to rescue your ass."

"Nuh ah, I will call Gia!"

Gianna laughs. "Yep, it will be me she calls."

"Ouch, the pain of being second choice."

"Well, whose fault is that, mister Alpha in training, and doesn't have time for us anymore."

"My father's?"

Zara and Gianna laugh. "Don't tell him that. We will all end up doing thirty laps around the pack territory."

"My lips are sealed." The limo cruises down the highway, as Zach gives them a running commentary of what they are seeing on their left and right of them.

Sebastian turns to Zara. "You spoke while in our realm that you do not ride horses anymore because of these carriages. How fast are we going in comparison?"

Zara shakes her head. "I am not sure. Let me check." She pulls her phone out and googles a horse's speed. "It looks like the average horse travels at thirty miles per hour. Quarter horses can run at fifty for about twenty minutes. Right now we are on a highway, so we should be doing about seventy, but with Zach driving, probably eighty to ninety. So three times as fast as a horse."

"Impressive."

"Yes, but there are rules and we need roads to drive on. You need to pass a test and get a license. With horses, you can go where you want to."

Eighteen

Mall Crawl

Forty minutes later, Zach pulls the limo into the mall parking lot, finding a place along the back to park it. Once he's securely parked, he hops out and opens the door for the others. Chuckling at Anthony's distress at being locked in, he reaches around and pushes the button, unbuckling him. "Alright, this is the mall. Mostly a human city. Shifters and vampires are pretty much myth and legend to them and we like to keep it that way, so all talk of that ends now. We are simply humans on a shopping trip, with a lot of moolah!"

"Moolah?"

"Cash."

Sebastian looks at Zara. "Cash?"

"Gold Seb."

"You have gold?"

"Yes, and no. We don't use it to buy stuff. Here we have plastic." She winks at him and takes his hand. "You'll see."

The group heads into the mall with Zara, Zach, and Gianna keeping a close eye on Sebastian and his crew, knowing it's going to be overwhelming. Zara smiles at their amazed expressions, squeezing Sebastian's hand gently, drawing his attention to her. "What do you think?"

"It is like a market, but bigger and covered. And I see what you mean by colored hair. Some look quite striking."

"Yes, I tried blue to match my eyes. It didn't last. Now, let's find some clothes for you guys."

"We have clothes, my queen."

"Yes, and you are here for ten days. You kinda standout as different."

Sebastian looks around at the other people wandering, seeing a few of them stop to stare. "Perhaps you are right."

"I know I am!" She pulls him into a shop and looks at the clothing, holding it up against him, before placing it back on the rack. "Hmmm, I don't really like anything here." She turns to the others. "Guys, if you see something you want. Let me know. I am taking Seb to the store next door."

Gianna laughs. "Let me guess, the suit store?"

"Yes, that's the one."

"How did I know? Have fun. I got Nero covered. Zach's got Anthony."

"Mathew, Theodore and Julian, you come with me then."

"Yes, my queen."

Zara rolls her eyes, directing a scowl at Sebastian for his chuckle, and pulls him into the shop next door. She decides on a few dress pants and casual button down dress shirts. "Here, hold these Seb. They're for you. Now, you three. Let's see, being guards, you might want more flexible attire. We have zippers here and not laces, just pull the tab up and it closes." She picks up a few pieces, holding them up to them as the sales clerk comes over. "I didn't know there was a Ren Faire in town."

Zara catches the bewildered look from Sebastian and his guards. Her gaze moves to the tag adorned to her shirt. "There isn't Jenna. They are from out of town."

"Wait, I'm confused. Why are they still dressed in costume then?"

Zara laughs, fully expecting the questions. "It seems they got distracted at the fair and didn't watch the time. When they realized how late it was, they had to book it to catch the plane, fully planning to change when they arrived here. But, you know airlines. Their luggage got lost along the way, so we are buying a few things to tide them over."

"Well then, how can I help you?" Her eyes look over the men intently, liking the look of all of them.

"I need a more casual suit for them, then we are gonna get some jeans and T's." Zara bristles when her gaze roams over Sebastian.

Sebastian steps forward, sensing Zara's angst, and kisses her cheek. His free hand wraps around her waist and pulls her against him. "My love. We should pick something and get back to the others. I don't like us being separated."

"Right, Sorry Seb. You need to try them on to make sure they fit."

Sebastian looks around at the open story, furrowing his brows, suspecting asking aloud would make the clerk question them more. *'Here?'*

DRAGONSCALES DIVIDE 149

'Nope. In a change room. No way I am letting her see you in your skivvies.'

'Skivvies?'

'Undergarments.'

'You know I love only you?'

'I know Seb. It's just different with humans. They do not see mates as sacred and try to steal them away from us. Sometimes unintentionally, other times deliberate. They don't understand the concept and a lot of human marriages end up in divorces. Besides, she is eyeing the lot of you like you are fresh meat and I don't like it.' Zara watches Jenna move off and return with a few choices.

'Divorces?'

'Yes, it's the equivalent of splitting up after mate marking. Another thing to add to the list of explaining later and not in front of a human.'

Jenna returns with an armful of clothing. "How about these? Casual but somewhat dressy. It would suit them."

Zara laughs. "Suit them, good one."

"I try. Let's get them into the changing rooms." Jenna leads them towards the back of the store, where booths with curtains drawn across them sit. "We have four, so you are in luck. If you find they do not fit, let me know. I will bring the next size up or down."

Sebastian pauses and kisses Zara's lips softly. "Don't move my queen."

"I won't."

"I promised Mama-bear I would not let you out of my sight."

"You're not. If you leave the curtain open a crack, you can see that I will be right here."

Jenna leaves to ring another customer in, returning shortly to give a once over of Zara. "That's so sweet. He even calls you his queen. Are the others available?"

"Unfortunately, no, they are all spoken for."

"So where are they? I would never leave their side!"

Zara sighs, struggling with the overly chatty sales clerk and what to tell her. "Back home, where they came from."

"They travel without them?"

Sebastian steps out and looks over the pair of women, dressed in black dress pants and a navy blue shirt with hints of a pattern woven into it. "I come from a position of power and they are my bodyguards. So yes, they travel without them."

"Wow." Zara gasps, her eyes roaming over Sebastian, desire instantly heating her core. She steps forward and unbuttons the top few buttons, her fingers lingering on his skin. *'Never all the way to the top unless you have a tie.'*

Sebastian grasps her hand to his chest, staring into her eyes, reading the desire and love in them before bringing it up to kiss the back of it. "I am glad you approve, my queen."

Zara blushes, pulling her hand away, knowing where her thoughts are going, and pushes them aside as she spots the curtains opening from the other stalls. Diverting her attention to them, she looks them up and down, each sporting more of a casual suit look, with tan pants and light tops. "You all clean up nicely. Do you like them?"

"Yes, my queen."

Jenna snaps her gaze to Zara. "Wait, they all call you queen?"

"Ah yes, it's a Ren Faire thing. I keep telling them to stop, but they don't. I am pretty certain they do it to annoy me."

"Where is your outfit?"

"Oh, it's at home. I live here, so I have a change of clothing."

"It must be beautiful."

Zara thinks back to the blue dress that Sebastian had dressed her in first. "Yes, it is. Super soft blue velvet with some lacings to tie it on. Full skirt that flows nicely when you walk and it spins like a poodle skirt."

Sebastian reaches over and squeezes her hand, knowing the dress she was speaking of. *'You will need to explain this Ren Faire later. Yes? Also, that was not a queen's dress, my dear. I will have you wearing what you rightfully should when we return.'*

'I will put on A Knight's Tale when we get home and you can watch it. And it was for me. I felt special in the dresses you gave me.' Zara blushes softly and turns to Jenna. "They will wear them out, if that's alright. We will need bags for their clothing."

"Of course. I just need the tags. How will you be paying?"

Zara pulls the price tags off the clothing and hands them to the clerk so that she can scan them at the till. "Card." Turning back to the others. "You should get your outfits. We will bag them up and carry them out to the limo."

"Right this way." Jenna looks over them again, specifically at Sebastian. "Wait, limo?"

"Ah, yes, we have a limo."

"What exactly does he do?"

"It's not actually his Limo, it's my friend's fathers. We just borrowed it for the day."

"Wow... To be able to borrow a limo."

"It's our first time, to be honest, and it took some begging, pleading, and batting lashes."

Jenna laughs. "I can imagine!"

Seeing they have collected their clothes, Zara leads them back to the till as Jenna rings the items through. "Do you have any scissors that I can cut the plastic off?"

"Of course." Jenna hands Zara a pair.

Zara works on cutting the plastic pieces out of their clothes, smiling at Sebastian's expression while she digs into his guards' clothes. *'Remember, I love you.'*

'I think, my love, they are quite uncomfortable with their queen touching them.'

'It's fine. If I don't cut these out, they will irritate the skin. You can tell them that.'

'You can tell them that yourself.'

'RIGHT! I can mind-link them.' She focuses inward as she continues her task, reaching out to them. *'It's a little plastic piece that needs cutting out. Normally, you don't wear clothes out of the store and you cut the tags off when you get home. If I don't do this, it will mark you.'*

'Of course, my queen. We were just wondering what you were doing exactly.'

She hands a piece over to each of them, placing the rest on the counter. Pulling out her card, she slides it across the counter to Jenna. "Thank you." Turning back to size them up, her gaze lingering on Sebastian, noticing how the dark blue enhances the color of his eyes. "Next up, Shoes to go with those. We should hook back up with the others cause they will need shoes too."

Jenna finishes tallying all the tags. "That will be eight hundred and forty-eight dollars."

Sebastian frowns at the number quoted. *'It seems high. Could you not barter her down?'*

'No Seb, we don't. You pay what's on the tag. It's the way of the world here.' She leans up and caresses his cheek. *'I got you covered. Being a Beta's daughter has its perks.'*

'I don't like it.'

'You don't have you. You took care of me. I will take care of you.'

Once the sale is done, Zara retrieves her card and stuffs it into her purse. "Thank you for your help."

"You are welcome back anytime."

Catching the clerk's wistful sigh, Zara forces a smile as her possessive nature kicks in. She grabs Sebastian's hand and pulls him from the store, ignoring his chuckle as they meet up with Nero and Gianna. Gianna elbows Nero. "Damn! Had I known how well you all would look in suits, I would have shopped there first! Let's get you one."

Zara laughs at Gianna. "You know I have always preferred a man in a suit, but be careful, the sales clerk is looking to latch onto one of them. Just so our stories are clear, I told her they were at a Ren Faire and late for a plane. They arrived but their luggage did not. Seb did state they were his guards when she questioned why they traveled without the ladies, so that's safe to use. Oh, and we begged and pleaded for use of the limo."

"Understood." Gianna drags Nero to the suit store.

Zach chuckles as he approaches, doing a once over of their new attire. "Let me guess, Nero is getting one?"

"Yes, shoes next, then perhaps jeans and t's and some training clothes." Zara looks over the patterned shirt and casual khaki pants that Anthony is sporting, smiling in approval. "Did Zach choose those, Anthony?"

"Yes, my queen."

"Do you like them?"

"It's very different from what I am accustomed to. Much lighter, free'er in some regards and more restricting in others. This zipper thing is amazing. How it opens and closes." He lowers his hands to his zipper.

Zara places her hands up in dismay and spins her back to him. "Don't need to see how it works, Anthony! I already know. Zach, Control your man!"

Zach laughs, grasping Anthony's hands. "Not here. Later."

"Ugh. Zach! Don't want to hear that either. Lets get shoes now, alright."

"That sounds good." He turns to Anthony. "Did you want a suit as well?"

Anthony shakes his head. "They look formal. I am more casual than that. What I am wearing is good."

Zach chuckles. "Oh, it definitely is... but it's not enough. We have money to burn and you are getting spoiled by our pack. Let's head with them and get shoes. Your footwear still stands out."

Sebastian places an arm over Zara's shoulder. "My queen, is everything alright?"

"Yes."

"Your thoughts speak otherwise, and everyone but Zach can hear them."

Zara buries her face in Sebastian's chest. "I don't want to talk about it."

Zach turns to Zara, "Wait, what am I missing?"

Zara scowls at both Sebastian and Zach. "Nothing... You are missing nothing."

"I think it's something Zara."

"No Zach. It's just that we are with a group that can read thoughts. Even without that ability, I know where your thoughts went, and being that I grew up with you as a bestie, I don't want to even think about that!"

"Seriously? You are the first to explore that unknown territory with Sebastian here. Perhaps you should give Gia and I pointers."

"Oh gawd, Zach! NOT discussing it! NOT at all, so don't even go there. Let's go now before I tackle you."

Zach winks her way. "Later than."

"Yes." Zara mutters. "Later. I just need to stay away from you till Alpha Madison comes to get us."

They peek into the suit store. "Gia, Nero, we are heading to the shoe store. Meet you there."

The clerk gasps and points at them. "They are with you?"

"Yes."

"Where did you find them?"

"Not from around here."

"I need to go to more Ren Faires."

"Yep, you probably do."

Gianna giggles. "We won't be long. Nero just needs one, and we will meet you there."

Nero stands behind Gianna and whispers. "My queen, save me!"

Gianna spins and scowls at him. "I heard that Nero!"

"My dear, I should be guarding the Ki...Sebastian. Not separated from him."

"Then make it quick. Pick something."

"Poor Nero. You thought I was a handful, Seb. Gia is double me and then some." Zara shakes her head and leads them toward one of the shoe stores.

"I am getting that impression. I believe Anthony got the calmest of you all. Are all shifters like that?"

Zara shakes her head. "No, just us. I would refrain from making that opinion until you see Zach's wild side. Though he is curbing it in, what with training to be an Alpha and all."

Zach gasps. "What! I am so NOT curbing my wild side. I will show you Zara!"

"Oh, no! Please wait till we have finished shopping!"

Zach sighs heavily in exasperation. "If you insist."

"I do. I don't want us kicked out of the mall."

"I can agree with that."

They spend a few hours buying all the necessities for Sebastian and his men. Ensuring that they covered all basic's in the clothing, shoe and personal hygiene department, even adding a few books and bottles of wine for them. Each one picks out a style that appeals to them. Carrying their loot back to the limo, they lock it in the trunk and agree to head back into the food court and grab an afternoon snack. While they are laughing and joking at a table, a group of girls sits at their table, flirting with the men.

Zara arches a brow, her eyes locking on Gianna's for a moment, each of them in shock at the audacity of them.

'Humans, right?'

'Yes, like clearly we are a group. What the hell?'

Zara turns to the three, keeping her voice polite. "Can I help you?"

"Oh no, it's quite alright."

Zara watches Julian shift slightly closer to their end of the table, clearly uncomfortable with their level of flirtation. *'Switch places with me, Julian. Mathew, switch with Gianna.'* She stands up and settles in his chair while Gianna does the same with Mathew. "So, what made you decide to sit at our table?"

"Oh, come on, you can't keep all these hunks to yourselves. Share the love."

Zara smiles coolly. "I'm not, but since the men happily changed seats with us, it implies they do not desire your flirtations."

"You don't know that. Tall, dark and handsome is watching us pretty closely."

"Oh, but I do. You see, three of us are engaged to three of them, including tall, dark and handsome, who happens to be mine. That leaves three remaining and two of those just traded places with us willingly." Zara turns to Theodore. "Do you have any interest in these women?"

Theodore shakes his head. "No, my queen."

"There you have it. Please find another table."

"Bitch, you just want them all for yourself."

"Oh babe, how wrong you are! I only want one and I have him. The rest come with him." She watches them storm off to a nearby table, sending dark glares their way.

Sebastian observes their actions, turning his attention to Gianna and Zara. "Why would they challenge you on this?"

"Sebastian, my love. You all have an aura that radiates from you. One of authority, power and wealth. It speaks that you will protect whoever is beside you, and women desire that. Look around at the other men or even the women in the mall. Who here screams power like you do. Very few have that aura. Those that do, have people vying for their attention. They are drawn to it, like a moth to a flame. Shifters suffer the same when we come to town, so we try to avoid it and keep to the pack town, but I wanted you to experience the most that you can while you are here."

Sebastian looks around the food court, noticing Zara's astute observation, not feeling power or threat coming from any in the nearby vicinity. Even the three glaring at the party did not worry him, for he could feel the pettiness of their thoughts. "Humans in our world are very different."

"I suspect they are, especially if they are forming a resistance. Some of them here would, but most wouldn't know where to begin. They are happy with their day-to-day lives. Shall we continue shopping, or do you want to head home?"

"Did we buy enough?"

"Yes Seb, we got you enough. I just wasn't certain if you wanted to see more."

"I have what I want to see beside me, my queen. Let's go home. Perhaps we can watch another one of those moving pictures with the quilt again."

"Deal!"

"Restroom first though. It's a long drive."

Nineteen

Queen Bee

They rise, pushing their chairs in, catching the glares from the three. Zara winks at them as she loops her arm into Sebastian's. The rest fan out and protect her and Gianna as they leave the food court, knowing if looks could kill, they would be dead three times over. Zara leads them to the mall washrooms, the men waiting as Zara and Gianna enter and return, before some of them enter themselves. She groans, seeing one of her high school tormentors walking down the hallway towards them. "Damn, what the hell is with all the trollops in the mall today?"

"Oh no, that must be busy bee, Bianca. Only she has earned that name." Gianna bursts out laughing, her eyes doing a sweep and seeing their arch nemesis approaching. Dressed in a yellow dress, a black belt at her waist, with matching black pumps. Her dark brown hair tied back in a ponytail, with makeup that borders on excessive. Behind her are two she doesn't recognise, each with light brown hair and brown eyes. One dressed in a pair of jeans and a blue t-shirt, the other in black dress pants and a button down patterned silk shirt.

Bianca strolls up to them, the loud clack of her heels on the floor echoing around them. "Well, well, well. What do we have here?"

Zara stiffens and steps closer to Sebastian. "Bianca. Shouldn't you be in class?"

"I can ask the same thing about training. Does the Alpha know you are here?"

Zach comes out of the restroom, distaste laced in his voice at seeing Bianca. "He does."

"Does he know you are slumming it with vamps?"

Zara smiles coldly. "We are slumming it by talking to you. These men have a hundred percent more class than you ever could."

Bianca narrows her eyes, watching as four vampires move to stand in a protective box around Zara. "Ah Zara, ever the wannabe popular girl. Had to find it with blood suckers cause you couldn't find it with wolves."

Zara growls softly. "I am not like you, Bianca. I don't need to be the popular queen bee. I have friends who are loyal to me. Can you say the same for those you run with?"

"Of course. They are loyal to the core. What does Jeremy think of his mate playing in the gutter? I bet he rejects you when he finds out."

Zara laughs. "I was never and will never be his mate, so he can't reject what isn't his. I have my mate and I don't really care what your assholic brother's opinion is of me. Besides, as you say, he's slumming it in the pack dungeons for ten days."

"WHAT?"

"Aww, are you saying the queen bee is not up to date on her news? Tsk tsk, that poor little me knew before you. It seems he threw a tantrum and challenged my mate to a death match."

"So let me get this straight. Your precious mate had him tossed in the dungeons instead of fighting. Who is the loser?"

Sebastian places a hand on Zara's back before she can answer. "I am the mate in question and I defeated him fair and square. With the pack as witnesses. Alpha Darian had him taken to the cells because of his deplorable actions."

Bianca laughs hysterically. "Oh, my Goddess. This just gets even more precious. You... Mated to a vampire? What did you do to piss off the Goddess?"

Zach and Gianna both growl at the same time. "We all are actually."

Bianca glares at Zach, then at the one he moves beside. "Your father won't accept it. Reject him now."

"He has, and I won't"

"I doubt that. Have you marked him yet?"

"That is none of your damn business."

The two girls beside Bianca snicker. "When Alpha Landon returns and takes Nightshade Howlers back from that new wretched Alpha, we won't be allowing no vamps in our domain."

Zara turns to the two beside Bianca in shock. "You know it's forbidden to mention that pack."

"No, it's not. It's our pack. Just because Silvermoon invaded doesn't mean we need to accept it."

"Invaded? Did you even read the King's newsletter? I mean, I know that's hard for some of you society bumbles, especially since your queen bee can't comprehend what she reads. But really, it talked about why the takeover happened. Secondly, does Alpha D'andre know this? He seems pretty cool."

"How would you know, bitch? I hear you are nothing but a low-class omega born into a beta position. That you haven't even earned that title."

"Hmm, let's see, cause we were there a couple of months ago. Perhaps I should call him and let him know."

"Doubtful an omega like you would be hobnobbing with another alpha."

Zara pulls out her phone and dials, hearing it ring a few times. "Alpha D'andre. Zara here. I have a couple of your people at our local mall. Yes, in Stormfang." She pulls the phone away. "What did you say your names were?"

"We didn't."

Sebastian trails his fingers along Zara's back, his eyes studying the trio intently. "One's name is Layla Monroe, and the other is Yvonne Steckles."

The two snap their gaze to Sebastian. "How do you know that?"

"Us vampires have our ways of knowing things." He wraps an arm around Zara's waist and pulls her closer. *'My queen, you best call your Alpha as well. These three, along with a group of others, are planning to commit treason on both your pack and this Alpha D'andre's.'*

'Seriously? I didn't think they would have it in them.'

'Yes, my queen. Do not let them walk away from us.'

'Got it... Zach, call your father. Sebastian's reading bad things in their thoughts.'

Zara returns her attention to the call and repeats the names to D'andre. "Anyway, you should really have a talk with them, Alpha. It seems they still think they belong to the pack whose name was stricken and that its leader is going to return. Yes, they did. Alright, I will let Zach know. He's going to call his dad."

She hangs up and tucks her phone away. "Oh, I believe you girls are in trouble now. They might even strip your school funding."

"Whatever. You probably just called another friend and pretended it was the Alpha."

"Either way, we are to keep you contained until further notice." ... *'Zach, Alpha D'andre is getting Alpha Madison to bring him to the pack house.'*

"I was with her. Are you accusing my Beta of lying? On Stormfang pack grounds?" Zach growls and pulls his phone out, dialing his father.

"Who are you exactly?"

"Alpha Zach Ravenwind, first born to Alpha Darian Ravenwind."

Both pale and glance at Bianca. "We should go."

"My Beta said you were to stay." Zach glares at the three of them as the phone rings. "Dad, we have a problem. No, it's Jeremy's sister and two townies from Silvermoon. They are skipping class and are here at the mall." Zach watches the three girls bolt, only to be swiftly caught by Sebastian's guards. "They just tried to run, but Sebastian's guards have them contained. Yes, we will take them to the mall office and wait. I believe Alpha D'andre is on his way to you. Ohhh. He's already texted. Damn. Alright, see you soon." He hangs up. "We are to take them to the mall office and wait."

Bianca screeches. "You can't do this to me! Unhand me, you filthy vamps."

"Our queen commanded you to stay."

Zach grins coolly. "Actually, both Alpha's ordered it. Let's go to the main office."

Sebastian's guards force the girls to walk, who struggle and scream, trying to draw attention to them. To those that step forward to help, Zach simply replies, "Caught shoplifting," which causes them to back off, though a few follow at a respectable pace to the office doors. A few minutes later, Zach holds the door open as Anthony, Mathew and Julian push the girls in and sit them on chairs. Theodore crosses to the other side and stands near a door there. Sebastian and Nero follow Gianna and Zara in, remaining at the door closing behind them. The secretaries look over the group entering, as Zach moves to the counter. "We are waiting for my father."

"Understood Master Zach. He called. He will be here shortly."

Five minutes later, the door opens beside Sebastian and Nero. Sebastian steps aside and studies the six that walk in, recognizing Alpha Darian. His attention turns to the woman that steps in next. Stunning aquamarine eyes meet his gaze, and he smiles at the partial block on her mind. Intrigued by her because she is the first of this realm to have it. Behind her is a tall man, tanned, friendly, his thoughts bouncing between concern and curiosity. Sebastian feels the power radiating off the fourth with two guards at his side, despite being in casual clothing, catching the subtle stiffening, and the rage in his thoughts, knowing he is fighting control of it. Two females walk in and stand in the back corner silently with him, each one meeting Sebastian's gaze. Knowing by their thoughts that they are the witches of this realm. He is curious to know more, making a mental note to speak with them afterwards. His attention returns to the others, seeing Zara, Gianna and Zach all bowing to authority, whereas the three girls are clearly clueless at the power now standing in the room.

Alpha Darian gestures to the secretaries. "Leave. Take lunch now." Waiting until they have vacated, Darian turns to his son, Zach. "Alright Son, what's going on exactly?"

"Well, Bianca approached us, being catty as usual, but Zara said we needed to contain them."

"Zara, please explain."

Zara looks up at Alpha Darian, drifting her gaze to the others that just came into the room with her Alpha, recognizing Alpha D'andre, Alpha Madison and their witch Amara. Her gaze lingers on the unknown four, suspecting one is the king, though she's never seen him in person, along with his guards and his witch. "Alpha, Sebastian read their thoughts. He told me these three are planning treason."

Darian frowns at his friend's daughter. "Treason is a strong word to throw around Zara."

Sebastian steps forward. "If I may Alpha Darian. This one, Bianca, as you call her, has some witch's token in the top drawer of her dresser in her dorm. She also has a powder she was planning on feeding Alpha Zach. Her plan is to drug him and get him to mate mark her. Then control him with the charm and take over the pack. The two girls in question have a group of shifters, also at their dorm, that seek to take down their current Alpha and reinstate one Alpha Landon. They believe their territory was unfairly invaded and have no desire to swear allegiance to the new Alpha."

All three pale drastically but scream at Sebastian. "Those are lies! You can't possibly believe what a blood sucker says!"

"Are they now?" Madison steps forward, her eyes looking over Sebastian carefully. "If I may ask questions, Alpha Darian."

Darian frowns but nods. "By all means."

"Let's find out, shall we?" Madison murmurs a few words as soft aqua lights surround the three girls, as well as Sebastian. "Now, what are your full names?"

"Bianca Hillock."

"Layla Monroe."

"Yvonne Steckles."

Madison smiles at them coldly. "Bianca. We will start with you. Do you have a mate?"

"No."

"Did you have a mate?"

"I ah..." She struggles to fight the magic instilled upon her. "Yes."

"Where is he?"

"I rejected him."

"Why?"

"He was a filthy omega and worked as a janitor at the school. I can do better than that."

"I see. You know the Goddess matches us with a perfect mate."

"She is wrong."

"Such entitlement. What are your plans with Alpha Zach?"

"He is going to mate and mark me."

"And how do you see that happening if he is mated to another?"

"He won't have a mate."

"But it looks like he does have a mate."

"I will just get Jeremy to take him out for me. It's not like he hasn't done it before."

Madison's aqua eyes flash in anger, having dealt with someone trying to force a mate mark on her. "We will come back to that. What happens if Zach resents you for killing his mate?"

"He won't. Once we mark each other, he won't be able to resist me."

"I very much doubt he will mark you if you kill his mate."

"Doesn't matter. I have drugs and a talisman to help make him compliant to me."

"And where are these located?"

"In my dorm."

"I see. How are you planning on administering them when you live on campus?"

"I am still working on that."

"How long have you had these items?"

"Just over a month, I guess."

"Where did you get them from?"

"A witch on campus."

"What is her name?"

"Stella Kaala."

"Back to Jeremy. What did you mean when he has done it before?"

"When I don't like someone, he takes them away."

"He will just take anyone away?"

Bianca pouts. "No, they can't be people like Zara that everyone knows. I tried, but he denied me. I think it's 'cause he loves her. Only the loser loners that annoy me."

"Do you know what he does with them?"

"Don't know, don't care. They just never irritate me again, and I am good with that."

Madison's aqua eyes darken dangerously as she turns to Alpha Darian. "I will speak with this Jeremy upon our return."

Darian frowns at Bianca's words, knowing they have had a few pack members go missing, but had put it down to the battles at the border or the messages from the King that someone was stealing shifters. He hadn't thought someone in his own pack was so traitorous. Two actually. Rage flows through him, as his hands clench in balls, knowing both are never seeing the light of day again. "Of course, he's already in the cells for challenging Zara's mate."

Madison nods, returning her attention to the other two. "Layla, Yvonne, you are from Silvermoon?"

"No, we are Nightshade Howlers."

"That pack does not exist. The King himself has stricken the name. Do you want to correct your pack and Alpha?"

"No. The invasion against Alpha Landon was unjust."

"He was kidnapping supernatural creatures and selling them to witches who were killing them."

"Those are just lies created by the new Alpha to breed fear into the pack. The King is weak for believing such nonsense from that Alpha."

A deep growl in the back of the room draws everyone's attention, one that causes everyone in the room to bare their necks except Madison and the vampires.

Madison growls back. "Gran-pappy! Stop or I will have your witch Thalia, silence you. I cannot question them if you fear them into submission." She returns her attention back to the three, seeing their eyes staring at the man in the back. "Never mind him. He's just cranky right now. How many of you believe this?"

"About twelve of us."

"All from school?"

"Yes."

"Were you all at school when Alpha D'andre invaded your lands?"

"Yes, Alpha Landon sent us here to learn."

"Interesting he would send you to a university so far away from his pack."

"Not at all, actually. He sends students all over. He pays for our schooling and we keep an eye on everything here for him."

"An eye on what, exactly?"

"Who has magic and who doesn't? Who has families? Loners who don't get along in school and where they hang out? People like you with strange colored eyes. That sort of thing."

"And you never questioned this?"

"Why would we? It's easy and we get everything paid for, including clothes and stuff."

"And so I ask you. What are your plans?"

"Plans?"

"Clearly you are unhappy with Alpha D'andre and want Alpha Landon back. Yes?"

"Of course, he's the rightful ruler."

"How were you planning on replacing D'andre with Landon?"

"Poison."

"Wait, you were going to poison D'andre?"

"Yes, and Alpha Darian. That way, we would get Alpha Landon back and Luna Bianca would rule Stormfang. Our packs would be best friends."

Madison's eyes flash in annoyance at the stupidity of the girls. "Do you know where Landon is?"

"He's in hiding. He will come out when the false Alpha is gone and reward us handsomely for our loyalty."

"I'm sure he will." Madison turns to Sebastian, having deliberately wrapped her aqua magic around him, but notices he refrained from answering when she asked their names. "You are a vampire, like five others in this room. I get the impression they all defer to you."

Sebastian smiles, offering a slight bow. "Indeed, and your truth magic will have no effect on me. You are not a witch like the two in the back, but you have magic like one. I sense two entities inside you, whereas everyone else I have met has one. You shield some of your thoughts, but not all Alpha Madison. I find I am curious to know more."

Madison arches a brow, glancing over at Zara for a moment. "A clever vampire. Unheard of in this realm. We shall see if you bend to my magic. What is your name?"

"I don't feel the need to answer that." Sebastian winks at Madison.

"She said you were strong." A grin tugs at the corners of Madison's lips as she draws on more magic, emphasizing her command. "Tell me your name."

"I think not, Alpha Madison. Not until I prove your magic has no effect on me."

Madison laughs. "Stubborn. I can see why you won Zara over."

"That I will choose to comment on. I admit, I was uncertain whether I would win her over despite her wolf falling in love with me instantly."

"It seems like you succeeded. Now, without magic, may I have your name?"

"Sebastian Darkholme at your service. These are my men, Nero, Anthony, Julian, Theodore and Mathew. Two of whom have accepted Zach and Gianna as mates."

"Yes, Alpha Darian mentioned it when we arrived." Madison turns her gaze to Alpha Darian. "Three shifters mated to vampires. I feel there is some importance to this."

Alpha Darian glances at the three girls glaring at the group of them. "Yes, and we can discuss that after."

"Agreed. Now Sebastian, Zara, I was to come and get you tomorrow, but since I am here, did you want to leave now?"

Sebastian looks at Zara, seeing her blush. "We had plans to spend the night alone. If you can grant this, then her family would be grateful not to be kicked out of their house."

She laughs and turns to Caden. "Sire, you heard the man. Can you grant this pair a room in your castle?"

Bianca, Layla and Yvonne gasp as they direct their gazes at the King, a sinking feeling growing in the pit of their stomachs.

Caden turns back to the vampire he has been watching. "I can, but there will be guards. Just because Alpha Darian trusts them does not mean I will blindly accept them."

DRAGONSCALES DIVIDE

"Understood."

Zara gasps. "Wait. No, I need to say goodbye to my parents and pack. I would rather leave tomorrow as planned. Besides, I gotta trounce Nero in the training rings tomorrow since I didn't get to today."

Madison laughs. "A fighter after my own heart. Tomorrow it is then."

"Thank you." Zara nods and leans against Sebastian, wrapping her arms around his waist.

Madison returns her attention to the others in the room. "Well, you heard them beneath the truth magic. Sounds like treason to me. I would suggest that we take them to the school campus. Find the poison and the witch's stock as evidence. Then compel them to call their friends forward, arrest them all, including this Jeremy. Hopefully, the witch is ignorant enough to answer the summons as well. If she walks the dark side, she will need to be bound along with her sisters." Her eyes stray to Thalia, knowing she can do the binding. "Gran-pappy, if you need it, I will happily question them more upon arrival in the royal prisons." She lifts her hand, twisting it slightly as aqua magic surges from it, snapping the phone out of Bianca's hands and into hers. She turns it over and reads the message on it. "It seems Miss Bianca was planning to warn her friends. Confiscate the other two phones and let's get going. Alpha Darian, can your witch portal us there? I cannot fey-step where I have not seen?"

"She can, but she has limited uses."

"She just needs to get us there. I can get everyone back here or your pack house."

Zach glances over at Madison. "We need to come back here. I drove the limo to take them shopping."

"Got it. Sebastian, are your men skilled enough to arrest twelve shifters?"

"Of course."

"Perfect. So let's get to the university and get this done."

Amara steps forward and chants a few words, a portal opening up into an empty office designed for it. Mathew, Julian and Theodore guide the three young ladies through the portal as the rest follow. They head first to Bianca's dorm, finding the items in question that she had to taint Zach, condemning her to at the very least, life in prison. As they search the room, they find a notebook with a list of names, some of which Darian recognizes as missing shifters. He mutters a string of curses under his breath at the two in question, and himself for not catching it sooner.

Madison places a hand on Darian's shoulder. "It's not your fault, Alpha Darian. Trust me, I went through this with my old pack. Those responsible are in the royal prisons. This group will join them. After that, I do believe I will make a tour of all the pack universities and see if there are other Landon or Davis wannabes out there."

"Thank you Madison. Internal pack betrayal hurts."

"It does. When I return, you should call a pack meeting. I would suggest Sebastian and I watch to see who reacts to Jeremy and Bianca being imprisoned and from there, we will move forward."

"Thank you"

Once Bianca's room is done, they head over to Yvonne and Layla's room and search it, finding the poison in question. A mix of silver dust, wolfsbane and mistletoe. Madison frowns as she hands the mixture over to King Caden. "They meant business, sire. This mixture would have easily taken out Alpha Darian and D'andre."

Caden growls deeply. "Get the rest of them here. I want them all in my prisons now."

Madison turns to the three girls. "You are going to call your friends now."

"Not a chance. We won't snitch on our friends."

"Allow me Alpha Madison." Sebastian smiles and steps forward, meeting each of their gazes while gently caressing their cheeks before focusing on Yvonne. His voice is soft and compelling, as it works its way into her mind and soul. "Shifters are really an extraordinary species. We do not have them in our realm. I find I desire to meet more. You feel the urge to help me with that by calling your friends here. Specifically, the ones in your inner circle. Can you do that for me, Yvonne? Can you mind-link your group and bring them here?"

"Not over the mind-link. The Alpha will hear. I will need my phone to text them."

"What color is it?"

"It's not one that you have. It's hidden in my dresser."

Sebastian shakes his head at the others wanting to ask questions. Moving to the dresser, he rifles through until he finds the box. Moving back, he sits next to her. Placing an arm over her shoulders, he hands the new phone over. "Thank you Yvonne, I really look forward to this." Feeling Zara's confusion and possessiveness, he winks her way. *'My queen, I belong to you. Trust me.'*

DRAGONSCALES DIVIDE 167

Zara nods and moves over to Gianna and Nero, both drawing her into their arms.

Yvonne smiles up at Sebastian and types into her phone.

> Group meeting, my room, I have someone I would like you all to meet.

> Yvonne, we are in class. Shouldn't you be too?

> What… NOW?

> This better be important.

> Who is this person? You know it's dangerous to just message like this, especially when in class.

> Are they another for the cause?

> Yvonne, is everything alright? This is unusual.

Sebastian reads the messages as they pop up. "Tell them you have just discovered information regarding where Landon is hiding, but others overheard. You need to hurry."

> Yes, everything's good. I just found out where Landon is hiding, but we need to move fast. I think others were listening in on the conversation and I don't want them to find him first. He needs to know how loyal we are.

> Damn straight, OMW

> Me too

> Just need to get out of class. ASAP.

> Gonna tell my teach I have a headache

Approximately thirty messages later, with most saying they will be here soon,

Sebastian rises. "Thank you Yvonne. May I have the phone please now so that I might put it back?"

"Of course." She hands the phone over and Sebastian moves to the dresser, pretending to place it back. He slips it into Madison's hand as he walks past her to Zara. "I would suggest my guards stand on either side of the door. When they come in, we move them out of sight so others don't bolt."

Madison frowns. "They won't bolt. I have binding magic."

"Is it visible?"

"Yes."

"Not good enough. Someone in the hall will see. They will not see my compulsion."

Zara looks up at Sebastian, chewing on her lip, finding herself wondering if he used his powers of persuasion on her.

He kisses her cheek lightly, his mind touching her thoughts as he pulls her into a hug. *'I can hear those thoughts, my love, and so can the others. I won you over the hard way, perseverance, charm and a whole lot of hope.'*

'How can I be sure? You compelled her so easily.'

'Zara, my queen. First, her mind is open to be compelled. That's why I picked her. Yours was not. You were not letting a vampire tame your heart. Remember? Second, within the hour, she won't recall this conversation. That is the drawback to my compulsions. Do you have blank spots from your time with me?'

'No, but...'

Sebastian places a finger to her lips. *'I love you. I would not do such a thing to you, your friends or your family. If you have doubts, ask Nero.'*

Madison glances between them, her eyes finding Nero, who was also watching them intently. "What's going on?"

Nero shakes his head. "Nothing Sebastian cannot handle."

"Sebastian?"

He lifts his gaze to Madison. "Just alleviating some doubts, Alpha Madison."

"That's understandable. That's one hell of a power you have there, Sebastian. Enough to cause some concern whether you are using it now."

"It is and I am not. It comes in handy when running a kingdom. But it has its drawbacks. As I explained to Zara here via mind-link, they will not remember anything said or done under the compulsion once it wears off. So when you question them, please keep that in mind."

"Is there a way to make them remember?"

"No. That time will just be gone for them. A blank spot if you will, but you have proof in the written words on the boxes. And your truth magic will tap into before and after the compulsion."

"Very true."

All of them in the room shift at a knock on the door, moving out of direct line of sight of the door. Yvonne rises and opens the door, smiling and gesturing for them to enter. As soon as they step in, Sebastian speaks quietly, compelling them to find a space out of sight as he reads the thoughts in their mind. Within fifteen minutes, a mix of students fill the room, all looking around in confusion at the strangers in the room. "Yvonne, was Stella in the group text?"

"No, she's Bianca's friend."

Sebastian turns his attention to Bianca. "Bring her here."

"I can't. She's..."

"Shhh, Bianca, I have faith that you can do it for me. If not, do it for Zach."

Bianca nods. "I need my phone."

"Is it a special one like Yvonne's?"

"No, just my regular one."

Sebastian turns to Madison, who hands the phone back. He watches her closely as she texts Stella.

> Stells, can you come to Yvonne's room? We are having a meeting.

Not even on campus today, Bee. I am busy.

> Please, it's important. It's regarding Zach.

Zach? Your Stormfang Alpha, right?

> Yes

Has Jeremy said anything about visitors to the pack?

Sebastian places a hand on hers to stop typing. "No, he hasn't."

> **No, he hasn't.**

> **You'll let me know if he does, right?**

> **Of course. So can you get here?**

> **Yes, but I need about twenty minutes. I'm with Colten.**

> **Great. CU Soon.**

Sebastian takes the phone from her and hands it back to Madison. "Twenty minutes." He turns back to Bianca. "Who is Colten?"

"He's just a delivery driver for the local courier company. I think she likes him."

Gianna groans at the name. "Ugh. What are the chances?"

Zara laughs. "If he shows up, it's you and me, babes!"

Madison looks at the two of them. "Are we missing something?"

"Nah, Colten delivers to the pack. He has the biggest crush on Gia so we pretended to be mates, just to dissuade him."

"Did it work?"

"Doubtful; he certainly wasn't thrilled with the idea, but it was fun to pretend."

Sebastian chuckles "I see how you were spending your time while I was searching to get here."

"That's right Seb. Me, Gia, and Zach! Our own power trio."

Bianca rolls her eyes and mutters. "You wish. You will never be popular, and when Zach is my mate, I am kicking you out of the pack."

Sebastian turns his attention back to Bianca. "Why does Stella care about newcomers to the pack?"

"I don't know. I think she is looking for someone."

Madison glances at the others in the room. "Who?"

Bianca shrugs her shoulders. "I don't ask. I think it's a witchy thing."

Studying her thoughts carefully, Sebastian shakes his head. "She doesn't know. If a witch is arriving, I think we should have everyone removed from the room, except Bianca. We do not know the limits of her magic, or what path she walks on."

Thalia steps forward. "Agreed. I will open a portal to the royal cells. We should get them locked up before she arrives. Sire?"

"And before my compulsion wears off."

Caden steps forward, fighting the rage within, wanting to break all the students that are stoically standing next to the walls. He thought they were done with Nightshade and Duskrunner's treason and yet, twelve more appeared out of the woodwork that a vampire had discovered. Silently, he watched this vampire. One that his granddaughter had come to him about. Asking to let him into the archives when he arrived, along with a Beta shifter she had just met. He had objected, of course, because trusting a vampire was unheard of. Yet, here one stood, with a power and skill that was clearly beyond any he had seen. In fact, all six of them seemed to have a poise and grace to them; better than some shifters he knew, himself included. But would they still have poise and grace if there was blood in the room? He doubted it, but that was something for another day. "Agreed, Thalia, let's get them out of here." Watching her open the portal, they guide the students through it, locking them into cells for the time being until he could talk to them. "Looks like we are going to have a busy afternoon, Maddie. Sorting through them and speaking with their parents about their actions and whether they agree with them."

Madison laughs. "Damn, I will need to get my pup and let Lucian know I'm gonna be late. Perhaps Gran-mama can look after him in between feedings."

"She will love that, Maddie."

"Great." Madison turns to her best friend. "Thanks a lot, D'andre. You know I have my pack to run and a pup to take care of! I knew I shouldn't have added protection to the contract."

D'andre chuckles. "Oh, no! It's in the contract you wrote! You are not pinning this on me. Blame Zara! Or yourself, for that matter. You brought this trouble to my pack in the first place. I knew I should have rejected the strays at my door."

Madison moves over and hugs D'andre. "You love it! Besides, Zara wasn't the one that read the treasonous thoughts. Her mate was." She turns to Sebastian. "To which we are grateful, despite the complaints."

Sebastian nods. "You are welcome. I still need to learn pack structure and how it all works together, but even I know, thinking of poisoning your Alpha is treason, even if you do not follow through with it. Tricking another into a mate bond is cruel and unfair to anyone, but her thoughts were more sinister than just that.

She desired to control him like a puppet, taking away all his freewill."

"Can you read everyone's thoughts?"

"Here? Yes. Though, as I stated, you have a partial block on yours. It takes work to get past it to read them. Everyone else's is an open book. In my realm, most have learned the art of putting up walls to keep people out."

"So you cannot hear your men's thoughts?"

"No."

"What if there is treason in their thoughts?"

"There is not."

"How can you be sure?"

"Because they have pledged service to me of their own free will, and I trust them."

Caden steps forward. "And how trustworthy are they, exactly?"

Sebastian turns his attention to him. "Trustworthy enough. None of them will not react when you cut your hand to test their resistance to blood. They will harm no one in this realm and will not feed unless granted. My men will only fight to defend themselves and protect me from harm."

"They all defer to you. Why?"

"Because, like you, I am their king, and Zara is my queen."

"Vampires have a king?"

"In our realm, yes. Nero is my right-hand man. I cannot say in yours, but as I am to understand, the vampires here are wild, cruel, and feral. It doesn't sound as if they have a ruler. Our actions thus far should speak for what we are like."

A knock on the door interrupts them, each turning as Bianca rises and opens it. "Stella. Come on in."

Stella hesitates, sensing more in the room. "You know what Bee, I think now is not really a good time."

Bianca looks at her blankly. "Why wouldn't it be?"

"Because you are acting weird. I have to go." Stella backs up a step and runs down the hallway.

Realizing that the witch is running, Madison and Sebastian step out into the hall. Madison tries to cast a binding spell, only to have it deflected, while Sebastian locks his mind onto Stella's. *'You will stop right now and return to the room.'* He watches her stop and turn around, feeling her fight the command that he has issued. Knowing a lot of witches have the power to shrug off a vampire's dominance, he laces his thoughts with charm. *'Stella, I just want to speak with you.'*

'You are a vampire?'

'Indeed. Different from those you know.'

'Why are you here?'

'To talk about the magic items you granted Bianca.'

'You don't plan on killing me?'

'No. I will not kill you.' He focuses and wraps his magic around his words. *'Come back to the room, Stella.'*

Stella nods and saunters back to the room, struggling against the magic forcing her, knowing to step into a room with a vampire meant death. She fights within her mind, trying to recall a spell to portal her out, finding it hidden beneath the vampire's commands. She hesitates, smiling at the vampire and murmurs a few words, fading her from the hallway and into a random bathroom. Peeking out the door and not seeing the vampire, she runs down the hall and out of the school, heading to her car.

'Nicely done Stella, but you can't run forever. I have your presence now. I will find you.' Sebastian turns to Madison at his side. "I could not bring her back, but she's close, because I can feel her mind, although it's fading fast."

"You almost had her. She must be wearing an amulet against binding magic."

"Almost. In our realm, witches have the strength of mind to push aside a vampire's command. Clearly it is the same here, but it was worth a try. Shall we look for her?"

"That will be hard in a school full of students. Ask Bianca where her dorm is. We can check there. Otherwise, she is out of our grasp for now."

Sebastian heads back into the room. "Bianca. Where is Stella's dorm?"

"Oh, she doesn't have one. She lives off campus."

Madison sighs. "Right, that's it then. Unless you can track her."

Sebastian shakes his head. "I cannot, sorry."

Caden looks over at the pair. "Let me guess, she got away?"

"Yes, Gran-pappy. We both used magic to ensnare her. Sebastian almost had her, but she teleported away. For now, take Bianca away and deal with those we have. I'll return the others and meet you at the castle. We will come up with a plan on how to find this witch."

"Deal. Thalia, take us home." The King's guards grab Bianca, and step through the portal, followed by Caden and Thalia, closing the portal after them.

Madison turns to those remaining. "Take hands and let's get going. This differs from stepping through a portal. You might feel a touch dizzy upon landing." She fey-steps back to the office, hearing the gasps from the secretaries as they arrive, noticing more than a few green faces.

Alpha Darian turns to the ladies, smiling at them. "It's alright. Alpha Madison is just returning us."

Madison smiles. "Thanks. I thought they would be gone for an hour. I am used to dealing with packs that allow magic freely."

Alpha Darian glances their way. "They belong to the pack, but Amara is our only witch and doesn't use it around the entire pack. They won't say anything." He turns to his son. "Zach, I will see you at home within the hour. Zara, remember you are all invited into the pack house for dinner tonight. Mathew, Theodore and Julian are staying to play games. I expect Zach and Gia will want to steal their mates away as you are with yours, but they are welcome to stay as well. Sebastian. Thank you for all your help today. I really appreciate it."

Zach chuckles. "You're right about that Dad. I am taking mine to my room!"

Sebastian pulls Zara close at her groan. "Your welcome Alpha Darian. We will talk more at dinner."

Gianna laughs. "I gotta kick my parents out of the suite. Alpha Darian, can you invite my family down for dinner too?"

"Of course Gianna. I will mind-link them as soon as I get home."

Madison laughs. "Alright, let's get you home, Alpha Darian. Sounds like you have plans to make." She takes their hands, along with D'andres and steps to Stormfangs' pack house. Once there, she nods and releases Darian and Amara. "I will see you tomorrow morning. Once I deliver Zara and Sebastian to the castle, I will return and we can sort through your people."

"Perfect. See you tomorrow."

She nods and fades away with D'andre.

D'andre hugs Madison tightly when they arrive in Silvermoon. "Thanks Maddie, I think you just saved my life."

"Anytime. It concerns me, but we will figure it out. Do not hire anyone new in the pack house. I will talk to Thalia about finding you a witch to protect you until we are certain this is over."

"I really appreciate it." He watches her fade before seeking out his Luna.

Twenty

Crowned King

The group heads out to the parking lot, the jovial banter of earlier gone as each of them drift in thoughts to what just happened. A betrayal in the pack. One intent on killing their Alpha and destroying Zach. They clamber into the limo, with Zach and Anthony once more in the front seat. Sebastian speaks to them all when the limo moves.

"Zach, Zara, Gianna. Do not let it eat at you. People will always crave positions of power. They will seek to drag you down and will do whatever is necessary to see it happen. This is why you have guards you trust and friends who will stand by you, no matter what you face." He moves his gaze to the mirror in the front, meeting Zach's gaze. "Anthony is my guard for a reason, Alpha Zach. He will keep you safe. There is no question about that. Poison does not affect him the same as it will you. If you are worried about contamination, let him taste the food first. Right now, his oath is to me, but I will release him from his service to be with you, if that is both your desires. If Mathew, Theodore and Julian mate with she-wolves, they are also welcome to remain as your guards. We can discuss that further when and if it happens. In fact, if they desire to stay here, I have no qualms leaving them under you and your father. You both have proven to me to be honorable men and shifters."

Zach nods, sparing a glance at Anthony. "Thank you, Sebastian."

Sebastian turns his gaze to Gianna. "You will need to make a choice, but I suspect it isn't really a choice. Nero has stood by me for as far back as I can remember. I might be wrong, but I doubt he will leave my side, so that means you need to decide to return with him to my realm." His eyes travel to Nero, catching the slight nod. "As I explained to Zara, I have hired witches to realm hop me here. I will maintain their services, no matter the cost, so that Zara might visit her family as often as she can. But I cannot give you a time and how often that will be. It pains me that she is forced to choose, so I desire to make it as easy a transition as I can. The same goes for you. If you return, you will have the same options as Zara."

Gianna nods, looking up at Nero. "I am staying with Nero and Zara. I decided the second I saw him at fight practice."

"That will make Zara happy. Now, I know it was a rough day. Treason and betrayal within your own ranks is a bitter herb to drink. You need to look at those that stand with you, that support you. Those numbers are far greater than the ones that seek to tear you down. And before you go there, every tribe, pack, clan, community, even our resistance, and your rogues have someone striving to be on top. The thing to remember is, you learn from it, and you continue to push forward, bettering those around you."

Zara smiles and snuggles into his arms. "Bitter pill to swallow. You are the bestest Seb."

"Pill?"

"I will show you when we get home. Our herbs and medicine come in pills now."

Sebastian caresses her cheek and tightens his hold on her. "Your world is so strange."

"I know, but it's normal for us."

Forty-five minutes later, they arrive back at the pack house. They pile out of the car and collect their purchases from the trunk. Zach agrees to meet them after he parks the limo and talks to his dad. Gianna stays with Nero, returning to Zara's house to watch a movie. Zara tells them to store their stuff in their rooms as she runs into the office where her father sits working on his computer.

"Your home earlier than I expected, Zare-bear."

"Yes, we finished shopping and had an incident. So if it's alright with you, we are hijacking the living room for a movie."

"Incident? Are you alright? Is Sebastian alright?"

"Yes Papa. We are all good. It was Jeremy's sister. She was planning to betray the pack. You should talk to Alpha Darian about it."

Kieran rises from his chair, concern etched in his features. "That's not good, Zare-bear. I will head over to the pack house now and see you there later for dinner. Enjoy the movie."

"Thanks Papa." She heads to her room and collects her blanket along with the two bottles of wine they bought, bounding back down the stairs to the living room where the rest are getting settled. She drops it on the couch and carries the wine to the kitchen, where Gianna and Anthony are making popcorn. "Learning how to use the air popper Anthony?" Placing them on the counter, she rummages through the drawers. Finding the wine opener, she opens a bottle of red for Sebastian.

"Yes, my queen." His eyes focus on the gadget in question. "You have the most interesting magic things."

Zara giggles and pats his back gently, reaching for the glasses that are above him. "We do not have as many as the pack house, which you will see later. But the air popper is a necessity around here."

Gianna laughs, pulling the melted butter out of the microwave. "Damn straight it is. Zara and I live on the stuff."

"That's right." She pours out a glass for Sebastian and Nero and sets them on the tray. "Anthony, do you guys drink wine? I never saw you drink it at the castle."

"Yes, my queen. But I like that soda better."

Zara laughs. "It is good, isn't it? What about the others?"

"Bring the bottle in and let them decide." He pulls three glasses down and hands them to her.

Placing them on the tray, she opens the fridge and pulls out sodas for the group of them. She carefully carries the tray back to the living room and places it on the table, followed by Gianna and Anthony carrying the bowls of popcorn. "There is wine for Seb and Nero. Julian, Theodore, Mathew, if you want some, help yourself. Otherwise, I have soda for everyone." Her eyes lock on Mathew, looking through the movies, and moves to his side. "Nope, I'm picking. We are watching A Knight's Tale. It's one of the better ones that represents the Ren Faire we were talking about, even if it's not quite the same." She pulls the case out and hands it to him. Grabbing the remotes, she clicks both the player and TV on, along with the surround sound. *'Zach, Eta?'*

'Running there now Zara.'

'The doors unlocked.' Turning to the others settling onto the couches and tugging her blanket out from beneath them, she giggles and sits on the floor. "Zach's on his way."

Sebastian sighs, and sits down next to her. "You are damaging my image, my queen, having me sit on the floor with you."

Zara laughs, spreading the blanket over the two of them. "With who? They all know who their king is. Besides, if it was their mate wanting to sit on the floor, they would be here too."

Gianna settles in next to Zara and whispers. "I am making Nero do the same!" She tugs the blanket to spread it over her and Nero. "Na ah, you need to share the blankie."

Sebastian laughs as Nero sits on the other side of Gianna, who spreads the comforter over the four of them. "I can see why you and Zara are friends. She made us sit on the floor last night, too."

"Well, it's the best seat in the house!"

Zach steps into the house and closes the door after him, squeezing on the couch between Anthony and Theodore. "Sorry I am late. Did I miss anything?"

"Just getting out of making popcorn, but your mate took over for you."

Zach chuckles, his eyes drifting over Anthony as he drapes an arm over his shoulders. "Good to know. Movie time then!"

Zara snuggles into Sebastian and presses play on the remote, each of them becoming lost in the world of jousting knights and the medieval era. After the movie ends, they clean up the living room and head over to the pack house, discussing comparisons to Sebastian's world. Theodore and Mathew focus on the music, eager to hear more and wondering where they can find it. Zara laughs. "There are hundreds of thousands of songs out there. How about after dinner, we take you to the music room for dancing?"

Sebastian pulls her close and whispers in her ear. "Not for too long, I hope. We have plans."

Zara blushes. "Nope, just for a few songs."

"Good."

At the pack house, the six of them stop, with Zach and Gianna turning in confusion.

Zara smiles. "They have to be invited in, Zach. From what I have researched, vampires cannot enter a house uninvited."

"But most of the pack house is public domain."

"For wolves, yes, but you and your family still own it."

Zach nods. "You are all invited in."

Sebastian offers a slight bow. "Thank you for trusting us in your home, as Zara and her family have."

"Zara has always been an excellent judge of character and since she's mated with you, it means you are a good person, despite being vampires. I trust her and therefore trust you. On top of that, Anthony is my mate, so even if I had issues, I would need to deal with them fast."

Sebastian chuckles. "Your acceptance is better than someone else's when we first met."

Zara blushes and mumbles beneath her breath. "I would rather not discuss it."

Zach arches a brow. "You know I am going to ask about it later, right Zara?"

"Yes, and so is Gianna. I can tell by her expression. I already told you I was angry at him." She scowls at Sebastian. "Thanks a lot."

"You're welcome, my love."

"Yes, but it sounds like there is more to the story than you told us."

"There isn't. I yelled and screamed at him and called him names. He kicked me out of the library and locked me in our cell downstairs."

Gianna places a hand on her lips. "Oh, my!"

Zara glares at her friend, rolling her eyes. "You would too if you didn't know them. I would like to point out, you both accepted them on my word. You're weelll... commme!"

Gianna and Zach laugh as they enter the dining hall, where all their families are already sitting and chatting with each other. Their talk diminishes when the group enters.

"Alpha, Luna." Zara and Gianna bow and bare their necks momentarily and move to sit next to their parents.

Alpha Darian and Luna Willow watch their son, seeing the happiness in his expression as he walks hand in hand with Anthony. Gamma Luca and his wife, Paulette, skim over their daughter, their eyes narrowing on Nero.

Kieran nudges them gently. "Get to know him before you judge him. Nero is one hell of a guy and Sebastian's Beta."

Luca hisses softly. "He's a vampire. They all are."

Gianna scowls at her father. "Dad! He's my mate. Deal with it."

Darian sighs, understanding his Gamma's point of view. "Yes, they are. But they saved Zach's and my life today. They allowed Kieran and Zara to live when they arrived unexpectedly in their realm. Luca, you saw the fight against Jeremy. Sebastian had every right to kill him, but didn't. He also did not react to the blood flowing from Jeremy's chest. What other vampire do you know that can resist fresh blood?"

Sebastian settles beside Zara, his eyes accessing Gianna's parents, reading their thoughts and feeling the fear within them. He mind-links Nero. *'You are gonna have your work cut out with those two, Nero.'*

Nero sits next to him, rolling his eyes at his king's comments. *'You are just happy that you didn't have to suffer alone in winning the wolves over.'*

Sebastian chuckles, drawing the room's attention. "Sorry, you have your mind-link. We have ours. Nero was just reminding me of my courtship with Zara and how much of a chall... delight it was to win her over."

Zara scowls at Sebastian. "That's right. You better have switched those words, Seb."

Sebastian kisses her cheek. "I loved you the minute you stepped into my library, my dear."

"I am sure you did." She mutters under her breath.

Nero chuckles. "Perhaps not the minute, but definitely close to that lassie." He turns to the others at the table. "Alpha Darian, Luna Willow. It's a pleasure to see you again." He winks at Kieran and Lila before turning his attention to Gianna's parents. "Greeting Gamma Luca, Lady Paulette. Gianna speaks highly of you. Most especially your understanding nature regarding the mate bond. I want you to know that Gianna will be treated like a princess, and I will spoil her as she deserves. She is someone I would forfeit my life for to keep her safe. King Sebastian, has already stated that he intends to keep the witches that sent us here, so that the ladies may visit as often as the witches can send them back. I will admit, it is something we still need to discuss more fully because I am dedicated to my king. I also want you to know the witches will call the six of us back, plus one. Gianna and Zach were unexpected, so I will need to return for her and I cannot say what that time frame is, because I do not know. We are in unknown territory, so to speak; working with witches, trusting witches, leaving the kingdom for ten days to realm hop. This was a trial run for us. Who knows what we might find upon our return, but I will say this. Nothing I can foresee will stop me from returning for Gianna. I will find a way, just as my king did with Zara, our queen."

Kieran chokes on his drink and places it down, sending a look Nero's way while Lila pats his back gently. "Nero. What are you doing?"

"Just trying to alleviate the fears that they have roaming around in their head."

Paulette glances at her daughter, knowing her well enough to know she is seething inside. "Nero, you need to understand. You are a vampire, taking our daughter away. We've despised your kind since we were children, long before we even knew why. Our parents, and their parents before them, taught us that hatred. It's not something we can easily let go of in a single day."

"I understand. All I ask is that you give us a chance, as Zara and Kieran did. You will find we are not much different from you."

Paulette takes her husband's hand, her thumb rubbing circles over the top to soothe him. "Luca and I will try, but there are no guarantees."

"Thank you. I am certain that Gianna appreciates that."

Alpha Darian sighs, reading the tension in the air, suspecting this is going to be a long dinner. "Right, on that note. Let's bring in the food." He mind-links the maids as platters of food arrive in the dining hall. Throughout dinner, the tensions dissipate as Luca and Paulette see the vampires eating actual food, just as they do, curiosity driving them to ask more questions. By dinner's end, the air is relaxed with a teasing nature returning to the lot of them.

After dinner, Zara, Zach and Gianna drag everyone to the dance hall. Zach moves to the stereo and sets the music to play. Each of them teaches the other their own styles of dance, laughter filling the air as the group of them boogies on the dance floor.

An hour later, Sebastian walks with Zara back to the house, an arm draped over her shoulder, drifting in their own thoughts, with Sebastian listening to hers as well.

Zara stops to look up at him, her hand caressing his cheek lightly. "I love you Sebastian. I never expected to, but I really do."

Sebastian leans in and kisses her lips tenderly. "I love you too, Zara. Thank you for today. We saw so many sights, but spending it with you was the best part. How I have missed you these past few months."

"I missed you too, Sebastian." Zara hugs him tightly, holding him beneath the evening sky. She smiles and steps back, taking his hand. "Come, we have more time to spend together... Alone."

"As you wish, my queen."

She laughs and pulls him to the house, leading him upstairs to her bedroom. Zara moves to her computer and boots it up, picking a playlist for them and turns it on.

Sebastian closes the door behind them, smiling at the music in the room. "This

I will miss in my realm."

"So will I." Zara steps up to Sebastian. "May I have this dance?"

He bows and takes her hand, kissing the back of it. "You may."

Zara steps into arms, as his scent envelopes her. She rests her head on his chest, swaying to the music, safe and content, her thoughts drifting back to the last day at the castle.

Sebastian chuckles at her thoughts, his hands moving slowly over her back, as he whispers in her ear. "My queen, I can hear those thoughts."

"I know Seb, but I want this dance first."

He tightens his hold on her, swaying with her, resting his chin on her head, allowing the peace of the night to take over. When the song ends, he steps back and kisses her gently, feeling her soft gasp against his lips. He picks her up and carries her a few feet to the bed, placing her gently on it. He settles in beside her, studying her face, his fingers trailing lightly over her. "Thank you Zara, and Ember, for allowing me to win your heart."

Zara looks up at him and blushes, becoming lost in the depths of his blue eyes. "You had it from day one, Sebastian. I was just foolish."

"No, I had Embers. Yours I had to work for." Sebastian kisses her lightly, peppering kisses along her jaw to her ear, nibbling on it. "Now, we are alone and I intend to take full advantage of this."

Zara sighs, feeling the flames within from his touch as she succumbs to the passion he creates within her.

Later that night, Kieran and his family, as well as Mathew, Theodore and Julian, return to the house. Kieran pauses in the doorway, and tilts his head, catching the soft stable breathing of his daughter upstairs. "Seems like at least my daughter is asleep. Let's follow suit. Jayden, Jenson, please be quiet and do not wake your sister." Watching Lila lead them upstairs, he turns to the others. "Are you watching movies tonight?"

Mathew nods. "If that's alright with you?"

"Let me just make sure the surround sound is off." Kieran moves over to the remotes, checking the settings and adjusting them accordingly. "Did you need food or drinks?"

"No, we are good, thank you." Mathew nods and moves to the movie case, while Julian and Theodore settle onto the couch.

Kieran nods, "See you in the morning then." He heads up the stairs, pausing at Zara's door. "Night Sebastian. I hope you had a good night."

"Indeed, the whole day was special. Pleasant dreams Kieran."

"Thank you." He continues down to his room, seeing his wife already curled up in bed with her book. He crawls in next to her, kissing her gently. "What a day. Have I told you how much I love you today?"

Lila rests a hand on his chest. "You have. Several times."

"Good. Now, this old body needs to sleep." He drapes his arm over his wife's lap, and drifts off to sleep.

Around three in the morning, Alpha Darian groans as a mink-link interrupts his sleep.

'Alpha Darian, we have a problem!'

'What is it?' He glances over at the clock, grimacing at the time flashing on it.

'Alpha, there are vampires collecting at our border, not like Zara's mate and his guards. These are the frothing at the mouth kind. Our kind.'

'What side?'

'North.'

'Alpha, vampires at the eastern border.'

'West here too Alpha.'

He rubs his eyes and pushes himself up. Glancing down at his wife, he slips silently from the bed and dresses quickly. *'Shit, what are they doing?'*

'Besides growling and grabbing at their heads, they are kneeling. You might even say, bowing.'

'Wait, they are not attacking?'

'No. Initially, they looked like they would, but they aren't.'

'Refrain from attacking this moment. If they do, protect our lands and take them down.'

'Alpha, I don't think you realize how many are out here. They outnumber us ten to one on the north side.'

'About the same, if not more on the east.'

'Still gathering in the west, but if we start now, we might hold out a while.'

'No, don't attack. I think it's tied to Sebastian and his crew.'

'Why would Zara's mate have something to do with this? I thought he was trustworthy.'

'Because he's their king. Or at least, he is in their realm. I'm uncertain how it crosses over here.'

'FUCK, are you serious.... Sorry, Alpha.'

'It's all good. Luna Willow is looking into his background as we speak, but he is a Darkholme, the first of the first of vampires. His lineage is pure, much like the Lycan line. I have a suspicion his power is drawing them here. We will find out tomorrow when Zara and Sebastian head over to Whispering Pines. If they follow, it's tied to him. If not, we are in for a world of hurt.'

'Damn. I hope they follow, but I also hope they don't. That's the Lycan King's land. We don't want a war on his borders, especially if it comes from us, Alpha.'

Darian leaves the pack house running, heading to his Beta's house. 'I know. I will speak to Alpha Madison about this in the morning.'

'They still look like they are bowing, but they could be plotting. Never really interacted with vamps before, other than to kill on sight.'

'I understand. This is unprecedented and I am in unfamiliar territory with how to handle it. Kieran's house isn't suited for a full scale invasion if they mean him harm. Heading there now.'

'Won't he be asleep?'

'Yes, but the vampires won't be and it's their king I wish to speak with.' Darian arrives and knocks on the door lightly. "Sebastian. I know you can hear my thoughts. I need to speak to you. Outside please."

Sebastian sighs at Darian's request, glancing down at Zara curled up against him. He caresses her lightly and slips from the bed, turning at her murmur of dismay. "I shouldn't be long, my queen." Kissing her forehead to sooth her, he dresses and glides quietly down the stairs. His men suddenly stand in his presence and follow him to the door. Opening it, he looks over at Darian, reading the concern in both his expression and thoughts. "Alpha Darian. How can I help you?"

"I need you to come with me. We have vampires collecting at our borders."

"Strange. Why do you think this is?"

"Because you are their king?"

"I doubt it. This is not my realm, therefore, they are not my people."

"Sebastian, I don't have an explanation. My warriors have linked me and said they are grasping at their heads and bowing."

"Let me call Nero and Anthony." He reaches out into their thoughts. 'Sorry for disrupting your evenings, but I need you two. Appears we have a disturbance at the pack's borders.' He smiles as their replies echo in his mind. "They will be here shortly."

"How shortly?"

Thirty seconds later, Nero and Anthony appear at his side, each offering a bow to them both. "Sire, Alpha."

"Damn, I want your speed, Sebastian."

Sebastian chuckles. "I highly doubt you will ever get it, Alpha Darian."

"I know, but it doesn't stop me from desiring it. Come, let's see what's happening. You can clearly keep up if I shift?"

"Yes."

Darian nods and shifts into a large, deep brown wolf with golden eyes. He gives a nod and bolts into the woods, heading to the eastern borders, being that they are the closest. Sebastian and his guards follow, easily keeping pace with the wolf. Within the hour, they arrive at the borders, slowing as they spot the patrols crouching in the woods. Approaching them, his eyes take in the vampires, exactly as described.

Sebastian steps forward, studying the vampires before them. Pale, gaunt, some of their clothing in tatters, others barely dressed. Each resembles more of a wildling than a human, with eyes that glow in the darkness. Vicious fangs protrude, matching the claws on each hand. He can hear the drone of their thoughts in his mind, not coherent like his people, but clearly having some connection with him. Focusing inward and reading their thoughts, he realizes rather suddenly that most revolve around impulse, rather than cohesive thought. Speaking quietly to Darian and Nero. "They are not mine. I can read their thoughts as clearly as I can yours, but it feels like they are trying to connect with a mind-link. There is a sea of voices, all blending together, and I cannot separate them like I can with my clan. Even your mind-links between your pack members are clearer than what I am hearing from them."

"So what do we do? These are creatures that kill and destroy. Ones that deliberately create chaos."

"To be honest, I am uncertain. They are unlike any of our kind in my realm." Sebastian turns to a few that are approaching, holding his hand up to halt them. "Stop. Who do you serve?"

The closest grasps his head, rolling on the ground. "You!"

"No, I am not from this realm, therefore I am not your king. Who is your king?"

"Yooouuu."

Sebastian glances at Nero, who shakes his head. "Sire, perhaps they don't have a ruler and that is why they are here. They feel your power."

"No, they have a ruler. Someone controls them. That is why they grasp at their heads. They feel my power and it's conflicting with the one controlling them."

Nero glances their way. "Their sires?"

Sebastian's brows furrow as he turns to Darian. "I am assuming your vampires have sires?"

"Sires?"

"Ones that create them. I have a sire and I am the sire of any I create. Normally, you would automatically swear allegiance to your sire, but that is not always the case."

"Are you the sire of your guards?"

"No, I have only ever created one. These, though, are fighting something within their minds to be here." Sebastian turns to the wildlings again, focusing on the one before him. "You will disperse and leave this territory. Return to your home. The people in these lands are beneath my protection. You will not feed on them unless they grant consent. That means you will not command, dominate, coerce or force them. If it is granted willingly, you WILL take only what's necessary and let them live. After feeding, you will respect their boundaries and care for them until they can care for themselves. Then you will let them walk away. Is that understood?"

"Argh, how are we to survive with these rules?"

"The same way we do. With respect and permission. If you do not wish to abide by these rules, then you feed on the animals that I can smell around here. But as with the mortals, you do NOT kill them. Take only enough to appease the hunger."

"But sire."

"There are no buts. If you deem me to be your king, these are my demands. Disobey them and I will end you. Spread the word to your clan and the surrounding clans." Sebastian watches as they nod and slink back into the darkness of the woods.

Darian looks at Sebastian in shock. "Is it really going to be that easy?"

Sebastian shakes his head. "Not likely. Something is causing conflict in their mind, but I cannot determine what it is. The best way to know is to find a pattern from the previous kills and see if it continues. If it stops, then for how long and will it continue when I return to my realm in seven days? Another thing pointing towards the fact that we really need to find the other half of that scroll."

'Alpha, north borders here. The vamps are leaving.'

'Same with the west, Alpha.'

'Good. Sebastian commanded them down.'

'Does he rule them too?'

'It's a working theory. We won't know until we do some research. Just keep an eye out and look for them to return in seven days.'

'Understood.'

Darian turns to Sebastian. "Thanks. That could have been a bloodbath if they attacked."

"I am afraid to say it, but it's still possible. Their minds are feral, and wild, as you stated. When the witches call me back, it could drive them more insane than they already are and the blame could fall here. I will send Anthony back as soon as I can to protect you if we have not solved the prophecy. Perhaps some others as well."

"Thanks. Come, let's head home."

They travel back at a slower pace, talking about the differences in the vampires and how to combat them. At Kieran's' door, Darian bids them good night and returns to the pack house.

Sebastian turns to Nero and Anthony. "Thank you for coming. You may return to where you came from. You need not stay here."

They both bow, running to catch up with Darian, heading back to their mates in the pack house.

Sebastian heads into Zara's house, leaving Mathew, Julian and Theodore in the living room. He slips quietly into her room, only to find her curled up with a yellow bear in her arms, watching him. "Where did you go?"

Sebastian sits on the bed and caresses her cheek. "You should still be sleeping, my queen."

"I missed you here in bed. It woke me up."

"Your Alpha needed help. It seems the vampires of your world are collecting at your borders."

The warm flush of her cheeks pale as she crawls into his arms. "What does that mean?"

"I am uncertain. Some part of them recognized me as their king, but they struggled within their mind to accept it. I placed a command on them to stop feeding on the mortals of this world. Alpha Darian will watch for it during the next week. My concern is when I return home with you, and what will happen? If angered, they could turn on your pack. I am tempted to leave Mathew, Julian and Theodore here just to be certain they have protection, but I have no way to convey that to the witches calling us back."

"Would they stay without you? They are your guards."

"I will need to ask. I can only hope we solve the prophecy and won't need to worry about it."

Zara wraps her arms around him and tightens her hold on him. "I hope so too. I am sorry I wasn't able to find anything before you got here."

"Shh Zara, we discussed this. It's been hidden from me for hundreds of years. I wasn't expecting you to have it solved in a few months."

"I know Seb. I am just impatient."

Sebastian chuckles. "Indeed, you are."

Zara swats him. "You didn't need to agree so readily."

He tilts her chin and looks into her eyes. "I am not going to lie to you, my queen, even on something as simple as that. Trust is very important to me."

Zara murmurs, feeling herself drawn to his dark blue eyes. "I know Seb. I... "

He kisses her gently. "Shh my love. We will face everything together. Now, get more sleep. I don't want a grumpy wolf in the morning beating on my Beta."

Zara laughs and nudges him. "That's right, I still need to do that." She moves to lie down, waiting until he does and curls up in his arms, yawning happily at the security she feels wrapped in his embrace. "I love you."

"I love you too."

Twenty-One

Red Haze

The next morning, Zara wakes to the alarm, muttering under her breath against Sebastian. "One would think that being the Beta's daughter, I would have some sway in convincing my Papa that training can start an hour later."

He smiles. "I suspect you do, but I bet the Alpha has more sway with training time. You need to convince Zach to speak with his father."

Zara snuggles in closer, letting Sebastian's scent wrap around her. "He tried. He failed."

Chuckling as he draws her close. "I see. Is this something that I will have to look forward to in my realm?"

Zara grumbles against him. "If you are a morning person like the rest of the pack, yes."

"I don't sleep as you do, my love. Time is of little importance to me."

Muttering beneath her breath. "Then I guess it may or may not. Depends on when you wake me."

"I will keep that in mind."

An hour later, Zara stands in the training ring, facing Nero, her eyes studying him intently. Noticing that he is now sporting the training attire that they purchased in town, thinking it doesn't quite suit him. "Did you have a good night, Nero?"

"Yes, my queen."

"Aren't you going to ask me if I had a good night, Nero?"

He winks at her. "No, my queen. I know you did. I can read it in your thoughts."

Zara growls and launches at him, dragging him down to the ground. She feels him slip from her grip as he rolls away with a chuckle, returning to his feet quickly.

She follows, unrelenting in her attacks against him. "That's what got you into trouble in the first place, Nero."

"I know my queen. And I will admit, until you close your thoughts, it will continue to happen."

She dodges a few of his attacks while attempting to strike him, not realizing that a few of the others were watching the fight intently. Attempting to sweep his feet, she mutters beneath her breath as he jumps over it, feeling her own body being pulled over him and dropped to the ground. She kicks at his ankles, watching him dance away as she returns to her feet. She circles around him warily,

Sebastian sits with Julian, Theodore and Mathew, who talk between themselves about the fighting in the rings, comparing it to their own style, learning the differences. He lifts his gaze to a she-wolf heading his way, reading by her thoughts that she is on the prowl, wondering which one of the three guards she is going for. Distaste fills him as she sits down near him, placing a hand on his knee.

"Aren't you the handsome one?"

Zara catches movement out of the corner of her eyes, feeling a possessive rage flow through her blood at Megan's hand on Sebastian's knee, enough so that she missed the fact that Nero launched at her and now had her pinned to the ground. She hisses softly. "Let me go!"

"So you can rip a she-wolf apart, I think not. Nothing should distract you in the ring."

Zara growls deep in her chest and heaves against Nero, pushing him off to the side, rolling to get away from him. "You can't stop me, Nero. He's mine and everyone knows it."

"I can and I will." Nero grabs her wrist and locks onto it, dragging her back into the fight. "You're right. Sebastian is yours, lassie. Do not let another she-wolf push your buttons."

Zara slams her fist into Nero's wrist, causing his grip to loosen. She quickly scrambles back to her feet, only to feel his hands snake around her ankles, pulling her back to the ground. Lashing out, she attempts to kick herself free, finding Nero once more on top, straddling her and pinning her in place.

"Breathe lassie."

"Let me go, Nero." Zara growls. Her fists clench the dirt in her hands as she fights against the pin Nero has placed on her.

"I can't do that, my queen. Trust your mate." Nero releases some of his aura, forcing her into a calm state.

Zara slumps in the dirt, fighting the frustration within. "I do, Nero. I know he loves me and I love him. It's her. She's free with her body, especially if the other half is mated."

Sebastian picks up Megan's hand and removes it from his leg, keeping his gaze pinned to the fight in the arena. "Please refrain from touching that which is not yours."

"I am just trying to welcome you into the pack."

Iciness fills Sebastian's expression. "Do not presume to lie to me. It is disgraceful that you seek to steal me from Zara. It won't work."

"That is not true."

"It is. You are jealous that Zara landed a person of power. You aim to break us up by making it look as if I desire you. I can read your thoughts, Megan, and I am not interested. Neither are my men."

"But..."

"No buts." Sebastian leans into her, his face impassive, his midnight blue eyes flashing red for a brief second. A soft but deadly voice, filled with power, causes everyone in the area to shudder and submit. "I want you to understand this, Megan, so listen well. Zara is my mate and will rule by my side as QUEEN! NO ONE is getting between us. Not you. Not Jeremy. Not Anyone! I WILL fight anyone that challenges that and protect her with my life. So will my men. Is that clear?"

"Yes, sir." Megan bares her neck in submission.

"Good, Now leave. I was enjoying watching my Beta get beaten by my queen until you distracted her. It is in your best interest to avoid me for the foreseeable future." He watches Megan bolt from the arena, catching everyone in the vicinity looking their way in shock, including Alpha Darian and Alpha Madison

Sebastian's men chuckle beside him. "I think you made your point, sire, aura and all."

"I thought I made my point yesterday. Clearly it was not enough." He returns his gaze back to Nero, reading the defeat in Zara's body, feeling her anger and frustration along their bond. *'I love you, my queen, even if you let Nero beat you.'*

'I did NOT let... Arg Sebastian!'

Mathew follows his gaze to Zara. "It was. That she-wolf believes the world revolves around her. Hence her attempt. She will not do so again. In fact, I think you scared her enough that she won't try on anyone's mate again."

"Even better."

Madison stands with Darian, watching the sparring between Zara and Nero, reading their movements, knowing the vampire is pulling his punches and holding back. "She's good, Darian, but the vampire is pulling his punches, so she's not good enough."

Darian chuckles. "That's his queen he is fighting. I would pull my punches too, especially since I have seen Sebastian fight. I would not want to get on his bad side by accidentally hurting his mate. Jeremy, Bianca's brother, challenged him to a mate duel, and Sebastian took him down in less than ten seconds. Anthony, the one fighting my son, took me down in the same amount of time and he wasn't even paying attention."

Madison's brows furrow. "What do you mean?"

"I was talking to Sebastian at how fast he diffused Jeremy while Anthony was in the stands speaking to Zach. I commented that I hoped Anthony could fight, and he stated he was a guard for a reason. He dared me to attack him. We were in the rings. Anthony was standing about where they are now, not even facing me. Before I even connected with Sebastian, I was flat on my back by Anthonys hand. At which point, he informed me that if I was a genuine threat, all his guards would have shredded me. They might be passive, but they are beyond any skill I have seen as a fighter."

"Interesting. If you allow it, I might need to return and face one, learn their moves."

"You have my permission, but that's on them." Darian turns his head, feeling the power rolling off the king, and Megan slipping away from the ring. "When Zara and Kieran arrived in their realm, they killed three of Sebastian's men before being defeated. Sebastian spared the two of them. Even granting them access to live in his castle. They are unlike any vampires I have known and have more honor than a lot of wolves out there, including some of my own, apparently."

Madison smiles, placing a hand on Darian's shoulder. "There will always be wolves seeking power, not caring who they step on, or the cost. Deal with them efficiently, then step away. They are not worth your time. Focus on the good in your pack."

"I know...I have good wolves. The vampires are just pushing the buttons of the bad ones without even trying."

"That would happen no matter their race, be it elves, dragons, or faeries. It's an unknown entity. The power that comes from being different and some seek to claim it. Think back to before you met your mate. How many she-wolves vied for Luna position? How many tried to lure you off the mate path?"

Darian smiles "There were a few. How about you?"

"Some, but I will admit, most were ones my mom tried to set me up with. She wanted me to settle with a nice wolf when my heart was set on a dragon. She just didn't know it."

Darian laughs at her comment. "I know that situation very well. Come, let's go talk to Zara and Sebastian before they both kill Nero."

Nero relaxes his hold on Zara, chuckling. "Sebastian only has eyes on one body... Make that two. Though I doubt he desires mine quite like yours. I am currently getting the look for straddling you." He rolls off her and lies in the dirt beside her. "I will admit, these clothes make it much easier to fight."

"It's not really you, Nero."

"What do you mean, lassie?"

"Those clothes. You have too much class for that style. Like Sebastian. Both of you are suit and tie men."

Nero chuckles, propping himself up on his elbow. "Was that a compliment, lassie?"

Zara blushes and mutters under her breath. "No, it was just stating facts."

"I think it was." Laughter escapes him as he stands. He reaches down to help her up. "Come, enough fighting."

Zara swats at his hand before grasping it to pull herself up. "You are so bad, Nero. How is it possible that I like you?"

Nero winks. "Because I am both your mate's best friend and your best friend's mate. That's one hundred percent power right there, my queen."

Zara laughs, hugging Nero tightly. "Yes... Yes it is." Her eyes land on Alpha Darian and Alpha Madison approaching the rings. She steps away and bows to them both. "Alphas."

"Zara. Madison is here to take you to Whispering Pines."

"If I may, I would like a shower and need to say goodbye to my family."

"Of course. Take your time. We will be here analyzing the fighting."

"Thank you." She turns and runs toward Sebastian, who is approaching them.

"Seb, I need to say goodbye to my parents. I will grab our bags."

"I will join you."

"You will?"

"Yes, because I know you are planning to have a shower and I aim to join you."

Zara blushes deeply and looks at the ground. "Yes, well, I need to be presentable when meeting the King and Nero dragged me through the dirt."

Sebastian places a hand beneath her chin and lifts it gently. "Zara. My queen. I love you. Only you. Keep your attention on who you are fighting in the ring and not on who is annoying me."

"I know Sebastian. I just saw red."

Sebastian draws her into a tight hug, allowing his aura and bond to soothe and comfort her. "You are mine. I am never letting you go."

Zara clings to him tightly. "I understand... Just sometimes I doubt this is real."

"You don't need to doubt yourself. It's very much real. Now come, I wish for another shower before we leave."

Zara giggles. "You know there will be showers at the castle. Every house has them."

"But not every house has your scent through it."

"Sebastian! I see where Nero gets it from. Come, I doubt Alpha Madison will want to wait long."

Thirty minutes later, Zara and Sebastian approach the rings, seeing Madison fighting against both Nero and Anthony with Zach and Gianna on the sidelines watching. Moving over to Alpha Darian's side, Zara stands and watches the fight, seeing Madison holding her own against the two. "She's skilled."

Darian chuckles. "She's an Ironwood elite. She better be."

Sebastian turns to Darian. "What's an Ironwood elite?"

"They are the best warriors around and bring dread to any that hears their name."

"So she can take a hit then?"

Darian turns to Sebastian and studies him. "Damn, you are not saying what I think you are saying."

"I am just asking a question."

Darian's shoulder slump, his eyes drifting to the rings. "Let's see it then."

"Anthony or Nero?"

"Let's go with Anthony."

Sebastian nods, his mind reaching out to his warriors. *'Nero, bow and leave the ring. Anthony, no mercy, but do no harm.'*

Nero stops and bows to Madison. "It's been lovely sparring with you, Alpha Madison. Sebastian has requested I bow out. Be warned, the rules of the fight just changed."

"What do you mean by that exactly? Alpha Darian?"

"Apparently, Alpha Madison, the two were going easy on you. It's up to you whether you accept the challenge of my son's mate. No supernatural abilities. Just an all out sparring match. First one pinned, wins."

Madison smiles, looking over at Anthony. "I'm in."

Anthony glances over at Sebastian, catching his subtle nod. "I am too."

"Alright then. On my count. Three, two, one and go."

Anthony watches Madison circle the ring, having sparred with her and understanding her movements. He steps to the left, quickly pivots as she dodges and throws a punch. He grasps her extended upper arm, his other going to her waist, swiftly taking her off her feet and dropping her on the ground. Twisting the arm behind her, he presses down in between her shoulders, pinning her in place.

"Fuuuuccckk." Darian mutters beneath his breath, starting at the counter on the pin. "Ten, Nine, eight.."

"Bloody Hell." Madison growls into the dirt, feeling Somoko rising to the surface and pushes her down. *'No Somo. Down, girl.'*

'Let me take him, Maddie. I know I can.'

'Somo. It's a sparring match. We lost. Quickly. Darian warned us.'

'Next time Maddie, we beat the ten second mark.'

Madison laughs, drawing a confused look from Anthony. "Anthony, I give. You can release me."

"Not until the counter is done, Alpha Madison."

Madison nods, remaining still until Darian announces the match over. She feels the pressure release on her and rolls over, offering a hand to Anthony, who takes it and pulls her to her feet. "Nice match. Somo has informed me that next time, we will last longer than ten seconds. Be prepared."

Anthony chuckles. "I heard. My king said no mercy. Sorry."

"Dammit. I would hate to know what you fight like outside the ring. I would like to request that you come train with my men."

"If my king accepts, then I would be happy to."

"Great." Madison brushes herself off and turns to Sebastian. "No mercy, huh? Not playing fair with the wolf and dragon?"

Sebastian smiles, humor dancing in his eyes. "Correct. Heard this rumor you were the best of the best. That Ironwood elites are the most feared warriors in the land. My guards are in mine. I wanted a comparison."

"Bullshit. You wanted a win. You got it. Next time, Somo is coming out to play. I might last twenty seconds then."

Darian laughs. "Good to know I was not the only one trounced by his men."

Sebastian chuckles. "You're right, I wanted a win. I look forward to seeing Somo fight."

Madison tries to scowl at him. "Perhaps I shall challenge you to the duel, then."

He bows. "You may join Alpha Darian then, for he, too, has issued a challenge. Two on one, you might stand a chance."

Nero coughs softly. "Or not. Oh Look, there's Gianna! I think I need to go speak with my mate."

Madison's eyes follow Nero to the ring. "What did he mean by that?"

"Just that, I am king for a reason."

"Even a king can be defeated." Recalling her fight against their own Lycan king.

"Indeed, they can. I look forward to the challenge, Alpha Madison." Sebastian winks at her. "I will state this. My feet will remain firmly planted on the ground, unlike your kings."

Madison gasps. "How?"

Darian snaps his gaze between them. "Excuse me?"

Madison mutters beneath her breath. "The King and I might have had a disagreement at one point in time."

A cunning smile crosses Sebastian's lips. "A disagreement is an understatement, but your secret is mostly safe with me. You forget, I can read thoughts. Yours do have a partial block but they went right to it, clear as can be."

"Right, on that note. I should get you to the castle and said king. I would appreciate it if you didn't breathe a word about this conversation to him. It's one of those, what happened in that room, stays in that room."

"Understood."

She turns to Darian. "I will bring them back in about five days, though I might be back earlier to fight with those remaining. Depends on if I can convince Lucian or my parents to look after my pup for a few hours." Her gaze shifts to Sebastian. "If that's alright with you."

"My men will be under Alpha Darian's command for the duration of my absence. I see no reason they cannot train you."

"Thank you. Zara, are you ready to go?"

Zara glances between them all, her curiosity eating at her about Madison's fight with the King, knowing no one challenged him but not daring to ask. She offers her hand to Madison, understanding the drill from her travels before.

Madison smiles, giving a nod to Darian, takes Sebastian's hand, and fades from the compound, landing in a grand hall in a castle. She releases them and turns, seeing her Gran-pappy sitting on a throne.

"You're late Madison."

"Gran-pappy! Sorry, I got into the training ring and had my ass handed to me."

Caden coughs. "Excuse me? You? By who?"

"One of Sebastian's guards."

"Wait, a guard trounced you?"

"Yes, no mercy Gran-pappy, and he showed me none. I am going back there to train."

Caden chuckles, his eyes shifting to the pair he met yesterday. "Impressive. My granddaughter is quite skilled at fighting. The fact she admits to having her ass handed to her is a surprise."

"Indeed, she is. The difference is, we have hundreds of years on her. If she had that time, she would be as skilled, if not better, than my men."

Caden rises from the throne and moves to his granddaughter, hugging her gently. He faces Zara and Sebastian. "True. I had not thought about that. Now, down to business. You will have six guards while in the castle. They will also be your guides if you need something other than your rooms or the archives. I would say you are to remain in the unrestricted areas, but the library and archive fall under restricted and you have access to that. Breakfast will be in your room. Lunch brought to you and dinner in the banquet hall. There is a garden out back, along with a pool and hot tub. You are welcome to use them at any time. It is a public area, so please keep that in mind. Also, a lot of the wolves here may not approve of you, Sebastian. Vampires are... Not well liked. I ask that you try to avoid irritating them more than they already are, but we are Lycans and hotheaded. I think that's about everything at the moment. Did you wish to see your rooms, or the libraries first?"

"Yes, your Majesty." Zara curtsies and glances up to Sebastian, a blush staining her cheeks as her thoughts drift to the two of them in the hot tub. She looks down at the bags in her hand. "As much as I would like to say library, your Majesty, we should stash our duffle bags in our room."

"Fair enough. I will have the guards take you there first. If you need anything, let them know. If it's out of their hands, they can relay messages to me."

Fifteen minutes later, Zara and Sebastian stare in awe at the massive library, the musty smell of old books filling the air. Heavy wooden bookshelves line the walls, reaching three floors up with small balconies to walk along. Each balcony ending in a spiral staircase down to the next. Banks of drawers blend with the shelves, some holding a parchment in glass cases upon its surface, protected from the age of time. In the center sits a large table, a few maps spread out upon it, surrounded by sixteen very plush looking chairs. In the corners, matching chairs sit with tiny tables. On the walls hang old scrolls and paintings, each also protected from the elements.

"Damn! How are we supposed to find anything in here?"

Sebastian steps up to a bookshelf, his fingers skimming the spines gently, his love of books apparent in his action, "Well, we determine which ones are the oldest and start there."

"Sebastian! They all look old. We are never going to find it. Especially in five days!"

Sebastian returns to Zara's side and caresses her cheek. "Zara, my love. If we don't, then we ask if we can come back." He places his fingers beneath her chin, turning her gaze back to him as his thumb caresses her lower lip gently. "I have you. That's all that matters right now. It's possible the King has a system of some sorts on what books are where. I do at my castle, but it's only in Nero's and my mind. We spend a lot of time reading together."

"I gathered from when I was there." Zara smiles, and steps into his arms, holding him close for a moment. "If he has one, it will probably be digital. I will look for a computer. Thanks Seb."

"Good. Now, let's get started, shall we?"

The pair spend the day going through books, looking at scrolls and parchments, until they are called for dinner. After dinner they return, with Zara lasting until midnight, before she crashes on the sofa in the back corner. Sebastian smiles and looks towards the guards in the doorway. "Can we get a blanket for her?"

"Of course." His eyes glaze over and a few minutes later, a maid rushes in with a comforter and a pillow. She looks around and spots Zara on the couch, taking the blanket and placing it over her. She tucks the pillow beside her before bowing to Sebastian and hurrying from the room.

Sebastian rises and sits on the arm of the couch, gently stroking Zara's cheek. He lifts her upper body carefully, smiling at her murmurs of disapproval, and tucks the pillow beneath her head. Certain she is comfortable, he returns to the table where they have parchments and books spread out in ordered chaos.

At five in the morning, Zara wakes suddenly, her eyes finding Sebastian immediately. "The hourglass Seb." She pushes the cover off and slides from the couch, moving to one of the wall hangings.

"What hourglass Zara?" He rises and follows her, looking at the painting she is staring at. One of an hourglass with the sands appearing to be stopped mid time. A mountain scene behind with, with strange markings embedded into the background.

"This. It's not right."

"In what way?"

"The sand has stopped. An hourglass always runs if there is sand on the top."

"Could it be an artist's rendition?"

"No, even if it is, the date is wrong. They painted this before hourglasses even existed." She pulls her phone out of her pocket and takes a picture of the painting. Going into her settings, she plays with the filters, until the hidden words appear. *'Only when you still the sand, can peace return to the land.'* She turns her phone towards Sebastian, catching the widening of his eyes.

"How is it possible for your device to see this when it's not on the painting?"

"I did a report in school on paintings. A lot were painted on top of others because canvas was expensive. Now there are special lights to see what's underneath. My phone has the app to do that. I mean, it's not as good as the governments, but I installed it for my research. I didn't think anything of it, but clearly my subconscious did, because it came to me in a dream. Also, I know I saw a book with an hourglass on its spine. We need to find it."

"Do you remember where?"

Tears fill her eyes as she shakes her head. "No, I don't and I looked at so many today Seb. I'm sorry."

Sebastian pulls her into a hug. "Shhh Zara. It's a step. Whether it's tied to our step, you found something. Now, sleep for a few more hours. I will retrace your steps by following your scent and see if I can find it. If I do, I will wake you." He lifts her up and carries her back to the couch, placing her down carefully and tucking her back in. He runs his fingers along her cheek, dipping down to kiss her gently. "Now, don't dwell on it. We have only done the ground floor. I will find it."

"I love you Sebastian."

"I love you too, my queen." He sits beside her and caresses her gently, rising only when he feels her breathing stabilize and her thoughts quieten. He traces her smell through the passages, looking over the books at her eye level. A few hours later, he can hear Zara's thoughts returning to the room as she wakes up. He drifts back to the couch and sits down. "Good morning, my love."

Zara yawns sleepily, opening her eyes and meeting his gaze, feeling the immediate warmth flooding her at his look. She reaches up to trace her fingers along his jawline. "Morning Seb. Did you find it?"

He cups her hand close to his cheek, leaning into it and savors her touch. "Not yet. But we had almost all day yesterday. We will find it. We have a few hours before breakfast. After that, perhaps a shower or this hot tub to relax? Yes?"

A blush crosses her cheeks at his words and the fact that they will be alone in their room. "I would like that Seb."

A devilish light fills his eyes as he kisses her gently. "Perfect. You may continue to relax. I am going back to searching before I take you to the room now."

Zara laughs, pushing him off her. "I will help. I feel bad I slept while you worked."

Sebastian chuckles and rises, offering a hand to help her up. "You need to sleep more often than I do."

Zara rolls her eyes and stretches. "Yes, well, being mortal does that. So what shelves have you done?"

"That half over there."

"Right, let's get to it then." Zara moves to the other side and begins searching there, her eyes following Sebastian to where he left off.

Caden wakes in the morning, his nerves on edge that a vampire is roaming around his castle, despite Madison's reassurances. Suspecting he has enough power to dethrone him if he wants. He reaches out to his guards via the mind-link. *'Atticus. Tell me about our guests.'*

'Not much to tell, sire. They have been in the library. Only left for dinner with you and returned. The girl slept on the couch and he spent the night reading. Orion said she woke at one point and they moved over to a painting where she took a picture and they talked. Afterwards, she returned to the couch and slept and he started searching through the books.'

'Interesting. Do you know what he's looking for?'

'No sire. I can ask if you like.'

'No, I will ask at dinner. I suspect they will be there all day.'

'Sounds like they are planning to return to their room for breakfast, sire.'

'Just keep an eye on them.'

'Understood.'

Twenty-Two

Binding Nine

Hours later, after breakfast, a soak in the hot tub and some alone time, Sebastian and Zara return to the library with renewed purpose. To find the book with an hourglass on its spine. They travel through the rows and rows of books. Slowly closing the space between them. It isn't long before Zara finds it tucked near the bottom. "I found it Seb, but I don't remember it being this low."

Sebastian frowns, pulling another off at the same time. "Then there is more than one. I have one as well."

"Mine looks like it's about witches." Zara moves over and places her book down on the table. Her eyes follow Sebastian as he moves to stand beside her, setting his book next to hers.

"This one is on mystics."

"Other than the title, they look the same." She picks them up and looks over the outsides, comparing the hourglass on its spine. "Do you think it's the same author who did the painting?"

"I am uncertain, Zara. All we can do is read them."

Zara nods and sits down, cracking open her book carefully, her fingers tracing over the old parchment as she learns the origins of witchcraft. In the center of the book, she stops, staring at a clean page with only a line running through it at the top. "That's interesting."

"What is love?" Sebastian lifts his gaze and looks over at her.

"Right in the middle of the book is a straight line with some runes inscribed along it."

He leans over and looks at the page she has opened. "Wait, this one has something similar in the middle, but they are curved and have no definite runes. More of a speckled effect." Flipping back to the center, he slides the book over to her.

Zara chews on her lips, staring at the lines, shaking her head. "Oh, no way!"

"What are you seeing?"

She pulls her phone out and flips to the picture she took. "Look Seb, your lines are the center of the hourglass. Mine is probably the top. I think we need seven more books to make an hourglass!" Her gaze lifts to the floors about them. "Damn."

Sebastian chuckles. "Look at the bright side. We only need to find the hourglasses on the spines, and not read every book in here. Assuming it's tied to our prophecy."

Zara groans and tucks her phone back in her pocket. "You're not helping Seb."

He kisses her cheek. "Think of the discovery you have made, if nothing else."

She rolls her eyes. "Not exactly what I was hoping for, but let's see it out."

Sebastian rises, pulling her up. "Let's finish this floor. Then we split up for the upper levels."

"Got it."

Three hours later, the pair shares a look of accomplishment between them. Nine books sit on the table, each one different, both in title and the sands that sit within the glass, varying the times between them.

Sebastian reaches over and takes her hand, squeezing it gently. "Well, my love, I think you might be onto something. Shall we see what these books mean? Perhaps build an hourglass with them."

"Or a drawing of one." Zara giggles and moves to the wolf shifter book. She flips it open, riffling through until she finds the drawing. Looking at it carefully, she slides the book to the bottom. "It's gonna be like a puzzle with nine books."

"A puzzle?" Sebastian opens the vampire one, moving it to the top right corner.

"I will show you later, Seb. The pack house has them for those that enjoy fitting tiny little pieces of cardboard into other tiny pieces." She grabs the next one, reading fey in the title. Finding the drawing, she places it beside her wolf book, leaving a space on the opposite side.

Sebastian slides the witch book to the top. He grabs curses next, and looks through it, finding no lines, only a few runes in the middle. "Curious. This one has no lines, only runes."

Zara looks at it as she slides the mystic book into the center. "It will be on one side of the mystic because it's the center of the hourglass." She picks up dragons next and opens it, seeing it's the top right corner and places it down.

He places the book to the side and grabs runes, finding a similar entry. "Found the other side."

Zara laughs and snatches the shadow-walker book, opening it to the center. She slides it into place on the bottom beside wolves. "Right, so two remaining."

Sebastian nods, his eyes studying both pages, shifting his gaze to the books already spread out and open. He hands her the runes. "Here, put this on the left side."

"How do you know?"

"I don't, but see this symbol right here. It is from an old dialect in our realm, meaning ring."

"Ring?"

Sebastian places his book on the right. "Yes, the ring sits on the left hand."

Zara blushes and nods, placing her book down in place. She steps back into Sebastian as the black runes illuminate with golden light, moving across the page, fusing the books to those that are next to it. It spreads rapidly across the pages until the center one glows a light azure. Rising from it is an hourglass, the sands within glowing silver as scripture appears along the edges as in the drawing. It pulses nine times before a sudden flash floods the room.

Sebastian spins Zara to face his chest to protect her. Darkness and silence suddenly cut off the guard's cry of surprise, as if time itself is standing still. The air surrounding them holds a weightlessness to it. A book hitting the floor nearby echoes as the shadows fade. Sebastian's eyes adjust and he looks around at the room they have arrived in. Stone walls surround them, one containing an archway into another room. At the far end, a fire blazes in the hearth, warming the area. Two large chairs face the fire. A voice filters from one of them. "Who is in my castle, and what do you want?"

Back in the Stormfang pack, Nero staggers against Gianna. He sinks to his knees and clasps his head at the snapping of the link and emptiness inside. "Noooo, Sebastian! My queen."

Gianna falls to the ground with him, feeling Zara's link with the pack break. "Zara's gone too. Shit! This is just like before. We need to get to her family."

"And to the others." Nero struggles to his feet and lifts Gianna into his arms, bridal style. He uses his speed to return to Kieran's cottage where Mathew, Theodore and Julian have collapsed on the ground. *'Anthony. Kieran's, now.'*

'Nero! What's going on? I can't feel our king!'

'I suspect they realm hopped. I did not feel death in the break. Gianna confirmed she felt this when Zara came to our realm.'

'Damn. Do you think the clan felt this when we came here?'

'Likely. Let's hope Mason and the witches kept control.'

Anthony arrives at the door with Zach in his arms. "What are we going to do, Nero?"

"There is not much we can do. We don't know exactly what happened."

Kieran pushes the office door open and runs down the stairs to the others in the living room. "Nero! Where did my baby girl go?"

Nero shakes his head. "Wherever she is, Sebastian is with her, and he will keep her safe."

Kieran sags against the couch, struggling to hide the tears. "Oh Zare-bear. Please come home safely."

Gianna moves to Kieran, wrapping her arms around him. "She will. Somehow, we will get her back."

Nero's eyes move to the others, knowing they only had seven days to figure it out. "We need a witch that can trace them."

Zach shakes his head. "Amara can't. Trust me, we tried when Kieran and Zara disappeared the first time. Even called her coven members in."

At the palace, the guards blink their eyes, realizing rather suddenly that neither of them is standing in the room. *'Sire, we have a problem!'*

'Atticus, what sort of problem?'

'They are gone, sire. They are no longer in the room.'

'Gone? Well FIND them! I do not want them roaming the castle!'

'They didn't pass us, sire. They were working on something with the books. Putting them together. An hourglass appeared and flashed some bright blue light. When it stopped, they were gone.'

'Bloody Hell! I will be right there.' Caden runs through the corridors, arriving five minutes later. He enters the room and strides over to the table, seeing eight books lined up in a square with the middle one missing. "What is this supposed to be?"

"There was a ninth book, sire. I can only assume it went with them as it was where the hourglass spawned."

"Dammit. Alpha Darian will not be happy. I better call him." He pulls out his phone and sorts through his contacts, while staring at the books. "Impressive that they found this here. I have gone through my fair share of the books in the library and not seen this."

"I gather the vampire reads a lot. He was flipping pages twice as fast as her." Atticus points to the painting on the wall. "They were very interested in that painting when the girl woke up. Afterwards, they stopped reading and just started searching for these nine."

Caden listens to the phone ring as he picks up a book and looks it over. He closes it and looks at the cover, immediately noticing the hourglass on the spine. "FUCK!"

Darian pauses at the exclamation. "Sire? That is not exactly the greeting I expected when I saw your name on my call display."

"Sorry Darian. I gather you already know your wolf is missing."

"Yes, I felt the link drop. I was just on my way to find her father. What happened?"

"It seems the pair put some books together, created some sort of time jump."

"Time jump? Not a realm hop?"

"It's tied to an hourglass, hence time, but I will have my witches look into it immediately."

Darian grows thoughtful. "Damn, that's not good, Sire. The vampires are only here for ten days. Six left. Then their witches are calling them home. As I am to understand, with Zara. But what happens if they are not in our realm when the call comes in? Will they be left behind in some unknown realm?"

"I can't answer that at the moment, Darian. But I will pull in all my resources. I have a few planar travelers in the family. If my witches can't figure it out, they hopefully can."

"Thank you, your Majesty."

"Darian. I can hear it in your voice. Do not underestimate them. They found nine books in thousands that tied themselves together to create magic. Two books I have read and have been in my library for centuries. Yet they put it together because of a painting of an hourglass in less than a day. If anyone can figure out a way home, it is those two."

Darian chuckles. "Well, Zara was an honor student in school, despite causing trouble with Gianna and Zach. I am sure you are right. We will see them home soon."

"Yes, you will. Now, I need to go make other calls. I will keep in touch."

"Understood. Thank you again."

"You're welcome." Caden looks at the guards. "Keep someone posted here, just in case they return to where they left." He strides back upstairs, already calling his granddaughter's number. "Madison, we have to talk."

Darian hangs up the phone, his fingers tapping his desk for a moment, reaching out to find out where Kieran is. Realizing he is in his cottage, he rises and heads that way. *'Kieran, I am on my way to your cottage.'* Five minutes later, Alpha Darian knocks lightly and steps into the group meeting, his eyes landing on his son. "Let me guess. We are discussing what happened to Zara and Sebastian?"

"Yah Dad. What are we going to do?"

"I am not sure, but I know King Caden is calling in all his resources. He has powerful witches and apparently some realm hoppers in his family. We will find them."

"How do you know that?"

"I just got off the phone with him. Apparently, they figured out some sort of puzzle, put some books together and created a time jump. Or rather, he thinks that's what it is because it created an hourglass before they disappeared."

"Damn, so they might not be in another realm. They could be in the future?"

Nero shakes his head. "No, it will be another realm. Your time is more advanced than ours, so time was different in the first hop. I would wager it will be the same wherever they are, probably one tied to dragons or witches as they are the ones that started this all."

Kieran rises and studies Nero, a smile ghosting his lips. "That's a good point. It will narrow the search down." He turns to Darian. "Is there a way to let him know that?"

"Yes, I can call him."

"Thank you."

"For now, we...."

Lila runs in the front door, and straight into Kieran's arms, sobbing, interrupting Darian and the others. "Please, no Kieran. She can't be gone."

Kieran wraps his arms around his mate, tightening his hold to stop the shake in her body. "Shhh, Lila. She's fine. She's with Sebastian. We are gonna get her back. Nero and Darian already have ideas about where to find her."

Tears stream from her eyes. "I can't handle her gone."

Kieran lifts his mate into his arms, mind-linking Darian. *'I am gonna take her upstairs. You guys figure out what we need to do.'*

'Right now, I need to go call the King back and we wait. I will keep you posted, Kieran.' Darian turns to the rest of them. "For now, we carry on as normal. Work, train, and keep your eyes open. Especially tonight. Sebastian commanded the local vampires to stand down. I don't know what's going to happen now that he's gone."

"Shit Dad! I didn't even think about that."

"I did. I will double the patrols until further notice. Nero, if you and your men can each join a group, I would appreciate it. If the vampires appear, then perhaps they will listen to you if you speak on behalf of your king. Stand them down if you can."

Nero nods. "We will patrol on our own. We can cover the land faster, but they might not arrive tonight. It's very possible they gravitated towards Whispering pines last night. If so, they may take their temper out there at the sudden disappearance of our king. Or the one that they were fighting within their head might command them to return here."

"Damn, I will let the King know. I don't like this at all, Nero."

"I am sorry Alpha Darian. We did not plan to bring this trouble here. Only to retrieve Zara, learn of her world, and return home."

"I am not blaming you, Nero, or your men. It is what it is. I just hate complications. I prefer a nice orderly pack."

Nero laughs. "Don't we all? Ours changed as soon as Zara and Kieran arrived."

Darian chuckles. "Much like ours when they came back!"

"I can hear you blaming me! It's not my fault, it's my daughter's!" Kieran calls down the stairs, causing them all to laugh.

Nero chuckles. "You should learn to accept responsibility, Kieran, because I recall you blaming your wife for Zara's stubbornness."

Lila looks up at Kieran "YOU did WHAT? Oh, no Kieran. That is NOT my fault."

Kieran mutters, knowing Nero can hear it. "Thanks a lot!"

"As long as it distracts her."

Twenty-Three

Fangs and Fury

Steel places the glass of wine down on the table and rises from his chair. He turns to face the pair standing in the middle of the room, his silver eyes glittering in anger at the disruption as they roam over them.

Sebastian reads the rage in the man's posture and pushes Zara behind him. His gaze sweeps over him, the long black hair, the jagged scar that runs down the left side of his chiseled face. *'Stay there, my love.'*

A smile tips his lips as Steel casually approaches the vampire standing before him, feeling the power rolling off him, and knowing he was not weak by any means. His eyes drift to the blond hair hiding behind him, trying to get a better look at who he is protecting. "Aww look. A vampire is protecting the wolf pup. Isn't that interesting? What are you doing in my castle, and how did you get past the guards?"

"Magic apparently."

"Teleports and walkers cannot penetrate my castle's protection. Try again."

Sebastian nods to the book on the floor. "We were doing research. After aligning the books, they brought us here."

"Your saying a book brought you here?" Steel reaches down and picks the book up, feeling the faint traces of magic still within its cover. "Mystics. Powerful creatures. Don't live long, though."

"Nine books, actually. Each one covers a different topic. Dragons, wolves, vampires, among others. In the center of each is part of a drawing. We just connected the lines."

"Why?" His fingers caress the book, flipping it open to confirm his words as he returns his attention to them.

"Why what?"

"Why are mortal enemies working together?"

"Why is the dragon curious?"

"Ah, so you know I am a dragon."

"Yes, I can read your thoughts."

"Interesting. It is not a trait vampires normally have."

"It's one I have."

"Hmmm, you still haven't answered my question, vampire."

"We are trying to solve a prophecy."

"A prophecy..." Steel's gaze slides to Zara, peeking over Sebastian's shoulder. "Wait... You are the two?"

A wry smile crosses Sebastian's lips. "Are you referring to the one involving life and death?"

"Yes. Bound together... Damn... We cannot... Let's go." Steel hands the book back to Sebastian and guides them out of the room. Several twists and turns later, he opens the door into a small room. The room sparkles in a rainbow of color from the large diamond floating on the ceiling. "Please come in."

Sebastian's hand tightens on Zaras as he steps into the room, feeling her apprehension over their bonds. *It's fine, my love. I sense no dishonesty from this dragon.'*

Once both are inside the room, he closes the door. "Here we can talk privately. Probably said too much upstairs, so you both need to be very careful. You should not even be here. Now, the names Steel, who are you?"

"Sebastian, and this is my mate, Zara."

"Pleasure. Now, the prophecy." His eyes land on Zara now that she is not hiding. "Wow, you look exactly like her."

Zara looks up in confusion. "Like who?"

"The one in the prophecy. The girl that Coltrannax has been searching hundreds of years for. He thought he found you a century ago, but he never called the search off. Destiny has assigned you the task of restoring balance to the realms and returning the races of old to their original places. A merging, if you will."

She glances at Sebastian. "The other Zara?"

Sebastian frowns at the thought. "Is that the rest of the prophecy? We only have a part of it, along with a random line hidden in a painting. What do you mean by merging?"

"I will tell you what I know. About a thousand years ago, there was a black dragon called Obsidius the Night Stalker. He was as power hungry and cruel as

Coltrannax is now. In fact, there are whispers he is the offspring of Obsidius, but it has never been proven. Obsidius wanted to rule more than just this land. He wanted them all. Of course, the leaders and races of the other lands they governed took offense and defended themselves. Rightly so, in my opinion. This only angered him. He brought in witches, strong enough to force them to bow to him. Something backfired in the casting. The other lands disappeared. Entire races with them. People pulled from this existence, never to be seen again, while others arrived here. Dragons mostly, leaving their lives behind. In time, people have discovered through magic, different realms, alternate universes, so to speak, where the missing races live. Some peacefully, some cursed. I suspect the merging will bring those lands back, along with the races. Of course, I can't be certain. Logically speaking, if the lands disappeared during the break, then they should return for the repair."

"How do you know all this?"

"I am known as the Lore Master in this realm. It's hinted at in our history books."

"What happens to those who already have established lives?"

"It shouldn't affect them."

"It will though. My realm, for example, differs from Zaras. We use horses and carriages to get places. They have things called cars that move without horses. There is a buzzing noise that is not present in mine, or here for that matter. Our realm is simplistic in comparison. Without Zara as a guide, her world would be very intimidating, perhaps even terrifying. Now you would have people that live in my land thrust into an unknown world without a guide. On top of that, our race hides in her world. Just as hers does. Pretending to be humans. What happens when the realms shift and all these creatures suddenly become visible because they are unaware of those rules? Going the other way, I know what Zara's thoughts were when she arrived in my land. I imagine any taken from her world and thrust into mine would bear the same. It will be pure chaos for everyone and every realm. I do not think this is such a good idea."

"Then I cannot say. I just know that you have the power to stop Coltrannax's tyranny by restoring things as they once were. But you need to be careful. Dragons dominate this world. Although, logically, if you unite the lands, he can rule them all in one place again rather than needing to realm hop and spreading himself thin. Killing you would make it more difficult for that to happen."

Sebastian's brows furrow. "I believe I am missing something. A dragon rules this land, and yet dragons dominate it. Why not just overthrow him?"

Steel's gaze shifts from Sebastian to Zara. "We can't. You recall I said some are cursed. We are one race. We cannot attack the ruling monarch. They must die by another race's hands. Obsidius was killed by a race that walked as one with the shadows. Upon his death, he cursed them with his dying breath and so now they cannot leave their realm without shifting to a creature that steals the soul upon their touch."

"When and if we stop Coltrannax, will he curse us as well?"

"No, he shouldn't. It was Obsidius that carried the magic that separated the realms when he absorbed the witches. His dying at the walkers hands was a separate event. Coltrannax has witches in his employ, but is a dragon only. He has an amulet on him that allows him access to realm hops twice a week or a witch called Stella that sticks close to him."

Zara snaps her gaze to Steel. "Stella Kaala?"

"Yes, I believe that's her name."

Zara's body shakes as panic floods her. She grabs Sebastian's shirt. "We have to find a way back. Gianna's in trouble."

Sebastian covers her hands for a moment, and pulls her into a tight hug. "Nero will watch over her, Zara. She's safe."

"No, don't you see? Stella, the witch from the school, hangs out with Colten. The delivery driver that has a crush on Gianna. Who comes to our pack every few weeks and stays in the city center. Stella asked Bianca if there were new members in our pack. Colten is Coltrannax. He's the dragon Alpha Madison sensed. The one spying on us."

Sebastian runs his fingers through her hair, doing his best to soothe her. "Zara, my queen. All my guards are there. He is not getting Gianna." He looks over at Steel, reading the confirmation in his eyes that it's possible they were the same. "Where is the script of the prophecy? You indicated you have seen it."

"Yes. It's in Coltrannax's castle. The one you can see no matter where you are in the land. But you can't wander the streets like that. You two will stand out. Everyone here knows the bounty on your mate's head. Then you, being a vampire. Coltrannax has an intense hatred for your race and wants them all dead. Do you have any idea how much you are worth? Let alone her!"

"Is he a black?"

"Yes, he is."

"Then we met. Apparently, my sire killed his human father."

"That would explain it. It's interesting how you and her are connected to the prophecy. You called her queen. Title or nickname?"

"Title. There is more going on here. Assuming they are the same dragon, Coltrannax sent Zara to my realm, allowing us to meet. When she was trying to escape, he caught her and tossed her back. Why not just kill her then?"

"Escape?"

"Yes. In order to have a better standing with the witches in the resistance who could send her home, we set it up to look like she escaped."

"I see. All I know is that Coltrannax thrives on the cat-and-mouse game. He plays with his subjects before destroying them, breaking all those tied with them, before he ends them completely. The instant death bores him."

"That makes sense. He knew I didn't have access to witches and wanted her to be untouchable."

"Right now, he is off-world. You need to find the rebellion; the ones opposed to his rule. They are your way into his castle. The parchment hangs on the wall in his den."

Zara mutters softly. "What is with r words?"

Sebastian looks down at her. "R words?"

"Rogues, resistance, rebellion. Let's add rebels, revolution, revolt, renegades."

He chuckles. "Strong opposing factions, then. Does that work?"

She rolls her eyes. "I suppose."

"How do we find them before the others find us?"

"I will provide you with cloaks and a pouch to keep the book in. Keep your head down. Look for Drake or Amber at the inn in the center of town to the east. Enter via the back door. Both have red hair and golden eyes. Average build in that you are taller than him and Zara is about the same as her. Happily married, so likely to be all lovey with each other like you two are. Now, we have lingered too long. There are always eyes watching. Perhaps I will see you on the flip-side." He leads them out of the room, placing a finger to his lips, indicating silence. Winding back through the castle, he stops at a room and pulls two cloaks out of the wardrobe. Handing one to each of them. Once they dress and tuck the book away, he leads them to a small side passage, whispering quietly. "This will get you past the guards. Stick to the shadows. Don't get caught. Be careful and good luck."

"Thank you." Sebastian takes Zara's hand, following his instructions. Once outside, he lifts her into his arms and draws on his speed, racing through the shadows towards the town. At the back door of the inn, he stops and places Zara down. He scans the alleyway, watching for any shadows that appear to be paying more attention than they should.

Stepping inside, the scent of fresh bread, warm air, and a slightly run-down kitchen greets them. A hearth burns on the far side, casting a cozy glow, with loaves of bread cooling on racks nearby. Two doors lead off from the room, one to the side and a set of swinging double doors directly across from them. A large table sits in the center, surrounded by chairs, and a counter lines the far wall. The atmosphere is welcoming, despite the kitchen's worn appearance.

Sebastian studies the woman rolling dough on the table, her red hair bound up with a leather tie, flour dusting her face and hands. A graying apron, complete with burn marks, partially covers her. "Amber?"

"Who's asking?" Amber turns, her eyes narrowing at the vampire standing in her doorway.

"Sebastian and Zara. Steel sa..."

She cuts him off, her eyes warning him to speak no more. "Would you like a roll?"

Sebastian catches the warning and steps inside, closing the door after them. "Of course."

"Great, come this way then." She gestures for them to settle at the table. Moving to the counter, she pulls a sack of flour off it and a couple of buns, taking them back to her guests. "Fresh out of the fires." Scattering the flour on the table, she writes in it carefully. -*What do you want Vamp*-

Sebastian nods and flattens the flour out. -*Steel said we need to get to the resistance*- He smooths it out once more. -*We are wanted by Coltrannax*-

She sprinkles a bit more flour out and clanks a few pots before returning to the flour. -*why... Keep conversation going*-

Zara reads the message while munching on her bun. "This is very good. Thank you."

"Your welcome, little lady. What brings you here?"

-*Because we are tied to the prophecy in... Coltrannax's office*-

-*Shit, you can't stay here*- She moves to the oven and pulls out another tray, setting it on the block. Her gaze drifts out the window, scanning the alleyway for movement. After a moment, she pulls the curtains closed and returns to the table, resuming her work with a wary glance around the room. -*C has spies everywhere*- She wipes the message away. -*We need to get you underground fast*-

"We are just passing through and smelled your baking."

Sebastian nods. -*Agreed*-

"Thank you. It draws a lot of customers." -*You can't stay here... But you can't leave... I can hide you in the closet... Magical wards on it... stay there till nightfall*-

Zara shakes her head, her eyes darting between Sebastian and Amber.

Sebastian kisses her cheek, his fingers drifting through the flour. -*Deal. Lead the way*-

"Thank you for stopping by. Enjoy your travels." She moves to the backdoor, opening and closing it to make it sound as if they had left to anyone who might be listening. Gesturing with her hand to follow, Amber moves to the door opposite the ovens and opens it quietly. Inside is a pantry of sorts, filled with a variety of dried foods and baking supplies. She steps back, allowing them to enter. Once they are inside, she places a finger to her lips and closes the door behind her.

Sebastian steps into the pantry and finds a corner to settle in, planting himself on the floor with an inward chuckle. He pulls Zara down to snuggle with him, his hands wrapping around her tightly. '*Well, my love, once again, I am sitting on the floor with you. Three times in three days. Want to know how many times I have before that, none I tell you. Kings do not sit on the floor.*'

Zara covers her mouth, trying not to giggle. '*Oh Seb, you best get used to it. I practically live on the floor. So does Gia. The best position to talk on the phone is lying on your back with your feet on the bed.*'

'*Great, my queen is a rug.*'

'*I am not a rug!*'

'*You have fur right and you like the floor? That makes you a rug.*'

'*Ember has fur. You are calling her a rug!*'

He chuckles inwardly. '*I would never. Ember doesn't make me sit on the floor.*'

'*She would too. Oh wait, it would be lying in the dirt outside.*'

'*Ye' Gads! What did I get involved with!? Why you!?*'

Zara teases him gently. '*Cause you loved my outgoing personality when we first met.*'

'*Outgoing is an understatement, my queen. But you definitely intrigued me with your passion.'*

She cups his face and kisses him gently. *'And now you are sitting on the floor with me, because you moved me into your castle.'*

He nibbles on her lips. *'Your right, I was hooked. The second I heard your thoughts tumbling around in your head.'*

She sighs and rests her head against his chest. *'I love you Seb.'*

'I love you too, Zara.'

Hours pass as they hide in the closet, listening to the sounds of Amber working in the kitchen. Occasionally, they catch the odd voice of others, but the conversation remains muffled because of their secluded position in the back corner, separated by a solid wood door. They communicate through their mind-link, discussing their situation, expressing concern for the others, and wondering how they were reacting to the sudden break in the link, hoping they are alright.

Amidst these discussions, they comment on the differences between the three realms they have visited, marveling at the unique aspects of each one and how it contrasts with their own experiences. They strategize about what they need to do ~~from t.~~ weighing their options and planning their next moves, trying to stay calm and focused while they wait in the pantry.

Later in the evening, Zara dozes against him, while Sebastian watches her, knowing he is going to do everything in his power to keep her safe. If that means he needs to kill a dragon, so be it. He twines his finger in her long blond locks, fingering its softness, a smile crossing his lips as he imagines it blue. Knowing he might need to see that before they return to their realm. His hold tightens on her as the latch to the closet opens. Golden eyes flicker to them momentarily. His eyes follow Amber to the shelves as she collects some ingredients off them, clanging a few things as she whispers. "Another two hours. Drake will take you away."

Sebastian nods, remaining quiet as she turns and leaves with her hands full of items. The door closes and silence returns to the closet. He closes his eyes, listening to the soft pattern of Zara's breathing and the soft hum of Ember, each bringing a smile to his lips. An hour and a half later, the door opens again and draws his gaze upward, seeing a man step into the pantry and close the door. He turns a book in his hands to face him, while placing a finger to his lips.

-I hope you can read in the dark. We have a small window in which to move between the patrols. It seems word has already spread that you are here and arrived

in Steel's castle. They have questioned him for hours, but he is on our side and will not say a thing. He simply said he kicked you out. The guards at his door confirmed you headed into town. My wife has denied seeing you as they searched the rooms upstairs.-

Sebastian reads the script and nods, lifting Zara into his arms as he rises from the ground, his body complaining at being in the same position for so many hours.

Drake tears the page out and crumples it. Slipping out of the pantry, he holds his hand up to halt Sebastian, mouthing '*wait.*' Tossing the parchment in the fire, he moves to his wife, pulling her in front of the small kitchen window. He kisses her neck, moving along her skin as if she is the only thing in the room. All the while, his eyes watch for the patrols that pass. Once they do, he steps back, kisses her quickly and nods to Sebastian to follow. He peeks out of the inn, and glances both ways, before crossing into the shadows on the other side. Turning, he looks in confusion at Sebastian already standing beside him, whispering quietly. "How?"

"Just move. I will keep up."

Drake nods and bolts into the darkness, sensing rather than seeing Sebastian on his heels, winding through the streets, until they stop in front of a small house. He knocks quietly, a simple pattern to it, and steps inside. "Come in." He turns to close the door as Sebastian appears beside him, flipping the latch over to lock it. "Damn, I want that ability."

"Many do." Sebastian adjusts Zara and steps in. The simple cottage opens into a single room, warm and inviting, with shades of peach and silver adorning the space. A small dinette is tucked near the fireplace, which serves as both a cooking area and a source of warmth. Opposite the hearth, a nightstand and a small dresser flank a modest bed. In the far corner, an elderly woman sits quietly in a plush chair, her gnarled hands weaving yarn, her gaze fixed intently on the newcomers. Sebastian acknowledges her with a brief nod before his focus shifts back to Drake.

"Cindra."

"Drake. You bring unexpected guests."

"I do."

"A vampire? Carrying a she-wolf."

"Cindra. There is a bounty on their heads. We need to move them underground."

She places her weaving down and rises, hobbling over to Sebastian, peering up into his gaze. "What's wrong with her?"

Sebastian looks down at Zara. "Nothing, she's just sleeping."

"Why are you really here, vamp?"

"As Drake stated, we are wanted."

She taps her chin, her eyes glinting in the darkness. "That's only a partial truth. Tell me the entire truth, or you will get no help from me. I will take you to the guards myself."

Sebastian's eyes darken, swirling with a mix of red at her implied threat. "First, you would need to catch and contain me. Second, I know that the bed lifts and the passage to the rebellion lies beneath it by where your thoughts are. Third, I am calling your bluff."

She chuckles. "Clever vampire. Good call on the bluff. Despite this cottage having protection, we should not speak openly. This way." She lifts her hand and points to the bed. It rises along with the floor beneath it, revealing a hidden staircase below it. "Downstairs, quickly. I will see you soon."

Sebastian enters with Drake on his heels. He takes a moment to adjust to the darkness that surrounds them from the bed dropping above them. "Is she not joining us?"

"Not yet. She will later. I need to get you to headquarters and get back to my wife."

"Lead the way."

Drake runs through the passages, descending downward with Sebastian keeping pace. They arrive in an enormous cavern deep beneath the ground, a bustling hub of activity. The cavern is alive with movement: a small market thrives in one area, while bedrolls line the walls. People cook food over small fires, engaged in conversation with those around them. "We need to find Cindra's husband, Aethon." Drake says, glancing around the cavern. "He rules things down here."

Sebastian walks alongside Drake, observing the surrounding people with curiosity. For the first time in his life, he is on this side of the resistance, and it is not what he expected. Judging by their thoughts, they seem normal, many of them laced with fear but holding very little hostility. He looks down at Zara, remembering the intense anger she had when they first met, far greater than anything he senses in this group. Catching sight of Drake veering to the left, Sebastian follows and comes to a stop beside him.

Drake nods to an older man standing at a table, papers and maps scattered on a table, and he flips through them. "Aethon, I have new recruits."

Aethon sighs without looking up. "Find them a bed then."

"You want to pay attention to these ones, Aethon."

Aethon lifts his golden gaze from the papers, turning to Sebastian. He arches a brow at the unconscious she-wolf in his arms. "You're doing?"

Sebastian shakes his head, a cool tone in his voice. "Why would I harm my mate? She is simply sleeping."

Surprise fills his gaze as it darts to Drake. "A vampire, mated with a wolf?"

Drake smiles. "Look at her Aethon. I know it's hard with her face pressed against his chest, but really look. Steel sent them to Amber."

Aethon approaches Sebastian. He rises to his toes to peer into her face. "Wait, is it her?"

Sebastian's arms tighten on Zara, catching her murmur as she snuggles in closer. "Yes, she's life. I'm death. We need to get into the castle. The sooner the better, as I only have six days to solve the puzzle before we return to my realm."

Aethon backs up and leans against the table, his fingers tapping nervously against the edge. "Does he know you are here?"

"I don't believe so. Zara figured out a pattern tied to a painting and nine books that magically transported us here this morning. The one that brought us is in the pouch Steel gave us."

Drake shakes his head. "He's off-world, but the patrols know they are here. They sounded the alerts."

"Then we better work quickly. Get her a sleeping roll and a shelter. The others don't need to know just yet."

Drake races off, returning with a bedroll and a lean to, setting it up quickly. He does a slight bow to them all. "I need to get back to Amber. Been away too long."

Aethon nods. "Go, quickly."

Sebastian moves over and lays Zara down, smiling at her mumbles of discontent. He whispers softly as he pulls his cloak off and wraps it around her. "I am nearby." Once she is secure, he moves over to the table that Aethon is beside. "Tell me about Coltrannax and his castle."

"Well, he is a dictator and a tyrant, which I am certain you have figured out. Secure because us dragons can't dethrone him and he ends any races that arrive in our lands, besides humans, because he feels they are weak. Most of those down here are people we saved from his wrath, simply because they are not dragons."

"What are his motives?"

"To rule all with an iron fist. He seems to think the lands belong to him, even those in other realms."

"Yes, when he came to my land four months ago, he stated his desire to rule."

Aethon snaps his gaze up. "He was in your land?"

"Yes. He sent Zara there, then took her back, stating he would return her in exchange for me handing over my crown. I felt at the time, and still do, that it's a front for another reason. Why would he want to rule a vampire's land when he wants us all dead? Especially as my sire apparently killed his father 727 years ago. A human that took him in when he was a street rat. It begs the question how did he get to rule here, if he was a street rat in my land? The stories are not adding up."

Aethon rubs his chin as he looks over at Sebastian. "You're right. Coltrannax has always been here. Ruled since Obsidius disappeared. No one that has arrived is strong enough to face him, but I get the impression that you could"

"So what you are saying is that I will need to face a thousand year old dragon?"

"Give or take, yes. Some of us are older, but we cannot challenge or fight him."

Sebastian's gaze drifts to Zara. "I don't want to fight him either, to be honest. I have a queen to protect and I can't do that dead, or rather, more dead than I am. What I am after is a scroll in his castle. The one with the prophecy. My hope is if we can solve it, the curse will lift and you can stage a coup."

"That's a good plan. Let's figure it out and see if we can get you into the castle, shall we?" He pulls a map up and slides it over to Sebastian, the layout of the town and where the castle sits. The next one is the basic interior of the castle. "We don't have much information about the inside. He has Draconic guards patrolling the walls and stationary ones between the patrols. As with any dragon, they can sense tremors along the earth out to about a hundred feet. In order to get past them, he calls in witches to read your thoughts, though lately, it's just been the one. As you can guess, anyone with questionable thoughts never returns."

"I am hoping to avoid the witches. As for the guards, I just need to know the key ones to strike and the time frame in between."

Hours pass as they discuss strategies, putting out options, then tearing them apart with what ifs. Eventually, they decide on a few plans, with secondary options, in case things turn sour. Sebastian moves over to Zara's side, watching as

Aethon joins Cindra in a nearby tent. He slips in behind her and draws her into his arms, knowing tomorrow is going to test their skills and how well they work together. He closes his eyes and listens, hearing the thoughts of the rebellion, the soft dripping of water nearby, the footsteps of the guards as they patrol the area to keep them safe.

Morning arrives with Zara groaning in dismay, trying to stretch her body out but finding an arm wrapped tightly around her. She rolls over in his embrace, muttering against him. "Rebellion beds have to be the worst!"

Sebastian chuckles and kisses her forehead. "Indeed. Though it has you in it, so I can't complain."

She smiles and rests her head against him. "You are so sweet."

"Just remember that for later."

Zara's brows furrow as she looks into his gaze, reading the concern in his features. "You have a plan, but it's not one you like."

"You are correct, but it was the best option."

"What is it?"

He caresses her cheeks gently, his hold tightening on her. "We leave after breakfast. Aethon estimates it will take a few hours, as we need to wind through the underground caverns past the castle and end up an hour out of town on the west side. There are passages that open closer to the castle, but he doesn't want to risk them being found. Then we creep through the woods. His guards are Draconic in nature and patrol regularly around the castle. We are going to take the ones out at the main gate because he won't expect us to walk in the front door."

"If he has dragon guards, won't they sense us?"

"Yes, and no. They won't sense me, but they will sense Ember."

Zara's gaze snaps up. "Wait, you're using me as bait?"

Sebastian chuckles. "Correct. I am relying on the fact that Coltrannax has not told his guards to watch for a wolf. I will deal with them before they reach you."

"How?"

Sebastian winks. "You will see when we are close. I just need you to cross the road in front of them. About two hundred feet away. Make sure Ember stops to growl at them."

"We can do that. Are you sure about this?"

"No, but I trust you. Once I have dispatched the main guards, bolt for the gate. There is a small window where the patrols are on the far side of the ramparts. Once we are inside, we make haste to his office and avoid the servants working inside the castle. We need to be in and out in fifteen minutes. Aethon has men that will create distractions all around the castle and keep their focus outward, but none will risk their lives. If it gets dangerous, Aethon has ordered them to flee."

Zara chews on her bottom lip. "Do you think we can do it, Seb?"

He smiles, pulling her lip free with his thumb as he caresses it gently. "Yes, but it's not without risk. Should something happen, you run. Understand? I don't want to worry about you. Aethon and Cindra will watch over you. In six days, you will be called back to my realm. Nero will look after you from that point on. He is an excellent advisor."

"Sebastian?" Her eyes flood with unshed tears as she blinks them back. "You can't leave me. You need to come home with me."

"Zara, my queen. I will do everything in my power to keep us safe, but there is always the unexpected."

Zara wraps her arms around him and buries her face against his chest. "I don't want a life without you, Seb. You are everything to me."

He holds her silently, giving her a few moments, before pulling her back and placing a hand under her chin. "You won't have a life without me, Zara. I do not break my vows and I vowed I would do everything in my power to keep us together. I intend to keep that vow, and a dragon is not stopping that."

Twenty-Four

Unexpected Delivery

After sparing, Nero and Gianna chat while he walks her to her job along the main drag. Stopping at the entrance, he caresses her cheek softly. "When are you done?"

Gianna nods. "Five tonight. Do you think we are going to get her back, Nero?"

"We will. Apparently, your king is arriving in a few hours and we all have a meeting."

"Thank you Nero. For being my rock."

"Rock?"

"You know, someone solid like a rock to lean on."

Nero chuckles. "I see. Being called a rock is a first for me."

Gianna smiles and rises to her tiptoes, kissing his lips. "Yes, well, it's a fact, and you are amazing."

He draws her into a hug. "They will both return, Gianna."

Gianna takes a moment before pushing him away. "I hope so. Okay, I gotta get to work."

"Alright, I will wander by a few times and wink at you."

Gianna laughs. "Stalker much!"

"Oh course. Isn't that our job? I mean, Zara has books about vampires stalking their victims."

"Goooo Nero!!" She turns and heads into the restaurant, grabbing her apron and slipping it on. Noting which tables are hers today, she laughs out loud that her boss gave her the patio. "Fantastic." An hour later, as she steps outside to take a hamburger out to a customer, she spots Colten wave her down and approach the patio.

"Gianna!"

She inwardly cringes, forcing a smile to her face. "Colten. What brings you here?"

"Oh, I was just delivering a few packages and saw you working. Where is your girlfriend?"

"She left on a trip out of town."

"Really? Where?"

"I can't say."

His eyes narrow slightly, scanning the primary thoroughfare, his eyes stopping on Anthony and Zach. "I see there are a few strangers in town."

Gianna follows his gaze. "Yes, they are visiting Zach's family."

Colten eyes flash a brilliant red as they lock back on Gianna.

She takes a step back, suddenly realizing he is more than just the human he portrays. "Is everything alright Colten?"

"No, it's not alright. You have vampires here."

Shock flickers briefly in her eyes before she schools her expression. "Vampires? Are you crazy? They don't exist and even if they did, everyone knows they can't walk in the sun."

"Don't play games with me, Gianna. I can see one of them around your friend Zach." He points to the fighting pits. "And three are fighting over there. Where's their bastard leader?"

Gianna follows his gaze, seeing Nero and the others, teaching some wolves how to fight. "I don't know what you are talking about. As I said, they are Al... Darian's friends."

"Cut the crap Gianna. I know you are wolf shifters and they are vampires."

"How do you know that?"

"Let me see. Packages to Alpha, Luna, Delta, Beta and Gamma. I also see wolves running the borders when I drive in here to deliver mail. What I don't understand is how you can allow filthy blood sucking whores here. They are supposed to be your enemies."

Gianna's eyes dart back to Colten, doing her best to school the fear creeping in as she mind-links Darian. *'Alpha, we have a problem. You better get out here.'*

Colten grabs Gianna's wrist, pulling her close to him, his breath hot on her cheek. "DID you just call your Alpha? You think he's gonna save you? He's not. I don't really want you, Gianna. I was here to watch Zara. She's the special one. Tied to the bastard Sebastian, and it's him I want. I have been searching the packs for longer than you have been alive. Then when I found her, waiting until she came of age to find her mate. The wretched wannabe vampire king. But she refused to come to a border fight, and I couldn't just attack the pack. That would bring the Lycan king here. No, I played it cool. I waited. I bided my time. Well, time is up. I will kill them both now. Then I will kill all the vampires in his realm, and rule over all those that are left. NOW, where is he?"

"What the hell?" Gianna pushes against him, finding Colten's strength better than hers. "ZACH! NERO!"

Dragon's claws dig into her as Colten pulls her away from the restaurant, shifting into his Draconic form and holding Gianna in the air. "I am not asking again, Gianna."

"Colten! Let me go!" She gasps as he squeezes her tightly, pain flooding through her body. Catching all the people in the restaurant scattering in fear, none wanting to tangle with the dragon.

"No Gianna, you are precious to me now. A barter, if you will. I will release you in exchange for their king!"

Nero turns at Gianna's voice, fear coursing through him at the sight, recalling his queen in the same position. He runs forward among the people fleeing and stops Zach from attacking, whispering softly. "No Zach, let me handle it." He turns and faces the dragon. "The King is not here."

Colten turns his gaze to the others racing around, focusing on the four vampires and Zach, with the Alpha and Zara's father running towards them. "Then I suggest you get him, or I will end her."

A bitter smile crosses Nero's lips. "If only it were that easy. You see, my queen took him to the Lycan King's castle. It seems they solved some step towards the prophecy you want to stop. It formed a magical hourglass and realm hopped them somewhere."

"You're lying!"

"I wish I was. The connection between us broke two days ago."

Colten growls, reading the truth of the words in all of their expressions, just as the alarm goes off in his head. "That fucking bastard is in my castle!" A roar escapes him as he draws on the power of his amulet and creates a portal beside him. He jumps through and takes to the air, his eyes narrowing on his castle as his claws tighten around Gianna.

Twenty-Five

Wings of Wrath

S ebastian glances to the others in the rebellion traveling with them, a mix of
races but mostly dragons who want the ruling monarch defeated. "Stay back
and keep to the shadows. Zara and I enter the castle alone to get what we need.
The less we have, the easier it is to sneak past guards. We are not ready to fight yet.
Not until we have the scroll and know more of the prophecy."

Aethon nods. "No one is following you in. We will keep the ramparts occupied
by moving through the woods, just in range, then out of range."

"Got it." Sebastian turns to Zara. "Are you ready, my love?"

"As ready as I can be, Seb." She shifts, allowing Ember full control. She nudges
Sebastian and licks his face before slipping into the shadows of the forest.

Sebastian watches her leave and turns to Aethon. "If something happens to me,
you get her back downstairs. Knock her out if you have to. Tie her up. I don't care.
Keep her safe for the next five days."

"We will, Sebastian."

"Thank you." He shifts into a raven and flies towards the castle, settling into a
tree high enough to watch. Paying close attention to the patrols and their steps.
'Where are you, Ember?'

'Just on the outside of their radius. Ready to go.'

Fifteen minutes later, he takes to the air. *'Alright, go now.'*

Ember leaps onto the road, her eyes looking at the castle as she stills. Growling
softly at the guards to draw their attention, before bolting into the woods on the
other side.

Sebastian drops down and shifts behind the first guard, wrapping an arm
around his neck, his presence alerting the other guard. His eyes glow dangerously
as they narrow, drawing on his power to dominate him, wrapping it around the
one he holds as well. "You will both remain on guard, unmoving for the next hour.

Then you will forget we were even here." Smiling as they both freeze in place, he glances up at the guards on the ramparts, walking in the opposite direction. He mind-links Ember. *'Get here now.'*

Ember bolts from the shadows, racing towards the gate and Sebastian, her eyes darting to the guards, hoping they don't turn around. Just as she arrives next to him, she can hear their shouts, pointing at something in the woods.

Sebastian reaches down, drawing on his vampiric strength. He lifts the portcullis enough for a wolf to slide under. *'Get in.'*

'What about you?'

'Em, Now.'

She lies down and shimmies her way under, feeling a moment of fear and panic when the gate closes after her.

'Follow me.' Sebastian shifts back into a raven and flies through, guiding her along the shadows and out of range of the patrols.

'You could have told me you were shifting into a bird.' She growls softly in his mind. *'Zara read it was bats.'*

Sebastian chuckles in her mind. *'I can do that too, but prefer the raven. I can also shift into a wolf.'*

'Really? How did we not know these things?'

'You never asked.'

'Damn. We need to ask more questions.'

'And pay more attention.'

'What do you mean?'

'When the dragon captured you in my realm, I arrived as a raven after Nero called me.'

'We were focused on Papa.'

Once they reach the main doors, Sebastian shifts back, petting Ember's head lightly. *'It's alright, I know where I stand in your books.'*

Ember growls and snaps playfully at his hand. *'That is so not fair. It was Zara in charge then!'*

'Sure, blame Zara.' He grabs the handles and grows serious once more. *'Alright, in and out. We search quickly and take the scroll.'*

'Got it.'

He pushes the door open and they both slip inside. Sebastian guides them cautiously through the castle, recalling the floor plan that Aethon had, finding himself at the door to the office. Word was that Coltrannax was still off the realm, but it wasn't worth the risk of drawing his attention at this moment. Stepping into the room, they both stop in shock, seeing the scroll on display, protected by a glass case. Right next to is a painting depicting a very similar likeness of Zara.

Sebastian approaches it cautiously, feeling the magic radiating off it, even from the doorway. *'I have a bad feeling about this, Ember. We grab it and run as fast as we can.'*

Ember looks around nervously. *'Yes. It's too easy. It should be more protected. Glass isn't exactly conducive to that. It breaks easily.'*

'Agreed. Are you ready?'

'Yes.'

His hands caress the glass case, before driving his fist through the center, watching it shatter around the impact. Alarms suddenly surround them as he rips the scroll off the wall. Using his vampiric speed, he grabs Ember by the scruff and drags her from the room, just as the door slams shut after them.

Ember yelps in pain, her eyes snapping at the crashing sound beside her. *'It tried to lock us in there?'*

"Yes, let's go." Sebastian quickly rolls the scroll up and tucks it into a pocket in his cloak. He guides them back through the castle the way they came, stopping at the front door to watch the guards. "Alright Em. We are going to do the same pathing. Once you slide under the portcullis, bolt for the woods. I will follow in raven form."

'Got it Seb.'

Sebastian retraces their steps, seeing the guards alert, but facing outward, knowing they are cutting a fine line between the guards' ability to sense them. Once back at the portcullis, he lifts it high enough for Ember to slip out, placing it gently back down. A chill runs through him as his eyes land on the black dragon flying their way. "Ember. RUN!"

Nero bolts, drawing on his speed to follow the dragon and Gianna, feeling an immediate connection to Sebastian and Zara as he steps into the realm. *'My king.'*

'Nero? How?'

'The dragon's portal before it closed. He was in the pack wanting you. He has Gianna, sire.'

'We will get her back, Nero.'

'I know. I am following on foot. I believe he's heading to his castle.'

'Damn, that is him I see heading our way. We are just leaving after stealing the scroll.'

'Clearly there is an alarm, as he suddenly knew.'

'We heard it. Nearly got captured.'

Coltrannax spots the wolf running from his castle, with Sebastian on the other side of the portcullis. He drops Gianna and roars, his eyes narrowing dangerously on Zara.

Ember's heart skips a beat as her eyes lock onto the massive dragon barreling towards them. Gianna dangles momentarily in its grasp before plummeting through the air to the ground. Realizing too late that she is the target, Ember spins on her heels, her claws digging into the earth as she sprints in the opposite direction, breathing a mental sigh of relief at Gianna's curse in her thoughts via mind-link. *'Gianna?'*

'That bloody bastard! Gawd that fucking hurt... Colten, the delivery boy, is the dragon.'

'We know. How are you here?'

'He dropped me, the prick. He wanted to make a deal. Me for your mate and he fucking dropped me.'

'Can you run? Do you need help?'

'Barely. I feel like a truck hit me. I think I broke my ankle or leg or something. Wait, what the hell? Nero is here.'

Nero kneels next to Gianna, looking her over carefully. "Are you good to stay here for a bit?"

She nods. "Yes, go help him and Ember."

Sebastian shifts into a raven and takes to the air, heading straight for Ember, knowing she is not outrunning a dragon.

Coltrannax dives, crashing through the trees, his claws uprooting them up. Locking his jaw on Ember, he gives her a shake as his teeth sink into her. Delight fills him at the taste of her blood, the sweet taste of her power driving him to clamp down harder.

Ember howls in agony, trying to slip from his bite, only to feel her ribcage getting crushed in his jaws. She blinks in terror, white hot pain matching the sparks of lights flickering in her gaze.

Sebastian shifts back, staggering beneath the pain that he can feel in their bond. "EMBER!" He calls forth a sword and runs to the dragon, driving his blade into the dragon's side.

Coltrannax spits Ember out, as he breathes in, exhaling a blast of fire that billows out and engulfs the spot where Sebastian had been.

Ember groans at the impact and rolls over, rising unsteadily to her feet.

Coltrannax spins around at Ember's movement, his claws sinking into her and pinning her in place.

She drops again as his claws tear through her. Twisting her head, she clamps down on the underside of Coltrannax's foot, knowing he is killing her and wanting to make sure he remembers her. Tearing out a scale, she spits it aside, digging her teeth into the flesh beneath it.

Feeling the needling pain in his foot, Coltrannax slams his foot onto the ground, placing most of his weight on the wolf and grinding down, his lips curling in amusement as her body breaks. Picking her up, he tosses her away, watching her roll to a stop and lie still. Turning his attention to Sebastian, he laughs at his panic-stricken expression. "Aww, did you feel that? You didn't feel the other Zara die. That's how I knew she wasn't the right one. This one will die soon. Then you will die, but I want you to know what loss feels like first."

Sebastian's eyes shift, the dark blue fading as red floods them. A rage that he has never felt before, fills him as he faces the dragon before him. He tosses his sword at the dragon's throat, intending to race to Zara, only to be met with a wall of dirt and vines rising from the ground, blocking his path to her. He turns to the chanting, seeing the witch Stella up on the castle ramparts, fury in her eyes and a smirk plastered on her lips.

Coltrannax bats the flying sword away with ease, knowing after all this time, he will successfully take down the vampire kingdom.

Nero grimaces at Ember sailing through the air, feeling the precarious thread of life dangling along their bond. He races over to where she lies, grateful for the wall rising between them. He rolls her over carefully, sadness filling his gaze, knowing she is not surviving this. "Lassie."

Ember breathes raggedly. *'Nero, please tell Seb I love him. Zara does too.'*

"Ember, you will tell him yourself."

'No, Nero, I can feel darkness calling.'

Nero lifts her head, forcing her to look at him. "Fight it Ember!"

Ember cracks her eyes, her focus fading as she struggles to find him. *'It's too late.'*

"NO, it's not." Nero's claws extend on his left hand as he slices the palm of his right hand. "Bite me Ember."

'No...'

Nero growls, drawing on his aura to dominate her. "BITE ME!"

Ember succumbs to the command and sinks her teeth into his hand, tasting the cool metal of his blood with heady tones of cinnamon beneath it.

"That's it lassie. Latch on tightly." Nero grimaces in pain at the force of her bite. "Now shift."

'It hurts, Nero. I can't.'

"SHIFT Ember!"

Ember's teeth sink further into Nero's hand as she fights to shift back, her body arching in agony, as her growls of pain fill the air. Her body morphs back to her human shape, with her insides torn apart, ribs piercing through her skin. Zara gasps, turning her face away from Nero's hand, gagging on the blood filling her mouth and flowing down her throat. Her body shudders as her stomach churns at the taste. Blood drips from her mouth as her head lolls to the side, unable to fight anymore.

Nero takes her hand and squeezes it gently. "That's it Zara. I knew you could do it."

"Sebast..." Her eyes find Nero's through the shroud of darkness, tears creeping from the corners of her eyes and slipping down her face into her hair. She twitches her finger, showing Nero she feels his touch as the death claims her.

Nero hugs her close, feeling her heart stop and the link break through their bond, tears slipping from his own eyes. "My queen." He licks his palm and the bite marks to seal his wounds. Lifting her limp body into his arms, he carries her back to where he left Gianna. Placing Zara down, he kneels down next to a distraught Gianna, sobbing against the ground, knowing she felt the death of her friend. Wrapping his arms around her, he pulls her into his embrace. "Shhh Gia. We will get through this. I need to help Sebastian or we will lose them both."

"Why would he do this? I HATE him Nero! KILL that fucking bastard." Gianna rages against his chest.

"We will. But I need you to do me a favor first."

Sniffling, she brushes at the tears flowing down her cheek. "What favor?"

"Find some vines and tie her up."

"Who?"

"Zara."

"But she's dead."

"I know, but when she wakes, she's gonna be uncontrolled, hungry and far stronger than you, who she will see as a meal."

"You turned her?"

"I tried. But I cannot guarantee it worked."

Gianna smiles through her tears and nods. "Oh my Goddess Nero. Thank you! I will tie her up good!"

"That's my girl. Now, I will return. Stay hidden, but if you can get further away, do it."

Sebastian staggers back in agony as the link between him and Zara breaks, overriding the pain from the dragon's claw raking across his chest. He drops to his knees, his chest heaving as he struggles to comprehend his loss in the middle of the battle. The slam of the dragon slides him across the ground, just as Nero's thoughts radiate in his head.

'Fight Sebastian! She did!'

Sebastian's red eyes darken to blue as his drive and focus returns. He recalls his sword, striking the soft spot in the pad of Coltrannax's foot that appears to be missing a scale. Plunging it deep and stopping the descent, he rolls out from beneath it and rises to his feet once more. Chanting from behind him draws his attention to the glimmer of fire arcing his way. He shifts quickly to the back side, placing the dragon between them for some measure of concealment against her. *'Nero, Stella is here.'*

'On her soon. Zara's body is with Gianna.'

Sebastian glides around, slicing his blade through the hindfoot, knowing the first rule of fighting monsters is to aim for the heart. Of course, that is assuming the monster is not a gigantic dragon with a heart well above his reach. Next best thing is to take out the legs, to reach said heart.

Coltrannax breathes again, lighting the grasses and shrubs on fire around him to limit Sebastian's movements, knowing vampires are vulnerable to it whereas it doesn't affect him. His eyes trace Sebastian's movements, his fury growing when he notices Zara's body is missing from the other side of the wall. He sweeps his tail around, aiming to take Sebastian off his feet again, only to find he is no longer there, feeling the sting of his blade along his side and into the back of his front leg. Scanning the surrounding area, his gaze narrows on Gianna, dragging Zara's body deeper into the woods, struggling with a broken leg. "Aww Gianna. To lose your best friend. How you must hate me now."

Gianna pauses, lifting her chin in defiance. "I didn't like you as a delivery driver, Colten, and I like you even less as a dragon. I thought you were a pathetic piece of shit. Now I know just how pathetic you are. Killing a wolf while you're a dragon. Can we say Pa...THET...IC!!!!. The least you could have done was face her in your human form. But then she would have kicked your fuckin ass and you know it. You are a waste of space and I hope Sebastian rectifies it by destroying you for what you have done to her."

"You dare to speak to me like that, Gianna? You are also just as easily killed. Remember that, because when I am done with the king here, you're next." Coltrannax growls, slamming his tail into Sebastian as he feels the bite of his sword again, turning his focus back to the target at hand.

"That's right, you prick! Come and get me!" Gianna stiffens as a group of men surround her, one stepping in behind her and sliding a hand over her mouth to silence her. Panic floods her, darting her gaze to Nero and seeing him currently engaged with Stella. "Shh Gianna. We are not here to hurt you. No screaming alright."

Gianna nods. "What do you want?"

"We are part of the rebellion. Aethon has demanded we retrieve you and the body of Zara now that Coltrannax's attention is back on the vampire. Enough provoking him."

"Deal, but I can't walk and she still needs to be tied up."

"We know." He lifts her up as the other collects the broken remains of Zara, all of them fading into the woods away from the battle.

Zed and Brittany shimmer in, immediately taking in the scene before them. Brittany weaves a wall of air, stopping the group carrying the two girls away. "I do believe, boys, that those two girls belong to us."

The one carrying Zara turns, studying the newcomers intently. The human has white blonde hair floating about her as if a breeze is constantly running over her. Dressed in silver and pale blue robes, standing a good head shorter than the elf beside her. Her silver eyes glitter in the light, with a white mist swirling within them. The male elf, dressed in silk robes of a darker blue that complement hers, has ash blonde hair that appears dark in comparison, and his green eyes glow vibrantly. "Who the hell are you?"

Zed narrows his eyes, a gleam of red flickering behind his green depths. "We are here on behalf of the Lycan King to fetch Alpha Darian's missing pack members. That includes these two and the two vampires."

The man stiffens and pulls the body away, looking over the elf in dismay, feeling the powerful aura billowing out from him. "Well then, you need to take it up with the vampire fighting the dragon. His wish to Aethon is that we get the girl to safety."

"The girl is dead." Zed studies the group before him, while mind-linking Brittany. *'Brit, there is no aura on her. The others hold no shadows.'*

Drake nods. "Yes, that bastard of a dragon that rules this world killed her. If you want to help, kill that dragon and the witches tied to him. Now, if you don't mind, we need to get them to camp."

Brittany glances at her mate Zed, turning her eyes back to the man. "Once we are done, I will come for them." She turns her attention to the vampire fighting the witch on the ramparts. "I will get the witch. Zed, you help with the dragon."

"I will. Have fun Brit. I know how much you enjoy taking down dark witches." Zed kisses her lightly and races off toward Coltrannax and Sebastian.

"Yes, I do. Her and her sisters are going down." Her hands clench at her side, as she draws on her magic, stepping in beside Nero.

Nero spins at the presence beside him, the point of his sword stopping beneath her chin. "Friend or Foe?"

"Friend. Brittany. Used to work for King Caden. I got her. You help with the dragon."

Sebastian eyes the elf warily and shifts his position to face them both. Suspecting Coltrannax must have allies out there, but so far, none stepped in. He isn't taking any chances. "Touch me and I will kill you, too."

Zed chuckles. "Friend of yours... Sebastian, I presume. Enemy to the dragon here."

"Who the hell are you?" Coltrannax snaps at Zed. His teeth sink into his shoulder, lifting him off the ground.

"Your death." Shadows coalesce around Zed as his elfin form fades into shadows, calling forth the curse of his land. Red eyes glitter in delight at the aura before him, knowing the darkness is only going to feed his power, one that his mate Brittany has been teaching him to harness. His claws sink into the gumline of the dragon, drawing his essence inward, savoring the dragon's taste.

Coltrannax feels the drain on his soul and shakes his head, trying to dislodge the elf that he has just bitten. Not realizing it is a shadow walker in disguise. Every creature knows how dangerous they are. How they drain your life force until you are nothing but a husk. He slams his face into the wall, feeling the grip weaken, but not relinquish its hold, staggering back a few steps.

Sebastian jumps back at the dragon's head swiveling past him rapidly, shock filling him; both with the dragon's crazed actions and the fact that the elf just shifted to shadows. He dodges the claws as the dragon does his best to dislodge whoever or whatever is now latched on. Taking advantage of the distraction, he races around to the back of the dragon and crawls up his spine, knowing if he could get between the wings, he could hopefully find his heart.

Zed's teeth glitter like cut diamonds as his grin widens, feeling his shadowy form slam into the wall but maintaining his hold. Pulling himself up, he wraps around the neck, ensuring contact in more than one place, each touch drawing in his life force. "Ffinnaallsz lllastszz wooordss draagoonsz."

"Get the hell off me. This is NOT your fight." Coltrannax gnashes his teeth, trying to bite the hands off to no avail. Going for the next best thing, he swipes a claw through him, trying to dislodge him, only to feel the further drain against his claw. Panic floods him that a simple creature as a walker is going to defeat him, after all that he had set in motion. He hasn't even had the chance to kill the bloody vamp yet. Spinning suddenly, he beats his wings, intending to take to the air, needing to escape to fight another day.

Sebastian continues to move up his spine, positioning himself between the wings. Realizing that Coltrannax is planning to leave, he drives his blade into the wing leather, dragging his sword down its length and tearing it in two.

Coltrannax roars in pain, feeling his wing nearly removed from his body. He bucks frantically, trying to shake off his two attackers, as another sword drives into his side. Swiveling his gaze around, he sees the angry gaze of Nero, his own blood coating the hand of the blade he pierced him with. His gaze travels to Stella, stuck in a magical tornado, frozen and unable to move, with another witch he doesn't recognize, chanting nearby. He stumbles her way, breathing out a burst of flame. "Stella..."

Nero shifts at the dragon's lumbering movements, realizing as flames burst from his mouth, just who he is aiming for. "Brittany! Incoming."

She lifts a hand as a wall of air surrounds her; the flames rolling over her and into Stella, who screams in agony as the flames strike her. "I am surprised you don't have fire protection, considering you side with the dragon. Call the rest of your coven, Stella."

"I have no coven!"

"And yet, five witches attacked Zara and her father."

"They abandoned me! They could not see the true vision."

"Perhaps they did, and that's why they bailed."

"NO, they were wrong!"

Brittany laughs. "Either way, you are still going to pay a visit to my sisters." Brittany changes the nuances of her magic, calling forth a shimmering wall behind the cyclone holding Stella. With a flick of her wrist, she sends her through the portal to the prison waiting for her, knowing it's magically imbued to stop her from casting.

Stella smirks. "You can't keep me here. I can realm hop!"

"You could, but not anymore. Enjoy your stay." A sly grin crosses Brittany's lips, watching Stella realize her situation as the portal closes. Turning her attention to the dragon fight, she can see they have it well in hand.

Coltrannax slumps to the ground, feeling his energy depleting at a swift rate from the shadow walker, let alone the pain in his body from the vampires' blades. His heart sinks as he watches Stella burn from his breath, and then get banished, knowing he is never seeing her again. His witch. The one who supported him without question. The one he had failed. Hatred fills him with those who foiled his plans, knowing if he had a redo, he would have just killed the bloody wolf instead of playing the game he did. But he wanted more. Stella had warned him. Even her sisters decided they wanted no part of his plan, but she stuck with him. He should have listened. He closes his eyes, drifting into the endless darkness of death.

Sebastian drops his sword and sinks to his knees at the dragon's death, his shoulder slumping as grief floods him at the loss of his mate. Images flash through his mind of her broken body. Regret that they didn't move fast enough, or that he didn't protect her as he promised. He had failed her and now will suffer with her loss for an eternity. Somewhere in the reaches of his mind, he can feel Nero's hand on his shoulder, offering him some measure of comfort.

Feeling the life leave the dragon, Zed releases his grip upon him and rises to his full height of ten feet, towering over the two vampires, one looking at him warily, the other staring vacantly at the ground. He smiles, his white teeth looking all that more dangerous against the shadows that make up his form. Red eyes glitter as he moves forward, hesitating at Nero summoning his blade and standing protectively over his king. "Neeeroooz, Seeebastiannnz, Friiienndz... Heerrress toooz reetuurnsz yoouusz toooz Daarriiannzz."

Brittany flies over to the threesome and lands beside Zed. "Zed, I gather from their expressions, they don't know what you are. Nero, Sebastian. This is my mate Zed. He is a Shadow walker. After twenty-four hours outside their realm, a curse descends upon them, forcing them into this form. They can choose to accept it earlier if needed, which he has done to defeat the dragon. Lady luck was on your side, because we were already planning a visit and showed up unexpectedly. Caden informed us you needed our help. Otherwise, it would have been at least five days before we could rescue you."

Nero answers, knowing Sebastian is not in his right mind currently. "Thank you. We appreciate the help. The dragon is dead and judging by the surrounding cheers, people in this realm are happy. My king unfortunately needs time having felt his mate die at the dragon's hands, or rather, his claws."

Aethon hobbles over to the group, studying Sebastian carefully, not familiar enough with the workings of a vampire to know how he is going to react to her death. "Yes. And tonight, there will be parties in the streets. Those loyal to Coltrannax will still need to be weeded out." His eyes shift to meet Nero's, seeing what he had done with the wolf and judging by where his king knelt, hasn't told him yet. "Now, come, we need to get you underground. We will take the short path, like they took the girls?"

"Yes. The quicker we get to them, the better." Nero nods, and slips an arm beneath Sebastian, helping him to his feet. "Sire, let's go. Zara waits for you."

Sebastian turns his gaze to Nero, despair radiating from within their depths. "She died, Nero. He crushed her, and I felt her pain as my own. I could not stop it. I failed her."

"No, you did not. She loves you and will love you again."

"I do not have the power to bring back the dead, Nero."

"Sebastian. My brother, whom I love and support fully. You know this. I could not watch her die and so I fed her my blood. First as Ember and then as Zara."

Sebastian frowns, trying to comprehend what he is saying. "Wait. You bound her to you?"

"Yes. I did. To save her. When she returns, I will go through the ceremony to unbind her and hand her back where she belongs. She is my queen. Your mate, but I needed to save her and it was my only option."

Sebastian's eyes flood, tears escaping as he steps in and hugs Nero fiercely, despite the pain in his body from the dragon's strikes. "Thank you Nero. I owe you!"

"Sire, you owe me nothing. If you feel you must, then solve this prophecy so that we can live in harmony with our mates. That's what I want."

He chuckles and steps back, clasping Nero's shoulder. "I will. I have the scroll now. We can look at it downstairs."

Aethon shakes his head. "Right, now that the brotherly bonding is done, let's get downstairs. I am not sure how long it takes for your queen to return, but I want you there when she does. I don't need vampiric dragons, thank you very much. Coltrannax was enough."

"Agreed." Sebastian turns to Zed and Brittany. "Thank you for helping."

"Anytime. What I want to know is why it was just the three of you fighting them when others lurked nearby."

"Walk and talk. That's a thing you know," Aethon growls, gesturing to the lot of them, earning a chuckle from the group. Guards fall-in beside them as Aethon leads them into the woods nearby. He murmurs a few words as a large rock rolls to the side and steps into the darkness of the passage below it. "Quickly. It doesn't stay open for long." Once they are beneath the ground, the rock falls back into place, surrounding them in darkness. He guides them through the underground passage. "As for why we were not helping, we couldn't. Obsidius, the previous ruler, decided he wanted to rule all the lands. Things went badly with his spell. Entire land masses and races disappeared. Or we disappeared. Hard to say, actually. Dragons from other lands appeared here. With that, a curse settled upon this realm. A twisted protection that prevents us, the very people of this land, from overthrowing the ruler. Only an outsider, someone not of our kind, has the power to break his reign. We suspect he cast it to secure his own position, believing it would shield him indefinitely, but clearly, his foresight was flawed."

Brittany ponders it. "Interesting. My mate has a curse tied to his lands as well."

Aethon chuckles. "Indeed. I am guessing that you don't know it was Obsidius who cursed your mate's race."

Brittany snaps her gaze to his. "What do you mean?"

"My darling witch, Shadow walkers are the ones who killed Obsidius. On his dying breath, he cursed them with the powers of the witches he absorbed, banishing them back to their realms."

Brittany laughs. "That's it! The missing hole in our research. We didn't know where the curse originated from."

"Now you do. It's our hope that Zara and Sebastian here can break ours. Unfortunately, yours is an after-effect, so to speak."

"It's fine. We have a starting point now." Her eyes lift to Zeds, seeing the delight glittering in their red depths.

Meanwhile, downstairs, they place Gianna on a bedroll to rest while others carry Zara further into the camp.

Gianna hobbles after them as best as she can, resorting to crawling when the pain becomes too much. "No, I'm staying with her."

Drake glances at his companions, nodding to have someone assist her. Ten minutes later, he is on the outskirts of the camp, where stakes have been driven into the ground. He places Zara's body between them and quickly lashes her to them.

"Nooo. Nero just said, to tie her up. This is inhumane."

"If she comes back, she will break any ropes around her wrists or ankles. With her arms and legs spread like this, it limits her strength and keeps her contained until her mate can soothe her."

Gianna drops to her knees beside her and sobs. "She's my best friend. You are disrespecting her!"

"She's dead. There is no disrespect meant. It's not like she knows. Please. Just trust us. They did. Now, lets look at your legs and reset any bones that need it."

Gianna shakes her head. "I am not leaving her."

"That's fine. We can do it here. Lie down. Cindra will look you over. She's our healer."

Cindra approaches Gianna, giving her a once over. She kneels beside Gianna, running a hand over her legs, leaving a trail of amber lights. The glow increases as it embeds into Gianna's skin, sinking down to the bone and mending it. Giving a nod, Cindra rises and smiles at Gianna. "I healed the bones. But I would suggest staying off them for a few hours. Rest here with your friend." She looks up to the others. "Drake, get her a bedroll."

"Yes, ma'am."

A few minutes later, Drake reappears and lays a bedroll down. "Here you are, miss. The vampires are on their way. They should be here soon."

Gianna nods, shifting the bedroll closer to Zara and lies down on it.

"I would not suggest being that close to her."

"She's my best friend. She won't hurt me. I don't want her waking up and not having me here for her."

"And if she feeds off you?"

"Then she does. If she takes too much, I am quite certain you would stop her."

"Fine, but I don't think you understand how a hungry vampire works."

Gianna hisses angrily. "NO, you don't understand these vampires, or Zara, for that matter."

Drake lifts his hands in surrender, knowing better to argue with an angry woman. "You're correct. Just stay safe alright."

Aethon leads the group through the passages into the cavern. Guiding them through the tents, he leads them through to where he knows the she-wolves are. Sadness crosses his features, seeing the once vibrant shifter, dead, lashed to stacks. He flinches at Sebastian's growl.

"Untie her NOW!"

Nero steps up, placing a hand on his shoulder to calm him. "Sebastian, I requested it. We didn't know how long we would be. I didn't want her waking and going on a feeding spree."

Sebastian narrows his eyes, the rage and grief fighting for dominance within him. Closing his eyes, he focuses on stabilizing his emotions. "Untie her. I will care for her."

Nero's voice is quiet. "Sebastian, you can't. I bound her."

Pain fills Sebastian's voice. "Nero, please."

Nero moves over and unties Zara, lifting her into his arms. He carries her over to Sebastian and places her in his grasp. "If you need me, link me."

Gianna struggles to her feet, wrapping her arms around Nero and using him as a support. "If she needs to feed. I will feed her."

Brittany glances over at Aethon's men watching, knowing the situation is unprecedented. "We shouldn't stay. We need to return to your realm. Gianna, she may need more than you can offer."

Sebastian hugs her body close, absently listening to their conversation. "We have time. Her body has to mend before she wakes. Tomorrow morning, perhaps because of the damage." He lifts his gaze to Gianna. "Gia, Brittany is correct. Zara is going to need several blood donors. There is too much damage. The conversion is going to be rough on her. On top of that, she belongs to Nero, so my bond cannot soothe her."

Gianna's hands clench on Nero's arm. "What does that mean, exactly?"

Nero pulls Gianna in close. "When you sire a vampire, that childe, as they are called, belongs to them. I sired Zara because it was the only way I could save her. When she wakes, she is going to come looking for me. My blood in her will call to her, but her mate-bond with Sebastian will fight it. She will not understand what's happening and it will feel as if she is being torn in two."

"No... NO, Nero!" She grabs his shirt and twists her fingers through it. "You need to fix it! Have Sebastian give her blood. She's his mate, not yours! Why!?"

Nero clasps his hands over hers. "Gia, it doesn't affect us. It affects them. Let me put it another way. I went to the market and bought a horse. Zara is the horse and so she belongs to me. She, of course, prefers Sebastian when he walks into the barn. I have the bridle on her, controlling her, even if it's unintentional, and he has her love."

"So you can sell her to him?"

Sebastian chuckles. "Wait till I tell her you are selling her like chattel."

"But he can, right?"

"Yes. It's an extensive blood ceremony, and Nero has already offered to do it."

Gianna breathes a sigh of relief, her body collapsing against Nero's. "Right then, we do that, then solve the prophecy and we are golden!"

"Not golden. She will still wake with the battle of two bloods within her. I also need to face her family and tell them I failed to keep her safe."

Gianna pulls from Nero's grasp and stumbles over to Sebastian. "You cannot blame yourself. That fucking dragon is at fault. If he had faced her as a human, she would have kicked his ass and he knew it. He deliberately faced her as a dragon so you would both lose. You did what you could, Sebastian, keeping the dragon occupied while Nero saved her. They will understand."

"Let's hope so, Gianna."

Brittany glances between them all. "I think they are expecting you home tonight, but we can wait till morning if that is your desire. It will just cause them more stress as they wait."

Sebastian ponders it as he looks over Zara in his arms, something inside telling him to wait. He had not lived as long as he had, without learning to listen to the inner voice. "As much as it pains me to cause them stress, I would like to wait. A vampiric Zara returning home is far better than a dead one and, for some reason, I feel she needs to wake here."

"So be it. Listening to instincts trumps everything else. So, let's see the prophecy and start figuring it out while we wait."

Sebastian moves over to the bedroll Gianna was on and places her down. He brushes the hair off her face and kisses her forehead, missing her murmur of appreciation. He rises and steps back with a nod. Stepping over to the table that Aethon is standing near, he pulls the parchment out. Realizing that the dragon's claws had torn through it as well as his chest. He unrolls it carefully and lays it down before everyone. Finally, taking the time to read it, he leans over, taking in the details. The wolves were on one side, facing off against a black dragon. Men in armor stand beneath on each side, one basking in the light, the other shrouded in darkness. In the center between them is a large moon, adorned with runes, and below it, a set of vampire fangs.

When life and death walk as one,
The realms within become undone,
In the fires of chaos a new one begun.
Forged from the union of opposites,
A question of what shall be forfeit.
A world reborn, shifted by the prophecies.
Beyond the lingering animosity.
Through trials untold, they shall endure,
In unity forged, their strength secure.
With courage as their guiding light,
They'll face the darkness, embrace the fight.
Thus, from the ashes of turmoil and strife,
A new dawn emerges, brimming with life.
Only when you still the sands,
Can peace return to the lands.
All with the turning of six runes,
Under the light of the three full moons.

The others lean over and read it with him as he sighs at the newest puzzle they way. "When is the next full moon?"

"Here? Seven days."

Sebastian turns to Gianna. "Yours?"

"Seven days as well."

"So, who else has a moon? My realm does not."

Zed's voice causes a few of them to shudder. "Weez haaveesz onnez. I tthiinksz ittz soonnsz."

Brittany nods. "It is. But there is a glitch in that."

Sebastian turns to Brittany, his brows furrowing. "What do you mean by a glitch, exactly?"

"Well, there is a time difference between Zed's realm and this one. It's huge but seems stable, unlike the fey realms, which are all over the place. We are still trying to narrow it down, but we have figured out it's about one hour of their time to five days of this time, or rather Zara's, because we don't know about this realm yet. So if our moon is soon, that could be months, perhaps even a year, down the road before we all match. Even then, it will be hard to guarantee the timing because of being unable to communicate between the realms."

Sebastian groans and runs a hand through his hair. "So we have to be in three realms, at least. Possibly in seven days or longer, to turn six runes, all at the same time and with no communication. Wonderful."

Nero chuckles. "Hey! You figured this out. You could have waited and given yourself more time."

"Actually. Zara did. I was reading. She figured out the painting of the hourglass had the wrong date. She recalled seeing a book with an hourglass on its spine." He reaches into the satchel and pulls out the book on mystics. "One of nine, in fact." Turning it over to show them the spine. "Each hourglass is set to a different time and each book covers different things. This one is about mystics, but the others included dragons, vampires, wolves, shadow walkers, fey, witches, curses and runes." He flips it open to the lines in the center. "When all nine books were open, it formed a drawing of an hourglass. Lights flowed through the lines, with an hourglass rising from this book, being the center. It flashed nine times and then we were here."

"Wait, are you saying Caden has a book on Zed's race?"

"Yes."

"I will want to read that one. It might have clues to the curse or prophecy."

"Well, hopefully it's still in the King's library. Only this one came with us, so I cannot be certain what happened to the rest."

"He didn't tell me it was there."

Sebastian chuckles. "I have my doubts he knew it was there, Brittany. There are thousands of books in that library. Even I would be hard pressed to read them all in your lifetime and I don't sleep at night. Once Zara discovered the hour glasses, that's all we looked for, hoping it was tied to us."

"Clearly it was, because it brought you here."

"Yes, and now it looks like I will read about mystics while I wait for Zara's body to mend enough to return to life."

Nero reads through the scroll once more and looks over at his queen. "She was meant to die today."

Sebastian growls quietly, "Come again?"

"Look sire. These three lines, right here. They will face the darkness, Coltrannax, and embrace the fight. You both did. This line here." He places a finger down. "From the ashes of turmoil. Ashes implies someone dies. She did. A new dawn, brimming with life. Her life as a vampire can be considered a new dawn. She needs to be a vampire to turn the runes, whatever that means."

Sebastian stares at Nero, reading the hope in his eyes, knowing exactly what he was doing. "You cannot remove the guilt I feel for letting her die, Nero."

"You didn't let her die, sire. You fought. She fought. The dragon got lucky, but I still feel it was meant to be. The whole damn prophecy is about you and her. Life and death. Forged from the union of opposites. You won her over and in that you have a unity unlike any others I have seen. You should feel no guilt."

Sebastian whispers softly. "But I do. What if she blames me?"

"She won't sire. Your name was the last thing she spoke, after she told me to let you know how much she loved you. There was no blame in her voice or her thoughts."

Sebastian's gaze moves to Zara as he grows silent, contemplating Nero's words and what he knows of his queen. He suspects Nero is correct, but that doesn't stop the guilt from eating at him, knowing he is going to do everything in his power to help ease her transition. Especially if she loses Ember in the process, because they are still uncertain how it will work. "I hope you're right, Nero."

"I am sire. Now, as for the last few lines, where do we even begin to learn where the runes are?"

"Perhaps it's tied to the book on runes in the King's library. It was part of the nine in the... what was it she called it? The puzzle."

Aethon, who had been standing around listening, rolls up the scroll and hands it back to Sebastian. "Best to keep that with you. Cindra and I need to go above ground and face the ramifications of Coltrannax's death. But before we do, did you need Cindra to heal your wounds?"

"No, it will mend on its own. Thank you."

"No, thank you. I don't think I stated that. I am truly sorry he killed your mate, but I have to agree with your man here. It sounds like destiny had her hand in this and not much can stop her. You are welcome to stay down here until she wakes. Might be safer actually. You will get swarmed by those wishing to congratulate you for what you have done. Even down here, I can see them watching and waiting to approach. Then there will be the few that want to stab you in the back because technically, you are our new ruler... Or rather, the three of you are. His supporters might not take too kindly to you killing Coltrannax or that you are vampires and a walker."

"Excuse me?"

"The laws of the lands are as such. You defeat the current ruler, you adopt his position. The only reason the Shadow walkers didn't take over when they killed Obsidius is because he banished them at the same time. Coltrannax stepped up quickly after that."

"You are just telling me this now? I already rule a kingdom. I have no desire to rule another. Can I not appoint someone and hand it over?" He looks to Zed and Nero, understanding in at least Nero's expression, he has no desire to rule. Zed is more difficult to read with his piercing red eyes and white teeth, the only thing that stands out in his shadowy form that towered over him.

"You can, yes."

"Well, then, tell me who and I will see it done."

Nero chuckles, glancing at Zed. "Sire, I believe that's a, *we* will see it done."

"Yyyesss, wwwe'ss willsssszz."

Aethon smiles at the three of them. "I will put the call out, though I already have some ideas. We can vote on the new ruler and have a response by morning."

Sebastian tucks the scroll into his pouch. "Whoever it is, make sure you add Steel to that list."

"Why Steel?"

"Being the Lore Master, he knows the ins and outs of your history. He knows what people to trust and who not to. He also has the knowledge of success and mistakes at his fingertips. I think he would make an excellent ruler."

"I will consider this option and speak to him." Aethon gives a nod to the group. "I will return later."

Sebastian nods, picking up the book on mystics, his fingers caressing the edges of the cover, tucking the book away in his pouch as he watches Aethon leave with several of his men. "Nero, Gianna, Zed, Brittany, thank you for your help today. I am uncertain if I could have defeated the dragon and the witch without it."

Nero claps a hand on Sebastian's shoulder. "You would have, sire. It just would have taken longer. Besides, Zed here did most of the damage. I only stabbed it a few times."

Sebastian's gaze moves to Zeds. "Thank you."

"Haapppyyssz toosz hhellpsszz."

"Now, if you don't mind, I need to decompress and be with my queen. Perhaps read a bit."

Nero pulls Sebastian in and hugs him. "Gia and I will be close. Just call if you need us."

"I will." Sebastian returns the hug and gives a nod to Brittany and Zed. "And you?"

"We are going to explore Coltrannax's castle. Stella said she has no coven, but I want to make sure."

"Be careful. Some rooms contain traps."

"We will. Thank you for the warning. Zed can realm hop and I can portal. We will return later."

"Fair enough." Sebastian collects Zara and the bedroll she lies on and carries her into the darkness. Finding a small niche in the cavern wall, he settles into it. Drawing her into his arms, he holds her tightly, struggling with the loss, before breaking down and sobbing quietly into her hair as despair takes over. Some time later, he relinquishes his hold on her and tucks her up against him, caressing her skin lightly. "Look who's got me sitting on the ground again and doesn't even know it. I'm sorry Zara, my rug. I promise I will protect you better in the future."

He pulls out the book on mystics and settles in to read, the words clear on the page despite the darkness surrounding him. Learning on how mystics are considered a rare magic user, but their lifespans are short because of the power they wield. The dead giveaway is the purple eyes that each mystic carries because it is part of their heritage. Several pages list a few of their abilities; kinetic force, master of the elements, powers of persuasion, illusions, shields, mental capacity to read thoughts, but each is vague as it defines them. The common thread among them all is they all have the gift of foresight with the ability to rewrite timelines in the future.

Twenty-Six

Ink and Incantations

Hours later, Sebastian stops at a few lines in the book, the penmanship different from the rest of the book. He turns his attention to Zara's body for a moment, noticing it mending slowly. "Something else for you to solve when you return, my love. There is scripture in this book that differs from all the rest. Cross the veil and come to me. Mystic powers bring forth thee. But it seems too short to call forth a mystic. Most summoning spells requ..."

Swirling purple lights flicker before him, drawing his gaze upwards, as a ghostly image of a teenager appears. Violet eyes staring at him in shock, with shaggy black and red hair falling over his face. Dressed in clothing similar to Zara's world, blue jeans with a red plaid shirt over a white T-shirt. "What the? Bloody hell, you realm called me?"

"I did no such thing." Sebastian rises, studying the boy before him, knowing immediately that he had, in fact, called forth at least an illusion of a mystic. "You are a mystic."

A wide grin crosses his face as his eyes alight with excitement, his hand fisting as he swipes it in front of himself. "Yes, and you called. Damn, wait till Mom hears I finally got a summons! She warned me that the day would come, but I didn't see it happening. I wonder if she does. I will have to ask when she wakes up."

Sebastian tilts his head in confusion, knowing the book he just read stated several time they have brief lives. Not past twenty-five and yet, here is a teenager standing before him. "Your mother is still alive?"

"Yes, but she's in hibernation right now, so I guess that's why you got me."

"Hibernation?"

"A battle wore her out, so she's sleeping and Dad, well, he's just old, so he opted to hibernate with her."

"How old are you?"

"I am sure that's not the question you want to ask, but I am over three hundred years old."

"And you are still alive?"

"Clearly. Mom is powerful. She broke the rules of mystics only living twenty or so years and of their only being one, cause there are two of us. Well, I am only half mystic if truth be told, but we both have abilities. Mom is just way more powerful than I am. Now, what do you want?"

"Want?"

"Yes, you called me here for a reason."

"Actually, I was just reading a book on mystics. There was a scripture in it, but I didn't expect it to call you forth, if that's what you call this. It was only two lines and usually summons like that require a ritual with far more preparation. Though I suppose you are kind of transparent, almost wraith-like, so it's not a complete summons."

"Yes, well, I am not really in your realm, only my mind is. Let's see what's in your threads." His eyes glow softly as he studies Sebastian standing before him, his fingers flickering with small amethyst lights that dance between his hands. "Right, so you are a vampire and just lost your shifter mate in a battle. There is a prophecy with a set of runes tied to both of you. She is the gatekeeper and will return to set things right."

"Yes, we don't actually know how to find them."

"They are in the center of each connected realm. It does not matter which one she uses, but she needs to get the answers of all the races beforehand."

"Answers?"

"Yes, the hourglass will spawn a pillar. On the top, there are six races. Beneath each race are hieroglyphs that will need to be activated, but only if desired. Each race will have a representative that must choose their path for their realm."

"And what are these hieroglyphics, exactly?"

"The first one is Segregated. It seems when the pillar dropped into the earth, some races were divided. It is up to them whether to stay as a race-based land, or merge and mingle with others once again as they were before the break."

"And the second?"

"Realm. It is tied to the first. It will only activate if they choose to merge, for it will restore the lands from where they were taken, and those with it as if they never left."

"How many are there, exactly?"

"Five realms, but six races tied to the prophecy."

"Five? Mine, this one, who else?"

"The gatekeepers, walkers, and fey. The third is Limitless. When either of the aforementioned is chosen, it offers a choice to all citizens whether to accept the decisions made by the gatekeeper, or to remain as is. If they were pulled from a land other than the five in question, then the option is there for them to return and slide in as if they had never left."

"How would that work, exactly? If this realm returns and some citizens decide against it."

"The realms all existed before the break. Citizens just got shifted around with the lands. They will continue as they would have beforehand."

"You know a lot about this prophecy."

"Pretty much nothing, actually. I am simply responding to what I see in the variety of threads I am sorting through, tied to your present and future."

"So, do you know what choices Zara should make?"

The teenager's eyes glaze over. "I see each choice and the consequence of it, be they good or bad."

"Tell me the good ones."

He smiles and shakes his head. "I cannot take the choice from her hands, but she is clever; trust in her decisions. Now, the fourth is Chronos. It will remove the time anomalies between the realms, should they choose for this to happen. This will only activate if they opt to stay as a race and realm." The teenager's eyes focus on Zara's body, light dancing within their depths. "The fifth is Blestem, or rather cursed as you would know it. Activating it will remove the curses that were placed upon the lands by one of my own upon his death."

"One of your own?"

"Yes, I am a dragon, as are both my parents."

"The book does not speak of dragons being mystics, only humans."

"As I said, my mother broke a lot of rules. Now, back to the runes because I think these summons have a time limit. Mom only partially explained them." He frowns and grows silent, his eyes shifting back and forth as he sorts through the threads. "Hmm, the sixth is blank. I cannot see how it works. Perhaps it's tied to the gatekeeper and she will know. I cannot see all her threads, being that she is currently dead and her soul is elsewhere."

Sebastian frowns, not liking his words on Zara's soul. It means she disconnected from her body, probably from the damage and how long it is taking for her body to accept the transition. "Let's back up to the hourglass you spoke of. Do you mean the one the book created?"

"Kinda. That one was a magical illusion, but it looks exactly like it and is here in this realm. I can feel its power ticking with each grain of sand it drops. Find it, find the runes, and solve your prophecy. Now I must return to Cantara, where we have our own issues arising. Damn government, thinking they can play with powers they don't understand. Now the world is in chaos again and they somehow expect me to fix it. Idiots. Pleasure to meet you, King Sebastian, mate to the gatekeeper. Perhaps we will see each other again."

The image before Sebastian flickers as the dancing lights around him fade, leaving him once more in the darkness. He stares into it, unaware of time passing. His thoughts mull over the information given to him. *'Nero. We have a problem. We need to find an artifact. An hourglass somewhere in this realm.'*

'Sire? I will be right there.' A minute later, Nero stands in the dark with Sebastian. "So what's up? Clearly, the book told you something more."

Sebastian chuckles. "No, it summoned a mystic. It's outdated because the mystic I spoke to was a dragon over three hundred years old. The book states in many places that because of the power of mystics, they die young and only one may exist at any given time. Yet there are two. His mother is still around, who apparently is powerful enough to break the rules of mystics regarding them."

"Excuse me? Are you sure it was a mystic?"

"Yes. His thoughts blocked, his eyes violet, his body transparent with a purple glow surrounding him. He was pretty excited to finally be summoned. Plus, the power radiating off him was unlike any I have ever felt."

"So what did he say?"

"That Zara is the gatekeeper. He explained the runes and where to find the center one. But we need the hourglass that the books depicted to activate them. My guess is, it's in either Coltrannax's or Steel's castle."

"Do we go get it now?"

"No, I think we should wait until Zara wakes. I have a feeling that if it's magical, it will only react to her."

Nero hesitates. "It's possible she could be too hungry to function normally."

"Yes, it is something to consider, but I hope not. I would like to solve this sooner rather than later."

"I know Gianna has offered to feed. I will speak with Aethon and see if any of his people would be willing. Dragon's blood may be enough to tide her over until we can get more wolf blood in her."

"It's new territory for me, Nero. I am uncertain what blood she will need, if a dragon will even work."

"I know, sire. I know I put you in this position, but I am not sorry I turned her. If she rages, then you both can take it out on me."

Sebastian moves forward and places his hands on Nero's shoulders. "Nero, you are my brother, my favorite brother, but don't tell the others that. I cannot express in words how happy I am that you converted her. Never would I place blame on you for this situation we are in. I can't even place blame on the dragon at the moment, because if he had not intervened and sent her to me, I would never have met her and had her fill the emptiness inside me. Something I didn't know was there until it was gone, if that makes sense. I simply existed before her and now I exist because of her. There is light in so many things that only held darkness before. I find myself lost in the depths of her eyes, and the blush that creeps across her cheeks along with her shy smiles. Her runaway thoughts being completely opposite of the peaceful expression she has when she sleeps. Or the determination she has to beat on just you for reading those thoughts, even though the others can too. When she died, it felt like I broke inside. Darkness took over my soul. So much pain. To know she is coming back because of what you did. I can never repay that, Nero." His shaking voice lowers to a whisper. "Never..."

"Sire... Sebastian." Nero reaches up to clasp Sebastian's arms. "You never need to repay me. When you marked her and made her our queen, the entire clan felt the love between you. For those of us without a mate or wife, it only emphasized the emptiness within us. It is why you had so many offers to come to this land, or rather Zara's land. They want the same thing. When I saw her struggling to draw in her last breaths, I knew we couldn't survive without her. That complete feeling she brought to us by being your mate. I couldn't lose her either, and just knowing how I felt, I imagined yours to be a hundred times worse. I did it for you, for us, and for the clan. Now I have Gianna, so I know exactly how you are feeling, Seb."

Sebastian rolls his eyes at the nickname. "Not you too, Nero."

He chuckles and hugs his friend. "Alright sire, I will leave Seb to Zara."

Sebastian smiles as he steps back from the hug. "Thank you Nero. For being there for me. For everything. I could not do what I do without you."

"Your welcome, sire. Now. I will speak to Aethon about talking to Steel. Brittany and Zed are back from exploring Coltrannax's castle, so I will ask them if they saw it. You stay with Zara."

"I will." Sebastian returns to the small cubby hole and settles in, placing a comforting hand on Zara. He draws the book back into his lap, immediately noticing the summons was gone from the book. He chuckles, wondering how many old scripture books had that in it, knowing he would keep it locked away in his mind, in case he needed a mystic again. After all, he was intriguing, and the mother even more so that she could defy everything a mystic was with her power.

Twenty-Seven

Goddess's Embrace

In an unknown realm, Zara wanders through the darkness, a presence urging her to continue. Her pain diminishes with each step forward until she finds herself beside a small spring. She approaches cautiously, looking into the water, the depths unknown beneath its glasslike surface. A blonde wolf appears on the other side, drawing her attention. "Ember."

"Zara."

"We are dead, aren't we?"

"Yes."

Zara sinks to the grass, tears slipping down her cheeks. "Why Ember?"

Ember moves over and lays her head on Zara's lap. "Because we do not have the same power as a dragon."

"I didn't even get to say goodbye."

A soft musical voice appears behind Zara. "My child, you do not need to say goodbye."

Zara jumps up and spins around, resting her hand on Ember as she studies the woman before her. The woman's skin appears as if the moon has kissed it. Her eyes, dark as the night sky, flicker like stars lurk within their depths. White blonde hair, much like Gianna's, flows freely around her, nearly reaching her waist. Zara's gaze roams over her gown; silver, adorned with diamonds that glitter in the light. The sleeves are light, floating in the soft breeze that surrounds them. "You are the Moon Goddess," Zara whispers in awe.

"Indeed I am, child. Come, let me see you up close."

Zara approaches and stands before her. "Why do I not need to say goodbye? What do you mean?"

The Goddess takes her hand in hers, placing a mark of a crescent moon upon it. "Because you are the gatekeeper, meant to fix the realms. That and Nero is quick on his feet."

"All vampires are."

"Child. They are not. A vampire might look fast to you, but in reality, they are time weaving. Slowing everyone else down. You just cannot see it, but you will soon."

"How will I see it? I am dead."

"You are, for the moment, but you will return. Nero ensured you had the blood of a vampire in you before you died. You will return as one of them."

"Wait! What about Ember?"

"She will return with you. That is why he forced her to shift. He is rather clever, this Nero."

"But I thought vampires had to drain you to turn you into one of them."

"For the lesser ones, yes. Spawns, as they are called. Their blood is not pure enough, so they need to drain their victims and then have them feed, essentially replacing their blood to convert them. Sebastian and Nero are of the original royal bloodline and it only takes a drop in your system. Both powerful and both given willingly; One through a mate bond and one to revive you."

Zara chews on her lower lip. "Nero is a royal too?"

"Nero is Sebastian's brother, Zara. In fact, most of whom Sebastian keeps close to him are family."

"He called them family, but I took it the same way we call our pack a family. They look so different."

"Different parentage. His sire had four wives, all of royal blood."

"He didn't tell me."

"I suspect he keeps it close to his heart."

"Why?"

"Think about it. For anyone one of them, it takes but a drop of their blood to convert someone. Yes, you need to die in order for it to work, but in the wrong hands, it could be catastrophic. People would hunt them relentlessly for immortality and power. It is better to have the general populace believing they need to be drained completely by all vampires."

Zara's hand runs over Ember's blonde fur, twining her fingers through its softness as she grows lost in thought. "I won't say anything."

"Of course you won't. You are one of my sensible children."

Zara giggles at that. She tilts her head to study the Goddess. "Why am I here?"

"And clever too, knowing there is a reason! I came to offer a nudge in the right direction, since you died and all."

"I didn't intend to."

"We never intend to. But here we are. Now, your scroll. What it doesn't say is you need to communicate with the six races to decide their fate. Once they do, it is on you to choose the right hieroglyphics after you find the gatekeeper's hourglass, Zara."

"Wait. What do you mean by six races? We already found the hourglass in the books. Is there another?"

"Your clever Zara. Figure it out. Though I will say, your mate and his brother are helping faster than I expected. It seems your mate summoned a mystic in and asked the right questions." The Goddess fades from the spring.

"A mystic?" Zara looks around the clearing, seeing that she is gone. "Well, damn Ember. Now what do we do?"

Ember tilts her head, fading from her side. "We return to our mate."

Twenty-Eight

Broken Bond

Hours later, having finished the book, Sebastian tucks it away and draws Zara into his arms. His fingers gently caress her cheek and hair, enjoying the stillness of the cavern as everyone sleeps. The soft sounds of water dripping lulls him into a sense of peace, knowing she should be returning soon with how her body has mended.

Zara mumbles and reaches up to cover her ears. "Ugg, why is the water so loud? So hungry."

He smiles at her usual grumble while waking up. "Zara, my love. Welcome back."

"Sebastian?" Her eyes lift to his, seeing him clearly in the darkness but not feeling him. Panic floods her at the loss of their bond, grasping his shirt in her hand. "Why can I not feel you? Why do I feel Nero?"

"Zara, my queen. You are bonded to Nero right now."

She pushes off him and crawls away, her head spinning as white lights dot her vision. Hunger pains lance through her stomach, doubling her over. "No, Why? Why did you do that?"

'Nero, I need you and Gianna here. Zara is awake and panicking.' Sebastian moves over to her and rests a hand on her shoulder. "I didn't Zara. I failed to protect you and you died. Nero offered his blood because I couldn't get to you. He is your sire, hence the bond you feel."

'On our way sire.'

Zara kneels and clutches her head, shaking it madly as her blue eyes shift to red in the darkness. Fires rage inside as her teeth elongate into fangs, cutting through her lips. "NO!!! NO Sebastian. It's wrong. Everything feels wrong! Nero is not my mate. He can't be!! He's Gia's. Why is this happening? Why didn't you stop this?"

Nero places Gianna down and moves to kneel with Zara. Not wanting the rage to overtake her, he pulls her into his arms and strokes her back, allowing the blood bond between them to kick in. "Shh Zara. Sebastian is still your mate, just as Gianna is mine. Once you mark each other again, you will feel him, I promise."

Pain fills Sebastian as he watches Zara struggle with her transition. Regret floods him at not giving her his blood before entering the castle, but then he wasn't expecting to run into Coltrannax. He was off-world, and it was a simple enough mission. A sigh escapes him, knowing in hindsight that it would have made this much smoother for his queen.

Gianna, catching the conflicting emotions in Sebastian's eyes, moves over and hugs him. "She will be fine. She is already better than I expected, Sebastian. By the way Nero talked, I expected her to be more like ours."

Zara fights the pull of Nero, pushing against him, but his aura overpowers her and she settles against him, tears slipping from her eyes as she grips his hands. "Nero. I want Seb back. Wait, where is Ember?"

'I am here Zara. Just feeling very weak at the moment.'

"Ember..."

Nero rocks her gently, continuing to trace circles on her back, hearing Ember's reply, knowing the only way for both to get strong is to feed. "And you will soon. I promise. You are just going to have to accept me in the meantime. Now, I need you to feed. It will calm the raging emotions inside and strengthen both you and Ember. Alright?"

Zara nods, but does not move from Nero's arms. "I really just feel empty, Nero. Even when I came home from your realm, I had my pack. I feel... nothing. I don't like it. I want it back."

"I know, lassie. You will feel all that again." He lifts his gaze to Gianna and Sebastian. "Gia. Zara needs you now."

Gianna squeezes Sebastian's hand and moves over to kneel with Nero and Zara. "What do I do?"

"Hold out your wrist. I will hold her." Nero watches Gianna push her sleeve back and lift her wrist. His arm tightens around Zara's waist, switching to mind-link. *'When I tell you to stop, pull back as hard as you can. She's not going to let go because it's her first feed and she won't have control over her hunger.'*

'Got it Nero.'

'Ready?'

'As ready as I will be.'

Nero's claws lengthen and he slices through her wrist, watching the blood well instantly, hearing the frenzy in Zara's thoughts at the smell. He wraps his free arm back around her, pinning her in place, giving a nod that he is ready. "Alright. Lift it to her mouth. It will sting a bit initially."

Gianna shuffles closer and offers her wrist. "Alright Zara, just remember, you love me like a sister. Don't drain me, okay."

Zara's eyes flare red suddenly, her entire being quivering at the fresh blood. Finding herself unable to free herself from Nero's grasp, her claws elongate, only to have the sweet scent thrust into her face. She bites down, the alluring taste of honey blends with Gianna's blood, vaguely recalling that Nero's tasted of cinnamon. Her skin prickles with goosebumps as its warmth floods her body, calming the rage within.

Nero's eyes lock on her feeding off Gianna. Once he is certain she's had enough to get by, he pulls Zara away, earning a growl from her. "Enough Zara. Gianna has offered what she can. We need another donor, and we don't have one right now."

Gianna closes her eyes and pants in delight, feeling the pure bliss moving through her body. "Gawds Nero... It's almost as good as us! Is it always like this?"

"I think it's different for everyone, Gia, but all our feeders have stated it's quite euphoric."

She arches as another wave of emotions floods her, a low moan escaping her. "It issss..."

"I will get her on the bedroll." Sebastian rises and moves over to Gianna. He grabs her wrist and licks the wound closed, tasting her blood and savoring the little that there is. Gianna snuggles into his arms when lifts her off the ground, bringing a chuckle to his lips. "Well, never thought I would see the day that my mate is snuggling in your arms and yours in mine."

Nero laughs with him, keeping his arms tight around Zara, knowing she is far from sated and could still go on a binging spree. "No, sire, can't say that I have either."

Brittany steps forward, her eyes drifting to Gianna, whose hands are wandering over Sebastian with an expression of bliss. "I can offer."

"It's not expected of you." Nero lifts his gaze to the pair, uncertain when they actually arrived.

"I know, but the quicker you get her sated, the quicker we can get you back to your realm."

"Thank you."

Sebastian glances Brittany's way. "Thank you as well, but there are a few things we need to do before we leave."

"I heard. When we are ready, Aethon's men will take us to Steel's castle." She kneels before Zara, currently slumped in Nero's arms, and draws an athame out. She cuts her wrist carefully and holds it forward.

Zara turns instantly to the blood, her reactions more controlled as she sinks her teeth into the spot. She closes her eyes and moans, immediately noticing the power in the blood tied to the citrus flavor of Brittany. After a minute, she pulls out on her own and closes her eyes, her hands tracing lightly over Nero's arms.

Nero's brow furrows at her stopping. "Zara, you need to feed more."

"No, I am full."

He glances at Brittany, trying to stanch the flow of blood. "Lift your wrist, I will stop it." He glides his tongue over her wrist as she holds it up, sealing the wound. Tasting the power of the blood and understanding completely why Zara's full. "A witch's blood is potent. Damn, no wonder the witches of our realms hide from us."

"I suspected as much."

"I had no idea your blood was that fulfilling... Wait, why are you not euphoric?"

"Oh, I can feel it. The pleasure in my core makes me want to go home with Zed right now. But being a witch, you learn to control said emotions or spells can go awry. As for vampires drinking our blood. They have always chased us for that reason. Caden vouched for you, but upon meeting the lot of you, I instantly knew you were different. Neither one of you reacted to the fact that I was a witch, nor did your men at Stormfang... Well, not in the blood way. Spell wise, you did."

Sebastian places Gianna on the bedroll, doing his best to detangle himself from her roaming hands. "When I took over as king, my rules changed from my sires. No matter how sweet a person's blood smells, they are to be left alone unless freely offered. Key word being free. No compulsions, magic, manipulations or I end their existence." He sighs when Gianna's arms wrap around his legs, looking down at her sultry expression. "Nero, we need to switch. I have no room to lock her in."

Brittany glances his way. "Lock her in?"

"Yes, in our realm, we lock the feeders in a room, supplying them with beds, food and drink, so they can't get into trouble because they cannot control their actions." He grabs her hand, stopping it wandering up his thigh, only to feel the other squeezing his butt. "Gianna!" He jumps forward with a twist, reaching for her second hand to get it under control too. "Nero! Your mate!"

Nero chuckles, rising to his feet with Zara hugged to his chest. He carries her a few steps over to Sebastian and passes her over. "I will trade you. If she fusses, let me know."

Sebastian releases Gianna's hands, feeling them snake around his legs again. He takes Zara into his arms while Nero pulls Gianna off him and steps away. "Thank you."

Zara cracks her eyes, feeling the comfort leave her, her eyes scanning for Nero. "Nero?"

"Shh Zara. I have you now."

"Seb, I still love you, but I love Nero too now. Is that OK?"

Sebastian kisses her forehead lightly. "Of course. People can love more than one person."

"Good... Am I supposed to be tired?"

"Yes, usually feeding and sleeping go hand in hand, but you can't sleep yet. We need to find an hourglass and talk to the races before we get you home."

Zara's gaze snaps open as she struggles to get out of Sebastian's arms. "That's right, the Goddess said as much."

"Goddess?" He places her feet on the ground, his hands slipping around her waist to steady her.

Zara spins around to face him, her hand rubbing the back of her neck, knowing there should be more in her memory but it was already growing fuzzy. She lifts her gaze to Sebastian, studying his eyes in the darkness. "Yes... There was a field with a pond and Ember was there. Then a beautiful woman said that I would need to find the gatekeeper's hourglass."

Sebastian caresses her cheek. "You are the gatekeeper. I already know the hourglass is in this realm. We just don't know where."

"Coltrannax's castle?"

Brittany shakes her head. "Zed and I went through it. We did not see an hourglass."

Sebastian nods. "It's possible that it will only appear for her. If Steel does not have it, I would like to return to the castle."

"Fair enough. How long will it take for Gianna to return to normal?" She nods in Nero's direction where he is doing his best to stay dressed, but missing a few articles of clothing.

"Up to an hour."

"Perhaps I should magically bind her?"

Sebastian arches a brow at Nero's half dressed state. "Nero. Brittany here can bind Gianna."

"Yes, please do. She will be angry later, but damn, her hands are faster than I expected."

Brittany laughs and chants a few words, binding Gianna, who groans in frustration. "That will last about an hour as well."

Nero replaces his clothes and picks Gianna up, returning to stand with the group. "She should be fine to travel like this. Thank you Brittany."

Zara stares at her friend, trying to reach out for their connection. "Why can't I feel Gianna?"

"You died Zara. All your connections are going to be broken, except for the one with Nero, because he converted you. When I mark you, you will feel our bond and the clan again. Is there something that binds you to the pack?"

"Yes, Alpha Darian swears in new pack members with a blood oath."

"Then you will need to do it when we return." He brings her hand to his lips and kisses the back of it.

"Can you mark me now?"

"No..." Sebastian winces at her request and breaks eye contact. "Not until Nero does the transfer ceremony. Come, let's go find Aethon. The faster we get this done, the faster we can get you settled."

Zara gives a last look at Gianna and nods, drifting in thought as she walks silently alongside Sebastian. Desperately missing the pack's connections she took for granted her entire life and, even though it's still new, Sebastian's clan. It felt like home, and now home was gone. At least, she still had Ember. *'Em, I love you. How are you feeling?'*

'Still weak, but better after your feeding. I suspect I will have to feed too, but you need to get to full strength first before we can shift.'

'I will Em. I am glad you made it.'

'Me too Zara.'

Sebastian squeezes her hand, drawing her gaze up to his. "I am glad you both made it as well."

Zara smiles, her first one since dying. "Seb, you are not to be reading my thoughts!"

Nero chuckles. "He's not the only one, lassie."

Zara spins, a wicked smile crossing her lips. "I bet I could beat you now!"

Nero's shoulders shake as laughter spills from him. "Alas, not until you are unbound from me, my queen! Your body will naturally resist fighting me. But then, I welcome the challenge."

Zara's eyes dance in delight. "Then it's a date." She looks up at Sebastian. "How long?"

Sebastian smiles. "After we solve the prophecy because it depends on its outcome."

"Right, let's go then."

The group works their way back to the main table where Aethon's men wait. Seeing they are ready, they lead them out of the caverns and through the core of their town. People line the streets cheering, some even throwing flowers their way. Children weave through the feet of the crowds, trying to get a better look at the group that defeated their leader. Nero places Gianna down when he feels the effects wear off. She walks alongside him, a permanent blush staining her cheeks, refusing to look at either vampire. An hour later, they are walking through the gardens before Steel's castle.

Steel greets them at the front door, his eyes immediately straying to Zara, having heard that she had died in the battle. "Welcome back."

Sebastian catches his gaze moving to Zara and follows it. "Thank you. Is Aethon around?"

"Yes, he's in the meeting room. This way." Steel leads them through the castle to a large room. Sitting around a table are twelve other dragons, including Aethon, Cindra, Drake and Amber, each with parchments in front of them.

Sebastian gives a nod Aethon's way and guides Zara to a seat with two empty ones beside her, placing her between Nero and himself. Once they all settle in, he introduces his group, immediately noticing others shying away from Zed. "I guarantee Zed will not harm you."

Steel moves to the head of the table, introducing the others. "Apparently, there are things on the agenda. Like deciding on a new ruler and figuring out your prophecy. Which shall we do first?"

Sebastian reaches over to take Zara's hand. "Ruler. I have things that need to be said once a spokesperson for your realm is decided."

"Right then, let's get to work." The group goes through the papers, discussing the kingdom and what's entailed in ruling it. Along with the effects the prophecy may have that they are unaware of. A few hours later, Steel is nominated as the new ruler of the realm. Aethon smiles Sebastian's way. "You called it."

Sebastian nods. "It's in his blood. Now, the prophecy." He explains what happened down in the cavern, where he was reading the book on mystics and one came forth. Describing the teenager, repeating his conversation and what Zara needs to do. Part way through, he pauses, hearing Zara's thoughts panic. Both he and Nero place a hand on hers, calming her down. At the end, he turns to the others in the room, specifically Steel and Zed. "We need to find someone from the fey realm, but I believe as the ruler and the son of a ruler, the two of you can speak for your realm."

"I hhavesz soommesz iiddeaassz. Briitz anndzz I'zz haavves talkszz abbouttss zzittzz." Zed turns to Sebastian. "Hoowwzz diidds yoouuzz knoowwzz?"

"I can read thoughts and you carry yourself like royalty. Just like Steel and Aethon, but I knew by Aethon's, he has no interest in ruling."

Steel shakes his head. "We have no fey here that I am aware of."

"We do in Zara's realm." Brittany looks over at Sebastian. "My coven knows of a glen, but they are not the rulers. Just fey citizens, so to speak."

"Then we speak with them when we get back and see if we can get a decree from their royals."

"Fey are chaotic. It could be a problem, but I will text Thalia when we return."

Aethon and Steel glance at Brittany. "Text?"

Sebastian laughs, squeezing Zara's hand. "Yes, it's a small magical box that makes amazing paintings and sends messages we cannot hear."

Zara smiles up at him, recalling his first introduction. "But not here, cause I am certain there is no service. But I can take a painting." Rising from the chair, she pulls her phone out and backs up to get everyone in the picture. "Smile!" A soft click draws their attention. She flips to the picture and studies it. Returning to her seat, she slides her phone around to the others, each gasping in surprise at the mini painting.

"What magic is this?"

"Our magic. One you will have access to if you return to our realm, assuming it's my realm you merge into."

"Interesting. And who will teach us how to use it?"

Sebastian watches the phone move around the room. "If I am to understand, the rune magic will add it to your memories, as if you grew up with it."

"But you are not certain."

"Correct."

Steel turns the phone over in his hand. "What else is in your realm, Zara?"

"Too much to explain, to be honest. We have a lot of what we call technology. Magic boxes, as Anthony calls them. Cars, which function as a horse and carriage. Candles that turn on with a switch. Running water in our houses."

"And if we merge, how will the kingship here work? or Sebastian's for that matter?"

Zara glances up at Sebastian. "I suspect Sebastian will still be King of his kind."

Sebastian reaches out to Zara and caresses her cheek. "Our kind."

"Right." She mumbles. "It's still so new."

"I know my queen."

"Shit! That means I am really their queen now! Fuck Sebastian! I don't know how to be a queen!"

"You will do fine." Sebastian catches Nero's eyes, feeling the rising anxiety in Zara.

Nero reaches over and places a hand on her shoulder, instantly calming her. "Zara, you have already been a queen. The second we stepped foot in your realm."

"No, I was just showing you my world."

"Yes, and you didn't have to. Some would have left us to fend for ourselves."

"I couldn't do that to you or Seb."

"I know, and that's what makes you a queen. Now, back to decision making. We should return to your realm, find the fey and the stone before you get whisked away to our realm."

She returns her attention to the table. "Right, sorry. As for you, Steel. I don't know. There is Alpha Pierce, who has a pack of dragons beneath him but they fall under the Lycan King's rule."

"Lycan King?"

"He's a stronger wolf. Kinda like the original line that we all descend from. Royal blood. Like Sebastian is with his clan versus the vampires we have in our realm. I guess we could ask, but I don't know if we could make it back here before we need to turn these runes. Unless we wait until the next full moon."

"There is much to still talk about then."

Zara sits and listens as they break into talks as they decide what they all want to do, weighing out the pros and cons of each. A few hours later, the group has made the decisions that they need to, with Zara repeating them back to ensure that she got them correct. After memorizing them, she takes her phone back and opens the notepad, typing them in just in case.

Sebastian watches her fingers fly across the tiny screen. "Are you writing a book?"

"No, just taking notes. I don't want to make any mistakes."

He chuckles. "Do you know how long it took me to put mine in when we arrived?"

She lifts her gaze, her brows furrowing. "Not long?"

"In the time it has taken you to write all that, I was still on the first word."

"Really?"

"Really."

"You will get faster, I promise." She leans forward and kisses his cheek and returns to her typing. Once she finishes, she powers her phone off and looks back up to the group, noticing them all watching her intently. "Sorry, it's our version of quill and ink. Now we need to find an hourglass."

Steel nods and lifts his hand, snapping his finger, watching his butler enter carrying a wooden box. Placing it on the table, he bows and leaves the room. "This one perhaps?" He lifts the wooden box off and there, sitting in the middle of the table, is the hourglass of the painting. Gold framing with silver sands slowly flowing through it. A pulsing azure glow surrounds the runes embedded around the top and bottom.

"Wow, it's beautiful." Zara gasps and reaches for it, watching it slide across the table to her hands.

"And clearly reacting to you, because it's never glowed before, let alone moved on its own."

Zara caresses her fingers over the runes, feeling the power fill her as her eyes glow brightly in the room. The sands in the hourglass follow the magnetic pull of her touch, rolling along the glass, each one granting her a sliver of time. The runes along the top and bottom chase each other, their lights glitter as they brighten and fade.

"Zara?"

"I don't know if I can do it."

"You can Zara. Look at how the glass is responding to you."

"I can feel it, Seb, each life... each grain is a timeline... why me?"

Sebastian cups her face and directs her eyes his way. "Because you are special Zara."

Zara stares into his eyes, feeling his confidence wrapping around her as she struggles with insecurities. "Alright. We have three realms decided. The humans in our realm are clueless about the supernatural. They have a king we can talk to, assuming we can get an appointment. But it will put us on their radar or he might just pass us off as crazy and have us committed. We can talk to King Caden about the wolves and get Brittany to help us with the fey."

"Then it's decided. We return to your realm and start the process there."

Everyone rises and moves through the group, thanking Sebastian and Zara for what they have done, restoring the balance to their realm. They pack the hourglass back into the box and slip it into a sack for Zara to carry. Once all the goodbyes are done, they move over to Zed, knowing he is their means out of here.

"Whoever takes Zed's hand will feel a chill. This is normal."

Zara nods and moves to stand with him. "I will."

The rest form a ring, and give one last look to Aethon and Steel before they teleport out; back to King Caden's throne room. A shocked gasp causes them to turn, seeing a guard staring at them. "Brittany?"

"Atticus, it's us. We found them. Where is Caden?"

"He's in the library. I will mind-link him."... *'Sire, they are back.'*

'Where?'

'Throne room.'

'Be right there.'

A few minutes later Caden walks in, immediately noticing the difference in Zara. "Welcome back Brittany. I see you found them."

"Thank you, sire. I did, though not without complications." Her eyes slide to Zara, standing between Sebastian and Nero now.

"I see that. Zara?"

Zara lowers her gaze and bows, feeling Sebastian's and Nero's hand on hers, reassuring her. "Sire."

"What happened and why are you no longer part of my kingdom?"

"The dragon defeated me, but I will swear a blood oath to Alpha Darian. I promise."

"Do you have a wolf, Zara?"

"Yes, Ember is with me. Just weak at the moment, so she is sleeping a lot."

"It will be a first, having a vampire in the pack. And you Sebastian. You did this to her?"

"No. I tried to get to her, but the dragon's witch, Stella, blocked my way with her spell. Nero, thankfully, was on the other side and could save her."

Caden's keen eyes zero in on Nero, one hand in Gianna's, but another placed on Zara's back. "So she belongs to you now."

"Yes, until I pass her over to Sebastian in a blood ritual, which we will perform as soon as we can."

Brittany interrupts the proceedings. "Sire, we have limited time and need to discuss the prophecy with you, the human king and the faeries. We can talk about her death and who she belongs to after. She is still Sebastian's mate, and Nero is still Gianna's. It's just complicated now and not through any fault of theirs."

Gianna giggles. "Nah, we are just going to sell Zara like livestock."

Zara spins in surprise. "Excuse me?"

"That's how Nero explained it to me. You are the horse he bought, but you like Sebastian better cause he feeds you. So we have to sell you to Sebastian."

"And how much are you asking?"

"Oh, we haven't decided. I will talk to Nero and let you know my price."

Sebastian chuckles. "I am sure Nero will set a fair price."

She rolls her eyes. "I am sure he will. I am still beating on him as soon as I can."

Caden laughs at their antics. "I heard all about their fighting from my granddaughter. Come, let's go to a conference room and talk." He leads them out of the main room and into a smaller side room. Once they are all settled, he looks them over. "Now, what are we talking about and why are we going to the human king?"

Between the group of them, they explain to Caden what happened in the other realm, what the prophecy is about, and the choices they need to make and decide on, including the humans. "Damn. I will talk to my family about my decisions while you meet the fey. Going to the human king is a risk and I can connect you with him. I would not recommend it, but if it needs to happen, then all I can say is to be careful with your words."

"Thank you, sire."

"Now, you should get back to your pack. Even with the prophecy looming, they are more important. Brittany should be able to teleport you. Zed, you're staying here. Maddie wants a visit."

"Go, I will meet you at Maddie's after." Brittany smiles and turns to Zara. "Once I teleport you to your pack, I will contact my sisters. Fey are chaotic at best, but hopefully they meet you there in the morning. If all goes well, tomorrow or the next day, we can get in to see the human king."

"Thank you."

Darian slumps into his chair, dropping his arms and head onto his desk when he feels only Gianna's return to their realm. Praying to the Goddess that she just hadn't crossed over, but the chill running through him told him otherwise. How was he going to explain to his best friend that his daughter had not returned? A daughter that would have been safe if he had just not sent them to the borders. He knew, even back then, the feeling of dread was there, but he ignored it. He lifts his head as Zach steps into his office with Anthony.

"She's not coming back, is she?"

"I don't know, Son."

He blinks back the tears in his eyes. "Anthony can feel Sebastian and Nero, but not her. I can't feel her either."

Anthony places hands on Zach's shoulders. "There might be a reason we cannot feel her. Our queen is strong."

"Yes, it might be that Colten got her. I will find a way to kill that bastard."

Anthony wraps his arms around Zach, comforting him. "You won't be the only one."

A disturbance draws the group's attention to the door. Darian runs out and stops on the deck, with Zach and Anthony on his heels. His heart plummets as his eyes land on the five standing there, realizing there is something off with Zara. "Gianna, Zara, welcome back. Zara, why can't I feel you?"

Zara blinks back tears as she lifts her gaze to Darian. "Alpha. I lost the link. Please, can I swear a blood oath and return to the pack?"

Zach runs past his dad and draws them into a hug. "I was so worried about you two. Please tell me the bastard is dead."

"He is."

Anthony follows Zach to the girls, lifting his gaze to Sebastian, reading the strain in his expression, before moving to Nero's and seeing the same. *'Sire?'*

'Not now Anthony.'

Darian steps off the deck towards them, drawing Zara into his arms. "What happened?"

"The dragon trounced me and Nero saved me. Are Mama and Papa around?"

"They are at your cottage. They did not deal with it well."

"Can I go see them?"

"Of course. Once you are done, come back to the pack house."

"Thank you Alpha."

"I will go with you, my queen." Sebastian takes her hand in his and gives it a comforting squeeze. Leading her back to the cottage in silence, as he listens to her thoughts bouncing around in her head about how she is going to face her parents. He pauses outside the door and turns her to face him, placing a hand beneath her chin and lifting her gaze to his. "Zara, you are their daughter. If anything, it should be me who they take their anger out on and I deserve it. I did not keep you safe as I promised."

"It's not your fault, Seb. What if they don't like me as a vampire?"

"You are still their Zare-bear. They will love you no matter what. Just like I do."

Zara nods and pushes the door open, coming face to face with her parents. "Mama. Papa."

"Zare-bear? Thank the Goddess you are back." Both of them drag her into their arms, crying, hugging her tightly. "We were so worried about you."

"I'm sorry. We weren't expecting the books to realm hop us."

Kieran glances at Sebastian, watching them silently. "We are just glad to have you back. Is Ember around."

"Yes, she's just tired right now."

"Do you need to feed?"

"Papa!"

"Zare-bear. I am simply asking a question. Don't you think I can't tell you are a vampire now? What happened?"

Tears spill from her eyes as she snuggles into her parents' arms. "The dragon broke me. It hurt so bad but then Nero was there. He saved me, so now I am connected with him and not Sebastian. I can't feel anyone's links... except Nero's."

"Shhh Zare-bear." His eyes return to Sebastian. "We'll figure it out. I know

Darian will swear you back into the pack. I am uncertain about your situation with your mate, though."

She mutters against him. "Nero needs to sell me to him like cattle."

Sebastian chuckles. "That is not exactly how it works, Papa-bear, but that is how Nero explained it to Gianna. There is a ritual to perform to hand over a childe. Nero and I have talked about it and will do it as soon as we can. Then I will mark her again."

Kieran nods. "Good. Now what do we do?"

"We still have to finish the prophecy, Papa. King Caden is working on his side and Brittany is finding us faeries. Then I need to talk to the human king."

"What!! That is not a good idea, Zare-bear."

"I have to, Papa." She steps back and pulls the bag off her shoulders. Setting it on the desk beside them, she unboxes the hourglass. "This requires me to talk to the spokesperson of all the races involved. Humans, shifters, dragons, walkers, fey, and vampires. Apparently I am the gatekeeper to fixing what Obsidius broke. If I do it right, Sebastian's realm will return to this one and we can live here. Then you won't lose me, even though you have already."

Kieran spins her around to stare into her eyes, ignoring the artifact. "Zare-bear. We haven't lost you. Your mother and I don't care that you are a vampire and your brothers will probably think it's cool, or whatever their slang is for cool these days. You are our daughter and you always will be. We already expected Sebastian to turn you... perhaps not quite this soon though. If I need to be a feeder to keep you alive, then I will. Is that understood?"

Tears slip down Zara's cheeks as she steps into her father's arms, resting her head on his chest. "Thank you, Papa."

"We love you Zare-bear."

"I love you too."

"Now, what is this hourglass?"

"It's part of the prophecy. Tied to me." She swipes at her eyes and picks it up, the magic lighting up the room. Her gaze shifts to both her parents at their gasps of surprise. "Apparently I can stop timelines with this, or change them. See how the sands follow my touch? Each of those grains is someone tied to the prophecy."

"Zara, be careful with that power."

"I will, Papa." She tucks it back in the box and re-bags it. "I need to go to Thunderpaw, but I think by the time the full moon hits, I will be back in

Sebastian's realm. We only have four days left and the full moon is in six now. We will have to look there because apparently each realm has the piece it connects to."

"Alright then, so time is ticking. Let's get you to the pack house and be sworn in first. Sebastian; Mathew, Julian and Theodore are patrolling. They didn't trust those vampires not to come back. Anthony is with Zach wherever he might be. Now I can feel Gianna back in the pack link. Nero?"

Sebastian nods. "With Gianna. We left the group of them at the pack house."

Zara draws the bag over her shoulders and steps back outside, smiling as her mom laces her arms through hers and walks with her.

Sebastian falls back at Kieran's pointed expression, fully expecting it. "Papa-bear, be forewarned. She will hear your thoughts and whatever you speak of."

"I know. I just want to say thank you for bringing her back."

"I didn't. Nero did. I failed to keep her safe."

"Sebastian. I know you can read my thoughts and know I do not blame you in the least. You love her. You would have done everything in your power to keep her safe. The only reason you did not is because something stopped you, and my guess is that the blasted dragon did."

"Actually, it was his witch. She placed a wall between us after he crushed her and tossed her away."

Kieran grimaces at the thought. "He's dead, right?"

"He is."

"Did he suffer like my girl did?"

"I suspect so. A shadow walker stepped in to help. He drained him while Nero and I attacked him."

"Good."

Returning to the pack house, Zara finds them still outside talking. Anthony moves over and hugs Zara. "Welcome back my queen. The others are on their way here."

"Thank you, Anthony."

"Nero filled me in. We will get everything fixed as quickly as we can."

"Yes, we will." Darian steps forth. "And the first thing we do is get you back into the pack. Zach, blade?"

"Right here." Zach hands the blade over and stands beside his father.

Darian takes her hand and slices it carefully, before doing the same to his, placing them together. "Zara Lansdowne Darkholme. By the light of the moon and the strength of our bond, I welcome you into the heart of this pack. You are now one with us, bound by blood, honor, and loyalty. Stand with us as we stand with you, through the hunt, through the fight, and through the shadows of the night. From this day forward, you are under the protection of Stormfang, and together, we are unbreakable."

Feeling the connection clicking into place, her voice shakes as she replies quietly. "By the moon's light and the packs might, I pledge my loyalty, my strength, and my life, or rather un-life. I stand with you as a beta's daughter, bound by honor and blood. I will fight, I will protect, and I will never falter. From this day, I offer my allegiance to Stormfang, and together, we are unbreakable."

"Welcome back, Zara." Darian smiles and hugs Zara fiercely. Taking the knife and turning to Sebastian. "If you desire, I can swear you and your men in as well."

"Zara's pack is my pack. I will accept. My men are free to choose."

Several minutes later, having sworn in all the vampires, Darian turns to the pack members, watching. "As you can feel through the mind-link, they are now members of our pack. A first. Definitely. Unorthodox, one hundred percent. But they have proven themself to be members, even though they are vampires. Now, let's welcome them properly into the Stormfang Pack."

Darian watches a few rush forward, shaking hands or hugging, while others hesitantly approach, but overall, a joyous occasion. Once the greetings are done, he gestures to the group. "Come, I am certain you need a break and some rest, but I also know there are things that need to be said. Let's go into the pack house and get this done quickly."

An hour later, after discussing what happened and their next steps, the group heads into the theater room of the pack house and settles in to watch a movie to de-stress. Two movies later, they all part ways, with Nero and Anthony staying at the pack house, while Sebastian and his men follow Zara and her family home. Kieran and Lila bid Zara goodnight as she watches the other three settle into the couch.

Deciding not to join them, Zara heads upstairs to her room. Once inside, she pulls her phone out and plugs it in, placing the hourglass next to it. She undresses and pulls her pajamas on, knowing she should do her nightly routine, but finding herself crawling into bed instead, pulling her teddy into her arms.

Sebastian watches her, uncertain how to help her in her struggles. Recalling the last Zara wanted and accepted the transformation wholeheartedly. Undressing to his boxers, he crawls in beside her, drawing her into his arms. "Sleep Zara. You and Ember need it. I will sleep with you tonight."

"I love you Seb." She nods, tears slipping from her eyes as she curls up against him, feeling all the stresses of the past few days fading away to darkness.

"I love you too, Zara. Tomorrow is a new day." Sebastian kisses her forehead lightly, tracing a finger over their mark, missing the light that she used to be.

Twenty-Nine

A New Dawn

Sebastian wakes in the morning, realizing that Zara is still asleep, giving him a moment to contemplate how to help her get through this. A soft knock on the door draws him from his thoughts. "Kieran."

"Is she awake, Sebastian?"

"Not yet. Soon perhaps."

"Is this normal?"

"No, but normally when we convert someone, their body is intact. Her's was not. Nero's blood mended her, but it was still a drain. She should return to normal in a week."

"Should?"

"Kieran. Your daughter died. Her soul was taken from her body and sent to your Goddess. Apparently, they had a talk." He pauses at the gasp behind the door. "Her body is fine, but there is emotional turmoil she needs to face. That she did indeed die and is technically dead. Now she is immortal and will see everyone around her die. We had only touched on the topic and I told her I wouldn't convert her till I knew more. Add that to the fact that she is terrified of being a queen. It's a lot to process and she will need time. Normally, I would comfort her, but I can't. Nero has to, and her morals are in overdrive, objecting to having her best friend's mate call to her and soothe her."

"I never looked at it that way. Whatever she needs, we will provide it."

"I know Kieran and she knows it, too. She is just confused right now."

"Thanks for looking after my girl, Sebastian."

"You're welcome. We will be down when she wakes up." Sebastian listens to Kieran's footsteps padding down the stairs. Turning his attention back to Zara, he caresses her cheek, hoping that with a few more feedings, her color will return.

Lights flicker in the room, as his gaze shifts towards it, seeing a tiny little human with a rainbow of color glimmering on her wings that hold her up. Large amber eyes meet his midnight blue ones before dropping to Zara's still form. "She is the Gatekeeper?"

"Yes."

"Then tell her King Sebastian, that our queen has requested we stay exactly the way we are."

"I will do so."

"May you have a long reign like our queen has." The lights flicker and she disappears from the room.

"Thank you." He replies, despite knowing she is no longer in the room with them. "Well, my queen, just the shifters and the humans left. Then we can see where this prophecy takes us." An hour passes before she stirs in his arms, opening her eyes to his with a smile. "Seb."

"My love. How are you feeling?"

"Rested. A little hungry. Does eating real food help with that, or do I need to feed?"

"Probably feed. We only eat your food for pleasure."

She nods, growing silent. "I know Papa has offered, but will I always feel guilty about feeding?"

"I cannot answer that, but I believe so. They taught you that vampire feeding was bad. Now you are one and need to do it. Your mind realizes that it's a necessity, but your beautiful heart is fighting against it. Look at it this way. You're not killing them. I saw on one of the moving paintings, someone taking blood out of a human with a pointy thing for testing. Is it any different?"

"A bit, but I understand what you are saying. It just feels odd that it's Papa or Gianna."

Sebastian chuckles. "When we return, we have designated feeders. If you like, we can find one that suits you, as they all taste different."

"I noticed. Nero had cinnamon in his blood. You are vanilla. Gianna is honey and Brittany is citrus."

"Yes, once you decide on a taste, we can see if we can accommodate that."

"Thank you Sebastian. How long can I go hungry?"

"Not long after being newly turned. A day at most. Once fully attuned, a week to ten days."

"So you really are pushing it by being here without feeding."

"Yes, but everyone who came, swore an oath that we would not feed in your realm."

Zara giggles, "Then me and Papa offer and I go wreck it by dying."

"Indeed, it puts a crick in things. Shall we get up? Papa-bear already stopped by to check on you."

"Yes. I suppose I should be in the training ring."

"I think you have a pass this morning, but if you want, we can head that way. Also, a faerie stopped by and said to keep everything as is."

"Here?"

"Yes. I have never seen one, but it was about the size of your phone."

"Darn, I haven't either. You should have woken me."

Sebastian grows serious. "Zara. You cannot be woken when you sleep. It is why you are vulnerable in that state. The cottage could burn and you would sleep to your true death."

"Nero said something about that when I went to your room in the castle."

"He is correct. Come, I am sure the bond to Nero is calling."

"It is, but I am trying to ignore it."

"It will be hard to do." Sebastian chuckles and rises, offering a hand and helping her out of bed. "Let's get ready and head out to the training. You can probably feed around lunch." After spending time in a soothing shower, Zara and Sebastian dress and head downstairs, finding Kieran and Lila in the kitchen.

"Mama. Papa."

"Zare-bear. How are you feeling? Are you hungry?"

"A bit. Sebastian says I can wait until lunch."

"I will be here then."

"Thanks Papa. Did Jay and Jen go to school?"

"Yes, they wanted to see you, but we figured it would be best to keep things as normal as possible."

"Did you tell them?"

"Yes. As I expected, they jumped up saying dope. I said, they better not be doing that! Then shook their heads and said, cheugy Papa!"

Zara covers her mouth to stifle the laughter. "Oh Papa. you can Google their meanings. You know that, right?"

"Yah yah. I just want them to speak like a normal person."

Zara steps forward and hugs her father. "Alright, I keep you in the loop. Dope is cool and cheugy is very un-cool."

"Great. So much for being the fatherly idol."

Lila places a hand on Kieran, smiling at her daughter. "Kieran sweetheart, they love you."

"No, Zara loves me. They love you."

Zara hugs her mother. "Papa! I love Mama too."

Lila returns the hug. "Good, now, out you go. I think the others are at the training ring."

Zara smiles, her gaze lifting towards Sebastian. "Sounds good." Taking his hand, she heads out of the house to the training fields, immediately noticing Mathew, Anthony and Theodore in the ring with Zach and some shifters. Nero and Gianna stand with Julian watching. Zara moves over and stands next to them, feeling Gianna's hand on hers, and hearing the mind-link as she pulls her away.

'Can we talk?'

'Sure.'

They wander away from the group to the other side of the road, out of hearing range. "What is it, Gia?"

"I just want to say I am sorry for what I did to Sebastian. I feel so bad about feeling up your mate."

"Gia, it's not your fault. You don't need to apologize."

"Yes, I do. I wanted him, and I didn't care that he was yours, Zara. I even grabbed his ass."

"Gianna, Sebastian told me what that's like. You were not in your right mind. I don't blame you at all. If anything, blame me. I was cuddled in your mate's arms."

"I blame me."

"Fine, let's make it even then." Zara cups her face and kisses her. She spins and strolls over to Sebastian and Nero, forcing her thoughts to the how the trees grow around her, knowing they can read them as clear as day. She slips behind Nero and wraps a hand around his inner thigh, just as her other hand grasps his butt. "Was it like this?"

Nero launches forward, a strangled noise escaping him as he spins to stare at her. *'MY QUEEN!'*

Zara laughs at his reaction and places her hands on her hips. "So Gianna. Who jumped further? Nero or Seb."

Gianna giggles. "Nero, by a foot."

"Are you feeling better now?"

Gianna runs over and hugs Zara. "Yes. Thank you."

Sebastian turns to Nero's shocked exclamation, smiling at the laughter between the two girls. "May I ask what's going on?"

"Gianna was feeling bad about groping you, so I just groped Nero to make it fair."

"Ah yes. After the feeding, when she was trying to undress me with you tucked in Nero's arms. Did she forget about that?"

Gianna pouts. "No, I didn't forget about that, but being cuddled in someone's arms, and reaching up someone's leg with the intent to cop a feel is completely different. And I was going for the feel."

Laughter escapes Sebastian. "I know you were. I could feel your hand slipping up my thigh and where your thoughts were. That is precisely why we lock feeders in a room."

Zara nudges Gianna. "I think she did Seb. I told her there are no hard feelings, but she didn't believe me."

Nero chuckles. "None here either, but no more hands on me, my queen!"

"But Nero!!"

Nero shakes his head and steps back, tucking behind Sebastian. "No buts! You might be bonded to me, but there are lines drawn!"

Zara steps forward, pretending to chase him, only to step into Sebastian's arms. "You are safe, Nero. I just wanted to make Gia feel better. When we are alone, we will compare who has the better derriere."

"Compare? How?"

Both Gianna and Zara giggle at the same time. "Wouldn't you like to know? Girl stuff."

Sebastian squeezes Zara and kisses the top of her head. "Don't forget, we can hear those thoughts."

Zara elbows him. "Seb!"

"I love you."

She mutters under her breath. "I am sure you do."

Zach bounds up beside Zara and pulls her from Sebastian to hug her. "Zara! How are you feeling this morning? Are you hungry?"

Zara laughs and returns the hug. "Better than yesterday, and Papa already asked."

"Good, I want my Zara back. Not the melodramatic, broody vampiric one."
Zara slaps his shoulder. "I am not."

"Yes, you are. Do you even remember what movies we watched yesterday?"

Zara starts to answer and snaps her mouth shut, scowling at her friend. "It was a long day."

Zach rolls his eyes. "Yes, a long day of a TV dramatic vampire and a blushing bride over there."

"Right, well, perhaps I was going for the mysterious vampire vibe."

"You sooo Did NOT nail it!"

"I hate you!"

Zach kisses her cheek. "No, you don't. You could never hate me. I'm your Alpha! I will just command you to like me."

"You wouldn't dare!"

"I would if I don't get my Zara back."

Zara glares at him, despite the laughter dancing in his eyes. "You are so mean."

"That's right Babe. It's you, me and Gianna, remember. Always!" He turns to Gianna, reading the mirth in her expression. "Glad to have you back as well. The two of you yesterday were giving Dracula a run for his money."

Zara bites her lips to stop the laughter from escaping. "Dracula? Seriously Zach? You're comparing me to him?"

Sebastian glances between them. "Your thoughts say that Dracula is a vampire. Is he the leader around here?"

Zara giggles. "Only in the vampire movies. Others have tried to come close, but none have succeeded. He is the master."

"Can you show me?"

"Of course, we have it in the collections."

Zach grins. "So, what are your plans today, Zara?"

"I am waiting on King Caden to reply, and I need to see the human one as well. Otherwise, Nothing."

"Right. How about a day of broody vamps in the theater?" He nudges Anthony, winking his way. "Show these wannabes what real vamps are like."

Zara pushes him on the shoulder. "Are you trying to get into trouble?"

"Of course. I need to shower, but I will meet you at the pack house in ten." His eyes drift to Anthony. "Make that twenty."

Zara arches her brow, a teasing lilt to her voice. "Zach babe.... Twenty minutes.

Is that all?"

Zach grabs Anthony's hands. "For an extra long shower, hell ya. What were you thinking, Zara?"

A blush stains her cheeks. "Clearly things I didn't want to be."

Zach laughs as he drags Anthony away, with the others following, having all been in the fighting rings.

Sebastian kisses her on the cheek. "Come, take a walk with me for twenty minutes." He takes her hands and wanders towards the park, watching her grow lost in thought, knowing she missed the bond as much as he did. "Soon, my love. We will be back together in the way you want."

"I know Sebastian and I know I should have patience, but I don't like the wait. I want this done so we can get on with our lives."

"Five more days, six if you count the ceremony."

She stops, rising on her tiptoes and kisses him, feeling a mix of desire laced with pain. A sigh escapes her as she wraps her arms around him, resting her head on his chest.

Sebastian groans inwardly at her kiss, her scent and touch enveloping him, hearing and feeling her body react to him and the betrayal to Nero. He holds her close, resting his head on her head, knowing where her thoughts are going. Intent on distracting her, his fingers lightly roam her back. "Tell me about Dracula and the other broody vampires that us wannabees need to compete with."

Zara giggles, her hand tracing circles on his upper arm. "Dracula is the master that the others strive to achieve. There are lots of different takes on them by authors and producers, but none come close to the real thing."

"Good to know. Now, we have twenty minutes. You promised me a tour and I haven't officially gotten one yet. Only the pack house, your cottage, and the training grounds."

Her eyes snap up. "That's right, there have been so many distractions!" She takes his hands and pulls him back to the main town, pointing out the building where Gianna works and their local markets. "I know. There is one thing you haven't tried, Seb. Chocolate!"

"Chocolate?"

"Yes, it comes in white, light, and dark. I prefer dark, but let's get all three." She leads him into the market, heading to the candy aisle and walks down it. Watching Sebastian's eyes taking in all the different things. Deciding on a few and picking stuff up for the others, she carries it back balanced in her arms. At the till, she reaches into her pockets, realizing she doesn't have her card. "Shit, I don't have my card."

"Is it in the cottage?"

"No, it's probably still at the castle with our stuff that we forgot."

"That could pose a problem."

Zara holds a finger up to the teller. "Two secs." She mink-links her mother. *'Mama, what's our account number at the market?'*

'178612. Why?'

'I am buying chocolate for the group and I think my card is still at the castle.'

'I believe King Caden returned yours and Sebastian's things, but I don't know what your Papa did with them.'

'I will ask him later. Thanks.'

'Your welcome sweetie.'

Returning her attention back to the teller, Zara repeats the number, watching her punch it in and hand over the groceries. She accepts the bag with a smile and thank you, leading Sebastian out of the market.

"You can buy things with a number?"

"Yes, here in the pack, and not every family. Alpha, Beta and Gamma only I think." Knowing they were nearing the time, she winds her way back through town to the pack house, entering it just as Zach and Anthony bound down the stairs. "I brought chocolate."

"Yes! There's my Zara! Gia's making popcorn with Nero. The movies are set up! Let's go!"

Zara laughs and runs after him, while Sebastian and Nero exchange looks and follow.

Hours later, they pause the movie-a-thon for Zara to feed, locking Kieran in a room in the pack house with Darian watching over him. During dinner, Darian informs them that King Caden and his men will arrive in the morning at ten. They talk briefly about what his answers might be and how to go about talking with the human king. After dinner, they return to the theater for more vampire marathons. At the end of the evening, Sebastian walks Zara home with Theodore, Julian, and Mathew. They talk about the vampires they watched, comparing them to their lives and the lives of those here. Each one voting for their favorite one, and asking her opinion.

Zara smiles. "My favorite is Sebastian, but if I had to choose out of the TV ones, Dracula is it. And we only watched a few. There are a lot of vampire stories out there. But I am glad you enjoyed it. It's like us with werewolf movies. Strange views and I think humans would be disappointed to know we are much like them, just with gifts."

Sebastian squeezes her hand. "That depends. Your vampires are very different from ours. Something we will need to deal with when we return here."

"I suppose." She opens the door, and the group settles into the living room. Zara and Sebastian head upstairs, spending the night together, talking, reading, Zara showing him things on the computer, including Lassie.

Thirty

Moonlit Deadlines

M orning arrives all too quickly, with them getting ready to meet King Caden. Zara and Sebastian walk into Alpha Darian's office. Zara bows and bares her neck to everyone in the room. "Your Majesty, Alpha Darian and Alpha Madison."

Caden rises and shakes her hand. "You are looking better Zara. A bit more color to your cheeks. How are you feeling?"

"Better sire. Thank you."

"Hopefully, this will make you feel better. We have decided what's going to happen with the shifters. I also took the liberty to speak to the human king with Brittany's coven. They helped him to see that other species may arrive here, and will blend with society, so I have his choices too."

"Really?" Zara gasps, her mind whirling with the fact they are done with this section of the prophecy. "Do you think it's going to be okay?"

"Hard to say. But I don't expect a witch hunt from him, so to speak. Brittany and Thalia's coven were very specific about what would happen if he did. He agreed to do his best to make peace with the supernatural's, should the need arrive. This is going to be an unusual circumstance, not that it isn't already. Especially as I feel seven vampires in the pack now. Never thought I would see that day."

"That's amazing. I am so glad. So far, it's really just Sebastian's clan, though we haven't talked to all the people in his realm. We will when we get home. The others are staying in their own realms, some removing the time anomaly and curses, others leaving it as is."

"Good." He pulls out a piece of paper with handwriting and hands it over to Zara. "Here are our decisions. I hope to see you on the flip side of this Zara. It's pretty darn impressive what you two solved in my library. You are welcome in my archives anytime."

A deep blush creeps up Zara's cheeks. "Thank you sire. I will keep that in mind."

"Right, on that note. Maddie needs to take me home and get back to her son." He rises and takes her hand, shaking it firmly. "Good luck with turning those stones." He turns his gaze to Sebastian. "If all of your clan is like the six of you. I welcome you into my realm, and I look forward to the next full moon."

Madison steps forward, smiling at Zara and Sebastian. "Things like this can have after effects when you actually get time to relax. If you need to, call me at any time and I will take you away for some peace and quiet."

"I appreciate it. Thank you."

Madison nods, turning to Alpha Darian. "Darian. Thank you. We will talk soon." With that, she takes Caden's hand and fades from the room.

Zara stands in silence, feeling Sebastian's hand on her shoulder and Darian approaching her. She lifts her gaze to his "Alpha."

"Well Zara, it looks like you have two days to relax before you return with Sebastian. All your duties are suspended. Spend it with family and friends. Gianna and Zach are also relieved of their duties for the next two days. I know we will see you back, but this is my request, just in case."

Tears spring to her eyes as she hugs Darian. "Thank you Alpha."

He returns the hug, holding her close, knowing if she doesn't make it back, he's really going to miss her. Having considered her an adopted daughter the minute Kieran and Lila had her. He whispers softly to himself as his eyes meet Sebastian. "You will return."

Sebastian nods. "She will."

Darian releases her and stares at her for a moment. "Good, now go! Get out of here."

Zara smiles and grabs Sebastian's hand, leading him out of the pack house to have some fun with her family and friends. The next two days pass in a blur, spending their time equally among their families, knowing there is a real possibility of prophecy not working and never seeing each other again.

On the tenth morning, Zara gathers her stuff and tucks it into a backpack, along with the hourglass. Slipping her phone in her pocket, she bounds down the stairs, smiling at Sebastian talking to his men, with Zach and Gianna saying goodbye to theirs. She hugs her parents tightly, moving to her brothers who stand watching. "I will see you soon."

Kieran nods. "Take care Zare-bear. Don't push yourself. If you can't find it in two days, we will see you in a month. Understood?"

"I know Papa. I love you all."

Gianna and Zach hug her. "Don't listen to him Zara. Two days or we come hunting for our mates."

She laughs and hugs them back. "Deal. It's in the center. We can find it. I just have to hope it's less than two days by horseback. I really wish I could pack a car. Could you imagine all their faces?"

Zach chuckles. "You would need a jeep to go boonie bashing with. Your clunker could not handle it."

"My car is a perfect bucket of bolts; you leave her alone."

"That's right. She'd be in pieces after the first bump and you would be resorting to horses anyhow."

Zara rolls her eyes. "Doesn't matter. No cars are going with us."

Zach pulls her in for another hug. "We will see you soon Zara. Come back to us and bring our mates back."

Tears fill her eyes. "I will." She looks up to Sebastian. "Alright. Let's go." They leave the cottage, heading south to where they originally arrived. A few hours later, they stand overlooking the ocean, watching the waves crash, as they feel the call to another world and answer it.

Sebastian immediately feels his links snap in place, along with the collective sighs of relief at their return. His eyes turn to the five witches surrounding them, offering a bow and a smile to the head witch and his stand in. "Jeanette. Mason."

"Welcome back, sire." Jeanette's eyes drift to Zara standing in the middle of them, shock flickering across her expression. "She's been turned?"

Mason frowns. "I do not feel her as queen any longer, sire."

"Yes, we had some complications. She's bonded to Nero. I can explain as we travel."

Zara growls softly. "I am right here, and Nero is selling me as soon as he can."

"Travel? Selling?"

"Yes, we have less than two days to get to the center of our realm and find the runes." His eyes drift to Mason. "I will need you to man the castle for a few more days."

"Of course, sire. I will have Vincent saddle horses. How many?"

"At least three for Nero, Zara and I." He glances around, seeing Anthony step closer to Zara, along with the others.

"We are all in, sire."

"Thank you." Turning to the witches. "Jeanette, thank you for what you have done. I hope you and your coven enjoy the hospitality of my castle for a few more days."

Jeanette shakes her head. "Oh no, I am coming with you. I want to hear all about it. My sisters can stay here."

"So be it. We leave shortly. We need to place our belongings away and switch to traveling clothes."

"Yes, I do not think what you are wearing will hold up."

Zara shakes her head. "No, What Sebastian and Nero are wearing will not, but the others in their jeans are exactly what our cowboys wear."

"Cowboys?"

"People that ride horses a lot."

"Right, let's get moving. Meet at the stables as quickly as you can." Sebastian leads Zara into the castle and through the halls to his room. He drops his backpack on the bed and moves to his wardrobe, switching out of the suit and into his traveling clothes.

Zara watches him strip, sighing inwardly as her eyes roam over his body, wishing they had a bit more time and that she was not still bound to Nero.

"Soon my love."

"I know." She empties her pack and repacks a change of clothes and her hourglass.

Sebastian moves over to the bed and picks up the stuffed bear. "You brought a bear?"

"Yes. In case we don't make it back."

"You will, Zara. I promise."

A few minutes later, they meet Mason at the barn as Vincent leads the saddled horses out. "Mason. I need you to send missives out. Let them know in two days, the people of this realm will need to make a choice. A thousand years ago, realms were split and divided. What Zara is doing is undoing that break. I made the decision to return to Zara's realm, where we were taken from. But everyone has a choice in the matter. I want them to know that. Whoever wishes it is welcome to join us there."

"I will sire. I know the clan will follow you. It might make the resistance happy if we leave."

Jeanette walks up, catching the tail end of the conversation. "What will make them happy?"

"Us leaving. If Zara is successful, we as a clan will be returning to her realm."

"Then my sisters and I want to follow. Is there a way to do that?"

"Why?"

"Well, as I said when we answered your summons. You seemed fair, and Hazel was in love with one of yours. It was hard to be in the resistance and love one that's opposed to it. The gold you offered, as you know, was enough for us to test the waters. These waters are nicer than portrayed and we wish to stay in them. While you were gone, Endora also found a mate in one of your men."

"So be it. We will swear you into the clan and have Mason swear your sisters into it." Sebastian places Zara's pack in the saddlebags and lifts her onto the horse, before mounting up himself. He watches the rest mount up around him. "Mason, if all goes well, the realm will shift with the land, including the castle and surrounding area. Don't attack the wolves that may patrol past."

"Understood. Good luck, sire."

Sebastian nods and urges his horse into a gallop, with the others following, heading due north.

After two days of horseback, Zara slips off the horse stiffly, pain radiating through her body. She staggers and sinks to her knees, her fingers digging into the grass beneath her.

Sebastian dismounts and moves to her side. "Zara?"

"What I wouldn't give for a hot bath right now. This is worse than training."

Nero chuckles and slips off, moving to assist her with Sebastian. "I thought you were made of stronger stuff, my queen."

Zara shoots a glare his way. "I thought with at least being dead, I wouldn't have pain like this!"

Sebastian smiles. "We feel just as you do, my love. Come, it should be close and we are running out of time."

"I can feel its power, Zara. This way." Jeanette says.

She nods and rises unsteadily to her feet, her gaze turning at Jeanette's words. "You would think being a witch, you could just portal us here."

Jeanette snickers. "What, and miss out on your suffering? I think not."

Zara pouts, sending a look at Sebastian, as she unpacks her hourglass. "Can we fire her after this?"

"Fire her?"

"You know, send her back to where she came from."

Jeanette places her hands on her hips, returning the look. "No, you are stuck with me as your witch guardian. Deal with it."

"Great. Just what I wanted. Another guardian." Biting her lips to hide her smile, having truly enjoyed Jeanette's company immensely in their travels.

Jeanette laughs, leading her to the east and into the woods. Five minutes later, after winding through the dense forest, she steps into a clearing. She stares at the stone hexagon embedded in the ground with six runes surrounding a small circle in the middle. "How did we not know this was here before?"

Sebastian and Nero step up with Zara between them. "I suspect it's reacting to the hourglass." He lifts his gaze skyward. "I do not know when the moon is, but if I hazard a guess, it's really soon. You best get started."

Thirty-One

Realms Align

Z ara kneels down and unpacks the hourglass, watching it light up before her as she holds it in her hands. She rises and steps into the runes, catching the flickering from them as she does. Glancing around, she carefully places the hourglass in the circle. The runes race around the top, continuing its path along the bottom, before lighting up the ones at her feet. Walls of light suddenly surround her, as a hexagonal pillar rises from the center. Zara turns, her eyes noticing Sebastian and the others on the outside fading away. A gasp escapes her, knowing she is now on her own. She lifts her hand, catching the silver sands that fall around her, realizing rather suddenly that she is in an hourglass.

Turning her attention to the top, she can see a dragon. Her gaze travels down the six runes on this side and to the one that she is standing on. Noticing it seems to be a combination of all the ones on the pillar, but blended as one. The landscape around outside the glass is forest, but as she peers outside the golden walls, she can see Steel and Aethon watching her. A smile crosses her lips as she gives them a wave. Pulling out her phone, she flips it to notes and reads carefully, before turning her attention back to the hieroglyphs. She presses the first one, watching the others light up below it, and moves her way down the side. At the bottom, she touches the darkened rune, knowing instantly what it is. Caressing her fingers along it, she lights it up. Memories of the past and the present; and each race is going to get theirs.

As Zara steps onto the rune with the faerie etched into its surface, the world around her transforms in a cascade of shimmering light. The oaks of the previous realm fade away, replaced by the graceful, drooping branches of weeping trees. Soft motes of light drift lazily through the air like tiny, glowing spirits. The air feels lighter here, the atmosphere filled with magic, and a sense of serenity washes over her. Realization dawns on her with a burst of laughter. Each rune, each step, shifts her from realm to realm, allowing her to walk through the realms all at once, pausing time as the painting depicted. The panic she once felt dissipates, replaced by a sense of control, as Zara moves forward with renewed confidence. She works her way down their path, keeping everything the same. Noticing the memories at the bottom, do not light up.

After completing the faerie realm, Zara pauses, her eyes alighting on a tiny faerie watching her. She nods in her direction and steps onto the rune for the shadow walkers. As the world around her shifts once again, her eyes widen in awe. The trees here are unlike anything she's ever seen, their bark a deep, vibrant purple, with strange, twisted branches that seem to pulse with an otherworldly energy. Flowers with petals in hues of midnight blue and green dot the landscape, while vines twist and curl around the trunks of the trees, making the entire forest feel alive with a quiet, eerie beauty.

Realizing the rarity of this moment, Zara flips her camera to photo mode and begins snapping pictures of the surreal landscape, knowing that once she leaves, she may never have the chance to witness this again. Tucking her phone away and returning her attention to the pillar, she works her way through the shadow walkers' path, ensuring most of their world remains untouched and focusing on dissolving the time anomaly. With her task complete, she glances around once more, committing the strange, haunting beauty to memory.

As Zara lifts her gaze, the rune for the vampire realm is next. Taking a deep breath, she steps onto it, and the world around her changes once again. This time, a very familiar sight greets her. Sebastian and his crew appear outside a large hourglass, their faces etched with panic and concern. She can see the fear in their eyes, their worry for her clear as they watch her. Smiling softly, Zara raises her hand and blows them a kiss, hoping to calm their fears. Her gesture is small but filled with affection, silently telling them that she's alright. She knows they can't reach her yet, but their presence gives her strength as she turns her focus back to the task at hand. With practiced ease, Zara lights up the pathways, unlocking the glyphs that have been hidden away. As she reaches the bottom of their realm, the final step, she grants them their memories, feeling a surge of power as it flows through her and into the hourglass, completing the cycle.

She waves goodbye to the vampires as she steps onto the shifters' rune, expecting the familiar landscape of her own realm. Instead, she is met with darkness; a vast, eerie void illuminated only by a pale moon hanging high in the sky. She freezes, recognizing the woman stepping forward. It's the same figure she saw during her death. The Moon Goddess. Zara bows deeply, baring her neck in a show of respect. The Goddess remains silent, her presence radiant and all-encompassing. After a brief moment, Zara straightens and she slips out the note Caden had written for her. Her fingers glide gently over the glyphs, her touch sure and steady, carefully aligning each symbol of the shifter realm. Once complete, Zara nods once more to the Goddess and steps forward onto the next rune; the humans.

The rocky edges of mountains rise up around Zara. She feels their eyes on her before she even turns. Bears, larger than life, stand sentinel nearby, their eyes sharp and calculating, far more intelligent than they first appear. A lone human stands among them, observing her quietly, their presence commanding yet patient. The connection between them is palpable, a unity of nature and ancient power.

Zara lifts her gaze skyward, the full moon hanging low and bright above her, bathing the entire scene in silver light. A smile touches her lips; Sebastian had been right all along. Under the light of a full moon, the magic of this place thrummed with life. Acknowledging the bears with a respectful nod, Zara turns back to the stone. Her hands move swiftly now, shifting the runes with precision, adjusting the symbols into the correct sequence. One by one, they begin to glow, their light growing brighter with each passing second.

When the final rune locks into place, the ground trembles slightly beneath her feet. The hourglass pulses nine times, its rhythm echoing like a heartbeat through the realm. The sands within it slow, coming to a complete stop, suspended in time; floating in midair, frozen as if held by some unseen force. Everything around her stands still, as though time itself is waiting for her next move.

Suddenly, a storm rages within the hourglass, sand stinging her skin as it blows around. Zara pulls her shirt up to cover her face and nose, grateful she didn't have to breathe, wondering if it was, in fact, meant to be. She closes her eyes, and sinks to her knees, hearing the hum of the voices in the winds, each grain speaking to her as they make their decisions. Minds entered and rewritten to adapt to the changes. The sands dance, each taking on a silver glow, before winking out of the hourglass, finding its place among the occupant it belongs to. Time passes as the moon stretches over the sky, and just before dawn, Zara collapses into darkness.

She wakes, hearing the growl of something nearby and Sebastian's voice, blending with Nero, who she can feel nearby. "Seb?"

"I'm here, my love. We are all here. Well, not here exactly. But I can feel my clan. I just need to know where they landed."

She blinks, her eyes focusing on his concerned expression. "Who's growling?"

"Bear shifters. It seems we are trespassing in Thunderpaws territory. They are holding us captive until they receive confirmation from the Lycan King that we are who we say we are."

Zara giggles. "Damn, a prisoner again. At least you are captive with me this time... And Nero. That's gotta be new to you two."

Sebastian chuckles and helps her to sit up. "Actually... We are not exactly captive. We just chose not to fight them. All of us that traveled to the stone are here, horses included."

"How long have I been out?"

"I am uncertain. Since the magic ended, perhaps five minutes, but the bears said you dropped inside and time stood still. The sun is rising. I would hazard a guess it's been a while."

"I remember hearing the thoughts of everyone. It was overwhelming." She reaches into her pocket and pulls out her phone, powering it on. Lifting her gaze at some growls from the bears. "Oh please. King Caden will verify us. So will Alpha Darian, Alpha D'andre and Alpha Madison. I can give you their numbers. Well, not the Kings exactly. We went through Alpha Madison for that. But we disappeared from his archives if that counts for anything."

A tall burly man steps forward, his hair in a short crew cut, with a tattoo creeping out from beneath his shirt and up his neck. Dark eyes narrow on her sitting next to Sebastian. "You are a vampire. How can you know about these people?"

"Cause I was and still am, a wolf shifter first. Mixed breed mutt now, I suppose." She sends a scowl Nero's way. "Anyhow, Alpha Darian of Stormfang is my Alpha, and Sebastian here is my mate."

"Prove it."

Zara growls at him. "How do you propose I do that?"

"Shift."

"I can't. Ember is not strong enough yet. I was only recently turned after being mangled by a dragon. But I can call any of them on my phone."

"Then call D'andre."

"Fine." She places her phone on speaker and dials him up, hearing it ring before it's answered. "Zara?"

"Alpha D'andre. You are on speaker phone, and I am in a bit of a pickle."

"How can I help?"

"Well, you can tell Thunderpaw that we know each other and we are not bad people."

"What the hell are you doing in Thunderpaw?"

"You know that prophecy I was working on?"

"Of course."

"Well, I figured it out. It was tied to an hourglass, and I ended up here when I completed it."

"Where did you start?"

"Sebastian's realm."

"I am uncertain how I can help Zara. Maddie can only fey step to places she has seen. Caden's witch might be able to, though. You've met her, right?"

"I met two. Thalia when we dealt with Bianca and Brittany and Zed. He sent them for us when we accidentally put books together and realm hopped into a dragon realm."

"Wait! How am I just hearing about this now? Maddie and I need to talk."

"I am not sure Alpha Madison knows. We were in King Caden's library and disappeared from there. Then Brittany and Zed brought us home. Two days later, Sebastian's witches pulled us back to his realm. Jeanette from Sebs' realm came with us, but she also needs to have seen her location to portal us and this whole place is new to her."

"Alright, I will contact Caden."

"I think Thunderpaw has. They didn't believe I was part of a pack."

"Why wouldn't they?"

"Because I am a vampire now." Zara breaks the silence that ensues on the other end. "D'andre?"

"What happened Zara?"

"The dragon that started this. He wrecked me badly and I am still mending. Nero saved me or I wouldn't be here."

"The thing that matters is that you are here. Did Ember make it?"

"She did, but she's still weak. I haven't been able to shift to have her feed."

"It will happen. Now put Thunderpaw on the phone and let's see about getting you home."

Zara laughs, her eyes lifting to the surprised expressions on those surrounding them. "You've been on speaker Alpha D'andre. I think your words clarified everything. Thank you."

"Right, you said that. I expect a visit after this."

"Of course. Thank you Alpha. I will bring Sebastian, Zach and Anthony. And maybe Nero. Depends on if he has sold me back to Sebastian yet. It seems I can't be away from him for any length of time yet."

"Sold you?"

"Yes, Like a cow."

Nero chuckles. "It was a horse, lassie. I have more class than that."

Zara mutters under her breath. "Right, like that's any better."

"How does he own you Zara?"

"Cause he brought me back with..." Pausing when she recalls what the Goddess said about their lineage. "From dying with his vampire turny abilities."

"That's not good Zara."

"It's not so bad, Alpha D'andre. I'm here and Nero has agreed to sell me, just not what the price will be."

D'andre laughs. "Well, I hope Sebastian has lots of money."

"I hope so too. Alright, I better go. Thanks Alpha D'andre."

"Your welcome Zara. Tell Alpha Daniel to let you go."

"I will. Thank you." Zara hands up the phone and turns her attention to the one standing with the bears. "There you have it. Please tell Alpha Daniel to let us go."

Sebastian squeezes Zara's hand. "That is Alpha Daniel."

"WHAT?" Zara mutters quietly. "Why did I not feel that?"

"Because you are a queen and hold more power than him, Zara. You only react to Alpha Darian because he's always been your Alpha, and if you wanted, you can stand up to Caden because you are his equal."

"Alpha Darian will always be my Alpha."

"I know. That's why I never said anything. It is who you are."

Alpha Daniel steps forward. "Sorry, we don't deal with trespassers well, let alone vampires and strange magic. Come, I will take you to the pack house to rest. Then we will figure out a way to get you home."

Zara rises with Sebastian and Nero's help. "Ugh, my muscles feel like mush."

Alpha Daniel watches Sebastian lift Zara into her arms. He leads them back through the mountain passes, across lush valleys and through narrow crags in caverns. An hour later, as they cross another meadow, he turns back to those following. "The horses might want to stay in the valley. They will not like where we are going." Once they set the horses out to graze, he leads them into a cave and down into the depths of the mountain.

Jeanette murmurs a few words quietly and a soft glow surrounds her, causing the others to look back. "What? I can't see in the dark like you all can."

Sebastian smiles. "Sorry, I forgot about that."

"All good. I just don't want to break my neck in a bear's cave, even if he is delightful to look at."

"Vampires are not your type?"

"Oh they could be, but let's see, three of you are unavailable, and no offense to the other three pretty boys, but you just don't call to me the way that tattooed hunk of a bear does."

Laughter erupts around her as a heat crosses Alpha Daniel's cheeks. "I have a mate, thank you."

"Oh, I know, I see the mate mark. Doesn't mean I can't enjoy the landscape."

He huffs under his breath, "As long as that's all it is."

Jeanette's eyes grow serious. "I would never step on another mate's territory. I know better. Mom always said, you can always go window shopping, as long as you don't buy the merchandise. I get the impression there might be window shopping here. Wait, how is that in my mind? We never had that in the other realm."

Zara smiles. "The last rune added memories. I granted it to everyone that got shifted from their original realm as if raised in the new one. It's tied to a second mark, allowing you to know there is a difference."

"Clever."

Alpha Daniel leads them into a large cavern. Medieval torches line the walls, with oil lamps sitting on large wooden tables. Fire pits sit in nooks, smoke filtering up into the passage above them. Couches, chairs and tables sit near them with men and women in them talking. Children race around, laughing and playing, some of them stopping a moment to look at the newcomers before continuing in their game of chase.

Zara looks around as Sebastian places her on the ground. "This looks out of place in our time. More like Sebastian's or Steels."

"It is. All of us have houses with electricity, but as bears, we crave the cave. No modern technology down here and it brings a measure of calm and peace that a lot of us seek."

"I get that. When I was at Sebastian's castle, it was like that. It was hard to return home to the constant noise."

"Oh. don't get me wrong, there is noise here." He gestures to the kids running around. "But it is different. The cave system down here is extensive. Some families have chosen this as a permanent location to live." He guides them over to several vacant couches, waiting until they settle before finding one himself. "So this hourglass?"

Zara smiles, explaining to Daniel what she has been through, and what she did, with the others interjecting when she missed something. A few hours later, a runner comes down into the cave looking for them. "Alpha Daniel, King Caden has set up a flight from Hollowridge to Stoirme. It leaves at four this afternoon."

"Good, we have time then. It's about a two-hour drive to the airport. We will need to take two cars. What about the horses?"

"Can we not bring them?"

Zara giggles. "No Sebastian. We will need to come back for them. Perhaps a week? If that's Ok?"

Daniel nods "They should be fine to graze in the valley. I will have someone guard them from predators and get some troughs of water out for them. Let's get moving."

"Thank you."

Daniel rises and leads them through another passage, stepping out of the darkness into a small canyon. He winds his way through it and up some stone stairs, cresting into a small village. Zara glances around, seeing the modern cottages surrounding the larger pack house. Humans and bears mingle, with a group clustering to the left, where definite growling was coming from. Zara smiles at those that stop and stare, their glazed eyes meeting Daniel's, knowing they were asking about the vampires in their pack. Most of them continue on their way, but one stops to stare longer than the others. The white t-shirt does nothing to hide his muscles. Deep brown eyes stare at the group, his lips pursed into a frown. Tattoos of bear claws reach up from beneath his shirt. "Alpha?"

"Beta Quinn. I am taking our guests to the airport."

He points to Jeanette. "Her too?"

"Yes, why?"

"She's my mate."

"Then I guess you need to speak with her while the cars come around."

Jeanette squeals and runs straight into his arms. "Yes, I knew I needed to get me a bear! Sorry, sire. I am all his now."

Quinn growls protectively, his gaze trying to determine who she is talking about as his arms tighten around her.

Sebastian grins. "Fair enough. Does that mean you are breaking our contract?"

"Yes, and no. Your clan is here, so you won't need my realm hop services but my sisters and I will still help you, whenever you need it."

"Deal. Thank you, Jeanette, for everything you have done to get my mate back in my arms."

Quinn relaxes at those words, giving a nod to him, before tossing her over his shoulder and carrying her off.

Zara calls out. "Text me Jeanette!"

"I will! I will get hunky here to show me how it works!"

Danial laughs. "Well then. I guess I'll be seeing more of her."

Sebastian chuckles. "I suspect so. Take care of her. She's one that offered help when no others would."

"We will."

Hours later, the group minus one, is sitting on a private jet. Zara settles into a chair, while the others all move to peer out the windows. "You are saying this large contraption is going to fly?"

"Yep, that's what I am saying." She pulls her phone out and slips it into airplane mode. "Papa will be waiting on the other side." She tilts her head at the engines starting, feeling the jostling in her seat as it pulls onto the runway. "You should sit for takeoff. After that, you can wander." She watches them settle in the chairs, each looking at her with a slightly panicked expression on their faces. "I get this is new, but it will be fine. They fly these all the time." She shifts over, allowing Sebastian to sit beside the window, knowing it is a coveted position the first time anyone flies.

The roar of the engine drowns out conversations for a minute as the plane speeds down the runway, taking to the air with ease. Zara glances to the window, watching the mountains fading away. "There, see, no problem. After a few hours, we will be home. Then we can find out where your clan ended up and, hopefully, your castle."

Sebastian's eyes stare outside, feeling his stomach tighten at the sight of being so far off the ground. He turns to those on the plane, feeling their anxiety for the first time, being unable to mask their emotions. The only one that is calm is Zara. He chuckles, drawing the attention of the others.

"What?" Zara lifts her gaze to his.

"You Zara, teaching us new things; who we can read with ease is sitting there calm as can be. But for the first time in hundreds of years, I can actually feel their emotions. Their blocks have slipped."

"YES!"

Nero shakes his head. "I think I like my feet on the ground with the horses. My ears feel funny."

"Yes, it's the altitude. And if we did this by horse, it would be like three weeks. This is much faster and I won't die from my muscles rebelling against me."

"Lassie, I am quite certain you will adapt to riding."

Zara rolls her eyes. "Yes, that's right, when I have a car!"

He chuckles. "As long as it's not in another one of these things."

"Got it."

Two hours later, there were audible gasps from them as the plane touched the ground, bringing a smile to Zara's lips. She flips her phone off airplane mode and texts her father.

> Landed safe Papa though the others might disagree. See you soon.

> I am waiting.

Once the plane stops, the hostess opens the door and lets them out. Zara races across the tarmac to her father standing beside the limousine, throwing herself in his arms. "PAPA!"

"Zare-bear. I see you did it?"

"I did. We still need to find out where Sebastian's clan ended up."

"They are on our borders, west side, half here and half in Whispering pines."

"That's even better. Did the castle arrive?"

"By the looks of it, yes. Along with a variety of small cottages."

Sebastian steps up next to her and offers a handshake to Kieran. "Good to see you again."

Kieran releases his daughter. "You too. Now, Alpha Darian has requested we bring you to the pack house. But I think perhaps we should take you home, to your clan and castle. Tomorrow we can catch up. How does that sound?"

"That sounds great, Papa. It is good to be home with both my families."

"I am glad it worked out, Zare-bear."

"It seemed to Papa. I hope all the other realms and people involved are alright."

"I'm sure they are. Come, your limo awaits, Queen Zare-bear."

Zara smiles up at Sebastian and clambers into the limo, with the others following. She curls up in Sebastian's arms, feeling his love despite missing the bond. She closes her eyes, drifting in thoughts, realizing that she can hear someone else's. Lifting her head, she looks around.

"What is it Zara?"

"I can hear something."

"Most likely your Papa's thoughts."

"I can do that?"

"Of course. It will get stronger as you do."

"Can I move as fast as you do?"

"Yes, another thing we can teach you."

"I love you Sebastian."

"I love you too, my queen."

Thirty-Two

Epilogue

Four months later, Zara races around the castle, knowing people are going to be swarming en-mass to visit for her twentieth birthday. Part of her wishes the castle had come with modern technology, the other part loving the silence every night as she sits on their balcony, watching the ocean below them. She slides to a stop as Sebastian steps out of the library, phone in hand and dressed in a blend of modern and medieval clothes.

"Zara, my love. Stop. I can feel your stress. We have servants to do this."

"Staff Seb. It's paid help, so it's staff."

"Right, still learning your terms."

She giggles. "They should be in your memories."

"They are, but when you have had over five hundred years of the original terms, that's what you gravitate to."

"I know, and so do they. Since they all came with us."

"Yes, for which I am grateful."

"Me too."

His fingers trace over the mark on her neck, once again mated after performing the blood ritual to hand her over. "Now, as the saying goes, take a deep breath, even though we don't breathe. You got this. They have all been here before."

"But not together! All the Alphas, Darian, Madison, D'andre, Pierce and even Daniel, Quinn and Jeanette. King Caden is bringing the human king who I haven't met! Brittany and Zed are realm hopping Aethon, Cindra and Steel for the day. Then everyone else. Family, friends, my pack, your clan. Even some of the resistance that chose to come here, which I am surprised at. I don't think the castle is big enough."

"Our clan. You are their queen."

"Right, our clan. Still not used to that. But…What happens if the ferals attack?"

He places a finger to her lips, leaning in to kiss her forehead. "Shh, they won't. Too much power here. Now, the castle is fine. The bedroom, library, and treasure rooms are locked. Most will be outside in the courtyard where you have those tents set up. Let's go watch the ocean and enjoy your birthday together for ten minutes, before we get *swarmed* as your thoughts indicate. Shall we?"

Zara stares up into his eyes, feeling his calm wrap around her, drawing a soft sigh to her lips. She nods and takes his hand, following him to the back balcony. She moves to the stone wall, looking out over the cliffs, the water crashing two hundred feet below her soothing her.

Sebastian steps up next to her and places a small box on the wall. "A gift for my queen on her twentieth birthday."

Zara glances up at him. "You didn't have to Seb. Just being back with you is all I wanted. I mean, Nero is nice and all, but he belongs to Gianna."

He chuckles. "I know. Open it."

She lifts the box and pulls the top off, her eyes landing on a jeweled infinity necklace, the gems inlaid in gold matching her and Sebastian's eyes perfectly. "Sebastian, it's beautiful. I have never seen anything like it. Where did you find it?"

"I had it made for you when you left me the first time. It was always my plan to give it to you when I turned you. But it didn't quite work out that way."

Tears slip from her eyes as she hugs him fiercely. "I don't care. I love it and I love you."

"I love you too, my queen. More than I could ever have imagined. Here, let me put it on, and let's go out and greet our guests."

Zara hands him the necklace and turns around, feeling his hands caress her neck gently as he slips it in front and clasps it at the back. She places her fingers on the necklace, having never owned anything quite as exquisite as this. "Thank you Sebastian. It's beautiful."

"You are welcome. Not as beautiful as you." He takes her free hand and lifts it, kissing the back of it before leading her out to all the guests who are gathering.

The end

Thirty-Three

People

Alpha - Leader of the pack
   Luna - Leaders Mate
   Beta - 1st guard of the Alpha
   Gamma - 2nd guard of the Alpha
   Delta - Personal guard of the Luna
   Warrior - Other guards
   Omega - Working class, smaller wolves
   Hierarchy
   Lycan is top dawg (King and Queen)
   Alpha and Luna (Think Baron and Baroness)
   Dragon, Wolf, Fey, Vampire, Shifters, Witches, all battle it out below Lycan (Think Nobles)
   Rogues - Wolves with no pack, either banished or disowned. (Think Rebels)

Stormfang Clan

Alpha - Darian Ravenwind (Brown hair, green eyes)
   Wolf - Orion
   Luna - Willow (Red hair, green eyes)
   Wolf - Autumn
   Son - Zach (Auburn hair, green eyes 5'9)
   Wolf - Atlas
   Son - Ben
   Daughter - Sophie
   Beta - Kieran Lansdowne (Brown hair, Hazel eyes, 6'3 Fit build. 45)
   Wolf - Emeric

Wife - Lila (Ash blonde, blue eyes)

Wolf - Sienna

Daughter - Zara (Ash blonde hair, blue eyes, tanned skin 5'6)

Wolf - Ember   (Gold and red fur, white muzzle. White socks)

Son - Jayden - Older twin (Ash blonde. Hazel eyes)

Son - Jenson - Younger twin

Gamma - Luca Hansley

Wife - Paulette

Daughter - Gianna (White blonde hair, Pale complexion, green eyes 5'7)

Wolf - Sable

White Witch - Amara

Healer - Ashlyn

Warrior - Jeremy Hillock

Sister - Bianca Hillock

Witch - Stella Kaala

Amazon driver - Colten

Sales clerk - Jenna

Town - Stoirme

Whispering Pines

Lycan King - Caden Sylvanax
   White witches - Thalia, Brittany
   Shadow walker - Zed
   Kings guards - Orion, Atticus

Wildfire Crescent (Madison's Web)

Alpha Madison Marzire - Fey touched (Aquamarine eyes, brown hair, freckles)
   Dragon - Somoko
   Wolf - Zuri
   Mate - Lucian Marzire (Blonde hair, blue eyes)
   Delta - Victor Martinez (Brown hair, Brown eyes)
   Beta - Clarice Martinez

Frostbite Syndicate

Alpha - Pierce Marzire
Luna - Violet Marzire

Thunderpaw

Alpha - Daniel Clawrick
Beta - Quinn
Town - Hollowridge

Silvermoon

Alpha - D'andre Camdon (Short brown hair, hazel eyes, goatee)
Luna - Erica (Blonde, hair, gray eyes)
Children - Archer and Mila
Beta - Terrence
Student - Layla Monroe
Student - Yvonne Steckles

Darkholme

King - Sebastian Darkholme
(Tall, 6'3 Black hair, dark blue eyes, pale skin, trim lean build)
1st in command - Nero
(Blonde hair, green eyes, 5'9 Trim build)
2nd in command - Mason
Kieran's guards - Mathew, Anthony, Vincent, Logan
Zara's guards - Seth, Mason, Theodore, Julian
Sire - Silas Darkholme
Witches - Jeanette, Hazel, Endora

Dragon realm

Current ruler - Coltrannax
    Previous ruler - Obsidius the Night Stalker
    Lore master - Steel Vortrax
    Rebellion leader - Aethon
    Rebellion healer - Cindra
    Rebellion members - Drake and Amber

Darian Ravenwind

Kieran Lansdowne

Zara Lansdowne

Nero Darkholme

Sebastian Darkholme

Gianna Hansley

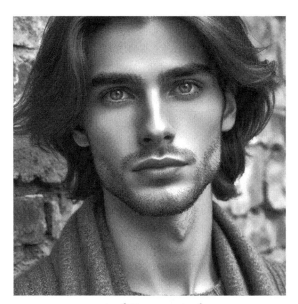

Zach Ravenwind

Anthony Darkholme

Thirty-Five

Contributors

Cover Design - R Dey

Bing Portraits - Edited by R Dey

Cover Silhouettes - Dover Royalty-Free Images - Approval granted by A Sliwoski at Dover inc.

Beta readers - M Verronneau, N Doyle

Proofreader - N Doyle (She called Dibs on Sebastian)

Editor - T Street, N Peterman

Editing Software - ProWritingAid, Google Docs with Grammarly, Impact, Atticus.

Author Portrait - G Woodward

Assists - M Harris R Marie

Thirty-Six

Extras

Thank you for taking the time to read my stories and I hope that you enjoyed them. If you like this, here are other books released or upcoming. Please feel free to follow me on the pages for the books, or add me via Goodreads or Facebook. Also, reviews are important to self published authors, so please take the time to leave one. Thank you.

Social media - www.facebook.com/AuthorRandiAnneDey
www.goodreads.com/author/show/45347028.Randi_Anne_Dey
www.facebook.com/groups/randiswriting
The King's Mystic: Oct 2023
The Dragon's Mystic: May 2024
Cantara's Mystic: Eta 2025
Madison's Web: Mar 2024
Dragonscales Divide: Oct 2024
Chahaya Durmada - Five Swords of Power: Book 1- Eta 2025
Royal Deception: Tails Scales and Tiaras Anthology (short story) June 2024

Fun side note – When I was writing this, I Googled – Can vampires turn into crows? Answer – No, Vampires are not real. Therefore they cannot turn into birds in 'real life.' I laughed. Really? Not real? And because the next line down, it stated, 'Vampires can turn into bats, rats, owls, moths, foxes and wolves.'

Yes they are real in our hearts + minds.

About the Author

Randi lives in Victoria, BC. Canada. She is a dog groomer by day and a writer/gamer by night. She loves to read and write fantasy and has been for years, only now trying her hand at publishing. She partook in the SCA and taught medieval dance for nearly fifteen years. Since 2004, she attended the Faerieworlds festival yearly, keeping fantasy alive in her heart until they closed it down in 2022. (Now its Realms Unknown.) She hopes her books draw you away from the modern world and into a land of intrigue and fantasy, where magic, dragons, shifters, vampires and kings roam the lands.

Manufactured by Amazon.ca
Bolton, ON

41214847R00181